W9-AGD-870

"A surprisingly intimate view of the relationship and mutual respect between this deputy and her inmates. It's a must-read!"

~Rosalie Pope, Author of *Puppies for Sale $25*,
winner of the Next Generation Indie Book Award

"Through my career as a business owner, state assemblywoman, and even first lady of Nevada, there were tough times when determination and perseverance carried me through. In *Dishrags to Dirtbags*, Beth is tested, finds her inner strength, and transforms to succeed in a male-dominated world, and with all odds stacked against her. I can relate to her character and appreciate this witty and touching story."

~Dawn Gibbons, Former First Lady of Nevada

"A story to which any woman who has considered reinventing herself can relate. *Dishrags to Dirtbags* weaves a story proving transformation is not only possible, but it's worthwhile as well. It's fantastic. Like a good first date, it leaves you wanting more."

~Sarah Johns, Anchor, KOLO-TV

"A story that needs to be told! An adventure of personal growth told from a unique perspective. A housewife transitions from one very important job to another and learns just how big her world has become. Each of us could take a lesson in perseverance, drive, and humility from this character. *Dishrags to Dirtbags* is a fun and interesting read."

~Michael Haley, Sheriff of Washoe County

A Lucky Bat Book

Dishrags to Dirtbags
Copyright 2013 by Brooke Santina
Cover Artist: Nuno Moreira
Author photo by Dana Nollsch

All rights reserved

ISBN 978-1-939051-36-3

This is a work of fiction. Names, characters, places, and incidents either are the product of the author's imagination or are used fictitiously. Any resemblance to actual persons, living or dead, events, or locales is entirely coincidental.

Published by
Lucky Bat Books
LuckyBatBooks.com
10 9 8 7 6 5 4 3 2 1

DISHRAGS
TO
DIRT
BAGS

BROOKE SANTINA

6/8/14

So nice meeting you at Lit Fest in Carson!

To anyone who doubts their potential or their ability to achieve it, this book's for you.

Lois,

Happy Reading!

PROLOGUE

"STOP SMILING! THIS IS JAIL!" my training officer instructed as I stood at the deputy station preparing to feed about a hundred hungry male inmates, each peering out his cell window, staring down at me.

"Yes, Sir!" I said with a big grin on my face. I couldn't help it. This was exciting!

"Get your poker face on, Dolinsky," he said. "I mean it!"

Biting the inside of my cheek to remind myself not to smile, I pushed the button and twenty-five blue steel doors on the upstairs tier popped open. Fifty rough, hard-looking men exited the cells, stood by their doors, and glared down at me, sending shivers up my spine. I swore they looked right through me, with no respect for me; it was only out of respect for my trainer that they behaved. All races were represented. Each prisoner was dressed in gray pants and a gray smock. What skin I could see—primarily arms thick from exercise—was tattooed heavily with every frightening image I could have imagined—swastikas, skulls, gang symbols, racial pride statements, and even pictures of naked women.

House Two was a maximum security unit filled with convicts among whom many had done more years in prison than I'd been alive, and who were now in jail for everything from trespassing to sexual assault, burglary to murder.

Tension hung in the air, my heart nervously pounded in my chest, and I felt beads of sweat accumulating on my brow.

"Bring it around!" I yelled while making an arm motion like that of a cowboy with a lasso.

The line of hard-edged criminals walked slowly down the green painted staircase to my left and toward the center of the day room where the lunch cart stood.

"Dolinsky!" hollered my trainer in a tone reminiscent of his years as a Marine. "How many times are you gonna let him clown you like that?"

I looked up quickly and noticed Mr. Rodriguez, a short, Hispanic inmate who was at that moment strolling out of Cell Forty-two with his shirt up over his head and his arms sticking out the top. He slowly slid it into place as he walked along the top tier. The strict jail rules stated that each inmate must be fully dressed before exiting his or her cell, and Rodriguez was clearly not fully dressed. Yesterday this inmate had played the same game with me and I had missed it, but my trainer was quick to bring it to my attention this time.

"Dolinsky! What's it gonna take for you to gain control here? This is YOUR housing unit! Run it as such!" he hollered at my back loudly enough for all to hear. My confidence crumbled. *Why must he always communicate by yelling at me?*

"Yes, Sir," I answered, not really certain what I was supposed to do to Rodriguez for his indiscriminate "clowning." The men trudged by, their orange Croc-like shoes dragging on the gray cement floor. I watched for signs of a rule violation, such as a note passed between inmates, or the sharing of food or personal items, but I caught nothing.

Each man took a lunch, then headed up the green painted stairs to my right and back to his respective cell, completing a full circle of the room. It was the same procedure every meal.

Watching Rodriguez smile smugly as he took his lunch and wandered back to his cell, I felt completely defeated. It seemed an impossible task to monitor fifty inmates at one time and respond to every rule violation; there were too many possibilities!

Once the top-tier inmates had returned to their cells and the last door had slammed shut, I let out the inmates on the bottom tier to get their lunch, visually scouring each door as it opened to see that each inmate emerged fully dressed. My eyes darted between the men as they walked up to the lunch cart to receive their helping of a lunch consisting of a ground bologna sandwich, a cup of salad, a piece of fruit, and a cookie. It was the same lunch every day.

As they headed back to their cells suddenly, my training officer leaped from behind the deputy station and moved quickly toward an inmate in line.

"How many sandwiches does each person get?" he hollered across the day room, his boots thumping on the floor with each exaggerated stride.

"One, Sir," responded the inmate in question, with beads of sweat now emerging from his bald head as he stood nose to nose with my trainer. Paxton continued his boot-camp style of questioning.

"Tell me, then, why do you have two?"

"Because I'm hungry, Sir," the inmate answered coyly.

"So you get two when everyone else gets one, right?" my trainer went on. "You just lost your tier time. Lock down!"

The inmate left the food line and swaggered off to his cell, grumbling "This is fucking bullshit ..." loudly enough for us to hear and causing some of his peers to chuckle. Once inside his cell, he slammed the door.

"Dolinsky, you should have caught that!"

"Yes, Sir, if I had a nickel for every time I've missed something today," I joked, "I could retire before I even complete my one-year probation!"

"Very funny, Dolinsky, but this is not a joke," he replied, straight-faced and stern. "I think you're smart enough to do this job, but you're fucking killing me here. You need to have a poker face and officer presence to make it. Right now, as far as I can see, you have neither."

It was true. One year ago I had been a stay-at-home mom with no immediate worries, and now I was inside a jail, training to become a deputy sheriff. There had been no choice in the matter; I *had* to pass this training, for myself and for my family.

The end of shift couldn't come soon enough, and with a loud crack, the blue slider door opened to let us out of the secured facility. Our boots clomped on the cement as we walked through the slider. Keys, a set of which I had yet to earn, rattled on Paxton's belt as we moved down the glossy white corridor to leave. We passed inmates in the hallway and they quickly stopped, turned, and faced the wall. This always made me feel uncomfortable.

"Tomorrow will be the last day of your training," Deputy Paxton said calmly (for what felt like the first time that day). "I need to be able to tell the Sergeant that you got it ... got it?"

"Yeah, I know. I'll study the rules again tonight and I'll be ready for to-morrow, I promise." I smiled at him. Paxton looked frustrated, yet something in his expression led me to believe that, deep down, he wanted me to succeed.

As we navigated the hallway maze on our way out, heavy, steel doors slammed in the distance and echoed loudly. The first few times I'd heard the sound I had been startled, but now, weeks into my training, I was getting used to the dramatic sounds of jail life—the scratchy voices blaring over police radios, people yelling and sometimes screaming at the top of their lungs. Jail was never quiet. Never.

That night, before bed, I again read the inmate handbook and policies of the jail, and replayed everything my trainer had said, or yelled, through my head in hopes of making it stick. This was my last chance; I'd come too far to fail.

The next day, back in Housing Unit Two, Paxton was evaluating me, and I knew what I had to do. At lunchtime, I pressed the intercom button.

"Top Tier, step outside your cell if you want to eat, Top Tier!" I called half the inmates to come downstairs and pick up their food, but this time I was focused on Cell Forty-two, to catch Rodriguez in the act. He exited the cell half-dressed, as he had done for the past two days. I took a deep breath and yelled, "Rodriguez!"

He ignored me. Louder, I bellowed, "Rod-*ri*-guez!"

Again, he gave me no response. In fact, none of the inmates gave me a second look. Out of the corner of my eye, I could see my training officer watching disapprovingly, shaking his head from side to side. It was time.

I stood up, pushed my shoulders back, and walked into the middle of the housing unit, right up to the line of inmates. With a very deep breath, I employed my loudest, deepest voice.

"God-*dammit*, Rodriguez! You have fucking clowned me for the last time! Get back in your cell! You are locked down for the rest of the day!" I glared at Rodriguez, who by now was halfway down the staircase and had stopped moving mid-step. He looked up at me with a stunned expression. I didn't say another word, just pointed to his cell and glared at him like I would my children when they misbehaved.

"Aww, man," he grumbled and shuffled back to Cell Forty-two, looked back over his shoulder at me, and slammed the door.

It was then that I noticed the line of felons had come to an abrupt and complete stop. In my effort to control Rodriguez, I had, in fact, controlled every inmate in the room. As I stood among the line of lawbreakers, I looked to my left. A crew-cut-wearing Native American fellow three times my size looked down at me with surprise in his eyes. I looked to my right and noticed two elbows clad in spider-web tattoos attached to a burly white male inmate, who also towered above me. My gaze slowly walked up his back to find him stiffly facing forward, not daring to move. Nobody gave an inch. I felt as if I were among wild animals; I expected, at any second, a stampede to start, but it didn't. On the contrary, the inmates waited, patiently, quietly, and respectfully.

It was then that I noticed the strong scent of body odor, and realized I didn't want to overstay my welcome. After all, I was the sole obstacle between these men and their meal. I glanced up at the Native American man, who gave me an uncomfortable grin.

"Anyone else gonna try to clown me today?" I added for good measure, holding back a smile.

"No, Ma'am," was the chorus.

I turned and walked back to the deputy station, breathed a huge sigh of relief, then waved my arm around, signaling for the line of men to proceed. The inmates began moving slowly, each picking up one sandwich, a cup of salad, a piece of fruit, and a cookie; then, without exception, each walked briskly to his cell and quietly closed the door.

I passed my training that day. No longer a recruit, I was a full-fledged deputy sheriff. Everything had hinged on me proving my ability to confront and control situations. Yet, as a fledgling in this newfound career, one question remained present in my mind: How did my success in life come to depend on my ability to shout the f-word across a room full of strangers to make a point?

One

IIIIIIIIIIIIIIIII

BEING A HOUSEWIFE had never been my dream. But being a mother was, and like my mother used to say, "There are times we must sacrifice for the good of the family." This was one of those times. My husband and I believed in traditional family values, that a parent should stay home and raise the children, if possible, and a man's home is his castle, its cleanliness a reflection of his wife.

As a housewife, I spent my days ensuring that my children ate a well-balanced diet, that my husband had a row of cleaned and pressed uniforms in the closet at all times, and that my house was spotless and well stocked with the necessities.

Garrett was my high school sweetheart ... almost. We met senior year in French class; he sat next to me in the back of the room. From his six-foot-two frame and jet-black hair to his perfect olive skin and deep brown eyes that resembled pools of chocolate I wanted to melt right into, he was out of my league and I knew it. I was short, ordinary, with reddish-brown hair, fair skin, and freckles. I felt certain that Garrett Dolinsky would never be interested in me.

Twenty years had gone by since that day in French class when he stood up for me. As I vacuumed the carpets in our old home in South Reno, I would often daydream about the day we met. Days that change your life don't happen often, and I wanted to remember it forever.

"Mademoiselle Scott ..." the teacher said one day as I sat staring out the window and daydreaming, deep in thought about what life would be like if my parents weren't splitting up.

"*Comment allez-vous*, Mademoiselle Scott?" he persisted. "Eh-hem, Elizabeth Scott."

I was seriously oblivious.

"Are you with us Miss Scott?" Mr. Brown called to me, again.

A pencil poked my ribs and Garrett nodded toward the front of the room where our instructor stood glaring at me.

"Sorry! What was the question?" I asked, startled and then mortified, my face redder than a stop sign. The class broke out into laughter while I broke out in a sweat. Being singled out was my worst nightmare.

"He asked how you are," Garrett whispered to me, then said, "Relax, I got this."

His hand shot into the air, and he waved it, calling, "Mr. Brown?" attempting to divert everyone's attention away from me.

"*En français, s'il vous plaît*, Monsieur Dolinsky," barked Mr. Brown. How he hated when we forgot to speak in French.

"Uh, oh, *oui*, uh … *la jeune fille est très bien*, Monsieur Brown." Garrett told him that I was "very well."

"Very good, very good …" said Mr. Brown.

"Oh no! Monsieur Brown, *en français, s'il vous plaît*," said Garrett. The class erupted in laughter.

Mr. Brown, a bit annoyed and squinting his eyes, replied, "*Oui*, Monsieur, *très bien*." Then he went looking for another student to question.

"Thanks" I whispered.

"It's okay, Emerald Eyes," Garrett said, and he smiled, so confident and kind. I gave him a quick smile then looked down at my desk. My bright green eyes were the only things that set me apart from complete anonymity, and I kept them aimed downward toward my desk most of the time. Stunned that the Adonis in the neighboring seat had noticed me, and even given me a nickname, I could never have dreamed that, years later, I'd be vacuuming his carpet, doing his laundry, or wiping his pee off the toilet seat.

While I cleaned and put away dishes in our small but workable kitchen, I relived our high school graduation day, some twenty years ago, when he had asked for my address so that he could write me. Through his ten weeks of boot camp, I didn't hear from him, and didn't expect to. I was busy myself, buying books, moving into a dorm, and getting established in my college classes, so he rarely crossed my mind.

Until the day I received a letter that began, "My Dear Emerald," and went on to describe his ten weeks of physical and mental hell that was Army Basic Training. It sounded like a movie script: getting up early to a Sergeant's booming voice echoing through the barracks, pushing himself to complete obstacle courses, learning to shoot many different automatic weapons, all the things he needed to accomplish to become a soldier. He wrote about times during his training, when I would just pop into his mind, and how, unbelievably to me, the thought of me helped him get through. He wrote of his parents being present at his graduation from Basic, and how he wished I could have been there, too.

I read the letter over and over, trying to grasp that Garrett actually missed me ... me! When I wrote back, I told him about my crazy professors, and how I had a roommate who kept me up with her snoring; it was hardly a fitting response to his seven pages of adventure, but it seemed to work, because after that, he wrote religiously, twice a week. It always felt as if my heart would beat out of my chest when I opened the post office box to find an envelope addressed in his handwriting. It was sure to be filled with sweet comments, always beginning with "My Dear Emerald" and signed "Your Most Humble Warrior."

We were so young then, so inexperienced, so idealistic. So many years had gone by, and it felt good to think of those times as I moved through our kitchen, wiping down the counters and cleaning the sink.

Our relationship had grown through our letters. That's where I learned we were much the same, sharing conservative beliefs, similar upbringings and strong faiths. He would occasionally mention a weekend party at which he and his buddies had had a few too many beers. His stories were hilarious and always made me laugh.

The day I received The Big Phone Call, I had just walked into the dorm after working at the coffee shop, when my floor advisor waved to me to pick up the phone in the hallway.

"Hi, Emerald!" I was thrilled to hear his voice!

"Hi, Warrior!"

"I have to tell you something, so you can hear it. So ... I had to call."

He sounded so strange ... nervous. I'd never heard him sound nervous before.

"Oh, it's so good to hear your voice! Are you okay? What is it?" I asked cautiously.

"I uh … Yeah, I'm okay, but I have to tell you … Well, I need you to know, I think … Well, I think … I love you." He spit it out, his voice cracking. My heart stopped completely. I felt excited and terrified at the same time. There was a long silence and I realized it was my turn to speak.

"Wow … I … I … feel … the same way. I guess, I love you, too." *There. I said it.*

My heart began to beat again, with force. We were official.

Those were the days, I thought as I flopped down on the couch after folding a week's worth of laundry and putting it all away. I was so intoxicated by him, I'd quit school and moved that following summer to be with him, without a care in the world. I'd left myself with no college degree, nothing to fall back on if things got rough. Who cared? I had Garrett. That was pre-marriage, pre-babies, pre-responsibility … back then, I was free.

These days, I felt confined to the house, as if my work was never ending, with a constant line of dishes, dusting, vacuuming, and laundry that seemed to multiply every week. Sometimes I wished I could do what I had done during college—working part-time in a coffee shop. I had worked the register, but enjoyed the camaraderie of the waitresses and the cooks; someone was always playing a practical joke, and something happened every day that was worth a laugh.

I collapsed on the sofa for a much-needed break from cleaning. *How can there still be so much cleaning to do? There are only four of us!*

Our life hadn't always been like this. I recalled all the moves we'd made after we were married, to wherever the military wanted Garrett. A couple of years at Fort Lewis, then on to Fort Bragg, and then Corpus Christi Army Depot in Texas. We had even spent three years in Germany. Ours was an adventuresome life. All the while, I rarely left the base, and would take part-time positions stocking shelves in the community stores, helping teachers at the elementary schools, and, of course, volunteering at church. Garrett didn't want me getting a "real job" because we were certain we would be starting a family soon. We were actively trying to get pregnant, though we could never have anticipated how very long it would take.

Forcing myself off the couch, I picked up the broom and began to sweep the kitchen. At least now that we were back in Reno, I was near Gwen and her family. I had felt so guilty for not being around when my sister had given birth. I was so far away, disconnected, missing out on the joys of her pregnancy. Mom had sent a few photos of her holding my nephew, and in each picture she had worn a smile wider than any I had ever seen. At the time, I had been excited for Gwen, but that was mixed with my own feelings of failure, and I'd be lying if I said I hadn't been jealous. Month after month I had anticipated pregnancy, expecting to be expecting, hoping this would be the month it would happen, but it didn't … no matter how much I'd prayed.

Garrett had repeatedly put in for a transfer to a base near Reno; when he was given his new assignment, the one that finally enabled us to move home, we were thrilled. Stationed in Herlong, about seventy-five miles north of Reno, he began commuting weekly to the Army Depot, there for a few days, then home for a few. By then I'd hit my thirties and felt that time was running out on the baby front. We visited a fertility specialist and after a couple of months of hormone shots, I was finally pregnant … with twins!

I smiled as I stood in the kitchen, leaning on the broom handle and admiring the boys' artwork on the refrigerator. Those months before the boys were born had been the most joyous of my life, but I began to sense Garrett didn't share my joy. We had informed the family right away; Gwen loaned me books on the subject while Mom began sewing a green and yellow baby quilt. But we waited a few months to tell friends at church and at Garrett's work, until we were sure. By the time I was showing, my husband was getting nervous about our impending life changes, or so I told myself. He would call me once or twice a week on his way home to say that he'd be late.

Whenever I answered the phone, he'd begin with, "Hey, Babe, how are you doing?" I could hear the tipsy in Garrett's voice.

"Where are you?" I'd ask. "I expected you home by now—your dinner is getting cold."

"Stopped at the bar with the guys," he'd say, then yell something to his buddies. Male mumbling could be heard in the background, then lots of laughing. "Beth, I'll be home when the game is over, just stopped in for a beer. Bye, Babe!" And he'd hang up.

"Love you, too, bye," I'd say into the air as I disappointedly hung up the phone.

Mothers go into the hospital expecting to know their offspring intimately from the moment they arrive. But after the cesarean section, when I came out of anesthesia, I didn't know these two creatures at all. Garrett nervously held Colton as the nurse placed Jacob on the bed next to me. Here I was, being presented with my baby boys, yet it felt so foreign. I had expected to feel like jumping for joy, but I could barely sit up in bed. Throughout my stay in the hospital, nurses would come in periodically and press on my stomach like they were kneading bread. I felt a flood of emotions, not all of them joyful, and everything hurt. On top of that, while all the books said "breastfeeding is best," nursing didn't come as automatically to me as I'd expected. Birthing was a completely humbling experience.

Once we were home from the hospital, Garrett had figured he'd instinctively know what to do as a father. Meanwhile, I'd studied and prepared myself by reading every book on motherhood that I could find. Yet, experts espousing parenting's best practices paled dismally in comparison to the actual doing. My mother had been a great help, coming over to our apartment every day to help me change diapers, bathe and feed the boys. How I worried about the feeding part, fearing my tiny A-cups would never hold enough milk to sustain hungry twins. Trying to train my mammary glands to produce enough, I had become a pumping maniac, and what a weird sensation. Parts of my body that had been previously used for nothing but foreplay were transformed into life-sustaining mounds of gelatinous flesh. And I would never forget the feeling, a whoosh of warmth through my chest, and if the baby, or the pump, wasn't locked on tight, I sprayed warm milk at high velocity across the room. Garrett watched perplexed while my mother laughed and grabbed a dishtowel, unfazed, to clean it up.

Soon, my life revolved around those tiny creatures. I was in motherhood orbit, their every need my concern. Within weeks, Garrett was back at work and I'd morphed into someone new—the resident expert on Jacob and Colton Dolinsky. Recognizing what each coo or cry meant and knowing the difference in their voices, I knew an earache cry from an erupting tooth cry, and how to soothe each. I knew whether one had a fever as soon as I picked him up, and had the emergency phone number to the pediatrician memorized. As they grew, I knew their favorite toys, blankets, foods … I examined every bite that went into them and every poop that came out. And through it all, my heart filled with love for these little people, and I knew this was the "job" I had been born to do.

Shaking myself from my daydreaming about bygone days, I finished cleaning the kitchen and walked down to the mailbox to get the day's bills. As the boys had grown, I realized Garrett's and my relationship had changed. We moved from our apartment into a small house, and I thought things would improve, but our initial friendship, the foundation on which we had built our marriage seemed non-existent, and our sex life was suffering, too. Being a stay-at-home mom, I expected to cook and clean and, of course, take care of the boys. Yet, there never seemed enough time in a day to do it all. And Garrett would always notice.

"Babe, how can you be home all day and still have dishes in the sink from yesterday?" he'd say.

"Well, Jake puked all over his bed this morning, so I changed the sheets. Then Colton pulled all the pots and pans out of the cabinets in the kitchen, and as I was putting them back, my friend Sylvia called, and ..." He would stand there with his arms crossed, just shaking his head from side to side, as if I were a child being scolded. It was the same thing every week when he returned from the depot.

My husband had duties, too, and I learned the hard way not to encroach on his responsibilities. Each week he would take my car to the car wash and fill it with gas. He mowed the lawn and did yard work. He handled the finances. Once, shortly after we'd moved into the house, I mowed the lawn in our tiny back yard, thinking I would do him a favor since his weekends were so short. I figured I would do his weekend work, so that he could play with the boys, practice his guitar, or do whatever he wanted to do instead of chores when he returned home.

"Ta-da!" I exclaimed, pointing to the back window as he walked in the front door of our small home, his duffle full of dirty clothes slung over his shoulder.

"'Ta-da' what?" he grumbled as he dropped the canvas bag on the living room floor.

"I mowed the lawn so you don't have to!" I chirped proudly.

"Why would you do that, Beth? You know that's my job!" he replied, actually sounding upset.

"Well, I wanted you to be able to relax. Play with the boys, enjoy your ..."

"So you don't even need me here, then? Why did I even come home?" And with that, he walked into the bedroom and slammed the door. My husband was traditional in every sense, and in my attempt to be helpful, I had apparently confiscated his man card.

Two

DEPLOYMENT WAS INEVITABLE; we knew he would be leaving soon, and I would be taking care of the house alone. Garrett invited a buddy and his wife over for dinner to introduce us, so that I might have a friend during his time away. We could talk about "women's work" and they could discuss their impending overseas trip. The moment Cheryl and Jeff walked into our home, I could tell we probably would not hit it off.

"Isn't this quaint, such a tiny home!" Cheryl said patronizingly. "How do you do it?" Cheryl didn't hold back.

"How do I do *what*?" I asked.

"How do you raise children in such a tiny home? Jeff, could you imagine us in such a tiny place?"

"Even without children, we have too much stuff. At least you don't need a housekeeper, right, Garrett?" Jeff added.

"Nope, this is my housekeeper right here." Garrett squeezed me around the middle, then quickly let go. "Hey, Babe, could you bring us out a couple of beers? I want to show him the Harley."

Off they went to the garage where they could drink and talk in peace. I headed to the kitchen, picked up two beers, and delivered them to our tiny garage, which seemed even tinier since these two people had arrived. The guys were discussing "promotion points"—I knew Garrett had been vying to become a First Sergeant for some time.

"Craig's sitting on seven-hundred-twenty points this month, but I don't think he really wants it," said Jeff. I had no idea of whom they were speaking and realized that there must be a lot Garrett wasn't sharing with me.

"Marta wants it bad ... I can't see her being any good in the position, but if they want to promote a split-tail, that's the one they'll take ... pisses me off," Garrett complained.

"Uh-huh," Jeff corroborated as I placed the beers on my old desk, which doubled as a workbench for Garrett.

"Oh well, Essayon, brotha," Jeff offered their combat engineer slogan as he picked up a beer, held it up, then took a swig.

"Essayon," Garrett repeated. Feeling like an eavesdropper, I hurried back into the house, slamming the door behind me.

"So what do *you* do?" I asked Cheryl, trying to be friendly while getting the upper hand in the conversation upon returning.

"I do hair."

"You're a stylist?"

"Yes!" and she handed me her card.

"Thanks, I could use a haircut," I said as I placed the card under a magnet on the refrigerator.

"Yes, I was gonna say ..." Then she giggled and asked, "So what do you do?"

"I volunteer in the boys' classes and at church," I said in my typical self-deprecating way. "And, you know, the usual stay-at-home mom stuff around here, cooking, cleaning ..." It didn't sound like much, though it felt like a lot.

"Are you worried about the deployment?" she asked.

"A little. I just want him to be safe and come home to us. But Garrett is really good at what he does. I know he will do his best to stay safe."

"Really, Elizabeth? Hmm ... Isn't he a combat engineer? I'm not sure how someone stays safe clearing land mines ..."

As soon as she removed herself from my kitchen to join the guys, I ripped her card off my fridge and threw it in the trash. Then I did something I rarely ever did: I poured myself a beer. It was going to be a long evening.

About four hours later, the pain-in-the-neck couple left, but not before they got in a few more jabs about the size of our home compared to the enormity of theirs. I was thankful that the boys had been playing at the neighbor's house while the "grown-ups" had been here, so they had been spared Cheryl's wit.

We hadn't set out to live in a small house. We rented from Garrett's mom, Marge; this was the home Garrett had grown up in, and it seemed important to raise our boys here. And the rental income provided Marge's only income since her husband had died five years prior. We wanted to move into a larger place, of course, but we also felt obligated to help Marge any way we could. She didn't trust strangers in her home, and with her health failing, what else could we do? I didn't mind. After all, it was in a great school district for Colton and Jake; at six years old, they were finishing up a great first-grade year.

Once Cheryl and Jeff left, I called the boys home and got them into bed; it was a school night. That done, I entered our bedroom, exhausted from the stress of entertaining the awful couple, and found Garrett, passed out on the floor of the closet, using my sandal as a pillow. My heart sank. This was not the first time I'd found him like this.

"Okay, Baby, come on up." I tugged on his arm and he roused enough to clumsily stand up. My shoe fell from his face to the floor, but the footprint was still pressed into his cheek. He fell toward me, as if all five feet of me could possibly hold up his six feet and two inches. "Whoa there, Warrior, aim at the bed," I said as he stumbled toward the bed and landed perpendicular across it, groaning. He lay there, and I knew he'd passed out again. His clothes and shoes were still on. I sighed deeply, then began removing his clothes and maneuvering his underwear-clad body under the covers.

"Okay, Babe, there you go," I said to his unconscious figure. I slid into bed next to him. His breath filled the room with the smell of beer; it was a disturbingly sweet smell that reminded me of my childhood, when mom would go to bed full of alcohol. Garrett had always enjoyed a drink or two, but he had seemed to lose count in recent months. I made the decision that in the morning I would talk to him about curbing his drinking. We needed to get our relationship back on track before he left for Iraq. The truth was, I was yearning for what we'd used to have, back when we had been close, and were a team.

My parents had done their best, but had never been much of a team. Dad had a career in the casino industry while Mom had been an unhappy housewife with an affinity for cheap wine. The more she consumed, the meaner she got and the longer Dad stayed at work. Pretty soon he had a girlfriend and they were separated. Months later they were back together, but eventually they divorced. I knew from watching them that the elusive happy marriage was the key to a joyful life, and I wanted both. When Garrett and I married, we agreed that the D-word was not an option. We would never divorce. There was nothing we couldn't get through.

But here we were, nineteen years later, and things were so different.

The next morning, he was seriously hungover and slept most of the day away, so my window for having that conversation remained closed. Then, the next day, he got the call: Their battalion was deploying in the morning … and he was gone, just like that.

THE FIRST WEEK WITHOUT HIM, I felt helpless and unsure about the basic logistics of running the house. After all, he'd had no time to fill me in on the details of his household duties. I didn't even know where he kept the checkbook; how could I keep up with the bills? Then, during the first weekend without him, it was time to find it.

"Dammit!" I yelled as I scoured the bedroom looking for the checkbook.

"What is it, Mom!?" Jake ran in the room, alerted by my outburst. Colton was right behind him.

"Sorry, Sweetie, it's okay, boys, I'm just looking for the checkbook." Colton ran out of the room, only to return a moment later.

"Is this it?" asked my son as he stood holding our checkbook in his hand.

"Yes! Where did you find it?" Colton took my hand, led me to the dining room, and pointed to a space between two books entitled *Beers of the World* and *You, Too, Can Become a Master Brewer.*

Of course! I should've known, I thought to myself wryly.

"Who keeps the checkbook in the dining room?" I mused aloud to myself.

"Dad!" said the boys, and they ran down the hall to their room to play.

I sat and paid the bills, slid the checkbook back between the books where Colton had found it, placed stamps on the envelopes, and walked them to the mailbox.

That afternoon, I mowed the lawn for the second time in my life. Then I loaded the boys into the minivan to get it washed and filled with gas. My van felt like a boat floating down the road, and I was reminded of how much I hated it. It had been a gift from Garrett when the boys had been babies. I'd wanted an SUV—to be specific, I'd wanted a black Toyota 4Runner V-8. Instead, he had gotten me the "next best thing," a two-tone, brown Ford Aerostar minivan that seated eight. Then, a year later, when it was time for him to purchase a new vehicle, he had bought himself a black Toyota 4Runner V-8. He had wanted a Dodge truck, but felt I couldn't handle a truck, and he wanted me to be able to drive his vehicle if needed. When he brought it home, I'd been frustrated and hurt, but had told myself that with his weekly commute he needed four-wheel drive more than I did.

As in any marriage, we'd had our troubles, but with Garrett's extended absence came a strong sense of aloneness. Those first few days, it felt normal, like it did when he was away at work and would be home in a day or two. But after a few weeks, I began to miss him. Lying alone in bed each night, I'd catch myself touching his pillow and wondering where he was at that very moment, curious about whether he missed me, too. I'd remember the positive things about him, how his strong arms felt wrapped around me in a hug, and how much fun we had when he told his crazy stories and the kids would laugh for hours. After a few months, I'd forgotten about our problems and begun to glamorize his return. Would we be able to meet him on the tarmac at the airport? Would he look as handsome as ever when he stepped off the plane? What should I wear in order to look particularly appealing to him, after a year of being apart?

After a few months, I had mastered the basic day-to-day workings of home, with one exception: I could never remember to take the garbage can to the curb on trash day. On more than one occasion, my neighbors witnessed me in my pink robe, rushing to pull the can to the curb just as the truck pulled up in front of my neighbor's house. I would run back in and the trash men would empty it as my screen door slammed behind me. Then, as soon as they left, I would sneak back to the curb and race the empty can to its home on the side of the garage. This happened every Wednesday until one morning when I startled awake with the usual, "Oh no! I didn't take the can to the curb!" I began to jump out of bed, and then another thought appeared: Who cares? Who really cared if I missed the trash pick-up one week?

If I was honest with myself, my daily housework was feeling tedious and dull, not fulfilling, as I liked to portray it to others. In an attempt to keep myself busy, I spent more time helping out at the kids' school, and, afterward, the three of us would go and visit Marge, to keep her mind off her son's deployment. Her assisted-living home was just a few miles from ours.

During one visit, I asked her whether she would mind if I did a little redecorating to the interior of her little brick house. "You know, just a paint job and some new curtains?" I asked.

"No, I don't mind," she said, but something in her resigned voice told me that perhaps, down deep, she did.

During that year of Garrett's deployment, I felt it was important for him to feel a part of things at home, like the boys' birthday party. In his care package that month, I sent him lots of photos of the kids opening gifts and eating cake. One photo was cute; in it, the boys held a sign they had made, which read, "We miss you Dad!" I wanted him to know life wasn't the same without him home.

When we spoke by phone, about once a week, he revealed little of his experiences; our conversations dealt mostly with what the boys had been up to, and the day-to-day business of our life here at home. And though, in the beginning, I watched the news on TV each night, trying to grasp any tidbit of his life in the desert, eventually I avoided all television because it made me feel overwhelmed and frightened. There were stories of the Iraqi army disbanding and pictures of heavily armed men shooting automatic weapons in the city streets. Iraq seemed like a violent place with "weapons of mass destruction" and "biological warfare," and so many other terrors for which I couldn't comprehend a purpose. I didn't want to lose my husband, and during his deployment, all I could do for him was pray.

One of the few stories Garrett did share with me was horrifying, but the fact that he confided in me made me thankful. It gave me hope that we would be able to reconnect when he returned. He mentioned the day his buddy had been in a vehicle that ran over an IED, an improvised explosive device. He had been killed when the truck he had been riding in flipped over on top of him, and Garrett had been the first on the scene. He didn't cry on the phone as he told me the story of how he had tried with all his might to move the wedged vehicle. Then my husband had held his friend's hand as he coughed, spit up blood, and, moments later, took his last breath. Garrett spoke so matter-of-factly; this was a normal occurrence in Iraq. It was heartbreaking.

So, really, who cared if the dishes were done? So what if I had a pile of laundry to do? Jake and Colton didn't care, and neither did I. Besides, the work just needed to be done again the next day.

But decorating only needed to be done once, and that held a satisfying appeal for me. While my husband fought for freedom. I threw myself into beautifying our home. It became my creative outlet, where my imagination danced wildly and freely, moving effortlessly from room to room. Garrett didn't care about styles or colors. Plus, I reasoned, it would be a great surprise for him when he returned. I became obsessed with changing every room in the house, putting my stamp on it. And since there was no man of the house, I had to do all the work myself. While the boys were in school, I could be found scraping off the old, striped wallpaper from the living room walls, then painting them "Summer Cantaloupe," and sewing curtains and valances to replace the dated gold ones that had hung there for thirty years. I even stained the fireplace mantel to enhance its function as the focal point of the room. By the time Garrett returned home, I would have an intimate and up-close relationship with every square inch of our brick home; the colors, fabrics, and textures would all be my doing and chosen with care. The next time Garrett walked through the front door, our home would look like a page out of *Better Homes and Gardens*.

During one morning of painting, I turned on the TV to find *Gone with the Wind*, one of my mom's favorite movies. I couldn't bring myself to turn it off. She always loved the classics. I popped the top off a paint can and went to work, crying myself right through all five hours of the film plus commercials, as I painted the living room. Up the ladder, down the ladder, blow my nose … I missed my mother, who had had been gone just over a year.

Each day, while the boys were in school, I decorated while old movies played in the background. *Meet Me in St. Louis* got me through painting my bedroom. *Annie Get Your Gun* ran as I wallpapered and installed wainscoting in the dining room, and *The Sound of Music* played as I hung bright blue curtains in the boys' bedroom. I was on a mission like never before, dancing and singing along with the greats, and had finished the house in just a few weeks. Friends from church stopped by and were impressed. They couldn't believe I had done all the work myself—now I felt even more anxious for Garrett's return.

On the Tuesday he was scheduled to return home, the three of us were on the tarmac, anxiously waiting to meet him, just as the many other families standing with us waited for their own loved ones. I caught a glimpse of Cheryl standing there to meet Jeff, but I quickly looked away and decided to avoid her. I couldn't wait to see my husband; my warrior was finally home. I began to feel I could breathe again, could relax knowing he would be with us, safe, to share once again in all our family's events. I had kept him apprised of everything that had happened at home in the twelve months since his deployment, including what role Jake played in the Christmas play, the troubles Colton had been having with math this year, and even that we had adopted a little dog while he was away. I kept him abreast of everything but the new interior décor, which I had saved as a surprise.

THREE

IIIIIIIIIIIIIIIIIII

AS SOON AS HIS FACE PEEKED OUT the back of the C-17 aircraft, the boys took off running to greet him. Garrett scooped them both up simultaneously, one in each arm, and nuzzled his face into theirs. My arms ached to hold him, and when he knelt to place the boys on the ground, I reached out and he lifted me up. I clung to him, filled with so much pride, yet even more relief to have him home in one piece, and just hugged him as hard as I could. With his arms tight around my ribs, I had to remind myself to breathe.

Arriving home, I opened the door and let him enter first. He said nothing, just walked into the kitchen and grabbed a beer out of the fridge.

"What do you think of the colors in here?" I asked him.

"Oh, yeah! Hey, you had the place painted!"

"*I* painted it," I said proudly. "*And* made new curtains, *and* bought new rugs and covers for the old couch, *and* ..."

"Okay, okay! Looks good, Beth."

The boys began yelling excitedly to their dad, anxious to have his attention. "Dad! Here's Magnum, you gotta meet Magnum!" Colton, on tippy-toes, held the small Pomeranian up as high as he could, in a proud attempt to show his father. For the dog's safety, I took her from his grasp and placed her on the floor. She promptly ran away from all the commotion.

"Dad! Come see our room! Come on, Dad!" yelled Jake, as he jumped up and down in the hallway.

"I'm comin', I'm comin'!" Garrett said as he tossed the can in the sink and grabbed another beer from the fridge, hurrying so as not to disappoint his boys. I couldn't help but notice, he hadn't even been home ten minutes, yet he'd powered down a beer and was opening another.

I made spaghetti for dinner while he played with the kids. By the sound of their giggling, it was like I had three eight-year-olds running loose in a room full of trucks. I heard "Vroom, vroom, crash!" followed by uncontrollable laughter. Garrett could relate so well to the boys. I had to admit, there were times I felt jealous. Though I had done my best to play trucks, the boys would ruthlessly remind me, I didn't play "good like Dad does." I was like a tiny drop of estrogen living in a lake of testosterone.

He drank a few more beers with dinner, and before the night was through he had polished off the entire twelve-pack. While I was brushing my teeth and getting ready for bed, in my new pink nightie that I had bought just for the occasion, Garrett passed out on the sofa. It was as if the last year had never happened. I left him there. Then, to soften my disappointment, I let Magnum sleep on the bed with me that night.

A FEW WEEKS AFTER GARRETT'S RETURN, I took the kids with me to the grocery store. The kitchen was pretty empty; I'd forgotten what it was like to cook for four of us, and we had plowed through what I had stocked the kitchen with in no time. Per usual, the boys were trying their best to get me to buy them something special.

"Mom, can we get some cereal?" Jake hollered from halfway down the aisle.

"I have boxes of Rice Puffs and Corn Krunchies in our cart already. That's enough cereal."

"Oh come on, Mom, please!?" whined Colton. They were teaming up on me, but I was onto their ploys.

"What cereal do you want?" I asked, knowing full well their favorite.

"Peanut Butter Oogles," they snapped in unison.

"Oogles? Again?" I teased as the boys stared up at me with their big brown eyes.

"Please?" their whining escalated.

"Here's the deal. You can have the cinnamon rolls you already picked as a treat, or the Oogles, but not both. And you have to eat all of your vegetables at dinner tonight or no treat. Is that clear?"

"Aw! Mom!"

"That's the deal. Take it or leave it."

"Okay, I say cinnamon rolls," Jake led this decision.

"Yeah, cinnamon rolls," Colton agreed.

"Okay, boys, put the Oogles back where you found them."

The three of us scoured each aisle of the store to be sure we didn't miss anything we might need for the week ahead, then went to stand in the long checkout line. It was Saturday afternoon and the store was very busy.

"Hey, Elizabeth!" The clerk greeted me. Her son was in Jake's class.

"Hey, Joan! How's everything?"

"Great!" she said as she rang up my purchases.

"And that comes to $172.56, Ma'am!" Joan said to me cheerily when she'd finished ringing up our items. I handed her my debit card and she swiped it as the young man bagged the last of my groceries.

"Elizabeth, Honey, um … it says it was declined," Joan said quietly.

"What? Oh, my! Well, it must be a mistake … can you try it again? Can you?" Joan nodded once in assent and swiped my card again.

"I know we have enough in the account," I said nervously as we waited to see.

"Hmm. Declined again. Beth, I am so sorry, I don't know what's going on … Do you have another card we could try?"

Joan was very kind but the line was growing behind me and the other shoppers were getting restless, sighing loudly, moving their weight from foot to foot and rolling their eyes.

"Hmmmm," I mused, and put my fingers on my brow, trying to concentrate and block out the crowd forming behind me. "Let's just put it on the credit card." I handed her my card. "There must be some mistake, probably a bank error. Guess I'll be visiting them tomorrow." I smiled, trying to act casual and mask my embarrassment. She swiped my credit card and we waited.

"I hate to tell you, but this card was declined, too." Joan looked at me, clearly sorry for me.

Fear shot through me. I felt like I had been hit in the stomach with a bowling ball. I looked at the grocery cart full of bagged groceries awaiting the trip to the minivan, and stammered, "Gosh, I don't know what …" and didn't know what else to say. I checked for cash in my wallet. "I only have fourteen dollars."

Joan smiled at me and looked back at the ever-growing line of customers. "I am so sorry to do this to you, but can I just have the milk, bread, cheese, and ... eggs?"

"Sure," she said, and beckoned to a manager to void the transaction. Up my groceries went, back onto the belt, and they deleted the items one by one. It was excruciating, standing there waiting as my fellow customers' impatience grew. Most found other checkout lines.

Once we'd sorted out the four items I'd be taking with me, Joan said, "Okay, Elizabeth, that's twelve dollars and ninety cents."

"Okay, thanks so much," I told her, humiliated, and handed her the bills. I timidly took my change. "I'm so sorry!" I apologized as I grabbed the two bags and headed for the door.

"Mom! What about the cinnamon rolls?" Jake, who had been too busy goofing around with Colton to notice the trouble, asked.

Then his brother piped up, "Yeah, what about ..."

"I'll tell you in the van, just keep moving!" I interrupted. I could hear the panic in my own voice.

Reaching the minivan, we piled in. I felt tears welling up but held them back.

"We had a little trouble, boys, I'll get you cinnamon rolls next time." I hit the gas pedal with force and the boat lurched forward, bouncing off the curb as we accelerated. My mind was numb as we floated down the road toward home.

As I parked in the driveway, expecting to find Garrett at home, instead the house was unusually dark. I stormed inside, calling to him.

"Garrett! Garrett!" I called at the top of my lungs. There was no sign of my husband.

"Boys, go to your room. I'll call you when dinner is ready," I said as I pulled out a pan to scramble some eggs. I didn't have a lot of choice. It was breakfast for dinner or nothing. My hair was hanging in my face, so, before I started cooking, I headed into my bedroom to grab a hair tie off the dresser. I started at the sight of Garrett's feet sticking out from beside the bed. My panic over potentially finding him dead quickly subsided when he emitted a loud snore.

After quickly locking our bedroom door to guard against curious kids, I returned to Garrett, who was clearly very, very drunk.

"Hey, Emerald ..." he said sleepily when he opened his eyes and saw me standing over him. "Ammmember when I used to call you that? Emmm-mmmrald?" he said, slurring every syllable. I knelt down and grabbed his arm helping him to sit up.

"Sure, Baby, I remember ..." I said patronizingly. Then, calmly, "Garrett, what happened to our money?"

"I should've ennnnded it ..." he said. "I should've ..."

"Garrett, listen to me! My cards were declined at the store! I need to know what happened to all our money."

"I ... I ..." he said, then started sobbing uncontrollably. It was then that I knew this wasn't just some bank error. We were broke.

I stood up and shakily took a few steps back, finally perching on the edge of the bed, still staring in shock at my intoxicated husband. I was unsure how to feel.

"What happened? What did you do? I need to know."

"I ax ... I ax-idennnally lost it," he said, then rolled over and began leaning his body to reach under the bed.

"You LOST IT? Eight hundred dollars! Garrett, we had eight hundred dollars in the checking account, and you *lost* it?"

"I'm so sooorrrrrry." He pulled a black gun from under the bed and held it up in the air. I gasped and just stood there in horror, holding my breath.

"I shooo-d just end it, you can have ... insurrrrance, I'll do it now." And he placed the gun's barrel toward his temple.

"No! Babe! No!" I yelled then looked toward the door hoping the boys didn't hear me. "No, please, please, Babe! Don't!" I begged quietly, having no idea what to do, what to say. He sat leaning against the wall, legs straight in front of him, gun in his right hand.

"You don't even need me anymore!" he said with unusual clarity, as he swept the room with the gun. "Look at this room! I'm not neeeeded here." And he was sobbing again.

"I need you more than ever, Garrett! The boys need you! We love you!" Tears were slipping off each cheek, smacking my shirt, while my gaze remained on the weapon in his grip. I tried to make him feel better and come up with a way to get the gun from his grasp.

"Honey, we have two beautiful boys who need their father! Please stop ... just hand me the gun, Baby."

"I don't want to live anymore," he said, disgusted, as he put the gun again to his temple. My heart stopped and I froze. I prayed silently, "God help him! God help him!" over and over in my mind. It felt like an eternity, but it was only seconds before Garrett dropped the gun to the floor and put his hands to his face. I quickly kicked the weapon under the bed and out of his reach.

I helped my sobbing husband into bed, as my mind flashed a memory from my eighth-grade year. My mother had consumed so much wine she was unable to walk herself down the hall to bed. Dad had left the house, and Gwen and I didn't blame him. Mom had been exceedingly vicious that night, accusing him of cheating, among other things, and had thrown a wine glass full of merlot at his head. She'd scared us that night, but Gwen and I knew that if we could get her into bed, she would fall asleep quickly. We were right. I wondered why this memory had only just returned to me, despite the many other times I had put Garrett to bed drunk? Perhaps because he had scared me tonight, truly scared me, just as my mother had truly scared me that night long ago. He had never done that before.

Shortly after, Garrett fell deeply asleep. I clambered under the bed and retrieved the gun, and then carried it with three fingers out to the garage, placing it in the open gun safe. Most of Garrett's weapons he kept at work, with the exception of two handguns he kept in his dad's old safe in the garage. It was small, and so old there was only one key to it. I collected the only other handgun I knew of from under the seat in his vehicle, and locked it safely away, putting the key in my purse. Ten minutes later, I realized that this was just exactly where he would go looking for it. I pulled it out, and tossed it into the bottom of a box of tampons under the sink in the bathroom.

While I made eggs and toast for the boys, the pistons in my brain fired in all directions. *Now what do I do? Do I call the VA Hospital? Do I call his friends? His first sergeant? Do I call other army wives, like Cheryl, ask how Jeff is holding up? No ... And what did he mean LOST it?* In the morning I would visit the bank and see what damage had actually been done.

Once the boys were in bed, I climbed into ours. I stared at my sleeping spouse, then at the ceiling, for hours. He'd been drunk many times during our marriage; why had I never addressed it? Was I numb? How had I been conditioned, like Pavlov's dog, to accept the apology in the morning and never question? As the dog was taught to salivate at the sound of the bell, had I been taught to retreat from a fight? And if I did finally address the issue, might it push him to choose drinking over us?

That night I decided I needed to make some changes in my life, though I was unsure what exactly they might be. I felt a multitude of emotions as Garrett slept—pity after seeing how badly he was hurting, anger at him for frightening me like that, helplessness and fear for my children's futures, irritation at myself for becoming completely financially and emotionally dependent upon another person, especially one so unstable. Mom had always said, "Every housewife should have her own savings account." Now I knew why.

FOUR

[|||||||||||||||]

AFTER MY LONG, SLEEPLESS NIGHT, Garrett called in "sick" from work and I left the house early to drop the boys at school. I wanted to be at the bank right when they opened to discover the truth, so I sat in the car in the parking lot for twenty minutes, fretting, chewing my cuticles and mulling over worst-case scenarios in my mind. The second the doors were unlocked I darted into the bank and approached the first person I saw with a name tag.

"Excuse me, I have some questions about my accounts?"

"Yes, Ma'am, I can help you." The well-dressed young man gestured for me to follow him and said, "Have a seat, please," directing me to a seat in front of his desk, in a small office just off of the lobby.

"Your last name?"

"Dolinsky." His fingers clicked on the computer keyboard.

"Elizabeth and Garrett Dolinsky?"

"Yes."

"Okay, Mrs. Dolinsky, what can I help you with today?"

"My card was declined yesterday at the grocery store, and I need to know why."

"Well, let me see …" More typing. "Okay, that would be because you have no money in your checking account," he said matter-of-factly.

"How can that be? I know there were eight hundred dollars in there a few days ago."

"Yes, but I'm showing that was taken out on the fifteenth."

"By whom? Can you tell me that?"

"No, Ma'am, I'm sorry, I don't have that information. I assume it was either you or your husband, as your names are on the account." He looked at me, unsure of what else to say to me. "Anything else I can help you with?"

Maybe he's made a mistake, I thought. *How old is this kid, anyway? I need to calm down! My hands are shaking like a leaf!*

"Yes, my credit card. Can you tell me how it got maxed out?" My voice cracked.

"Let's see … It looks like your last statement … the balance was at just under twelve hundred."

"Yes, I recently redecorated the house and spent some money. That sounds right."

"Well, Ma'am, I'm showing a cash advance of one thousand dollars on the eighth. Then, another two thousand was taken the ninth, and the rest came out on the sixteenth. All from Lucky Harvey's Truck Stop and Casino."

"Lucky Harvey's? Isn't that the casino north of here? Near Herlong?"

"I'm not sure, Ma'am, sorry."

"So, he's been gambling …" I said to myself. My face felt flushed.

"Are you okay, Mrs. Dolinsky? You look a little sick."

I pulled myself together. "So, what exactly do we owe on the credit card right now?"

"Six thousand dollars."

I was stunned. I got up to leave and remembered our children's savings accounts. We had put money away for college since the boys were born. Every holiday, their grandparents, aunts, and uncles would give the kids money and we had added to it when we could. When I had last looked, each boy had had just over thirty-five hundred dollars in his account. Surely, Garrett wouldn't have touched our boys' money, would he?

"Oh! One more thing," I stopped and turned back toward the man before reaching his doorway. He had just risen from his desk. "Could you please tell me the balances of our savings accounts?"

"Oh, sure," he said, seeming genuinely concerned. He sat and began typing again. "Let's see … You have the minimum balances of fifty dollars in each of the savings accounts."

I couldn't even say thank you. Nausea overwhelmed me. I ran to the minivan and skidded out of the parking lot. We had no cash, no available credit. The seven years of savings for our sons' college education had just been gambled away. Unbelieving, I began doing the math in my head. *Over twelve thousand dollars my husband gambled away in three weeks! Why? What was he thinking? Was he crazy? Who is this man?*

Halfway home, I realized that I couldn't face him. Not yet. I was too angry, afraid, and sick to my stomach. I didn't know what I might do and I wasn't prepared for the excuses he might offer. I stopped at the elementary school to see if either boy's teacher needed any help, to throw myself into something constructive.

I reached Jake's classroom and was startled when a woman in a police uniform walked in front of me into the classroom. "Excuse me," she said, moving past me and proceeding up in the front of the class to talk about her career in law enforcement.

I followed her into the room, then stopped to speak to the teacher who was standing nearby.

"You need any help today?" I asked, quietly.

"Not really, it's Career Day, so there isn't much for even me to do," she whispered. "You're welcome to stay, Beth, if you'd like."

"Thanks," I said and moved to lean up against the back wall and listen to the speakers. Jake noticed me and waved; I waved back.

The sight of the officer's gun belt brought back the gut-wrenching image of my husband, holding a gun to his head, which made it impossible to concentrate.

A terrible fear rushed over me about what would happen to Garrett if I confronted him about all this. Most of all, I just wanted him to be all right. But how could I forgive him? Twelve thousand dollars! And how would we pay our bills? How would we eat? What could I do to keep us afloat financially? I had no skills, no degree, little experience. What about Marge? How would we pay her rent? I tried desperately to slow the pace of my brain, to make some sense out of all this. While I stood leaning, resting really, against the back wall of the classroom, I reminded myself to open up my eyes and smile, to not let my troubles show on my face.

The officer took questions from twenty-three curious children and discussed each tool on her striking black belt. While I contemplated, I listened.

"Not everyone is cut out for this line of work," she explained, and my mind flashed to an aptitude test I had completed years prior. When the boys had been very little, I had considered going back to college, but had no idea what I would study. I had invested in formal testing to see where my personality and abilities would best be suited. Law enforcement had been my top career match.

In my mind, police officers were like superheroes—able to leap tall buildings in a single bound (well, at least to overpower the bad guy with a single punch). *I could never do that!* I told myself as I listened to the woman and grew calmer. *Besides, Jake and Colton are my priority. That was the deal, and that's how it will be until they're grown.* Standing in the back of the classroom, I remembered the disappointment I'd felt, years ago, when I had tossed the test results into my bottom desk drawer, realizing I would do nothing with them.

Now, things were different. I had to do something, I couldn't afford not to, literally. I had loved being with my children each day, having the ability to see them grow, to see the little daily moments, the many firsts—first steps, first words, first day of school. Still, I had always hoped to finish college someday and be a career woman, someone with power to make a positive difference in people's lives, someone *I* could respect. The highest position I had held in the workforce was a cashier at a coffee shop, and that level of income wouldn't even cover our rent, much less any other bills. I would need to research what positions were available in the area and find out what, if anything, I was qualified to do.

As the officer left the classroom, I felt a need to connect with her, so I followed her out the door and walked with her down the hall.

"It sounds like you love your job," I called, hoping to start a conversation.

"Yeah, I really do," she said, turning and smiling. She stopped and I approached her. I was surprised, as I stood next to her, to find that we were approximately the same size. My initial impression had been that she was much bigger.

"I was thinking, as you spoke ..." I began. "I wondered if there is an age limit to, uh, doing what you do?"

"No! In fact, we have a brand-new recruit who is forty-two," she replied encouragingly. "Are you thinking of applying?"

"Maybe. I'm just, you know, thinking about it."

"You should do it! We're always looking for women on the force," she said.

"I can't imagine being on the streets, it seems so frightening," I mused.

"The county is hiring right now, and as a deputy, you have the option to work in the jail. Here's my card, just call me if you have any questions," she said, and handed me her business card, which I promptly slid into the back pocket of my jeans.

At home that afternoon, I walked into the crowded one-car garage where my old desk sat stuffed into a corner, because there had been no room in the house. I opened the bottom drawer and dug out the old test results. There it was, in black and white: "Police Officer." *Why did I bother to take the test if I wasn't going to seriously consider the outcome?* I reasoned. *The university testing service placed me in this line of work for a reason. Maybe I could do it.*

I yawned and stretched my arms high over my head, walked into the house and found Garrett resting on the sofa, watching TV.

"You hungry?" I called to him from the kitchen.

"No, had some soup."

"Okay," was all I could say. I knew that if I said anything more, we would certainly fight, and I wasn't ready for that yet. My night with little sleep was catching up to me, so I went to our bedroom and flung myself face up on the bed. It felt good to lie down, away from everyone, where I could relax a minute. After about thirty seconds, I felt the pricking in my back pocket—the officer's business card. I got up, pulled the card out, and placed it on the dresser where Garrett's wallet lay. Quickly, I opened it, inspected the many receipts stuffed inside, and located those with dates and amounts matching the withdrawals I'd discovered at the bank that morning. He had been at work those days, and must have gone out afterward. I had felt panicked most of the day, but realized payday would be in two days and calmed a little. Quickly, I yanked his debit and credit cards from the leather pocket, and hid them in my underwear drawer, knowing he would never look in there. It made my heart hurt to realize the extent of Garrett's problem, our problem.

It was then that I noticed myself in the mirror. I stared deeply into my own green eyes for guidance. They looked dark, worn out, with lids heavy from lack of sleep, and with reddish-brown bangs dangling over them. The rest of my straight hair fell down the sides of my cheeks to my chin. *Is that the face of a cop?* I wondered. Then, *man, am I ever tired.* At that moment, there was only one thing I knew for sure. I needed to get some sleep.

FIVE

UUUUUUUUUU

UNLESS YOU CONSIDER BAKING COOKIES for my children's elementary school
or teaching hormone-laden teenagers at church about abstinence (a
message rarely heard), I had not held a job in seven years. Even when I had
worked, it had only been part time. But now, I knew it was up to me to land
a full-time position, a real job, and I felt a little guilty because I was getting
excited about it.

At church the next Sunday, my friends wavered as we discussed my
options in the job market. Sure, I had explained to them a little about our
marital issues, why I needed work, but they hadn't seemed to take me seriously. Then again, I hadn't told them everything. Just after services ended, I
cornered them in the nursery where they were working, to get their take on
my possible new career choices. Children were crawling everywhere, and
parents stopped in to pick up their little ones as we talked.

"Okay, ladies, I have searched through the paper and the only jobs
available in Reno right now that I'm qualified for are ..." I fumbled in my
purse and pulled out the classified ads folded up. I shook them open and
cleared my throat, "Cocktail waitress, substitute teacher, hair salon receptionist, fast food manager or deputy sheriff."

"*What?!* Deputy sheriff? You?" laughed my friend Sylvia, a heavy brunette from Georgia with a contractor husband, two children, and a beautiful singing voice. Sylvia was a solid Christian who would do anything to
help a friend. "Oh, Beth, that is a riot!"

"Thanks for the vote of confidence there, Syl," I said wryly.

"No! Oh, I'm sorry, I don't mean it like thaaat," she drawled, laughing. "But, really, Beth, you are a Sunday school teacher, not some … some cop. You aren't, I don't know, *manly* enough." Sylvia chortled as she sat down, picked up her two-year-old son, and wiped the baby's nose with a tissue.

"Fine, what can I do then?" I asked.

"Okay, seriously now, give us those choices again, please," piped up Mandy, who was tall and strikingly pretty with blue eyes and long blonde hair to her waist that was held in one thick braid. Much younger than her doctor husband, Mandy had three kids and no money worries.

I repeated my list, which still included deputy sheriff. "Oh, and I could be a hooker, there's always that." The ladies both swung their heads around toward me so quickly; I thought Mandy's braid might choke her. Now it was my turn to chuckle.

"The things you say sometimes! Geez," Mandy scolded as she shook her head. Ten children remained in the nursery waiting for their families to pick them up, all playing on the floor and chattering loudly. "I think the hair salon receptionist sounds good."

"It pays ten dollars an hour, less than twenty-thousand dollars a year." I told her. "We can't live on that."

"Live on it? Who said anything about living on your income?" Sylvia said loudly to be heard over the children. "You told me on the phone that you were going to work to supplement *his* income"

"Did I?" I replied innocently. "Well, that's the plan, but you never know. Garrett's drinking has escalated. We may not always have *his* income. I'm trying to think ahead. You guys …" I stopped and motioned with my fingers for them to come closer. The ladies leaned in and I continued in a whisper to keep it just between the three of us. "If you had seen Garrett a few nights ago, drunk on the floor, you would understand."

"He looks fine now," Mandy replied and pointed out through the large glass window that separated the nursery from the main auditorium. My husband was on the stage, chatting with the band members as they packed up their equipment. An excellent guitarist, Garrett had played with the guys often before his deployment. Today, he was putting on a good show, all smiles, which reminded me of something my mother had once said: "The most depressed people are often the life of the party." It had never dawned

on me, until this moment, staring at my husband, that she had been referring to herself.

"Okay, so, I say substitute teacher" said Sylvia, shifting our attention
back to our conversation. "Then you could still be home with the boys, have
the same vacations, that kind of thing."

"The only trouble with that one is, it's intermittent. I need something
full time."

"Hmmm, true," Mandy said. "That leaves fast food manager, because
you can't be a cocktail waitress and wear one of those skimpy outfits running around a casino."

"Sure she could! It beats walkin' the streets!" said Sylvia, smiling as she
placed her son back on the floor.

"Well, not by much. Those girls in the casinos have to put up with a lot
of stuff, sexual harassment and other things like that, just to live off tips.
You really want to do that?" Mandy chided.

"No, I don't really."

"Then it's settled. Fast food manager it is," Mandy confirmed, waving a
hand in the air.

"There's one problem with the manager job," I said.

"What now?" griped Mandy.

"I'm not interested in it."

Mandy threw her hands up in the air. Sylvia stared at me with a blaze in
her eye that could burn paper and said, "You are *not* seriously considering
that deputy position."

"I made an appointment to go on a tour of the jail next week to see what
I think."

"Girl, you're crazy if you want to work in a jail with criminals!" Sylvia was
adamant. "What is wrong with you? It's dangerous!" Her southern drawl
was always more evident when she was feeling stressed.

"What if you get shot? Who will raise your kids? Have you thought of
that?" Mandy spoke quietly so as not to alarm the families in the room.

"Of course I've thought of that," I said calmly as we waved "Bye-bye" to
three families who had picked up their children and were leaving the nursery. The noise in the room instantly softened.

"I just don't understand why you can't just be a manager or something.
Why do you have to be a ... sheriff?" Sylvia questioned, pronouncing the
word as if it tasted bad.

"I've always wanted to challenge myself. The deputy position pays twice what any of the others do to start, and it has better benefits. Don't forget, my options are somewhat limited. I never finished college."

"Yeah, I still say there has to be something else you could do," Sylvia added, and then noticed her son's nose bubble re-emerging and rolled her eyes.

I countered, "Besides, if you remember, that test I took a few years ago said I should consider police work."

"That's right! I forgot about that!" Mandy said, picking up her own child.

"Beth Dolinsky, you knew all along you were going to pick that job, you just played us like a deck 'a cards," Sylvia said.

"Was it 'Go Fish' we played?" Mandy joked.

"More like 'Crazy Eights,' because our dearest friend has lost it!" Sylvia shot back.

"Honestly, guys, I hadn't realized I had made the decision until we talked about it, just now." I added, "Maybe I played ya … just a little."

Suddenly we were interrupted.

"What would Jesus say about a woman in a position of authority over a man?" blurted out an elder's wife who had just happened to walk in on our conversation and was now waving one finger in the air as if I were a child being scolded. "You know what the Bible says."

"Yes, I know what it says, thanks for your insight, Mrs. Green," I responded sweetly as the three of us smiled and nodded unnaturally, mechanically, while we waited until she had collected her grandchildren and left the nursery. Once the coast was clear I spoke up.

"Perhaps I'm being led to this career for a reason?" Neither friend would look at me as I spoke, but I continued. "God knows what's in store for me. Maybe I should practice what we always hear from the pulpit, 'trust in Him.' I think I will trust Him and go for it. It just seems like the right thing for me to do. And with Garrett's troubles right now, well … I'm going to need your support, ladies. He can't know about this decision or he would flip."

"Of course, we'll be there for you, and we can keep a secret. But you can't expect us to like it," said Mandy. "And, of course, we will pray for you."

"Yes, I will pray that you come to your senses and take the fast food manager job. That's what I'm prayin'," said Sylvia tongue-in-cheek. She then smiled at me as she picked up her son, who promptly wiped his runny nose on the shoulder of her blouse.

After church, we drove through a fast food restaurant to grab the family some lunch. Payday had come and we were solvent again. I studied the people working with curiosity as the cute female clerk handed us bags loaded with burgers and fries. The manager stood behind her with a clipboard doing some sort of inventory. I considered it for a moment. *Nope, not interested.*

WE ATE LUNCH IN THE CAR on the way home. I needed to test the waters a bit to see if there was any hope of Garrett's approval. Not that it mattered; he certainly hadn't asked my permission before he had gambled away our money. Still, I felt the need to bring up the idea of my getting a job.

"So, I talked to the ladies today about my maybe going back to work."

"I'll fix everything," Garrett said. "You don't need to work, Baby."

"But I feel like it's the right thing to do. I'm planning to drop off my application at the human resources office in the morning," I said with some trepidation over Garrett's response.

"Okay," he shrugged.

"That's it? Okay?" I pushed.

"What do they have openings for? Receptionist?"

"Well, yeah. Among other things. They also have some jobs, uh ... at the jail."

"Ha! What the hell would you do at a jail?"

"I'm not really sure, but I'm going to take a tour of the place next Wednesday. You want to come, too?"

"Nah, it's your thing, I don't need to go," he said. "Besides, you're jumping the gun. You don't *need* to work. I told you, I'll take care of everything."

"It would help if you went, too, you'd understand where I might be and ..."

Before I could finish the thought, Garrett interjected, "No, thanks. If you *really* get the job, *then* I'll check the place out."

"What does that mean, 'really get the job?'" I prodded, my feelings hurt.

"Nothing. I don't want to fight," he tried to pacify me, but it was too late.

"You don't think I can get hired, do you?" I pushed as he turned the minivan down our street.

"Hey, don't be twisting my words! I didn't say that!" he backpedalled.

Garrett pulled the boat into our driveway and stopped. I turned in my seat to face my husband. "Garrett, please, tell me the truth. Do you think I have what it takes to be a deputy sheriff?"

"Deputy sheriff! You never said anything about being a dep-..." then he burst into laughter. I sat staring at him while he laughed the kind of laugh that would have had me or the boys peeing in our pants if it had been one of us. He gathered his thoughts and said. "Come on, Beth, be serious. You? You're not tough enough to be a cop." His words stung.

"Oh," my eyes welled up. "'Least you were honest," I said, my voice cracking. I slid out of the car, eager to get away from him and the boys before the water works started, and hurried into the house. I felt like I'd been punched in the chest. It was the same hurt I had felt when my mother had told me, from her hospital bed, that she had removed my name as the executor of her will because she didn't think I "could handle it."

Heading straight to my closet to change clothes and put on something more appropriate for housework, I recalled how my mom had held my hand there in the hospital room. She had said, "I don't mean to hurt your feelings, but I switched the responsibility of handling my affairs to Gwen. I just think you're going to have too hard of a time; you're too emotional." At that moment, my sister and I had looked at each other with the same confused expression. No matter, we would both honor her wishes regardless.

I stood in my closet, in my underwear, listening to Garrett and the boys banging around in the kitchen. My heart felt heavy. *Why doesn't he check on me? Doesn't he care that I'm hurting?* Then the old guilt and sense of obligation kicked in, and replaced that thought with another: *I shouldn't be so hard on him; he's struggling, too.*

As I slid into a pair of sweats and t-shirt, my mind replayed another conversation with my mother that had occurred during one morning visit in the hospital. She had begged me to get her home to her own room, where she could die in peace.

"No matter what that doctor says, I want to go home with hospice." She stared at me with eyes that were already dead. "It's just gone too far already."

"It's your call, Mom, but are you sure? People have different reactions, it might not be as bad as you expect." I knew better than to try to make her change her mind; it never worked.

"I want to go home with hospice. That is what I want." She had sounded strong for a moment, then weak and frail again as she said, "Please, get me home."

I left my mother in the hospital and placed a call to her surgeon on the way to Colton's classroom for parents' reading group. Surprisingly, the receptionist put the doctor on the phone so I could express my mother's wishes.

"I see no need for hospice, not yet," the doctor said.

"Well, she's telling me hospice is what she wants."

"Well, this morning she told me she would try radiation treatment, which means there is hope. Mrs. Dolinsky, I'm not in the habit of giving up on my patients." He said this as if I were throwing in the towel, an unloving daughter who didn't care.

"*I'm* certainly not giving up on her either! Just honoring her wishes. She's not being honest with you. She wants to go home with hospice."

"What if she's not being honest with *you*?" he asked me.

"She begged me to call you today and get this taken care of. She wants hospice." I understood he was in the business of extending lives, but my mother had made up her mind. Even he wasn't going to win against her cancer. He was the one that had told us that she had "maybe six months" left. After a pause, he spoke.

"I'm not sure you understand how ..."

I cut him off. "Please, just send her home with hospice."

"But it goes against my ethics to ..."

"PLEASE!" I begged. "Send her home with hospice!"

"I'm not sure what I should do here ..."

"*Send her home with hospice!*" I yelled into the phone. At that, he hung up.

That was one of the toughest things I had ever had to do, fighting for my mother's right to die on her own terms. I drove her home from the hospital the next day. Now, some eighteen months later, my unrestrained husband didn't think I was tough enough to be a deputy sheriff? Didn't anyone think I was capable of anything? Standing there in my closet, I just wanted to scream.

SIX

THERE WAS NO DOUBT IN MY MIND. I felt compelled, really. Come Monday morning, I would apply for the deputy job. In the past, I had relied on my mother's approval, calling her daily and discussing even the smallest decisions. Since her death, I had looked to Garrett or friends for support. But this time, I couldn't get it from them. I was on my own. I needed to do this for me, and their opinions mattered less than usual. Feeling empowered by the decision, I was smiling ear to ear as I drove to the county human resources office to drop off my application, the first step of the process.

"You'll be hearing from us in a few weeks," said the clerk, a grumpy woman.

"Weeks?" I asked.

"It takes a while to get hired here, usually about six months" she said. *Six months!* "First, you'll take a test to see where you fall on the list. You'll get more information by mail in a few weeks. Next!" she called, dismissing me.

Walking out to the car, I wondered how Garrett was doing back at work. He had seriously curbed his drinking since that fateful night, and had apologized profusely for his behavior. He hadn't even argued with me when I had said I would be handling all the finances from then on; he knew he had no other choice. I had opened a new account, one that he would not have any access to, and we set up direct deposit so that his paycheck would automatically go into the new account.

Then we discussed our budget and allowances. It was the only way. He didn't like it, and I had to remind him of something before he conceded.

"If we don't have money for rent, Marge moves in here with us, in this nine-hundred-seventy-five-square-foot, two-bedroom, one-bath home! Think about that for a moment, please. You want your mother living back here, too?"

That did it; he consented. I felt better because we were communicating again, but forgiveness—that would take me significantly more time.

I also encouraged him to visit a doctor. Garrett had developed what seemed to me like night terrors. He would wake up sweating and yelling, and it was getting frightening for both of us.

"Honey, I know you're having trouble sleeping. Maybe you should visit the veterans' hospital, or see our family doctor? I'm sure a professional could help."

"Nah," he said, "I'm trying melatonin tonight."

"I still say you should see the doc. Besides, think of how much better you'll feel once you get through this." There was a silence.

"Fine! Geez!" he agreed, frustrated by the control that was slipping from his grasp. "I'll go to our GP, if *you* make the appointment."

Despite his resentment, I was thrilled. The next morning, I called our family doctor's office and scheduled an appointment for Garrett's day off.

The next step in my hiring process was going on the jail tour, and I couldn't wait. I wondered as I got dressed that morning, what is the appropriate attire to wear to a jail? I had an appointment at the Reno Sheriff's Department for a tour, and quickly chose the same clothing I wore every day: jeans, a t-shirt, and slip-on flats. I didn't have much else.

Deputy Smythe, my tour guide, was waiting in the lobby to greet me. He was a tall, thin guy with a long, thin face to match, and a full head of hair that was cut short. He seemed like a nice enough fellow, but nervous, though; he repeatedly looked around the room suspiciously at all the people in the lobby as he took my driver's license and gave me an ID badge to clip to my shirt. My expectations were high; this trip through the jail would clarify my decision. One way or the other, I was searching for a deal-breaker.

Smythe wore a black polo shirt with a badge embroidered over his heart, khaki military pants, and black army boots; a black belt and holster complete with gun sat on his hip. *I can't imagine wearing a gun on my hip,* I thought.

We started by taking an elevator down one floor. I halfway expected to see some type of dungeon, a wall of bars from floor to ceiling behind which prisoners hung their arms out with tin cups begging for food.

"So, you're thinking of working here, huh?" Smythe asked as we boarded the elevator.

"Yeah, I put in my application, and I'm waiting."

"What makes you think you want to do this type of work?"

I told him about the test, the officer in my son's class, my conscious reasons.

"Well, because you aren't just some lookie-loo and have already applied, I'll take you on a custom tour. You know, really give you a good idea of what it's like to work here. Ask any questions, too. There are no dumb questions," he instructed.

My only jail experiences had come from books, movies, and TV, so my curiosity was piqued. As the elevator door opened, we stepped out into a small hallway with lockers on the walls. He placed his gun and cell phone in the locker.

"You bring a cell phone?" he asked.

"No, I left everything in the car."

"Good. See? You're already thinking like a cop." He smiled.

"Why can't you have cell phones in the jail?" I asked.

"It's a safety precaution," he said, "If an inmate gets a hold of one, he could plan an escape or something. Too risky." I nodded.

We walked up to a huge, windowed sliding door that was bright blue like the color of the new curtains in the boys' room. Smythe pushed a button on the wall and we waited in silence. Suddenly, a deputy appeared on the other side of the door, and as he strode down the hallway, he banged the window with his fist so hard it rattled, almost startling me out of my shoes. Smythe laughed at my reaction and waved at the deputy, who had never stopped walking and was now disappearing quickly down the hall and around a bend. He was followed by three men dressed in black-and-white-striped clothes like scrubs, with chains around their waists and wrists. They shuffled along in plastic orange Croc-style shoes, with their ankles in shackles.

"Where are they going?" I asked.

"To court," Smythe replied.

While waiting for the door to open, I read a sign posted on the window just above my head, which read, "No weapons allowed beyond this point." *Wow, that's something you don't see every day*, I said to myself.

The sliding door opened with a loud *crack!* Startled again, I tried not to show it this time. We entered the jail and walked a short way down a glossy, white hallway. When I heard the door slide closed behind me, my heart jumped a little with both excitement and apprehension. I realized that I had no control of the doors. I couldn't get out of this place on my own.

We walked through two more of the same kind of sliding doors before arriving in a room that had a floor made of bright red tiles, and where bright blue mats hung on three of the four walls. Already I was surprised they had chosen such upbeat colors with which to decorate a jail. The tan shirts and deep green pants of the deputies' uniforms stood out against the primary-hued surroundings. I watched two deputies working on a handcuffed man who stood facing the wall. One was writing on a clipboard while the other took the man's belt off, dropping it into a gray bin placed on a nearby plastic chair. Though brightly colored, the smell in the room was repugnant, like dirty feet.

"Welcome to the Sally Port, the first stop for an arrestee," Smythe narrated to me. "The deputies are searching pockets, purses ... any item the inmates bring with them must be documented. They're doing the inventory search now." Smythe then walked over to a gray mat on the fourth wall, slapping it with his hand.

"This is where all mug shots are taken. The inmate stands in the tape square on the floor," he said, pointing to the floor by his feet. "He then leans his head on the mat, and *she* takes the photo." He waved to a pretty woman sitting at a desk, safely behind a window. She waved back.

"Come on in here," Smythe directed and I followed him through yet another sliding door, to an area with cells with wall-sized windows large enough that I could easily see everything inside. Oddly, there was no furniture in these cells, just an old, dirty man lying on the floor in one room, and a young man who looked like a college student in the other.

"These 'seeps' are not arrested, just kept here until they sober up," he explained.

"Seeps?" I asked.

"C-P-C's. It stands for Civil Protective Custody; we call them 'seeps.' These fellas were too intoxicated to care for themselves on the streets, so they were brought here."

"Like a drunk tank?" As I said it, I thanked God that Garrett had never ended up there.

"Yeah, sort of. I'll show you what *we* consider the drunk tank." I followed him about one hundred yards to another area of Intake that seemed to be nothing more than stark white walls and bright blue doors, all numbered. "Go look in Cell Three," he directed. Hesitantly, I walked over to the door of Cell Three and peeked in through the thin, dirty window, which was only as wide as my face. Inside, I saw a few men lying on the floor, sleeping, in a dark brown room.

"Why are they not with the seeps?"

"These guys were arrested, maybe for DUI, maybe for Domestic Battery, but they've been charged with something, unlike seeps."

Suddenly a scream came from the cell directly next to me. It scared me; I gasped and jumped, bringing both hands to my chest. I could see the man who had screamed lying on a wooden bench in the cell, his eyes closed.

"This is a loud place, you'd better get used to that!" Smythe said, completely composed and looking at a whiteboard affixed to the wall near the door to the cell. Someone had handwritten "Hargreaves, 10-96, .215, 2300" on the board.

"That's just Hargreaves. He comes in all the time and screams bloody murder every visit." Another high-pitched scream came from the cell. It was so unnerving! What would make a person scream like that, so loudly, and for no reason?

"What do the numbers mean?" I asked, pointing at the board.

"The 'ten-ninety-six' means mentally ill," Smythe explained. "'Point two-one-five' is his blood-alcohol level, and 'twenty-three hundred' is military time for eleven o' clock p.m., the time he arrived." Then Smythe added, "Don't feel bad, the screams used to bother me, too. Now I'm used to it. Come on."

As we left Hargreaves and Cells One through Eight, we entered a very large room and I could see a carpeted area where a number of people in regular clothes sat in more cheap plastic chairs like the one in the Sally Port. The ceiling was painted a bright, bubblegum pink! *A pink ceiling? In a jail?*

Smythe explained the folks seated were inmates waiting to be booked. "See the red line around the carpeted area? If an inmate crosses the red line, he gets thrown into a holding cell. He'll have to wait until we feel he's able to follow the rules before we let him out to complete the booking process."

We walked near the carpeted area toward another hallway, where a man with a scraggly beard and clothes way too large for his thin frame was peeling an orange over a garbage can. He smiled a toothless grin at me as we passed. I returned the greeting. Some of the people looked rough, like a woman who sat in the back of the room with overly bleached hair and tattoos on both arms; others I guessed to be homeless, but the vast majority seemed like regular, clean-cut folks. One man was in a dress shirt and pants, like he had just come from work. *I wonder what HE did to land in here?*

There was certainly much more to working in a jail than I could have anticipated. All the inmates in the lobby area were wearing only their socks, so I asked about it. "It hurts less if they kick us with socks than it would with shoes," Smythe answered as he escorted me down yet another glossy white hallway toward another blue sliding door.

We saw a few different housing units where inmates were "locked down" in their cells. The rooms seemed enormous. Bright, cheerful colors covered the staircases and railings, up and around the top tiers—a bright blue, green, or pink, depending on the unit we were visiting. Common to all were stark white walls and bright blue, numbered doors, with one exception: Housing Unit Five.

To get to House Five, which was identified by the "HU-5" emblazoned above its door, we had to walk through a dismal, cement courtyard surrounded by chain-link fencing, which was wrapped all the way to the top with coil after coil of razor wire. It felt like we walking into a World War II-era concentration camp, and I was instantly uncomfortable.

"That's a Housing Unit?" I expressed my surprise as we walked toward a semi-permanent building that resembled a large white circus tent from the outside.

"That is Housing Unit Five, a place where you will spend a lot of time if you get hired here," Smythe said. "I don't believe the building was designed to house humans, but we've had so many more females committing crimes, they had to open it temporarily. That was years ago; it still works just fine."

He opened the door and I entered; immediately, the women seated at tables turned their heads my way and froze. I gasped. All the noise stopped, and I don't remember another time in my life when I felt as much like an intruder. Clad in blue shirts and gray pants, the women glared at me like I had done something wrong. Smythe walked over to a deputy who was seated at a perch-like desk a few feet higher than the floor.

"Hey! Welcome to the Pussy Palace," she said, looking down at me.

"The *what*? Connor, you're bad!" Smythe scolded.

"What? It's the perfect name for this hellhole."

"This is Elizabeth Dolinsky. She's applied to work here, so I'm showin' her the ropes," said Smythe. Then he turned his attention to me and said, "This is Deputy Connor."

"Hi! You can call me Beth." I said waving a hand and smiling uncomfortably, my back to the inmates. I stole a glance behind me, to see if they were still staring, but none were. In fact, it surprised me how quickly they had gotten back to braiding each other's hair, playing cards, whatever they had been doing prior to the interruption. Connor invited me up the stairs to her perch to have a seat. Younger than me with piercing blue eyes and long blonde hair pinned up in a bun, she seemed so sure of herself, so confident, even tough. There was just enough room for two chairs, so Smythe sat on the desk, while I watched the female deputy with amazement.

"What are most of these ladies here for?" I asked Connor.

"Most of them are in custody for drug charges, prostitution, burglary, things like that, they're all minimum security." Connor then added to Smythe, "I'm maxed out!"

"You have seventy?" Smythe chirped.

"Yes. They even called to send me more today!" replied Connor.

"You should involve the association if they do." Smythe seemed upset.

"Goddamned right, and you know I will, too, brother."

Connor looked at a young inmate who had approached the desk. "What do you need?" she snapped.

"Permission to get supplies, Ma'am," said the girl who couldn't have been much older than eighteen.

"Yeah, hurry up," said Connor, who then looked at me and said, "These girls can be so annoying!" Connor hadn't finished her sentence before the young girl was back at the desk. "What now?" she yelled at the girl.

"We're out."

"Of *what*?!" Connor yelled.

"Tampons and pads."

"Oh, great! You ladies go through cotton rockets and launching pads like they're candy!" The inmate tried not to laugh. "I'll have to order more, but we won't get them until this afternoon. Borrow some for now." The inmate turned and walked away.

"This is way too much information for me," teased Smythe.

"Do you have any questions for me?" Connor asked, softening as she turned toward me and tapped my knee with her hand.

"Are you always by yourself out here?" I asked.

"Yup, all the time, unarmed and with seventy female inmates."

"Then how do you keep them in line?"

"I keep them in line because they let me. It's 'officer presence,' how you handle yourself. And you gotta stay on 'em, you know. You can't let anything by. The rules are posted and they have to abide by them or else," said Connor, her blue eyes squinting.

"Or else *what* happens?" I asked, amazed.

"Or they get rolled up to the 'shu,'" she said.

"Shu?" I quizzed.

"S-H-U," Connor explained. "That's disciplinary segregation, where they have to earn everything in their cell back, starting with a mattress."

"You take everything away and the inmate has to earn it all back?" I confirmed.

"Right," Connor and Smythe both nodded in unison.

"I should try that with my kids!" I joked.

"Well, maybe!" Smythe said brightly. He looked at his watch and said to Connor, "Hey, we gotta go. See ya, and thanks!" Connor waved us out.

Leaving House Five, I tried to retrace our steps mentally but was completely lost. Identical blue sliding doors existed around every curve, and the halls all looked the same. *How does anyone get around in here?* I wondered. Once back in the elevator, Smythe asked me what I thought.

"I'm intrigued, but House Five was a little freaky—so many inmates with one deputy!"

"Yeah, Connor's quite a character. It's not a hard job, really. Remember, we're trained, it's not like you just come to work one day and sit with all the inmates. You'd have to go through a ton of training before you were left alone with inmates, so by the time you get here, you'll know what to do."

His words comforted me a bit.

We reached the entrance where our tour had begun. "I enjoyed the tour. Thank you so much," I said to him as I took off my visitor's badge and handed it to him. I tried to hide how overwhelmed I felt.

As Smythe exchanged the visitor's badge for my driver's license, he seemed to sense my feelings. "I'm sure you can do it, Beth. It was nice meeting you. Good luck!" And with a little wave, he disappeared down the elevator to return to the unusually bright, yet very dark, jail.

Three and a half weeks went by before I received a letter from the county. Seeing the return address, I ripped it open and read it right there at the mailbox, bouncing up and down anxiously on my toes as I stood on the sidewalk. The letter thanked me for my application, and invited me to take the written test, the next step in the hiring process. Gleeful, I skipped into the house to mark my calendar.

THREE WEEKS LATER was my testing day, and I was a nervous wreck. Garrett wished me luck, which was nice, just before he left to go to work for a few days. The test was to be held at the convention center, a vast building in the center of town, and, for some reason, I was concerned that I would stick out like a sore thumb. As if, due to my age or inexperience or something unforeseen, it would be obvious to everyone that I didn't belong. Dressed in my mom uniform—jeans, t-shirt, and flats—I entered the auditorium. There were people of every color, age, shape, and size, all seated with test booklets closed on the desks before them. Some were quite heavy, and I wondered how they expected to handle the rigorous job. Some looked like they were fresh out of high school, while others seemed as if they could be older than me. I guessed that there were at least two hundred people in all. The room was packed.

Expecting a true challenge of my mental capabilities, I had visited a library and studied about a week before the exam. But instead, this was a simple test of analytical thinking and deductive reasoning. The questions were multiple choice with some true/false and some photos to study, but nothing too difficult. I finished quickly, but checked my answers twice, worrying that I had missed some section and would automatically be disqualified. I got up to leave, feeling sorry for the applicants who were seriously struggling through this testing process; now all I could do was wait to be contacted again by mail.

On the home front, meanwhile, we had learned from our general practitioner that Garrett exhibited the symptoms of Post-Traumatic Stress Disorder, or PTSD. The doctor recommended that he utilize the services offered through the Veteran's Hospital, but Garrett refused, without offering a reason. I think he feared his records and diagnosis would get back to the military and he might somehow lose his position. Military life was all he'd ever known. So the doctor recommended a private psychologist who specialized in treating PTSD. On the way home, we stopped at the grocery store to pick up some newly prescribed medications to help him deal with his depression and anxiety.

"So, I'll make the appointment for you to see the new doctor and ..." I began.

"Who ... the shrink?" he asked.

"Yeah, Babe, the psychologist he recommended."

"I'm not going to a shrink."

"Garrett, why not?"

"I'll take these pills, but I'm not going to a shrink, I'm telling you right now! Don't bug me about this, Beth." And with a heavy sigh, I consented.

It wasn't long before the pills went by the wayside, too. I learned this a few weeks later when I was heading to the store.

"Babe, I'm going out to the grocery store. Do you need me to pick up your prescription?" I asked as I picked up my purse and threw it over my shoulder. The boys and Garrett were seated in the living room watching television.

"Nah, I'm not taking them anymore," he yelled a little too loudly.

"What? Why not?"

"They don't work."

"But the doctor said it would be awhile before you felt ..."

"*Not taking them!*" he hollered at me, cutting me off.

I took a deep breath, waited a beat, and then tried another tack. "I'm not trying to upset you ... but how can you tell they don't work?" I asked politely. I approached him and made my voice as calm as possible, so as not to sound antagonistic.

"I was driving yesterday, I heard a car backfire, and I panicked." As he relayed the story to me, I could see that beads of sweat were glistening on his forehead. "It felt like I was back in Iraq ... in combat."

"Do you remember waking up in the middle of the night sweating?" I asked.

"Yeah."

"So maybe you should take the pills," I prodded.

"No. They didn't help."

I felt badly for him, but was getting angry at his refusal to follow through with the help offered.

"The doctor said you ..."

"Quit givin' me shit about it!" he interrupted again. "I'm not taking the pills!" And with that, he turned his attention back to the TV.

"Okay," I replied. "And do you have to talk like that in front of the boys?" He ignored me. I sighed and walked out the front door. *If only there were a handbook on how to fix a broken husband ...*

SEVEN

BOUT FIVE WEEKS after my test—two months after originally applying for the job—I received a letter from the county and ran into the house to read it to Garrett. He was in bed, home sick because he wasn't feeling well, when I ripped open the envelope and quickly unfolded the letter.

"I … I passed the test!" I read to Garrett excitedly. "I'm number forty-one on the list of possible new recruits! Whoo-hoo!" I squealed, jumping up and down. "So far so good!" I boasted, approaching Garrett, who was propped up in bed watching TV. I shook the letter in front of him.

"Good for you! That's great!" he said, with almost no enthusiasm. "But don't get too excited, you haven't really done anything yet."

"Way to rain on my parade," I said, my excitement grinding to a halt. I squinted my face at him and abruptly left the room. I determined that his attitude was not going to ruin my enthusiasm. Why did he always have to do that? Was he angry? Was he jealous of my building a future while he lay around drinking his life away? I wondered, did he recognize that he was letting down the family and think I was rubbing it in his face? I couldn't figure out why he resented my actions so much, but I'd gone too far to turn back.

I reread the letter more closely and saw that the next step was a test designed to measure my physical strength and agility. I had two months to prepare.

According to the standards and training manual for police officers, I needed to be able to do a number of exercises ranging from bending and jumping to completing eighteen push-ups and twenty-seven sit-ups. And I had to run a mile and a half in fifteen minutes and twenty seconds.

The more I thought about the testing, the more my excitement waned. Now my stomach hurt and I lost my appetite.

Unsure as to whether I could accomplish any of these feats, I got up early the next morning, put on some shorts, laced up the closest thing I had resembling athletic shoes, and prepared to give it a try. After picking up small children for many years, I had good upper-body strength, so push-ups were a cinch. Sit-ups were easy, too. The run was my main concern.

Summer was coming to a close, but it was still very warm where we lived, good running weather, or so I thought. Optimistically, I drove my brown boat three-quarters of a mile from home, measuring it on the trip-o-meter. Once it reached three quarters of a mile, I searched for a landmark that would help me to remember the spot and focused on an ivy-covered telephone pole near the street on the corner. *Perfect!*

"I will run to that telephone pole and back," I repeated to myself, as if I needed to hear it to motivate me to do it. Then I drove home and parked in the driveway. I went in the house, grabbed a hat and drink of water, then ran out the front door to complete the task at hand, or at least to attempt it. *I can do this, it's just one foot in front of the other. Let's go.*

Jogging felt familiar, yet brand new at the same time. At first I felt I could run forever—listening to the slap of my old shoes on the asphalt, breathing in and out methodically, I felt fabulous. But this was short-lived. By the end of the street, I was winded and had to walk. *I am certainly not in cop shape!* For the next few weeks I would need to get up earlier than usual each morning and jog the neighborhood, pushing myself to go just a little bit further each day. So while the boys slept, I exercised. This was a first. But it didn't take long, and within just a few days I could keep moving for a mile and a half at a very slow pace. The question remained: Just how slow was I?

Armed with a digital egg timer, I ran to the telephone pole and back, clocking a time of sixteen minutes, thirty seconds, which meant I had to shave off a minute and ten seconds in only a few weeks. It didn't sound like much, but when discussing one's physical ability to move through space, one minute could seem an eternity. I needed all the help I could get.

"You're only as good as your tools," my dad's voice rattled around in my head as I laced up my worn old athletic shoes one morning. I remembered that growing up, when he hadn't been at work, my Dad had been quite the handyman around the house. Often he could be found fixing something, with me glued to his side, watching. I remembered him working on the back fence one day, and I must've been about ten years old. I watched with amazement as he shot long screws into each slat of the fence to keep our dog from visiting the neighbor's yard. My awe of the power of an electric screwdriver had prompted him to tell me the importance of having the right tools, and it had stuck with me all these years. It was obvious that I needed some better tools, starting with a new pair of running shoes.

The boys needed shoes, too, so we went to the store after school, and, as always, I was determined to find a deal. This was not the time to spend money needlessly; on the contrary, I felt guilty even thinking about new shoes for myself. My boys were rough and ready as they come, and even at seven years old, they knew what they liked, which often cost more money than I was willing to pay. The boys were alike in many ways, but when it came to fashion they had very different styles, which I tried to respect. Growing up, though my sister, Gwen, was younger, I had been smaller and repeatedly had to wear her hand-me-downs, which never seemed right to me.

While my sons searched for the perfect footwear, I located some good quality running shoes in my size (albeit, in an ungodly shade of purple, which was probably why they were on sale). But they were comfortable and half price. I put them on and jogged around the shoe department to see how they would feel in action.

"Ma'am, why are you running around the store?" asked a woman with a name tag who was about as round as she was tall. She had come over to see what I was up to.

"I'm testing my shoes," I replied on my lap around the shoe aisle.

"Well, please stop before you run over someone!" she demanded.

"I'll be careful!" I said, concentrating on the feel of my heel as it hit the floor with each step. I wasn't worried; no other shoppers were currently in the footwear department.

"I'm going to have to get my manager," she warned.

I slowed and stopped, quite pleased with the feel of the shoes but not so with the clerk who had obviously never purchased a pair of running shoes in her life. But who was I kidding? Neither had I.

"These are running shoes. How do I know if they'll work for me if I don't run in them?"

The round woman turned and walked away from me, mumbling. I could hear the word "crazy" slide out under her breath.

I grinned while taking off my dreadfully purple runners just as my sons came over carrying shoeboxes.

"Mom, why was that lady mad at you?" Colton asked as I packed up my runners in the box and slid on my old shoes. He added, "She was mean."

"I think she was crazy," said Jake.

"I think she thought I was crazy," I answered.

"She did, Mom, she said so," Colton added. I shrugged.

Colton picked up a pair of shoes and the soles lit up. He lit up, too.

"Mom! I had these shoes in kindergarten! Remember, Mom?" he bellowed as he bopped up and down. "Mom!"

"Yup, you did. You want some of those now?"

"No way! We're too big for light-up shoes!" Jake said. Colton shot him a dirty look.

"And if I remember correctly, you guys ran around the store like I did today, just to see them light up."

"No, Mom, we ran around to see if they made us go faster," Jake clarified as he sat on a bench, opened a box of canvas shoes, and began to wriggle his foot inside. Colton was furiously trying to untie the light-up shoes.

"I thought you were too big for these?" I questioned as I reached for the shoe.

"No, *he* is too big for these," Colton said, pointing at his brother. "*I* like them still." He handed me the shoe and I unraveled the knot, then handed it to him as the sole blinked red and blue.

"Mom, too bad these don't fit you, huh?" Colton added, sitting on the bench next to Jake. As he struggled to put them on he added, "They're like police shoes, Mom, see? Red and blue lights."

"That's true."

"Yeah, Mom, that's what I think."

"Okay, buddy. Now you two hold still while I check the fit." I knelt down and felt the toes of each of the boys' new shoes. Both showed plenty of room for growth. Just then Colton took off running while Jake rolled his eyes at his brother.

"How do they feel?" I asked.

"Great!" said Colton.

"So you can run around to test your speed, and that's okay?" I teased him.

"Yeah, uh-huh, kids can do it. But grown-ups who run around stores are crazy," Jake put in his two cents. His eagerness to share his opinions was often exhausting for me, even though most of the time I loved that he had them, and the confidence to share them.

All the crazy talk reminded me of Mr. Hargreaves' unwarranted, ear-piercing screams emitted while he reclined on the long wooden bench in the cell during my tour of the jail.

"Grown-ups running through a store may be silly, but crazy is something entirely different," I stated.

"How do *you* know?" Jake asked in a snooty voice, then climbed on the bench and immediately jumped off, presumably testing his shoes, and certainly my nerves.

"No jumping, young man. Stop! Sit down and I'll tell you how I know." He stopped and sat. Colton sat, too, next to his brother. Both boys slipped off their shoes and placed them into their respective boxes, and I waited until I had their undivided attention. Once both sets of big brown eyes were aimed straight at me, I began.

"When I toured the jail, I saw a person who was mentally ill. He was screaming and screaming, for no reason at all," I explained.

"That's weird, why would a person do that?" Jake asked.

"I don't know why, Honey, but they do … I know they do." And I realized the job, which I had yet to get, had already taught me and my boys a lesson.

That afternoon, I picked up a pair of black running shorts, an athletic bra, a good pair of running socks, and a pink wicking t-shirt, all on sale and reasonably priced so I could feel good about the purchases. You're only as good as your tools, and like my son with his light-up shoes, I expected my new purple monstrosities to make me fly.

EIGHT

IIIIIIIIIIIIIIIII

IN THE PEACEFUL QUIET—with the exception of my footsteps—of the crisp morning air, I ran to the telephone pole and back each morning, before showering and getting lunches ready for my family. I felt one with the world watching the sun rise each dawn, peeking over the huge trees lining the street in our mature neighborhood. Colors and shadows I would never see during the bright daylight caught my attention. Birds, squirrels, and an occasional bunny crossed my path, as did other joggers. It was September, and the weather in Northern Nevada had abruptly changed, to my benefit. Running in eighty-five-degree heat only a few weeks before, I had been huffing and puffing the whole way, but in fifty-five-degree weather it seemed to take much less effort. That coupled with my new gear did make me faster, and my time showed a difference. Within a few weeks, I had mastered the mile and a half at fifteen minutes and twenty seconds, and I was confidently ready for the test.

Beyond birthing babies, there had been few times in my adult life when I had been expected to perform extraordinary physical tasks. This was one of those times. But babies arrive regardless. Mothers can change their minds in the home stretch and it doesn't matter, that baby will still come out. Like most young mothers, I hoped and prayed for simple births. My own mother popped me out almost before arriving at the hospital, and I figured I would do the same. But the twins were born cesarean section, as a precaution; the doctor stepped in and, exercising skill and precision, made it happen, within minutes handing each of us an incredibly beautiful baby boy, pink and perfect, with little work on my part.

In this testing situation, however, no one was waiting in the wings able to cut the pain and deliver the goods. This task was entirely up to me, every inch of it. If I didn't succeed, I'd be back at home, still dependent on someone else for every single thing in my life. The thought of failure turned my stomach.

The letter said to meet at the sheriff's department at ten o'clock in the morning, upstairs in the deputies' weight room. I almost didn't trust it; I brought the letter with me, in case they didn't have my name on the list and I would need some sort of proof I belonged there. I entered the building and took the elevator to the second floor. Two muscular, rather intimidating deputies greeted me.

"Name."

"Excuse me?"

"Your name. What it is your name?" said the stone-faced deputy.

"Oh, sorry, Elizabeth Dolinsky, but I go by Beth."

"In here, you go by Dolinsky. Go in and find a seat, Dolinsky."

Their abruptness stunned me. So did the fact there were no chairs in the weight room, so those of us in attendance were forced to sit on used workout equipment that looked like it had seen better days. I found an empty weight bench, sat down, and waited, glancing occasionally at the two deputies at the door. *I bet they work out together,* I thought. *They're symmetrical, like bookends. "Deputy One" and "Deputy Two," like characters from Dr. Seuss.*

The room was very cold and quiet, with the exception of heavy metal music playing softly from a boom box in the corner. My hands and knees were shaking, and I could barely sit still when Deputy Two took my blood pressure. Knowing it had a tendency to run high, I closed my eyes, breathing deeply to calm myself; it read 128/72. Normal.

Dismissal came quickly for one overweight young man with high blood pressure, and as the door slammed behind him, the rest of us lined up to begin the push-ups. Deputy One went over the very specific requirements.

"Push-ups must be done on your toes, feet together, with your legs and back straight," he demanded in a low monotone voice, as if he were reading to himself. "Hands must be aligned under your shoulders. Eighteen is what we need to see. Does everyone understand?"

"So, no *girl* push-ups," said one of the young ladies, giggling and flirting as best she could, and it seemed to work.

"Exactly, no girl push-ups," reiterated Deputy One, looking at her with the first big smile I'd seen him give. "All right people, let's go … two at a time."

The first two applicants striving for push-up prowess were sent home, one having only reached fourteen, the other just twelve. It was my turn.

As I placed my hands on the cracked blue mat and arranged my feet together, legs and back straight, I could smell the cologne of the fellow who had just failed lingering in the air, and hoped it wasn't a bad omen. As soon as I began, Deputy One counted, "One, two, three …" and my pink, wicking t-shirt floated up to meet my abdomen with a tap, in rhythm with his voice. I pumped out the required number easily, just as I'd expected. My face flushed when I stood, unaccountably embarrassed to have completed the task when the younger people couldn't.

Once each applicant had completed the push-ups, the deputies placed us into teams; one recruit was to kneel and hold the ankles of the other while he or she completed the sit-ups, then we would switch places. Partnered with a tiny female who looked thin and frail, with accentuated collar bones and a soft, wispy voice, I wondered if she had the strength to hold even one of my feet down on the mat, much less both together. We were lined up in the first group of four teams to attempt the task and listened to Deputy Two give the instructions.

"All right, people, twenty-seven sit-ups is the requirement. The only thing to remember here is that your shoulders must touch the mat with each repetition, or it will not count. You guys got that?" The crowd mumbled.

"I can't hear you! You got that?"

"Yes, Sir!" we shouted.

"That's better. Okay, begin."

With abdomen muscles still sore from practicing at home, I began doing my sit-ups in time to Deputy One's counting off, "One! Two! Three!" I was careful to lie all the way down each time. It felt odd having a complete stranger holding my ankles, and I tried not to breathe on her as I exhaled on the up-swing. My partner smiled when I reached my twenty-seventh sit-up. She was a lot stronger than she seemed, holding my ankles perfectly stiff, like they were dipped in cement. I did the same for her as she completed her twenty-seven even more smoothly and speedily than I had.

The day was not so bright for one heavy, young man that went after us and failed the testing process when he was unable to exert one last sit-up.

One sit-up! The trainers cheered for him to push just a little harder. "You can do it!" they prodded and encouraged this poor young man who, by the looks of it, could really use the experience and training of a police academy. In the end, he could not muster that final "up" and was sent home. I was astounded. Why would an applicant contend for this job without having tried the exercises, at least one time, to assess his skills before testing day?

A few feet away, a female applicant failed the vertical jump, which concerned me since I had yet to do it. As the disappointed woman walked toward the door to leave, the deputy called me up to attempt it.

"Dolinsky, over here," called Deputy Two, standing near the wall. I hurried to where he stood. Up close, this man was huge, with biceps that were roughly the same circumference as my thighs. He put some blue chalk on the fingertips of my right hand, held my arm up above my head, and pressed my fingers to the white wall to mark it. Then, re-chalking my fingers, he said, "To pass the jump you need to touch sixteen inches above the mark on the wall. Okay?"

I nodded.

"Well, then, whenever you're ready."

I bent my knees, jumped with all my might, and slapped the wall as high as I could manage. Landing, I stepped back and watched the deputy measure my attempt.

"Only fourteen and a half; you have two more tries," he said. He grabbed my right hand and looked at my fingers to be sure I still wore enough chalk to mark the wall. Then he said, "Go ahead, but try it like this." I watched as this enormous man leaned forward, knees bent in a skier position, swinging his arms back and forth. He looked ridiculous, like a little kid, and I held in a laugh.

"Okay," I said, mimicking his actions. Lowering myself forward, I swung my arms forward, back, then forward again and jumped, this time stretching my abdomen upward as high as I could, I slapped the wall. He measured.

"Nice, sixteen and a half," he announced, seeming proud of me, then turning his attention to the line. "Who's next?"

I beamed. With relief, I quickly returned to the pool of waiting recruits, which had dwindled down to twelve.

TO COMPLETE THE RUNNING portion of the test, we had to drive to a nearby high school to use its running track. I could feel my heart beat in my throat and swallowed hard to push it down, as I parked in the school parking lot. The track surrounded the football field, and it was obvious the grass had recently been cut and watered because the scent of mown grass was strong and sweet.

Today we would complete six laps. The first task was a three-hundred-yard sprint that was to be completed in seventy-seven seconds or less.

In a few moments, all the applicants were standing on the track. We were split up into three groups of four, and I was in Group Two. All of us were led across the wet grass, shoes sinking a little in the muddy spots as we crossed. We reached the starting point and waited for the signal, a wave of an arm from the timekeeper standing on the finish line. Deputy One, who stood at the finish, waved for Group One to begin. They ran quickly, one man way ahead of the other three runners as they strode by the deputy.

All of us in Group Two lined up and waited for the wave. When it came, I was all focus, intensity furrowing my brow. I ran as if everything in my whole life depended on it, because it did.

I was so focused on the run that I paid no attention to my time when the deputy shouted it to me as my foot crossed the finish line. I didn't care what it was, only whether I had passed. And when I heard him yell "Seventy-four seconds!" to the last runner in my group as she crossed the line, I knew I had been within the required time limit. I had passed. With only one more trial, the mile and a half, soon this nerve-wracking experience would be over. I was going to do this!

Breathing the crisp autumn morning air deeply into my lungs, I relaxed a little, confident that I would soon be on to the next phase. Everything was going my way, even the weather, which was an impeccable fifty-five degrees with no wind.

We started the run as a group lined across the track. After the "Ready, go!" my body pulsed with adrenaline. My competitiveness kicked in; I wanted to pass people and pull ahead of the pack, but I reminded myself that this was not a race against them, only the clock.

Once we'd rounded the first curve, the cluster of runners fragmented into smaller groups. A few of the fastest runners took off, pulling far out on their own. I was in the middle of the crowd, running alongside a few really slow people who seemed almost to be walking. I pulled forward slightly and began keeping pace with a woman next to me whose pace was quicker than mine. This was fine with me; I felt strong and capable, and the sound of our steps in unison helped me to focus. With each stride our shoes crunched into the rubberized track under foot.

According to the cheap watch I had purchased for the occasion (figuring it would be a bad idea to bring my egg timer), if I could just maintain my current pace, I would finish at right about fifteen minutes flat.

By the third lap I was winded. I started counting my breaths to take my mind off the importance of finishing. *Relax, you got this!* I told myself to counteract my waning confidence. By the fourth lap I began to see spots. I focused on the crunch, crunch, crunch underfoot.

I slowed a little to let the faster woman go ahead of me, but she slowed too. We were in this together, I realized, and we continued together around the track. I wondered as I ran, sweat now rolling off my forehead and into my eyes, what reasons were motivating these other runners here today. What was driving them to become sheriff's deputies?

I reached my arm above my head and wiped my forehead on my shirt sleeve, then rolled my shoulders a few times, to relax them. Now we were in the home stretch. When we were about half way around in the sixth and final lap, Deputy One began yelling.

"Hurry! You aren't gonna make it!" he hollered at us. I was certain my pace was faster than any I had practiced. Surely I was within the allotted time. Stretching my stride, I pushed with all my power, quickening my speed across the finish line, certain I had passed the test. I slowed to a jog and checked my watch: It read fifteen minutes, three seconds.

"Sorry, ladies, you'll have to try again," the deputy said.

What?! How could that be? I checked my watch again to make sure the sweat hadn't clouded my vision.

Barely able to catch my breath, I huffed, addressing him between gulps of air. "What ... do you mean ... try again?" I held up my watch and pointed at it with my other hand. "Look!" I huffed, inhaling deeply, "we made it ... with seventeen seconds to spare!"

"Sorry," he said, dismissively. "You'll have to start over with the application process, and test again." With that, he turned and walked away, unconcerned about having dashed my hopes for my future; any ability I might have had to control my own destiny had been crushed by seventeen measly seconds.

No. No way. I made it in time. I knew with such certainty that I had been successful, I became enraged. I turned to look for an ally, someone who could back me up. I looked pleadingly to the woman who had run beside me. She only shrugged.

So that was it? A shrug? No support? No debating? No fighting for what was ours? Well, her household may not have been falling apart like mine was, but I wasn't ready to accept defeat.

Standing there in disbelief, disappointment an unending well inside me, I watched the applicants that had passed their run line up in front of Deputy Two to receive envelopes full of information for the next step of the process. The rest walked dejectedly back to their vehicles.

Am I the only one upset about this? I spun around, looking for anyone at all who could tell me I wasn't crazy, that this guy obviously didn't know how to work a stopwatch. But I was alone, and out of options. I could do nothing.

My eyes were full of tears as I drove home to tell Garrett. He had been right. I hadn't *really* gotten the job after all. Still completely baffled by what had occurred, I arrived home and saw with relief that my husband had already left for work. I felt a tiny bit of joy when I realized that by the time he returned from Herlong in three days, he likely wouldn't even remember I had taken my test. Perhaps I'd never need to tell him I had failed.

All I wanted to do was crawl into bed and stare at the ceiling. But there were kids to feed, things that needed to be prepared for the next day. Everything in my life felt so unfair.

I got the boys ready for bed early—so early, in fact, that it was still light out when I dragged myself into bed, stared at the ceiling, and began talking to myself. *It just wasn't meant to be. Maybe something else will come along. Maybe I should be the squeaky wheel and call them tomorrow. Dammit! Why did this happen? There's not a doubt in my mind, I passed that run! I know I did!*

NINE

THE NEXT DAY I AWOKE prepared to call the sheriff's department to question their timing tactics. But as I sat in the kitchen drinking my morning coffee, I convinced myself that it was of no use. Why would today be any different than yesterday? I had no evidence, nothing but my cheap watch and strong convictions. I reluctantly forced myself to accept the inevitable: I would not be a sheriff's deputy. Time for a new plan.

At one-thirty that afternoon, Garrett called from work. He was having flashbacks and still hadn't been sleeping well. I couldn't help but feel irritated, because I knew that this might not be happening if he had listened to the doctor the first time, and had stayed on his medications. It had been four months since he had threatened to kill himself, and he hadn't taken any of the suggestions made by our doctor, nor had he visited the recommended psychologist. Down deep, I still loved Garrett, but I realized that I didn't like him much.

When it had become evident he was not going to get help from the VA, our family doctor, or the recommended psychologist, I had encouraged him to talk with the men at the church. There were many veterans at church who might be able to help. From what I had read about Post-Traumatic Stress, he needed to know he wasn't alone. If he could only connect with someone who understood, someone who had been there, it might make a difference. I bought him a book on recovering from PTSD, and I had begun giving him back rubs before bed to help him sleep. There was little more I could do.

At four o' clock that afternoon, the phone rang, interrupting my day-long funk.

"Hello?"

"Hi, Elizabeth Dolinsky?

"Yes, that's me."

"This is Deputy Rowland from the Reno Sheriff's Department. Since we had so many people fail the run yesterday, we've decided to offer those recruits one more opportunity to re-test in two weeks. Would you be interested in testing again?"

"Absolutely!" I said, exhilarated. Then, my curiosity getting the best of me, I asked, "Does this happen often?"

"No, I've never seen them do this before ..." Then he seemed to catch himself having said too much. "But, uh, well ... uh ... okay, so, we'll see you the morning of the fifth at ten a.m., in the deputy weight room." And then he abruptly hung up.

I understood. He knew they had made a mistake, but was afraid to admit it. But that was all right, it didn't really matter to me. I was just so excited to have the opportunity again, something to look forward to. A shred of hope.

Two WEEKS LATER, on the fifth of October, it was another beautiful day. I needed to complete each of the tests again in the same order, and by now I was well prepared to do so. The cold weight room gave me chills when I opened the door. It was much busier this time, with many more new applicants compared to my first visit, and four of us previous hopefuls retesting. I breezed through the weight room portion of the test, including the jump, to my relief. Then, again, we drove ourselves to the nearby high school to use its track. I noticed a different deputy handling the stopwatch, which reassured me, though I hoped not mistakenly, that we would have a competent timer this go round. We began with the three-hundred-yard sprint, five at a time, and though I wasn't the fastest in my heat, as was the case two weeks prior, I crossed the finish line at sixty-seven seconds and very pleased.

The line of recruits spread across the track like a ribbon. It was time for the mile and a half.

"Six laps everyone!" called the timekeeper. "Ready! And ... GO!"

I looked for my former running partner, but she apparently wasn't testing, at least not today. Running in much the same mode as my previous effort, I enjoyed the scent of fresh grass and the constant crunch of shoe strikes, counting breaths through my fatigue and wiping sweat drops from my brow. Out of breath but optimistic, I crossed the finish line.

"Fifteen-o-eight. Nice work," the timer announced. I had done it! This time my watch was almost in sync with theirs at fifteen-o-nine.

Once the last runner had finished, the new timekeeper handed me that coveted thick manila envelope. "Don't leave any lines blank. We begin the background check as soon as it arrives on our desk. Good luck!!" he said.

The background packet had to be returned to them within two weeks. Only then would they schedule a physical exam, psychological exam, and Computer Voice Stress Analysis, or CVSA. All of it had to be completed as soon as possible if I was to make it into the January academy. *Me, in the police academy?* I thought to myself. *Could this be real?*

Garrett, who had forgotten all about my test, as I'd suspected he would, was at work in Herlong when I returned home that day. I decided not to call him for fear of upsetting him further. But just a few minutes after I got home, he called me to say that he had been invited to join the group "Lead Cross," our church band, as the new lead guitarist. He'd hung around with the guys in the band in the past; the drummer also worked at the depot with him. I was pleased because it gave his confidence a needed boost, and gave him something to look forward to. I could hardly stand his gloominess lately. Perhaps getting in with the band would help him to curb his drinking. I felt happy for him. It seemed things might be getting back to normal.

HALLOWEEN WAS RIGHT AROUND THE CORNER and the boys had a harvest party to attend, one of our biggest events of the year. Their costumes had to be just right. Colton and Jake were usually pretty easy-going; I'd dressed them as Mickey Mouse or Sponge Bob Square Pants in years past. This year, both boys had to use their imaginations. Colton wanted to be a football player, and Jake a hobo. I visited a number of thrift stores to find shoulder pads and a helmet, and for Jake I sought overalls, a stick-on beard, and a gray wig. We still needed a jersey for Colton and a beat-up old hat for Jake, both of which we knew could be borrowed from their cousins. Gwen's kids had everything.

Gwen was two years younger and the complete opposite of me—loud, boisterous, naturally blonde, the life of every party, and a little self-absorbed.

In high school, she was a cheerleader, the prom queen, the quarterback's girlfriend … basically, every girl's nemesis. In college, she married her physics professor, who was a whiz at the stock market. They lived lavishly and wanted for nothing, and, in my opinion, their children were somewhat spoiled. When Gwen wasn't attending a pageant with her six-year-old daughter, or watching her nine-year-old son perform ballet, she was getting injections into her laugh lines or having her boobs done. If I'm being honest, we'd never been close, and I feared some things would never change.

"So … Dad said you're considering going to work?" she asked over coffee in her newly remodeled kitchen. "You sure you want to do that?"

"Well … yeah, why?"

"I dunno … Dad's a little worried about you, says you seem stressed."

"Yeah, well, I am! I've been nothing but a stay-at-home mom for eight years! The thought of starting a career at forty makes me a little nervous."

"Then why do it?" she asked. "I'm sure Garrett doesn't want you working."

"Garrett? He … uh … well … it's not entirely up to him," I replied. I debated telling her the truth about what had been going on at our house, but wasn't sure she'd understand. For a moment, I considered full disclosure, but only for a moment.

"I'm stressed out, too!" my sister said, naturally directing the conversation back to herself. "I got a letter in the mail this week saying we were late getting Chastity's application in for the regional finals! Can you imagine her sweet little face not going to finals? I've been on the phone all week about it!"

I chugged my coffee and got up to leave, realizing Gwen was not my sounding board for real issues. "So, thanks for loaning me the Halloween stuff." I made my way to the door. "The boys will be thrilled to have their costumes ready."

"You're taking off so soon?"

"Gotta go," I said as I accepted her hug. I thought how we both clearly wished we were closer, but neither knew how to make that happen. As I drove away, she waved to me through her front window. I waved back and then, in a flash, remembered that I had my appointment at the doctor's office for my exam, and drove straight there, hoping I wouldn't be late.

I was, but just by a few minutes. They ushered me right in, and within minutes the doctor was giving me a physical exam, checking everything from my height, weight, and body mass index to my hearing, vision, and lung capacity.

"Blood work looks good, eyesight, hearing … all good," said the doctor, rifling through my lab results and other papers pinned to the file on his lap. "Looks like you are fit for duty." And I watched as he wrote "FIT FOR DUTY" in large capital letters next to my name. I felt absurdly pretentious leaving his office, walking a little taller than I did when I entered, boosted only by my temporarily swollen ego. By the time I reached the minivan, my head was full of doubt. Next week was the psychological exam and, surely, if my family and friends were correct, the therapist would see right through me.

I ARRIVED EARLY the day of my appointment at the psychiatrist's office, which was a beautiful old home that had been converted into office space. Even though I was early, there were already three other women in the waiting room. I figured we must all be here for the same reason, so I said "Hello," and, to be neighborly, I began to ask if they were also here to complete police testing. But before I got it out of my mouth, the receptionist preemptively "shushed" me with a finger to her lips and pointed to a seat.

"Oh, sorry," I whispered, and I shut up and sat down. We waited in silence. All my life, I had prided myself on my positive attitude and friendly demeanor, and never understood such rudeness.

An assistant arrived from the back of the old house and explained the testing process. She was dressed in a designer suit, with perfect hair and makeup, and her bright red lipstick was so glossy I couldn't take my eyes off of it as she spoke.

"A portion of the test is written and a portion is to be taken on the computer," she said. "Once you begin, there will be no more talking."

What talking? I thought wryly.

"The questions are strategically worded so that your answers reveal something specific about your psyche; there is no right or wrong answer. Okay?" asked the assistant, lips glistening. "Any questions before you begin?"

"No," we said in unison.

She moved us to strategic computer locations in different rooms and gave us our packets to begin the test. As I followed the professional assistant down the hall to my computer, I felt a little envious. This young twenty-something was so poised, confident, and established in her career. Here I was, probably fifteen years her senior, just trying to start one, no makeup, no suit, no bright red lips, just a post-baby belly and a closet full of jeans. *She couldn't have kids,* I told myself.

"Do you have children?" I asked her.

"Yes, I have a three-year-old daughter and an eighteen-month-old son." Damn, there went that theory. *Well, good for her … she probably has a rich husband and a housekeeper, too.*

I opened the book to complete the written exam first there were almost six hundred questions, all true or false—questions like, "I almost always feel happy," or "Sometimes I am nervous for no reason." Then, about a hundred questions later, came; "You are happy most of the time," and "You occasionally feel very anxious." And so it went for over an hour, with questions repeating over and over, and me confused about whether to answer with "T" or "F."

The next test was to be completed on the computer. This one was as long, if not longer, than the written test. Going page by page on the monitor, it seemed to take forever. There were the same types of questions I'd seen on the written exam, but these were multiple-choice answers. It went on all morning, and by the time I was done, it was noon and I was starving.

While the perfect twenty-something assistant and mother of two hurried between our computer terminals, checking to see that we had each completed every portion. I sat quietly—or, all but my stomach, anyway, as it was growling so loudly I was convinced that people in the offices with closed doors could hear it.

Finally, when time was up, I left the psychiatrist's office with an appointment to return for the results.

Two weeks later, the psychiatrist ushered me into the beautiful old house, down the hall, and into his ornately decorated office. The doctor sat behind an enormous, wooden desk flanked by floor-to-ceiling bookshelves, and I sat in a very low chair, the only one offered, in front of his desk.

"So why do you think you're so perfect?" he began, his eyebrows squeezed together as he spoke, creating a unibrow.

"Perfect? Uh … not sure what you mean by that," I sputtered.

"You answered every question like you have the perfect life, like you have no troubles," he said, condescendingly. "Everyone has issues, and you are no exception." I felt like a child in trouble in the principal's office.

"If you only knew!" I exclaimed. "Honestly, I have been a housewife for as long as I can remember. I need to help support my family, so I applied for this job."

"So that's why you want the job? To support your family?"

I nodded to him.

"But why law enforcement? Seems like an odd job for someone like you."

"Uh, 'cause I don't type?" I smiled. I knew I was being a brat, but I figured after all those tests, he would know more about me than I did. I halfway expected him to tell *me* why I was going for this job. But he didn't move a hair, just sat quietly looking at me. And I, in turn, returned the stare over the enormous wooden desk. I wondered if he was searching for the dealbreaker that would keep me from becoming a deputy, the fatal flaw that all my friends and family seemed to recognize. Finally, he spoke.

"Well, all right, Elizabeth," he said. "I will forward my findings to Backgrounds, and you will be hearing from them." And in the blink of an eye, I was outside, standing on the front step of the old house, the door shut behind me. Later, I discovered that this doctor had used much the same approach with many of the other female recruits.

Deputy Rowland contacted me after receiving my psychological exam results and said that only one more mandatory exam stood between me and my new, exciting career: the voice-stress test. Then my file would be placed on the sheriff's desk for approval. Could I come in tomorrow?

So on that early November morning, I arrived at the sheriff's department to take the Computerized Voice Stress Analysis, which was administered by a female deputy with reddish-blonde hair who looked to be about my age. We entered a tiny room furnished only with two chairs and a table, on which sat a shoebox-sized machine. To date, every deputy I had met during this hiring process had been males who had worn casual uniforms with embroidered badges. This woman looked sharp in her crisply pressed, tan shirt, dark green trousers, spit-shined boots, and glistening badge on her chest. This could be me in a few months, if I could pass this last test.

"More people are let go due to lying than for any other reason," she said. "Better to just be honest about everything." Her warm demeanor put me at ease. Besides, this was a lie detector test. What did I have to lie about?

"Honesty is the best policy," I reiterated, demonstrating my earnestness. I felt certain this test would go without a hitch. Next, she explained how the test would work.

"I will ask questions such as, 'Is the sky blue?' and you respond with 'yes' or 'no.' It's that easy." I nodded my understanding, and we began.

"Am I wearing a watch?" She held up her arm for me to see her watch.

"Yes." The small machine made quick scratching noises with my words.

"Is the sky blue?"

"Yes." More scratching sounds.

"Have you ever used illegal drugs?"

"No."

"Is my shirt tan?" It was.

"Yes."

"Have you ever stolen items from a place of employment?"

"No."

"Have you ever stolen money from a place of employment?"

"No."

And so it went. After answering fifteen to twenty questions, she hit a button on the machine and stopped the test.

"Beth, I have to tell you, you are missing one vital question on the test. Without passing this question, I would have to disqualify you."

"What question?" I couldn't believe that I was failing an honesty test. I was a God-fearing woman, for goodness sakes! Lying wasn't in me.

"When I ask you if you've ever stolen anything from an employer, what's going through your head?"

"I was thinking of different jobs I'd held in high school and college. I'm thinking, maybe I took pens or paperclips, staples, or other office stuff over the years. You know, inadvertently."

The deputy laughed. "I won't let an overly sensitive internal guilt meter ruin your chances!" she said comfortingly. "Let's try this. Why don't you lie to me?"

"Lie to you?"

"Yes, I'll ask a question and you lie, so I can see how the machine measures a lie versus a panic. Ready? Here goes." She pushed the button to start the machine again.

"Is the wall gray?" It was.

"No," I lied.

She immediately stopped the test.

"That's it, you're fine. You pass," she said, smiling, just like that.

I gasped with excitement, somewhat embarrassing myself, and felt my face flush.

"Really?!" I cried.

"Yes! We'll be in touch soon to let you know what's next."

I gushed with thanks to her before heading out the door, resisting the urge to hug her. I felt triumphant. Only six months prior, I had handed the clerk at the human resources office my application. Now my testing was complete, and my fate was up to the sheriff. If he approved my file, I would hold the title "Deputy Sheriff Recruit." It hardly seemed real.

TEN

▯▯▯▯▯▯▯▯▯▯▯▯

THE HOLIDAYS WERE FAST APPROACHING, the city was abuzz with a feeling of Christmas spirit, and I seized the opportunity to decorate. I pulled advent calendars out of dusty boxes, and hung them where the boys could reach them, knowing they would be excited to open the tiny doors each morning. Stockings hung from the mantel, and I even baked my mom's favorite holiday pecan pie early this year. We hadn't even celebrated Thanksgiving yet, but all this took my mind off the fact that I had not heard from the sheriff's department. I was beginning to imagine other jobs that I might apply for, and promising myself that I would hit the streets with resumes right after New Year's. Garrett was feeling better—and, consequently, so was I—because he and the boys of "Lead Cross" had lined up a full calendar of paying gigs during the holiday season.

My time, when not completing my usual tasks, was spent volunteering with the elementary school parents' group fundraiser and planning what to bring to the church ladies' potluck, which would be at Sylvia's house this year. Still, on a warm Thursday afternoon, I stole away to do some holiday shopping and pulled my brown boat into the doughnut shop drive-through for a quick pick-me-up. I paid and thanked the girl working the window who handed me a warm, glazed doughnut, so fresh the coating hadn't even hardened yet. I promptly took a large bite, the warm fattening sweetness covered the inside of my mouth, and I heaved a blissful sigh of indescribable pleasure.

My phone rang. I sent my sticky fingers scurrying though my purse, and finally retrieved the phone. It was the Reno Sheriff's Department on the line.

"Hello?" I mumbled through a mouthful of doughnut. It was Deputy Rowland calling.

"Mrs. Dolinsky, we would like to offer you a job. Sorry for the long delay in getting back to you, but the academy starts mid-January, if you're still interested."

I struggled to swallow the enormous ball of doughnut in my mouth so that I could enthusiastically answer "Yes!" But trying not to appear too eager, I calmed myself, and instead replied a muffled, "Uh, yes, I am interested."

"Can you come here Tuesday to pick up your equipment?"

"Mm-hmm," I responded, and tried to thank him before hanging up the phone.

But the relief of getting the job opened up a floodgate of thoughts that rushed through my head as I hurried home to tell Garrett my news. It was time, after all, to fill him in, and I dreaded it. But then happiness overcame me as I told myself, in the car, "I'm going to the police academy! *Me!* A police officer!"

The irony of the doughnut was lost to me.

"No! I don't want you in law enforcement!" Garrett argued when I explained what I had been up to that night after dinner.

"And what are my choices?" I asked. "We have no savings! We live paycheck to paycheck. You make a good living, sure, but I can't trust that you'll always be here. It's time I help out."

"You do this, you're going against me!" he said loudly. It seemed lately that he always spoke louder than necessary. Then he softened. "Everyone makes mistakes. Come on, Babe. I need you to trust me, that I can make it right. I promise, I will never do it again. Don't do this."

I remained quiet. Oh, how I wanted to believe him. I never wanted to be against him.

"How do I know you won't have another episode where you drink and gamble?"

"I told you, I promise! You'll see! I'm a different guy!"

I thought a moment, debating how to convince him that this was a good thing without making him feel like the bad guy, then opted for flattery.

"You'll always be my warrior. You'll always be the man of the house, the one running our family." I spoke quietly, watching him grow more at ease. "But I need this. And I need your support, Babe. Nothing will change between us, because we're a team, right?"

"We agreed you'd stay home and raise the kids, remember? Not go to some academy," he argued, using guilt over our kids. But we both knew, standing there, that our marriage had outgrown those roles. I grew angry. I wanted to yell as loud as I could, right into his face "You gambled our money away, you idiot!" Instead, I calmly said, "Garrett, I love you, but I'm doing this, with or without your support. I have to."

"Fine," he said curtly, then left the room. With one word, he had spoken volumes.

ELEVEN RECRUITS MET TUESDAY morning and were seated at an oblong table in a conference room; only three were male. I recognized two women from the psychologist's office, and my pacer from the first mile-and-a-half run was there. We smiled across the table at each other. Curiosity and wonder filled my mind.

An older, skinny woman entered carrying two large bags—one full of black belts, the other full of items unrecognizable to me, all made of thick, black leather and obviously designed to fit on the belts. She poured the bag of items on the table before us and placed eleven boxes of handcuffs down as well.

"Everyone take one of everything. Then come over here, I need to get your measurements," she said. While she wrapped belts around people and used a measuring tape for necks, arm lengths, and inseams, I was studying what the other recruits were doing with their equipment.

"This is a guard for your mouth, in case you have to do CPR on someone," said one rather rough-looking woman as she held up a plastic item. She was wearing a tank top showing off her many tattoos. Her dark brown hair was short and spiked, and her teeth looked like she smoked a lot.

Neale was her last name, I heard someone say, and she continued in a whisper, "I'm not going mouth-to-mouth on any inmate, with or without this guard, no fuckin' way." My sensibilities were shocked by her attitude and language, but I also knew I'd need to get used to it. And I was thankful to have heard her, because never, ever, would I have guessed the item in question was used for mouth-to-mouth.

A few recruits were issued belts before it was my turn. I watched them putting the items on like stringing beads. I learned by listening that one item was a case for the cuffs, one was a holder for a collapsible baton, one was for a flashlight, and one was a case for the mouth guard thing. There were some pieces of leather with snaps; I asked Neale what they were.

"Keepers. They hold your belts together."

Once we were all measured, the skinny woman had us sign papers accepting responsibility for the equipment issued, and as we walked through the door to leave, she handed each of us a flashlight and a baton … that is, until she became irritated by having run out of belts.

"Some of you will get your belts when you pick up your uniforms. Give me at least two weeks," she said. Then, mumbling under her breath, she added, "'Be nice if they budgeted for all this."

Many of the recruits worked at the sheriff's department already; a few dated or even were married to deputies. All of them, it was obvious, knew more about the business than I did. Neale was very comfortable with many of the people at the table, and they were planning to leave the building and head to a uniform supply shop to buy boots, something I needed to do, too.

"May I tag along?" I asked.

"Sure, we gotta get boots soon so we can get 'em polished before the first day. They like to have an inspection on the first day of every academy, that's what my ex-husband said happened to him."

At the store, Neale knew the owners and was certain of exactly what she wanted. Six of us walked in and headed straight for the boot section. I tried on every style they had, but bought the same as Neale, which, according to the clerk, was their "bestseller for law enforcement." I felt pangs of guilt and stress spending two hundred dollars on boots for myself, but I reminded myself that it wasn't an option.

Two weeks later, we all met back at the sheriff's department to pick up our uniforms: two pairs of green pants, two tan shirts, and two belts, one for pants and a heavier one for equipment called a "Sam Brown," or duty belt. I also received a pouch each for pepper spray and a tape recorder, as well as a key clip and a radio holder, which was quite large. Then the skinny woman handing out equipment instructed me, "You can get your own gun, holster, and magazine case."

"Magazine case?" I asked her, wondering what the heck I'd need magazines for.

"Magazines. You know, they hold the bullets?" As she said this, a few of the recruits laughed. *I knew that,* I chided myself.

After arriving home, I laid the new items on our bed. The holster was the only piece whose best location I could estimate with any accuracy—on my right hip, of course. But I had yet to purchase it. Alone in my room, I grappled with what would be the most efficient way to organize my gear on my belt. I easily strung the black cases along the heavy leather belt, but my waist was too small to hold everything I had, much less the magazine case and holster to come. I left the radio and pepper spray pouches off for now.

In order to report back on whether anything didn't fit, I tried it all on for the first time. The crisply pressed, men's pants were awkward and ill-fitting on my body, and felt even weirder once I tucked in the short-sleeved shirt with dark green Sheriff's Department patches on the sleeves. Once the belt was through the loops and buckled, I grabbed the duty belt at each end, and jerked it off the bed up to my mid-back, leaning forward to steady it around my waist until I could get it clipped in the front. Everything felt completely foreign to me, and now I understood what they meant by "keepers." I slid one of the thin leather straps around both belts and snapped it into place, then a few more, and slipped on my boots. Then I stood there, staring at myself in the mirror, overwhelmed with pride, confusion, ineptitude, anxiety and, yet, deep down ... a sense of purpose.

Looking at myself in the mirror, I felt like a kid trying on a new Halloween costume. I walked into the living room, wearing all my gear, to give the boys a fashion show. Garrett was at a band rehearsal, but the boys were home watching cartoons. I entered the room and stood in front of them, feeling a bit silly, sort of like Ralphie in his bunny suit in *A Christmas Story.*

"Ha! Check out *Mom!*" Jake laughed and dove off the couch to inspect my belt.

"Wow, can I play with this?" said Colton excitedly, pointing to the baton.

"Hang on there, guys ... " But they were so excited to try pieces of the uniform on themselves that I soon relented. We sat on the floor in the living room, next to the Christmas tree, and played with the handcuffs and the other police equipment.

I saw an opportunity here to discuss how they felt about Mom going to work. Never had I missed a first day of school; never, not even once, had they returned home from school to find me not there. The thought was enough to break my heart and fill my eyes with tears. In their short academic careers, not a single school function or field trip had I missed. All that was going to change. There would be no missing a day of the academy. My complete dedication was expected, and I felt the need to explain this to my sons.

"Look at me!" Colton yelled as he turned on my flashlight and placed it under his chin, lighting up his face like a scary mask. His warm brown hair glowed from the light. Jake was busy trying to unlock my handcuffs, which he had tightened too tightly around his wrist in a matter of seconds. I handed him the cuff key, my only key, which looked so lonely hanging from the key clip on my belt.

"Hey, guys, when the academy starts, I'm going to be busier than I used to be. You know, I won't be able to go to your school for reading group or field trips for a while."

"We know, Mom, you told us that last night, remember?" Jake said as if I were an idiot.

Colton had always been so easygoing, sweet, and emotional. His brother? Well, not so much. But parenting my strong-minded boy often gave me a burst of pride. I loved his spunk, his "go for it" attitude. It enabled me to worry less about him being successful in life. Jake was a leader, never to be a "yes man," and he rarely took no for an answer.

While the boys and I talked, Magnum ambled over and curled up across my green, polyestered lap, ensuring I would need to de-hair my uniform before Monday.

"Well, I want to be sure you understand that I *want* to be there. Okay? It's just that I need to work now," I said. "I need to know you'll be okay."

"Mom," Jake added, "my friend's mom works. It's no big deal."

"Maybe for you it isn't a big deal, but for me, it feels like a *huge* deal." I said past the lump in my throat. "Dad may need a little help around the house, too, when I'm not here."

"We can cook and take care of ourselves. It's not like we're babies," Jake said. I found he exhibited many of Garrett's good qualities, and this independent streak warmed my heart at this moment.

"I know you can cook some things. You guys are pretty self-sufficient, and I'll show you how to do the laundry so you always have clean clothes for school." Then I added, "Thanks for being supportive, you two. It helps a lot."

Colton, who was now messing with the keepers, effectively punctuated the conversation with, "We know Mom, we'll be okay."

My heart swelled with pride over my boys. I smiled, hugged each of them, kissed their cheeks, and silently asked God to please watch over my two little men while I started this new adventure.

HAVING A HUSBAND in the Army and a father who had hunted, I was, of course, familiar with guns. But I hadn't fired one in fifteen, maybe twenty years, and the provided list of approved firearms was nothing but words on paper to me. I needed to purchase a gun before beginning at the academy, but I felt ill-equipped to do so alone, and I certainly was not going to ask Garrett for help. I thought of asking my dad. When Gwen and I were growing up, Dad's weapons came out of hiding occasionally, just prior to hunting trips, and were promptly cleaned and put right back into their mysterious hiding place, the location of which we never knew.

While I was Christmas shopping one afternoon, I decided to pay Dad a visit to talk about my impending purchase.

Though he and Mom had divorced long ago, they had reunited about six years ago and had together bought a small but comfortable home just north of our neighborhood. I never knew how they did it—put aside their problems, his memories of her drunken episodes, her feelings about his cheating. They had each said, "When you reach a certain age, none of it matters anymore."

At first I had been angry. If there had been the capacity to work things out, why hadn't they done it in the first place? Gwen and I never would have been forced to deal with all that came with being the kids of divorce— listening to one parent lament about the evils of the other, or wondering where to spend a holiday that wouldn't hurt one or the other's feelings, or hosting events so that they wouldn't have to be seated at the same table (or, if we could help it, in the same room).

When Mom was alive, I had spoken to her so much that Dad and I didn't need to do any talking; through her we shared the large and small details of each day, and she kept everyone apprised. So even though we hadn't established a pattern of talking on a regular basis, I felt close to my dad. He had been by her side through her cancer and had taken impeccable care of her, despite the fact that she had not been an easy patient.

Since her death, I had committed to making more of an effort to connect with him. Though he wasn't happy with my choice of career, he seemed to accept it, even trying to find the positive side. "When you get done with training, you'll be able to handle yourself, that's a plus!"

From our recent communications, I'd realized that Dad was inclined to see the positive side of pretty much everything. When the high Sierra winds had blown down his fence a few weeks earlier, he'd simply shrugged and said, "I needed to replace some slats in that fence, anyway." And when Jake had spilled his soda all over the floor in his kitchen, Dad simply smiled and said, "Well, guess I'm cleaning the kitchen floor today. It needed it anyway." There was always an upside, and it was his way to find it … with one exception: his hearing aids, which he utterly refused to wear.

"Hey, Dad?" I began. We were seated in his living room, I on the couch and he on the recliner. "Where did you keep the guns when Gwen and I were growing up?"

"In the gun safe," he said, rubbing his hand over the top of his balding head.

"Where was the gun safe?"

"In my closet, behind the clothes," he said. "Don'tcha remember the big boxy piece of furniture in the closet?" As if I'd spent hours in his closet as a kid. "I've gotten rid of most of the guns, but still got the safe in the garage. You wanna see it?"

"No, I don't need to see it."

"Huh?" he yelled, exasperatingly. "Well, come on out here, let me show it to you."

Dad, now in his seventies, had a way of getting me to do what he wanted to do, regardless of my interest. I wasn't sure whether it was his hearing or his attempt to just plain ignore me. But I didn't want to hurt his feelings, especially since I'd come to him for assistance, so I followed him into the garage.

"It's kind of a big safe. You can get a smaller one," he said.

"Dad, we have a gun safe already."

"You do?"

"Think about it, Dad. I'm married to the Army!"

"Oh, yeah, I forget sometimes." He kept talking in his rough, old-man voice, as we stood in front of a huge closet-like safe, which was old, outdated, and had nothing to do with why I came over.

"What kind of firearm are you going to get?" he asked as he opened the huge door to the safe.

"No clue, I have to ..."

"What? Huh?"

"I have no clue!" I yelled.

"I just don't understand why Garrett won't help you with this? Did you bring the list? Let's go in and look at the list, maybe I can help you." We walked back into the house, down the hall and past the master bedroom. I stared for a minute, halfway expecting to see Mom in there, but her hospital bed, of course, was gone, and only the queen bed she and Dad had shared remained. Everything here was tidy and perfect. No sign of her illness, or of her, with the exception of the blue-and-white checked décor, which was all her.

"I was once told by an old guy ... he was kinda crazy ... kind of a nut, this guy ..."

Dad reminisced as he entered the living room and sat in a recliner, "Anyway, he told me once, a long time ago ... he said, 'A gun is like a woman; you know the right one as soon as you hold it.' He believed finding a gun was like love at first sight. Kinda crazy, that guy, don't know that I ever had that experience."

"Really? That's funny," I said, pretending to be interested as I showed him the list. "Uh, here's my choices."

"Well, these are all really fine firearms on this list. You can't go wrong with a Smith and Wesson. That's for sure. I had a friend who had a Sig Sauer. He loved that gun ..." Then Dad started in to another story. "You know, when I was about your age ..."

I was growing impatient with him and was anxious to gather more information before it got too late in the day and the boys arrived home from school.

"You want to go to the range with me?" I interrupted him.

"Nope, I have a lunch date with the geriatric crowd," he said, referring to the bunch of retired casino buddies he met every week for lunch. At seventy-three, he was the youngest, most active of the bunch.

"Yeah, well, okay then. I'm gonna get going. Thanks for your help."

"What's that?"

"I'm gonna go now!" I yelled.

"Oh, okay, Honey." He sounded disappointed. "Not sure I helped much."

"You did. Just nice to see you, Dad!" I hugged him and was out the front door.

I nervously headed to the indoor shooting range in town, hoping to gain insight. I knew Garrett was a Beretta man, and though he had owned many handguns throughout our marriage, I wasn't welcome to use any of them. Nope, I needed to buy my own.

The range was located in a warehouse district in town, and the owner, an older gentleman named Bill, was very accommodating once he learned I was a recruit for the sheriff's department. He allowed me to test some firearms to get "a feel for them." Of the five approved brands, he had four on hand: Glock, Berretta, H & K, and Smith and Wesson. He took me into the range area to explain how to load and shoot.

The range was rather dark and somewhat creepy inside. Seeing the round targets all lined up at the end of the lanes reminded me of a bowling alley before the game begins, pins all lined up just waiting to be knocked down. Bill gave me a very quick lesson in handgun safety and provided eye and ear protection for me—large yellow glasses and what looked like 1980s headphones. He demonstrated aiming and shooting a few times, which, even with headphone protection, still left my ears ringing.

Each shooter had a lane. Targets hung from clips on a wire about thirty feet away, and Bill showed me how to bring my target closer or push it farther away using the ropes. He loaded just a few bullets into each of the four guns lined up on the table in front of me.

"I don't know what you've been told, but most cops carry Glocks," Bill said, picking up the Glock handgun. "You will hear a lot of people say you need a forty or forty-five for increased firepower," he went on. "I say accuracy is just as important. It won't matter what you carry if your shots miss the target." With that he placed the Glock in my hands, moving my fingers into proper positioning.

After a few safety instructions, Bill said, "This is not rocket science. Just place this sight," he pointed to a tiny bump on the top nose of the gun, "between these two sights, see?" He pointed to two bumps near the back of the gun. "Line them up and squeeze."

The Glock was cold and heavy in my hands. I was smart enough to know to keep the muzzle down range, but that was about the extent of my knowledge.

"Squeeze the trigger, nice and slow," Bill instructed. "Don't be in a hurry. I'll check back with you in a few minutes." He left me so that he could assist other customers in the store, and a wave of fear went through me as he walked away, leaving me standing there with a gun in my hand.

The only other person in the range was an old, gray-haired man using the target two down from mine. Scruffy and unshaven, he looked a little scary holding an enormous handgun that resembled something out of a Dirty Harry movie. I stood, holding the Glock out in front of me, ready to shoot, and stared at his target as he placed six bullets through the tiny center circle in a matter of seconds. He caught me staring at him; embarrassed, I quickly looked at my own target as if I had been aiming the whole time.

"Just squeeze, like he said, nice and slow. It should be a surprise when it shoots," he said to me, smiling. Then he packed up his enormous gun and walked out. It all felt surreal. Had someone said I'd entered some parallel universe, or told me I was in the Twilight Zone, I'd have believed them.

Alone now at the range, I closed one eye in an attempt to visually align the sights to aim. *Well, here goes.* I squeezed the trigger of the Glock and BOOM! My hands bounced upward, uncontrollably, with force, and I brought the gun back into position quickly. I held my breath as I shot twice more, until the semi-automatic was empty of rounds. Then I placed it back on the table. The feeling of power and strength from controlling an instrument of deadly force in the palms of my hands was captivating, sexy even. I tried the other three guns carefully, nervously keeping the muzzles aimed down range toward the target, so as not to make an unsafe movement.

I had pretty decent aim reaching the target with almost every shot, but no single firearm spoke to me more than the others. I gave Bill a wave through the window to indicate that I had finished, and he came back to the range to pick up the loaner firearms. He asked me what I thought.

"I learned the Smith and Wesson grip was too large for my hand, and the Beretta felt nose-heavy to me. Glock and H&K, well, I don't know, really."

"Then go to a gun shop where they sell Sig Sauer, and check that one out, too, just to be sure," he said thoughtfully. I paid him what I owed, and thanked him for his help.

Driving home, I passed a gun shop and stopped to do as he suggested. Sig Sauer was the last on the list, and there was a shiny new P226, nine millimeter handgun in the glass case, so I asked to see it. The man behind the counter was friendly as he checked the firearm to be certain it was unloaded before handing it to me. As soon as I held it, I knew. It fit my hand like none of the others, like it had belonged to me all along and had just been sitting in the case waiting for me to find it. I knew I couldn't settle for anything but the Sig. Although it was more expensive than the other firearms on the list, this was the one tool, I knew, that might save my life one day.

Altogether, the holster, magazine holders, and firearm came to just over eight hundred dollars. I asked them to hold the items for me overnight.

When Garrett got home that evening, I told him about my Sig and he agreed I had made the best choice; though I could see that he didn't want to seem interested, this, after all, was his forte. He went out to his car, returned to the house with a wad of cash, and handed it to me.

"What's this?" I asked.

"Get your gun tomorrow."

"Where did you get this money?"

"Don't worry about it, just go get it, you're gonna need it," he said calmly.

I suspected he'd won it gambling and was astounded that he'd so much as admitted it to me, since he'd so recently promised me never to gamble again.

"No! I don't want your gambling money!" I snapped.

"Don't give me that 'holier-than-thou' crap. Your dad was in the casino business your whole life! You've always lived off other people's losses! I'm letting you pay for something with winnings!"

I reluctantly took the money. He had a point.

"I know I can win all our money back, Beth, you gotta believe me," he continued with a gleam in his eye. I just shook my head, flabbergasted, and wondered just how long he'd been gambling and just how much money he'd won and lost over the months or years. Though I was excited to buy my gun, I felt more suspicious of him than ever before.

THANKSGIVING DINNER was always held at my sister's house. Every year, the whole family was in attendance. I would have loved to host everyone at my home, but there just wasn't enough room. It didn't really matter to me where we met, as long as we had dinner as a family. When my mom had been alive, dinner had been a team effort, all of us working together, taking turns basting the roasting bird and combining all the ingredients for mashed potatoes, candied yams, green bean casserole, cranberry sauce, and homemade bread, not to mention Mom's pies, made from scratch. Now it was up to me, the matriarch of the family, to continue the tradition. Even though Gwen had the bigger home and hosted the event, I felt responsible for it going off without a hitch. I was two years older, so the torch passed to me, and I had a list a mile long of things needing to be done prior to heading to Gwen's home.

On top of that, Colton needed to come up with a pilgrim costume for his part in the school play. Jake needed three dozen cupcakes for a bake sale to fund their class's year-end trip to the zoo. I needed to make centerpieces and get some of the cooking prep work done.

To save money, I made everything from scratch. I had been hoping to visit Bill at the range sometime to practice shooting my Sig, but I couldn't seem to make that happen.

After gluing a buckle on a hat that I had found at a secondhand store, making cupcakes, and completing much of the cooking prep work. I wound up so stressed and exhausted that I found myself, on Thanksgiving, with the flu. The boys and Garrett went to my sister's house while I stayed home in bed, awaiting the leftovers.

It took almost two weeks for me to get back on my feet—just in time for the academy to begin. I couldn't wait. Christmas parties in both kids' classrooms kept me baking cookies and wrapping gifts, and thankfully I had completed most of my Christmas shopping. Still recuperating, I was taking things a little slower in order to rest before beginning my new law enforcement adventure.

Christmas was emotional for me because it had been such an important holiday to my mother. She had always taken such pride in decorating her home, placing a huge tree in the middle of the house, each limb heavily adorned with one or more of her prized and meaningful ornaments. The boys loved her impressive Christmas village, complete with working train, which encircled the tree, and the mound of gifts underneath. Over the years, she'd decorated the living room ceiling with handmade beaded ornamental balls, which were suspended with satin ribbons. Walking into my parents' home during the Christmas season had been like entering a real-life gingerbread house.

But things were different now. Just two years ago, as the cancer claimed her body, it also ate away at her desire and ability to celebrate the holiday, and she died shortly thereafter. Last year's holiday season had been a blur. But this year, I didn't want to go to Gwen's house and see her happy family and have to answer her many questions about my recent life choices. I just wasn't up for it. So we had Marge over, and while the boys opened their gifts on the floor, Marge sat on the sofa and I balanced my behind on the sofa's armrest next to her. Garrett walked over to me, put his arm around my middle, and gave me a squeeze as if to say he approved of my holiday efforts. I appreciated that, though in my mind we were frauds. Though we looked like the subjects of a Norman Rockwell painting, the typical, wholesome American family (if there ever was such a thing). I wondered if, perhaps, behind the scenes, the families he painted were really just as dysfunctional as ours.

THE NIGHT BEFORE my first day in the academy, only one simple task remained: shining my boots. The task I'd assumed would be simple proved to be the opposite. The clerk at the boot store had told me to use rubbing alcohol with cream polish. Seated on the floor in front of the sofa while the boys watched television, I rubbed, then added polish, then rubbed some more. Garrett was at a band event, thank goodness, because I would have hated for him to see me struggling with something he had done a thousand times. The boots were clean but not shiny, and I wanted to see my face in the gleam, which was not the case. I had achieved no gleam at all.

Discouraged, I checked on the computer. We'd recently gotten Internet service, but the suggestions online were vast, everything from spitting on the boots to lighting them on fire. The latter was supposed to "burn off the residue so you can get into the leather." I was not accustomed to spending two hundred dollars for footwear only to destroy them right out of the box, so that method was swiftly excluded from my list. I dipped an old cotton shirt in polish and rubbed over the toes of my boots, over and over, for hours. By bedtime, they were close to shiny, which was going to have to do.

I knew it would be virtually impossible to sleep that night, and as I got ready for bed, I prayed that I would have the strength to complete this task ahead of me. I felt a bit like a kid the night before the first day of school. But like a kid, one who stays home for years until one day when he goes to kindergarten and his life changes forever, I was on the precipice of a new life, too. And while I thought I knew what to expect, I also knew that I couldn't possibly. I didn't see myself as a law enforcement officer any more than I saw myself as a lion tamer. If there had been a need for lion tamers, I might have considered that job too.

ELEVEN

‖‖‖‖‖‖‖‖‖‖‖‖

I FELT LIKE A CHILD playing dress-up in my uniform. Eating breakfast with the boys, I was extra cautious to avoid spilling cereal on my outfit or milk on my almost-shiny boots. Still, despite my best efforts, right before I left the house, Magnum ran over to me and wiped his furry little body up against my pristine pants. I sighed and hunted for the lint roller. My pants de-furred, I hugged the boys and left. For the first time in their young lives, I was leaving the house before they did in the morning. Garrett would drop them off at school that day, on his way to Herlong. They wanted to walk to school on their own, since it was just down the street. After all, they reminded me, they were in third grade now. I had to tell them that I just wasn't ready for that.

As I drove across town, I felt guilty, like I was abandoning my offspring in the wild to fend for themselves.

Pulling into the academy parking lot, I looked around. There were enormous pick-up trucks and other off-road vehicles, some sports cars, but, not surprisingly, no other two-tone minivans. I parked my ridiculously conspicuous vehicle and hurried to the big glass front door. It was chilly this January morning as I entered the cold cement building and wandered down the main hallway until I found the ladies locker room and went inside.

Three other female recruits were standing by their lockers discussing ways to pin their hair up. I wore my hair short, so I hadn't needed to worry about the regulation "off-the-collar" mandate. They looked at me and kept talking. I smiled awkwardly, located my locker, and dug into my pocket for the combination. I opened it, keeping my back to the women.

Another recruit, a tall woman with a man's haircut, was standing at her locker near mine. She nodded a greeting; I returned it with a grin.

After ironing my husband's uniforms for the past sixteen years, I was more than qualified to starch my uniform crisp and placed one suitably pressed shirt and pair of pants in the locker. The other set I wore. I also placed sweats, an extra set of clothes to change into at the end of the day, and my lunch in my locker, shut the door, and left the locker room, turning my attention to locating the academy classroom, just down the hall.

I entered the classroom grinning, unable to conceal my eagerness and anticipation of the many exciting adventures ahead. Still smiling, I greeted the other recruits.

"Good morning!" I nodded to the group. Most of my fellow recruits turned away and completely ignored me. One female recruit said "hello" and went back to reading. A few young men in the back of the room were discussing purchasing their holsters and why they had chosen Berettas over Glocks. A group of women were standing together, looking over each other's uniforms, reassuring themselves that they looked "squared away," a term I had heard Garrett use and one with which I would become intimately familiar.

The academy was designed to weed out those who didn't have the stuff to be deputy sheriffs, and rightly so. As the officer had told the children in Jake's class all those months ago, "Not everyone is cut out for this line of work." I'd learned on my jail tour that the sheriff's department was actively seeking women because of the increasing number of females committing crimes and becoming inmates in the jail. Soon I would realize that this academy, my key to a new career, a new lifestyle, was comprised of an unprecedented, disproportionate amount of females: thirteen men to fourteen women.

The classroom was cold and sterile, with large windows along the left side and three walls of painted cement block. *Would it kill them to put up a valance?* I thought. I wasn't sure what I had been expecting—cork boards with brightly colored crepe paper edging and cardboard cut-outs of snowmen for winter? Thick block letters that read, "Welcome new recruits"? I had to remind myself, *This isn't really a classroom; it's a law enforcement training center, for goodness' sakes.*

I found my seat thanks to a placard bearing my last name, which was strategically placed at one of the long, thin tables in the room. I was happy to be in the front row, on the far right side. A thick white binder sat on the table before me. I took my seat.

In what felt like an instant, recruits were scurrying to their places, standing at attention. The women from the locker room stumbled in and raced to stand behind their chairs. Everyone was at attention, rigidly facing forward with their heads high and their arms held taught, straight down by their sides. I stood, too, but never having stood "at attention," per se, I copied what my neighbor recruits were doing, and wondered what started the commotion in the first place. I turned my head slightly and watched.

In walked the administrative staff of the academy, a stiff, uncomfortable parade of three. It was made up of two men dressed in dark green battle dress uniforms, or BDUs, and one older gentleman in a fancy dress uniform; his brass badge glistened, as did the large chevrons tacked to his collar. I suddenly felt completely out of place and hoped uncertainty wasn't written all over my face like a billboard reading "clueless." At the same time, I couldn't help smiling at the irony of my presence in this room, and of the formality displayed, like the queen of England had just sauntered up the aisle.

The man wearing the brass was the academy commander, who, in no uncertain terms, told us how things stood in one sentence: "I am the academy commander, which means I am in charge of this academy." As if I'd had any doubt.

Very brusque and robotic in his mannerisms, he walked back and forth across the front of the classroom as he spoke, leaving long pauses between thoughts.

"This job isn't for everyone … Law enforcement is an honorable … exceptionally rewarding career … But make no mistake … This academy is going to be tough! … As recruits, just beginning your careers … you will be tested to see where you're at … in terms of fitness … in terms of skills … and in terms of trainability … And for some of you … in all probability, in all likelihood … this testing will be harder than you ever have been tested before." He walked across the length of the room slowly before continuing.

"Subsequently, some of you will not make it through this academy, if you do not demonstrate …" he stopped and looked at each of us, "the wherewithal necessary, compulsory really … to become … an exemplary law enforcement officer." He resumed his pacing. "But, for those of you that *do* make it … you will have an unbelievable opportunity … to be orientated into an amazing … a challenging … a gratifiably leading-edge career … And, like me, your talents and your skills may be recognized, and you possibly will demonstrate the propensities to move up through the ranks … as I have done, recently being promoted to Sergeant." He stated this last pompously, with his chin up and eyes closed.

The stiff sergeant continued talking for ten minutes about his career and how he had come here from Southern California, and how he had accomplished so much in a short time due to his "undying dedication, natural abilities, and willingness to do what it takes, irregardless of what that might be." He was obviously impressed with himself and wanted us to feel the same. I cringed as he spoke and repeatedly fought the urge to correct his poor grammar.

After only fifteen minutes (though it seemed much longer), the stiff sergeant left the room, and the mood lightened immediately once the door closed behind him. Our trainers took over explaining what we would be covering in the following fourteen weeks.

"The majority of the academy for a few weeks will be classroom and lecture, but don't worry, we will get to the fun stuff like driving fast and shooting guns," said Deputy Benetti in a scratchy voice that indicated to me that he smoked too much. Benetti had a hard, leathery face from years of working the streets, yet he wore a soft, comfortable expression. It was clear he had seen it all in this business.

"Look around this room. Look at each other's faces. Because, I'm tellin' ya straight up, these will be the people you will be closest to throughout your career. The men and women in this room will have your back like nobody else. There is a special bond. I mean, I don't want to sound corny …" Benetti seemed uncomfortable with the topic. He wore a thick moustache and perpetual smile, which made me curious whether he was honestly happy, or if his face was just stuck that way after years of squinting in the sun. "What I'm trying to say," he continued, "is it's a unique brotherhood that you will experience with the cops you meet in the academy. It's just different, don'tcha think so?"

With this, he looked to his partner, Deputy Smythe, the same man who had shown me around the jail. He looked much younger than Benetti and was quiet, serious, and seemingly nervous, with an apparent inability to stop bouncing his leg up and down while he sat on a stool in front of the class.

"Yeah, I would say that I have found it to be true," Smythe agreed. "My closest cop friends are the guys I met in the academy." Smythe's jumpiness was evident, but these fellows appeared much more approachable than the stiff sergeant, who wasn't a big man but in sheer command presence, and ego, seemed to tower over them both.

THE MORNING OF OUR FIRST DAY was full of preparation and paperwork. The deputies discussed their expectations of us and gave out the study guide for Friday's quiz. Not much else happened before lunch. I ate in the locker room, then dressed out in the gray sweats they issued, which had my last name emblazoned on the back, and met with the other recruits on the tarmac behind the building. The afternoon would be filled with physical training, or PT. I realized that acronyms would rapidly comprise much of my vocabulary.

Though it seemed to me that we had lined up quickly, it had not been quickly enough for Deputy Benetti, who yelled at the top of his lungs, "I'm gonna tell ya straight up, you people are slower than any academy I've ever seen! You're gonna have to pick it up, people!"

There was an icy cold wind blowing toward us as we did the first set of jumping jacks. Benetti walked between us, counting and trying to look like he was scowling, yet he had a smile on his face at the same time. He certainly enjoyed his work.

Deputy Smythe worked out with us, his thin face sporting very pink cheeks as the cold wind hit. He was stronger than he looked, showing us his impeccable physical condition throughout the workout. He never even broke a sweat. In comparison, his partner dragged his feet between the rows of jumping trainees, yelling, "If this is all you got, you all have tons of work to do before you will be able to graduate this academy! Our standards are high! You will all meet them, or you can get a barista job in a coffee house! Do you hear me?"

"Yes, Sir!" we cried in unison.

"What's that, recruits?" he called back.

"YES, SIR!"

There were three heavyset male recruits in front of me, one of whom, Phoenix, was having a difficult time. We began stretching our backs, then our sides and legs. Then we were directed to get into push-up position and a number of recruits groaned. Benetti yelled the count loudly, "One, two, three … elbows out! Four, five, six … let's go, ladies! What seems to be your problem, Mannington?"

Benetti had stopped pacing and was now standing over Recruit Mannington, a pretty twenty-something woman with stunning blue eyes and long brown hair pinned up in a bun, who lay on the ground on her belly. "You had better toughen up, Missy, or your dad will not like the report he receives from me, just tellin' ya, straight up!"

"Yes, Sir," she said and hopped back into push-up position, arms shaking. Pumping our arms this slowly was excruciatingly difficult. Even with a strong upper body and having practiced at home, I found this really tough. Benetti would occasionally stop the count while we were in the down position, just to mess with us. It worked. Holding myself up on my palms, with my elbows out, halfway through a push-up, I was beginning to sense sweat on my forehead despite the cold wind blowing. I was counting my breaths, like I did when I ran, just to take my mind off the discomfort, when Recruit Phoenix dropped in front of me. I peeked down the line at Mannington, who was holding firm. *Good girl!* I thought.

The burn in my abdomen and the cold wind on my extremities drowned out Benetti's yelling at the recruit who lay on the tarmac. Mannington never dropped again.

Suddenly, Benetti gave us the word to "line up and let's move your asses, people!" While he stood there shaking his head back and forth in disappointment, we sprang into position three wide.

Deputy Smythe yelled, "Be loud! Be proud!" to which we responded, "Yes, Sir!"

"I can't hear you!

"Yes, Sir!" we shouted louder into the icy wind.

Marching around the tarmac, Benetti paced us with a cadence: "I don't know if you've been told!"

"I don't know if you've been told!" we echoed in the old, familiar tune.

"Deputy Smythe is really old!"

"Deputy Smythe is really old!" we exuberantly echoed back.

"I don't know if it's been said!" he continued.

"I don't know if it's been said!" came our chorus.

"He's so old he's almost dead!"

"He's so old he's almost dead!"

My nose was running now, and I was trying to sniff hard before wiping it on my sleeve. We jogged about half a mile and then Benetti gave us a break. He led us back to the building and instructed us to "dress out and go home."

With fingers numb, I worked the combination to open my locker and changed my clothing. As the women filed into the locker room, they chirped.

"I can't believe they worked us that hard on the first day!" exclaimed Mannington.

"I knew what to expect, having my ex-husband on the force. I think I'm better prepared than most of you," Neale said casually. "I don't mean to be arrogant or anything, but there were no surprises for me today."

"Guess that's just good planning on your part," said Olin, a young single mother who had a ponytail of obviously-dyed, cherry red hair. Under her bright red bangs, she wore heavy makeup, especially eyeliner.

"And PT is only going to get worse," said Neale. "When it comes to the classroom work, I even got most of the studying done for the first week. Got my ten-codes already memorized."

"That hardly seems fair that you have access to all that when the rest of us didn't until today," said Olin, to which Neale responded coldly, "Guess it sucks to be you."

My ritual from that day forward was to leave my uniform in my locker and dress in sweats for the drive to and fro. It was what most recruits did, and it meant that I could keep my weapons somewhere other than my home. The gun wasn't loaded, anyway; I didn't own any bullets.

ON MONDAY MORNINGS, we received study guides for the quizzes, which were always on Friday and covered ten-codes, a few specific laws, and vocabulary words. The other days either began and ended with lectures or were the two PT days each week.

The lecturers were fascinating, and were all given by prominent community members such as judges, prosecuting attorneys, victim advocates, and undercover detectives who discussed actual cases with us as if we were already peers. Not one got through a presentation without commenting on the ratio of women to men in this academy. It seemed a joke to many of them, who often said, "I've never seen so many women in an academy; you guys better watch out with so much estrogen in the room." We would all fake a chuckle.

Female or male, there was so much for us to learn in a relatively short time, only fourteen weeks. Search and Seizure law was incredibly complicated and left me with more questions than answers, but as beginners we needed only a general understanding. I got excited reading the syllabus each night in preparation for the next day's events. Classes like investigative procedures, which covered securing a crime scene and gathering evidence, were captivating. I had no idea so many simple mistakes could compromise a case. Equally interesting was what to consider when responding to a HazMat incident, such as not being downwind. The list went on and on. Each topic brought new insights, and I was spellbound through each lecture.

So far, my favorite lecture was by a victims' advocate who told a story, complete with horrific photos, of a woman who was afraid to leave her husband, despite him beating her. Dressed in a dark suit with a head of long curly golden hair, the advocate impressed me with her style and professionalism as she discussed her client's torture at the hands of her dirtbag husband, and how she stayed with him out of fear that he would hurt their children if she left him.

"This is common in domestic abuse cases. Men will use the safety of the children as leverage because they know the women will never leave if it means harm might come to their children. It's the oldest trick in the book." The advocate flipped the slide to a particularly gory close-up of her client's head, still caked with blood, staples running in long, distinct lines around it. "This woman had been beaten so severely it took over one-hundred-eighty staples to repair her head alone." I looked away for a moment, but had to look back for fear I would miss something.

Listening to the advocate share the gruesome details of this woman's plight, I expected to hear that the woman had eventually been killed by the dirtbag husband, but that wasn't the case. The lecture ended with a photo of the woman in the hospital, her head shaved and lined with staples, the parts of her face and body that weren't in a cast and were visible were completely covered in red and blue bruises.

The woman concluded the lecture by asking, "Are any of you familiar with this story? Do any of you know this woman?" No response came from the recruits. We were all captivated, waiting on the edge of our seats to learn the truth. "Well," she said, "the truth is, you ALL know this woman, because this woman … is me." My jaw dropped.

It took me a while to process her story and her transformation. Days later, I would catch myself thinking of her and wondering how she did it, how she had overcome the fear and gotten help, and then found the strength to use her own painful story in such a powerful, thought-provoking way to help others. Would I be able to exact that type of meaning from my future work? How could I evoke positive change for people as the victim advocate had?

BY THE END OF THE THIRD WEEK, one male recruit had been caught cheating and was escorted off of the premises. The stiff sergeant entered the room and we jumped to our feet at attention, per usual. He walked to the front of the class to address us.

"Look around you, recruits. What do you notice? Yes … one of your peers … is absent … That is because that young man made an incredibly unwise … incredibly foolish choice … He decided it would be a good idea to cheat … on this morning's quiz … and was subsequently escorted off the property!"

Pacing again, he went on. "I predict … we will, in all probability, in all likelihood, lose another recruit or two … before the end of this academy." At this, I could have sworn he was staring at me. We were down to twenty-six recruits—twelve men and fourteen women—and so far, I'd been holding my own with these younger trainees. Neither my age nor inexperience had shown to be a performance factor, yet.

Not only had we lost a recruit, but we had something to gain this day, for it was payday, something I had not experienced for years since Garrett and I had made the decision for me to stay home. Many recruits in this room had not been hired on with any particular agency and had paid out of pocket to put themselves through this academy. But those of us lucky enough to be hired by a law enforcement agency, as I had been by the county, were to receive paychecks.

Anxious, I couldn't stand to wait, so at lunchtime I drove over to human resources to pick up my highly anticipated proof of employment. I wasn't alone—a line of recruits had formed. When I finally reached the desk and was handed my check, I quickly read the face of it: $505.07. I was elated despite the relatively small amount. Clearly, it didn't look like much to one arrogant recruit, who complained, as we paraded out of the administrative office, "Damn, I should have scored more whip!"

But the way I saw it, we were lucky. It hadn't even been a full pay period, so it reflected only one week of work. Besides, we weren't really working at all, we were learning, and in most situations, people paid to go to school, not the other way around. To me, it was a grand start. To finally bring home some bacon, dough, bread, or "whip" … whatever, felt extraordinary.

Garrett acted as if he didn't care about my check, like it was an inconsequential contribution. But I knew him well enough to know that he was pleased at the sight of an actual income, especially after all the money I had spent in preparation for the academy. Still, this check was a stepping stone. My goal remained to pass. I knew I would excel when it came to the academics. I had some college courses under my belt and knew how to study and test well. Physically, I was holding my own, even doing better than some. But with so much unknown still ahead, such as shooting, emergency driving, defensive tactics, and scenarios which we had been warned would be difficult, I was careful not to get complacent.

Another worry was brewing in my mind, about my inability to connect on a personal level with the other recruits. In an attempt to make friends, I smiled and greeted everyone I met, and each day the recruits ignored me or stared at me like I was crazy, which was difficult to understand. Maybe they didn't expect me to pass and so chose not to invest time in getting to know me. Or maybe, I told myself, they were just rude people. Friendliness had always paid off for me in the past, and we were told, repeatedly, that the people we met here would be our closest companions. If these were the people I would trust with my life, who would be my "go-to guys" throughout my career, then I was in trouble.

I could see most of the recruits were connecting on some level. I saw many leaving for lunch together and overheard women in the locker room discussing dinner or weekend plans. Being excluded socially was a phenomenon I hadn't experienced since high school; in every other situation in my life, making friends had been a cinch. This left me confused and hurt. Not willing to compromise my personality for the sake of others, I continued to be friendly and kind to those who were not. Though the academy was not as demanding as I had anticipated, it was more like high school than I could have predicted.

TWELVE

FROM THE WAY HE PRACTICALLY SKIPPED into the classroom and wore an enormous smile on his thin face, it was clear Deputy Smythe loved teaching this class. Our primary trainer for EVOC (Emergency Vehicle Operations Course—another acronym for the growing list), Smythe appeared more excited than we did. In his khaki BDU's and matching cap, he guarded the keys to the vehicles parked on the tarmac outside as if they were his babies. I liked seeing this fatherly side of him and I wondered if his actual children were treated as lovingly.

I was pining to get my chance to drive, anxious to try handling a Ford Crown Victoria police car. But before any of us newbies would score the keys to a patrol car, we had to watch a video about vehicle safety that described how to effectively turn, entering near the outside curb and leaving near the inside. We also had to prove our ability to shuffle steer.

"This is a fundamental basic. If any of you do not pass the driving portion of the academy, you can bet you will not see the streets as a patrol officer," Smythe reminded us. "And I know you all want that, right?"

We walked out the back doors of the building to the tarmac, where a steering wheel sat, oddly mounted on a stand, waiting for each of us to display our understanding of shuffle steering. Smythe excitedly explained what it meant to shuffle steer.

"You always keep your hands on the sides of the wheel; this is proven to be the most effective manner of driving. There will be no crisscrossing when turning, none of this holding the wheel with only your palm or one finger. Nope, none of that. Let me show you an example." He gestured for us to come closer.

We circled around the trainer as he stood in front of the posted wheel and continued his teaching. "To turn left, you would do this." He put his left hand at the top of the wheel and pulled it down to the left. Right hand met the left hand at the bottom, taking control and continuing the movement upward. The hands met again at the top and lefty took control. It looked like his hands remained on their own sides of the wheel. Each of us handled the wheel, sliding our hands up and down the sides to his approval. Then it was time to maneuver around the track made up of orange pylons glowing against the black asphalt.

Our academy was located in the center of town, so using sirens in training would be disruptive to the neighbors. As it was, they were already forced to live with the popping sounds of shooting practice on a regular basis, or so we'd heard, having not experienced range training yet ourselves. The administration, powerless to muffle the sounds of the range, compromised, and the stiff sergeant told us NOT to use sirens in driving practice. I recalled reading complaint letters written by unhappy residents that had been printed in the newspaper more than once. They concerned distressed pets and unwanted disruptions to relaxation due to noisy police training. So we were warned not to play with the sirens, and were only taught which toggle switch effectively turned on the red and blue lights on the roof.

There were three cars parked in a line on the tarmac, two black-and-whites and a third painted bubble gum pink so poorly that it looked as if household spray cans had been used. I wondered if it had been done as a joke, a dig at the number of females in this academy. The black-and-whites had badges on the sides, so smeared you couldn't tell for which department they had once patrolled. We were to "load up" three recruits per vehicle while the others waited near the building for their turns.

Before I could blink, the first vehicle was packed with three males; another three bolted toward the second car as I sprinted and reached the driver's side of the pink car. I slid in and noticed that in the passenger seat was an EVOC instructor. On his tan shirt, "Gruff" was embroidered in black lettering. I hoped it was his name and not his demeanor.

Two other female recruits had climbed in behind me to the back seat—
Mannington and Carnie, the tall woman whose locker was near mine. She
had short, brown hair and freckles across the bridge of her nose.

My heart raced as I sat in the driver's seat of a patrol car for the very first
time. I studied the car and found dirt and grime on the door handle, and
holes in the wooden panel where knobs used to be, which worked equipment no longer needed in this car. The center console had about twenty
different buttons and switches, all unmarked.

"Belt up and let's roll," said Gruff.

"Yes, Sir," I replied, and I struggled to get at my seatbelt, which was
wedged behind me. Finally I grasped it and pulled it across my body. As I
clicked it into place, my hand hit a nearby toggle switch—the one that happened to control the siren. It blasted a screeching wail so loud, I was stunned
and froze for a moment. After a second or two, I realized what I had done,
and fumbled to turn off the noise so as not to disturb the neighborhood.
But which switch, in the endless row of unlabeled switches on the console,
could it be? The deafening pitch startled the stiff sergeant, who was watching
us from the sidelines. He threw his arms in the air and yelled something to
Smythe, who was standing next to him while angrily pointing to my vehicle.

"There's one in every class," Gruff joked dryly as he reached over and
effortlessly clicked the siren toggle button into the off position.

"Thank you," I beamed at him, relieved, and he nodded a silent "You're
welcome."

Mannington and Carnie roared with laughter from the back seat, now
that they could hear again. I turned my attention to the task at hand and
watched as the first vehicle pulled into the pylon course.

"Thank God that wasn't me!" Mannington said.

"No shit!" said Carnie. "I would feel like an idiot."

Ignoring their comments, I shifted the car into drive and followed behind the second car as it entered the course of orange cones. I drove slowly
to make sure I didn't hit any pylons as I maneuvered through the course for
the first time. Gruff directed me to "speed it up and remember to enter the
corner near the outside pylons until the center of the curve, then move near
the inside pylons, okay?"

"Outside, outside, inside," he said. "Come on, Dolinsky, pick it up,
they're gaining on you." The first car, driven by a young male recruit named

Jarvis, was gaining on me fast. He drove like a maniac, screeching the tires with each turn, as I crawled along, concerned with avoiding the pylons and practicing shuffle steering. I picked up the pace in the second lap, ignoring the young recruit who was making up track behind me, and noticing that each turn was now missing one or more pylons due to his carelessness.

We were instructed to change drivers every three laps. By the time I reached the beginning of the course at the end of my third lap, both cars were right behind me and few pylons remained standing, although none of them had been knocked over by me. When I stopped my car, I looked in my rear-view mirror and saw a police car with lights blazing pulled up and stopped behind me, a familiar, dreadful sight that instinctively made me gasp.

The reckless trainees lunged out of their vehicles and were directed by Smythe to "clean up." As the drivers jogged onto the course to right the downed pylons, Gruff watched and commented as he opened the door for Carnie to get out of the back seat, "Recruit Jarvis seems pretty squared away."

I got out of the car, puzzled by the comment. *Squared away? He took out half the pylons on the track, and he's squared away?*

Mannington knocked on the window to get my attention; she couldn't open the back door to get out of the car.

"It's about time," she chided as I cracked her door open from the outside. She jumped out of the car, took a few steps, and slid into the driver's seat. Carnie walked around the car and hopped into the seat behind the driver while I ran around the back of the car and into her vacated seat, the back passenger's side.

"Why can't we get out of the backseats?" I asked as I slid into the uncomfortable seat made of hard plastic. There was barely enough room for my legs to fit sideways between the edge of my seat and the cage wall separating the front and back.

"Uh, duh!" Mannington said as I closed the door.

"The crooks ride in back. They could escape if we allowed their doors to open," Gruff put in.

"Aren't they adjustable? My car doors have child locks that can be turned on or off. Maybe these are the same?" I asked.

"Jesus, this is a cop car, not a minivan, Soccer Mom. You drive like a freakin' turtle," said Gruff, gruffly. "Let's see if Mannington's got some fire underfoot."

And we were off. Having had the benefit of knowing the course by watching my performance, Mannington was able to maneuver more rapidly right away, which made me look even more foolish.

In my seat in the back of the patrol car, I couldn't help but think about the fact that prisoners frequented this space, sat in this chair where my rump currently resided. I wondered who else had taken a ride in there, experienced these surroundings, and why. Had a murderer ever ridden in here?

Looking up at the cage designed to keep me out of the front seat, I realized that if we were to crash, and God forbid catch on fire, I would have no way to escape. The thought, along with the constant rocking of the car, made me feel queasy, so I asked Gruff to open the window as much as possible, and was relieved when Mannington's three laps were complete.

It was Carnie's turn. She slapped the pedal with her boot, hard, screeching around every curve, driving the way she'd seen the male recruits do it. "Outside, outside, inside!" yelled Gruff over the screeching noises coming from the tires below. In the back seat, I leaned hard left as she sped through a right turn, then right, and yet another right turn smashed me against the door. A hard u-turn and I was plastered to the back seat. It was exhilarating, but even with the window open, I was readily sick to my stomach. As soon as Carnie stopped at the end of her third lap and my door was opened, I hurriedly stumbled out of the back seat and made a beeline for the building, green-faced, frantic to make it to the restroom.

Benetti was waiting for me when I emerged from the restroom, my stomach still churning.

"Dolinsky, you have kids?" he asked.

"Yes, I have twin boys. Why?"

"Because you drive like a mother with kids in her car," he went on. "The academy is all about finding out if you're capable of being a cop. This job isn't for everyone. Straight up, you need to leave your mommy hat home tomorrow. Just bring your deputy recruit hat. Do you know what I'm saying?"

"Yes, I understand … I think."

"Go home and relax, get a good night's sleep, and then come here tomorrow with a clear head, ready to take it up a notch. All right?"

"Okay."

THERE WERE A LOT OF THINGS I learned my first day of EVOC, besides shuffle steering and rolling through a corner. First, I must never leave the house before taking a motion sickness pill, ever. Second, years of being responsible for two children had turned me into a safety nut, which works if I'm teaching the dangers of crossing the street to a six-year-old, but not if I'm trying to prove my abilities to trainers looking for courage and boldness profound enough to deem me badge-worthy. In order to become a deputy sheriff, I needed to "take it up a notch." It was time to toughen up.

That night at home, I decided to stop concerning myself with family stuff—the guilt I felt about leaving my kids each day, the worry over my husband's health, the anxiety over missing family events due to my new schedule. Then there was the worry about what my friends thought of my choice of career, the fear of not measuring up ... I had to face it, I worried about *everything*. But no more. From now on, when I was at the academy, I would clear my mind. It was a matter of actively putting things into perspective; it was time to focus on *me* and what *I* needed to do. And for eight hours each day, I would give myself permission to focus on nothing else.

For the next few days, we did the pylon course each morning and PT or some different type of driver training in the afternoon. One afternoon, our trainers added parallel parking to the agenda. It was a skill I already possessed after having driven my minivan for so many years. It was not difficult to maneuver the Crown Vic in and out of the parking spaces in both forward and reverse, and, to my enjoyment, most recruits had a difficult time with this task, knocking over pylons with almost every turn of the wheel. Not one pylon was moved by my bumper. I waited for an instructor to say "Good job," or something to that effect, but no one bothered. They high-fived the male recruits and those rude females that never spoke to me, even though during their parking exhibition most of the pylons were annihilated. I was beginning to feel that even when I did well, I wasn't considered "squared away" enough to be acknowledged, and by now I realized that accuracy was not as important as attitude to these trainers.

Though it surely went against my better judgment, I made a decision that afternoon as I drove home feeling frustrated and doomed to fail. From now on, I would start driving like the rude recruits who show no respect for the vehicles, the pylons, or the rules. I would play a game with myself, and mimic the behavior of the "squared-away" few. No car, no matter who was driving, would be allowed to catch me on the course, no matter what. If I broke a rule, great! If it felt dangerous to me, even better! If my behavior felt out of control, better still! Otherwise, I would surely not pass. And I needed to pass. When in Rome ...

The next morning, I stood out on the tarmac waiting with the other recruits as the trainers held a meeting inside. I took a good look at the cars we had driven for the past eight days. They were banged up and bruised, with tires so worn that frayed ends of the steel belts, which should reside deep under inches of tread, visibly stuck out from the sides of completely bald tires. It shocked me that I hadn't taken the time to really notice before now, and I started to go back into my safe way of thinking. *Dammit! Stop it!* I chastised myself. *No worry here! No soccer mom here! Go out there and show 'em you have the stuff.*

Once the trainers finally arrived and gave us the arm signal to load up, I jumped in the pink car first thing and started it. I hit the toggle and lit up the flashing red and blue lights on the roof.

Recruit Olin sat directly behind me and one of the male recruits, Phoenix, sat next to me. No trainers rode along in the cars today; they would evaluate us from outside the vehicles, where they could sit in the sun. My car was third to leave, which was nice, as it meant I didn't have my fellow academy mates on my tail. I punched the gas. *Show no fear, no matter what!* I commanded myself.

I was dead determined not to seem the slightest bit apprehensive today. Sliding my hands around the wheel, shuffle steering as we skidded into the first turn, I started to think "outside, outside, inside" in my head, and stopped myself, hoping to hit a pylon to make my point. I hit a pylon and sent it flying.

What little rubber was left on the tires burned, smelling up the track. Feeling reckless, I squealed my tires and raced as quickly as I could through the short straightaways to the next turn. We approached the largest curve, a u-turn which landed the cars close to the spot from which our trainers watched and evaluated. I focused and gave it all I had, tires screaming and me praying that I didn't lose control and send the bubblegum car careening into the trainers like bowling pins, clipboards flying. Around we went, and I hit the gas just at the midpoint of the curve to punch us into the straightaway at full acceleration.

I was working as hard as I could, left then right, through the pylons as if my life depended on it, and it was paying off. After completing the first lap of three, I noticed we were catching the car in front of us that was being driven by another female recruit. My heart pounded, loaded as it was with adrenaline, and my eyes watered as wind blew through the open windows. Every breath was filled with the scents of vehicle exhaust, burning rubber, and the warm plastic smell of the dirty dashboard cooking in the sun. I drove along the back stretch to the start of the track, then into my second lap, then my third.

Then it was time to switch drivers. We each drove three laps, four times each, before noon.

Benetti stopped me after my pylon course, just before we were headed out the door to go to lunch.

"Dolinsky! Come here a minute!" he yelled to me as I made my way to walk out the front door.

"Yes, Sir."

"You did all right today. You're starting to … uh …"

"Get squared away?" I cut in, hopefully.

"I wouldn't call you 'squared away' yet, but you *are* figuring things out," Benetti said. Then he added, "Nice job this morning."

"Thanks."

Delight and relief pumped though my veins, and I took myself out for a pizza lunch in celebration.

By the end of the day, I was drained but content with my performance. After tearing around a track in squad cars, my minivan felt very slow and boring to drive to the store. I picked up a few groceries and headed home to find my kids building spaceships with blocks on the floor. Garrett was on the computer. I noticed a photo of a motorcycle for sale on the monitor, but didn't mention it as I asked him how his day had been.

"Went to lunch with Jeff today." He was speaking loudly again, which I'd learned was another common symptom of PTSD.

"How is he?" I asked.

"He and Cheryl are having a baby."

"Oh, nice for them," I said, hoping he would ask me how my day had been. I was dying to tell him about my day of crazy driving.

"He's pretty excited," Garrett spoke, still staring at the screen.

"Why are you looking at bikes for sale?" I asked. "You aren't thinking of buying a bike now, are you?" Garrett smiled like a boy caught with his hand in the cookie jar. I pressed on reluctantly. "Sorry, Honey, but we still have about nine thousand dollars to pay back before we have money for extras like that." Then I used the opportunity to segue into my story. "And speaking of vehicles, I had such a crazy time driving ..."

He was not about to listen to me. "What's for dinner?" Garrett asked, stridently cutting me off.

"I don't know, but I want to tell you about my day." Then my dutiful side edged her way in, and I placated him. "How do grilled cheese sandwiches sound?"

"I had a sandwich for lunch. What else do we have?"

My exhaustion and stress had shortened my fuse, and my veneer cracked. "You know, there's nothing stopping you from looking in the kitchen and planning a dinner once in a while!" I yelled, feeling my face redden with every word.

"Not my job," was his cold response. As I stood looking at him, disbelieving, he continued looking at the computer.

"Whose job is it, then? Mine exclusively? I'm working, too!" I was determined not to back down. "How can I do everything? I assumed you would help me with the housework once I was in the academy."

"You knew the plan. You're the housewife. I'm not. So now you have a job, too, fine, but you can't expect me to do your work, I'm not the one who changed things." *What?* How could he say that?

"You most certainly *did* change things!" I argued, gathering a head of steam. "You gambled every last dime we had! Maybe you don't remember because you have nothing to show for it, but *I* remember, and every single time I'm at the store and swipe my card, I remember, again, how you let me be humiliated. You knew we had nothing in the accounts, and you watched me leave the house without saying a word!"

"Ya know, I was just sitting here minding my own business when *you* came over to me ..." he said, derailing the argument.

"Picking out bikes to buy? Is that what you're doing?" I asked. "You should be thinking of selling the one you *have* instead of dreaming about buying more!"

"Not happening! I'm not selling the Harley! We would have to be destitute before I'd sell it!"

All this time, I'd still been holding the groceries. Now, frustrated, I slammed the groceries on the counter. Garrett got up and walked out to the garage, slamming the door. *A new motorcycle? Really?*

The boys made scrambled eggs, bacon, and toast for dinner, with a little coaching from me as I sat at the counter and studied for the next morning's quiz. Colton took his dad a plate, which Garrett ate in the garage. That suited me just fine. I went to sleep that night feeling thrilled with my day, and still furious at my husband's refusal to face reality. I did feel a bit proud of myself for standing up to him, and had no idea where I had gotten the nerve.

THIRTEEN

▥▥▥▥▥▥▥▥▥▥▥▥

U P UNTIL NOW, PHYSICAL FIGHTING had played no role whatsoever in my life. The only physical altercation I could remember being part of had been in elementary school, when I punched a girl once in the chest for taking a toy I had brought for show and tell. It was hardly preparation for police work. Attending a class that trains recruits to go "hands on," in situations when a deputy sheriff would need to physically gain control of another human being, was certainly beyond my scope of experience. But I felt up for the challenge, especially after having received a "nice job" from Benetti the previous week, which instilled in me an ounce of confidence.

There was mumbling in the locker room that morning as all eleven of us female recruits changed into our PT gear. The first to emerge, I went directly to the mat room, which was at the opposite end of the hallway from the academy classroom. Upon entering, I was immediately drawn to the center of the room, where the floor was bright blue and entirely comprised of gymnastic mats. Blue mats also hung on three of the four walls. Curious, I walked into the middle of the mat floor and was surprised at how deeply the mats sank under my feet.

Deputy Benetti was the primary trainer, and was helped by Smythe and a female named Waverly, a heavy brunette. I couldn't help but notice how much her uniform bulged around the middle, and I wondered why she didn't have one that fit. While Benetti stood and explained what to expect from the next few weeks, and why we needed to master these techniques, one message became clear: In a fight for your life, anything goes.

"The moves we will show you today are to keep you safe and may, one day, save your life. More likely, though, you'll need to be able to articulate these moves in your reports. That is *very* important," Benetti explained. "But people, I'm gonna tell you straight up. The reality is, YOU are the POLICE! The COPS! The FUZZ! The PO-PO! You are the authority! And anyone who is going to attack you, anyone who is willing to come at a police officer, intends to kill you. They are fully aware of what they're doing, and it is a life-and-death situation! You must never, *ever* forget you are bringing a gun to the fight. And if the bad guy … I like to call him Joe Shit the Douche Bag …" the recruits chuckled. "Yeah, well, if Joe Shit the Douche Bag gets your gun, you're dead."

It sobered me to imagine being in a fight for my life. The female instructor, Deputy Waverly, remained in the background most of the morning. Benetti explained that this was due to her recent maternity leave.

"Did you have to tell everyone I just had a baby!" she snapped at Benetti. "Geez, I don't want them to think I'm weak! I can do the moves!"

"What does that have to do with having a baby?" he questioned her in front of the class. She just rolled her eyes, but it was obvious she was not happy to be there, and I understood. I had been fortunate that I'd not been forced to go back to work just weeks after having my children. But why would she feel that being a mother made her seem weak?

Quickly, Smythe and Benetti had us stretching in ways I had never done before, preparing arm and hand muscles to be pulled and manipulated during class. At one point, I lay on my back on the blue mats, right leg bent at the knee, my foot pinned under me, held there by my own weight, while the trainers counted. I relaxed and focused on the silver tubes of the sprinkler system hanging from the ceiling. Large, round light fixtures hung from long chains overhead as well. Rarely had I spent time staring at ceilings, but this one I studied like no other, stretching my right, then left sides.

After the stretching session, the trainers began demonstrating stances, evasive movements, and other basics. Easy stuff, or so I thought, but I learned right away that things are not always as easy as they seem.

"The position of advantage," demonstrated Benetti, "is standing tall, gun side back, knees slightly bent, hands resting in the belt area." I was standing in the front row attempting to get myself into the position of advantage when Benetti grabbed me. I had interlaced my fingers and he seized them, holding my fingers tightly with one hand. When he said, "Try to pull away," I couldn't. I couldn't move my fingers at all. My face flooded beet red, I could feel it. Benetti let go and said, "No interlacing fingers, people!" My initial embarrassment subsided as the instructors moved into demonstrations of "twist locks," "arm bars," and many other aptly named ways to immobilize a person.

"There are many ways you can twist a person's arm or wrist that won't hurt unless a slight bit of pressure is used, which creates pain," said Smythe, bouncing on his toes just a little as he spoke. "We do not want to cause a person pain, we simply want compliance. But sometimes pain will aid in compliance.

"It is imperative you master these techniques," he continued, in his typically enthusiastic, excited manner. "You must know how to place a person into a control hold, or grab them in a manner to gain control by pain compliance. We're going to practice this, but don't hurt your partners! I don't want to write paper, so give it about fifty percent, and if it hurts … say something! If you're on the ground, you slap the mat. That's the signal to tell your partner to let up. Got it?"

Partnered up, the recruits stood and watched as the trainers twisted each other's arms into pretzel-like positions, explaining each move slowly, step by step. Sometimes it looked like a dance as they stepped toward each other, grabbing hands, arms, elbows, and turning each other around. I imagined the trainers like Fred and Ginger doing these moves, in an old black-and-white movie—big band music, her dress floating like a wave of lace around her legs as they spun. But only for a moment, and then I was pulled back into reality.

For the next hour or so, we placed each other into these contorted, uncomfortable stances while the instructors walked among us. They stopped and worked with each team to be certain we had executed each hold correctly.

My partner was Olin, who was thin, wiry, and hard to hold onto. Training with her was good from a realistic standpoint; as the instructors had said, people on drugs move quickly and are hard to grasp. Still, I wished she would quit wiggling out of every hold I attempted on her, because we caught the eye of Deputy Waverly, who was unimpressed.

"You! Dolinsky! What seems to be the problem here? Why are you having such a hard time getting your partner, what's your name?" Waverly was yelling as she headed our way across the mats, while I continued struggling to get Olin's arm behind her. She pointed to Olin, who turned around, showing her the name on her shirt. "Okay, Dolinsky, why are you having such a hard time putting Olin into the reverse wrist lock? This is not rocket science!"

"I'm trying, but ..." Before I could finish the sentence, she grabbed Olin and had her arm twisted up behind her back like a pretzel. Once in position, Waverly moved one finger and Olin flinched—serious pain by simply adjusting one finger.

"Now, you try," she said confidently.

I began to grab Olin's arm in the manner the trainers had shown us, one hand near the elbow, one on the wrist, when Waverly yelled "Stop! Dolinsky, you're leaning backward. That puts you off balance, don't do that. See now, if you stand like this, you'll have the advantage. You'll be able to grab her hand and still have your feet on the ground and be stable. Try again."

Waverly stepped back and I stepped into the footsteps her shoes left on the mat. I positioned my upper body more forward as Waverly directed. I took Olin's right hand with mine, twisted it, pulled the elbow in, and voila! Waverly's way worked much better than what I'd been doing. Within seconds, I had Olin's arm wrapped up and had full control of her. I moved my finger.

"Ouch!" bellowed Olin. "What are you trying to do to me!" I loosened my grip.

"There you go! That's what I'm talkin' about!" Waverly praised me while Olin scowled at me from under her thick black eyeliner.

"Now, from this position, do you see how if she gets froggie, you can do a hair-pull takedown to the ground, where you could gain even more control?"

"Yes, Ma'am," I replied, though I wasn't exactly sure what she was talking about. I just felt pleased that she had been satisfied with my performance.

"Keep practicing," she said as she spotted another recruit visibly struggling and headed off across the mats to help.

While many of the trainees took to defensive tactics like fish to water, most of the females, Olin and me included, had some trouble mastering the techniques. When it was her turn to twist me up, I watched as she bit her lip in concentration. I also thought she was trying to avoid smiling. Smiling and laughing were the last things these trainers wanted to see. They were teaching us serious stuff we needed to learn, and no matter how awkward it felt, we needed to show them we meant business. Still, it helped me to know Olin was as uncomfortable as I was doing these moves.

We practiced over and over again. Then we were told to switch partners, and I ended up with Phoenix, who was very nice but at least three times my size. His arms were far less flexible than Olin's, but they were much easier to handle. It was likely due to the fact that he moved more slowly and was afraid to hurt me, so he didn't fight and wiggle to get out of my holds. My new partner was quiet and serious. He would just say, "Do it again," and I would, grabbing his arm and twisting until the wrist was contorted and I had it behind his back, secured.

It was weird to step up to Phoenix, a soft-spoken Native American man whom I didn't know well, grab his elbow with one hand and his hand with my other, and simultaneously pull his arm toward my stomach, all of which placed his body off balance and leaned it into mine. I actually felt stunned to get him into a secured hold, then have him flinch and yelp "Ow! Okay, let go!" It was acutely strange just being that close to someone other than my family, smelling his smells, getting his sweat on me. I wondered where I would be now if I had listened to Mandy and taken the fast food manager job. Yeah, this was weird.

After about an hour of control holds, it was break time and my wrists were sore and raw. The next hour was dedicated to "takedowns," and I was looking forward to discovering what exactly Deputy Waverly meant by "hair-pull," which turned out to be just what the name implied. While the instructors were quick to point out that these techniques were agency-approved and should most certainly be used in ideal situations, rarely were situations ideal.

"If someone is coming at you, you use whatever you have at your disposal," Deputy Smythe reminded us. "The point is to go home to your family at the end of shift. If you do that, then you were successful." *Holy cow, what have I gotten myself into?* I wondered.

Again the trainers demonstrated the different takedowns, many of which simply used particular body parts to direct the suspect. I learned that a person could be grounded by using their hair, arms, thumbs … there was even one that involved jetting your arm in front of the forehead of your suspect. But my lack of height made that awkward and challenging, especially with Phoenix as my partner. For sheer logistics, I was again partnered with Olin.

During takedown practice, she went first, coming up behind me, grabbing my hair and pulling straight down. My head cocked backward and I was flat on the floor, looking up at the big circular lights once again. I sat up quickly and rubbed my head, where I was certain a good chunk of hair was missing. Hopping to my feet, eager to try it on her, I thought how lucky the bald recruits were at the moment.

"I have a kink in my neck, could you please take it easy on me when you do the hair-pull thing?" pleaded Olin, looking innocently at me through her cherry red bangs. *How convenient!* Yet I acquiesced and tried to be gentler with her than she was with me.

We practiced throughout the morning, multiple bodies making contact with the mats at a consistent pace around me. This was a loud training, and often silliness and laughter followed because people didn't fall gracefully. I laughed a few times, I couldn't help it.

We broke for lunch. Trainees loaded up in vehicles and headed down the drive to some predetermined restaurant. I had brought my lunch and ate it alone in the mat room. I thought about my boys, speculating about whether or not I would be able to attend any of their school events this year. My thoughts went to my husband, and I felt the knot in my stomach tighten at the prospect of how upset I would be if I got home and he asked me what was for dinner.

Before long, recruits began to enter the mat room and it was time to get back to work.

"Handcuffing is next," hollered Waverly, as if we were yards away rather than inches from her. "Put on your duty belts and take your places on the mats. Get out your cuffs; this is how you hold them properly." She held up a pair in one hand. I pulled mine out of the case. They felt extraneous and clumsy in my hands. "Some of you females may want to get hinged cuffs; they're easier to use for little hands like ours," Waverly said. For now, I had the chain style that had been issued by the department.

Cuffing techniques intrigued me. Some of the techniques were rather complicated while others were ridiculously simple. We were given a demonstration on how to set up our subjects, then we were to do the same movements. Working again with Phoenix, I was meant to cuff him first, then be his practice subject. I began by giving him instructions.

"Sir, stop what you're doing! Place your hands on the back of your head" I yelled at him to be heard over all the other recruits' voices, copying what the trainers had just taught us. "Interlace your fingers, separate your feet, and face away from me."

I approached carefully, grabbed one wrist with my left hand, and cuffed his other with my right. I expected it to be simple, like it had been for Waverly when she had done it to Smythe moments before. But it was not so simple.

I held the cuffs by the center chain, but with my small hands, the cuff had to be in just the right position or it would flip sideways rather than wrench around my partner's wrist. When it finally did wrap around his mammoth wrist, I accidentally pinched the skin when the cuff arm cinched into place.

"Oh my gosh! I'm so sorry!" I cried as I removed the cuffs and noticed his wrist bleeding.

"It's okay, shit happens," he said in a monotone, and then began setting me up for his own practice session. "Ma'am, stop what you're doing, place your hands on the back of your head …"

I felt terrible having inflicted injury on a fellow trainee. I proceeded to place my hands on my head and look away from him. He snapped the cuffs on my wrists hard and my wrist bone resonated with pain. *Oh, well, shit happens,* I told myself.

The room smelled more and more like dirty gym socks. Toward the end of the day and after practicing cuffing for quite a while, I was feeling bruised and battered. Mannington had cuffed her partner and couldn't get the cuffs off. We each tried our different keys but none of us could remove them. After numerous attempts by both Deputies Smythe and Benetti to remove the cuffs, Deputy Waverly arrived with a very large bolt cutter and used the huge tool to cut the stainless steel from the wrists of the very relieved recruit. Mannington was directed to go visit "Supply" at the sheriff's department and retrieve a new set of cuffs while the rest of us were released for the day.

As I drove home, I replayed the movements we had practiced in my head in an attempt to cement them to memory. My heart felt light. I had gotten through one more day and I was proud of myself.

Once at home, I focused on making dinner. There wasn't much food in the house since I had not had time to get to a grocery store, but I found some noodles and a jar of spaghetti sauce, the old standby. After dinner, I excitedly asked Garrett to allow me to practice my techniques on him. He declined.

"Oh, come on, Honey, I need to practice this stuff at home. It's important for me to practice."

"No, thanks, I have things to do," he said and walked toward the garage.

"Did you make the appointment with the …"

"No," he interrupted, then mumbled something I couldn't hear before the door to the garage banged closed. I was disappointed and irritated, but not surprised.

Before being dismissed from the academy that day, Deputy Smythe had told us to "break in" our cuffs by pushing the moving arm through the cuffs repeatedly. I asked Colton to help me while we watched one of his favorite shows on television.

"Sure, Mom! I'll help!" he eagerly took the handcuffs from me and fumbled with them until I showed him how to do it. *Zip … Zip … Zip …* I took my second pair and sat next to my little dude on the floor, listening to the mindless goofiness of *Sponge Bob Square Pants. Zip … Zip … Zip …* We giggled as we tried to go faster and faster. Garrett entered the room and, with no expression on his face at all, sat down behind us on the sofa.

"I thought you were busy," I said. "The trainers told us to do this, it's supposed to make the cuffs work smoother." More annoying zipping sounds. *Zip...Zip...Zip.*

"Stop that noise, I'm trying to watch TV," Garrett said, his voice deeper than usual. Then he picked up the remote control and changed the channel.

"Awww, Dad, we were watching that!" Colton said, kneeling at his dad's feet. Garrett, wearing a disgusted expression, snagged the cuffs from Colton's hand and placed them on the table nearest the sofa. Colton dejectedly stood and walked to his room.

"You could've watched TV in the bedroom," I said, irritated.

"So could you," Garrett coldly responded.

"We were here first!" immediately maddened by his attitude. I picked myself up and went to our bedroom to seethe.

Seated on the bed, I tried to control my anger at him. I reminded myself that, sure, he was in the military, but that didn't mean he had asked to be traumatized. He didn't ask for this any more than I did. We knew there would be risks involved when he was deployed, and I always knew that if he were injured, I would be there to help him through it.

But then, I had never expected *this* to happen. If he had lost a limb, I would be driving him to physical therapy, and he would be getting stronger, learning to use a prosthetic limb. At least something tangible would be happening. But this? Garrett's problems were invisible. Unlike a missing limb, something that could not be ignored, my husband could ignore this, and live with the pain, for as long as he chose to do so. Until he wanted to heal, he wouldn't.

Which made me wonder, what had happened to him that was so painful he feared reliving it in a doctor's office? What was he really afraid of? Was he so scared that he preferred hurting to recovery? I felt sorry for him and sorry for myself for the changes that had occurred in our marriage. I needed to express these feelings to him, let him know I would help him through.

After I'd collected myself, a few minutes later, I went out to the living room and sat next to him on the sofa.

"Got a minute?" I asked in my softest, sweetest voice.

"Yeah," he sighed.

"I want you to know, whatever it is you're feeling, I'm here to help you get through it."

"I'm not feeling anything," he said dryly.

"I was just thinking, if you had been injured, lost a leg or something, we would be working toward your healing. We need to do that, as a couple."

"But I didn't get injured."

"PTSD is an injury. It's something that requires …"

"Is that what you think?!" he cut me off. "I'm mentally fucked up like if I lost a leg? What are you saying, that I lost my mind?" He glared at me.

"Babe, I'm just saying I will help …"

"Well I don't need your help!" he yelled as he retreated into the garage. I heard the big door open, the Harley start, and its distinct rumble getting softer as he drove away.

FOURTEEN

WE WERE A LITTLE OVER HALFWAY through the academy, and it was cus-
tomary for command staff and academy instructors to evaluate the
performance of each recruit and discuss our progress. It was near the end
of the day when I was called out of the class to the administrative offices to
speak to Deputy Benetti. I was relieved to see that it was a member of the
training staff and not the stiff sergeant that was going to talk with me. Still,
I was shocked at what he had to say.

"Recruit Dolinsky, have a seat."

"Yes, Sir."

"You have been doing well through the academic portion of the academy. Let's see, right now you are … Well, you are actually in the top third
of all recruits." He sounded surprised, though I wasn't at all. The academy
quizzes required nothing more than memorization and regurgitation.

"Yes, Sir, I've always been good in school," I said. Benetti went on.

"Well, um, that's good. Uh …" He cleared his throat. "I'm going to be
blunt and lay it out for you to understand. You will not pass if you don't
crank it up," he said, squinting.

"Sir?" I questioned, trying to understand what he meant. He had just
told me I had passed everything to date and was currently in the top of the
class academically.

He continued condescendingly in his smoker's voice. "I'm sure you're a
very nice lady, with a very nice family, and a very nice home, but that doesn't

mean squat here. Tellin' you straight up, this is a dangerous job, and you need to be able to react at a moment's notice, maybe even take a life if necessary. Do you think you're up to that, because I don't think you are."

"Yes, Sir," I replied uncomfortably. "I have considered that, Sir."

"Truth is, Dolinsky, you will not pass this academy unless you act more bull-dyke."

My eyes popped at his choice of words. "You mean you want me to act tougher?"

"This is a tough job, and you must be tough to be effective. We all want to go home at the end of the day. We need to know our partner has our back. You can go home to your nice home, your nice family, your nice car, your nice neighbors … you know not everyone is cut out for this line of work." He sat up tall in the chair, ran his fingers through his hair, looked me in the eye and said, "Straight up, you need to be more bull-dyke if you're going to pass the physical part of this academy."

Stunned, I didn't know what to say. "Uh, yes, Sir," was all I could muster.

"Understood?"

"Yes, Sir."

I wasn't sure whether I should be offended or thank him for his candor, so I left to go dress out in the locker room, where one other recruit, Carnie, was changing clothes, too. My shock over the feedback I'd just received was too much, and I couldn't restrain myself.

"You won't believe what he said in my evaluation," I said as I popped off my combination lock and opened the locker. "Apparently, they won't pass me unless I act more 'bull-dyke.'" A manly woman, Carnie had struck me as gay. I quickly realized what I had just said, gasped, and put my hand over my mouth in embarrassment. "Oh, I'm sorry if that offends you," I said.

"It's okay," she said, smiling slightly, but there was heaviness in her reply. Surrounded by silence, we changed our clothing, side by side.

Right before slamming her locker, she spoke. "They told me I should quit."

"WHAT?!" I exclaimed, absolutely amazed. "You can't! You aren't going to, are you?"

"Of course not. I wouldn't give them the satisfaction," she replied quietly. "But they said that I should consider quitting, because there's no place for people like me in this business."

"Oh, my goodness!" I replied again with my hand over my mouth, horrified. My insides boiled at her words. "I can't believe the attitudes of these people!" My hands were now in fists. "Don't they know that you could sue them? That's a lawsuit waiting to happen!"

"I know, but I don't want a lawsuit, I just want a job," she said, calmly and quietly. "My wife doesn't make enough to support us, and we have a son. I'm not interested in fighting for my rights at this time, I just need an income, and I'm afraid … well, I've never been much of a student. I might fail the academic stuff."

"I can help you with that!" I replied immediately. "Academics are easy for me. We could study together and I can help you pass that part. But how do I become more bull-dyke?"

She looked relieved as she laughed loudly for a few seconds. She had a warm, guttural laugh that was infectious, and I began to laugh, too, though I was certain there was nothing funny about this situation.

"That's no problem! I can help you with that," she chuckled, then slammed her locker hard. "You want to come on over this weekend? We can practice the defensive tactic moves and study."

"Sure!" I said, slamming my locker hard, too, but a piece of my uniform was in the way and the door flew back open, almost hitting me in the head. Embarrassed, I pushed the material in and softly clicked the locker door shut. We exchanged phone numbers before heading home.

I started the minivan and pulled out of the driveway, now feeling a bit apprehensive about visiting Carnie's home. Everything I knew about homosexuality, I had learned in church, through countless sermons damning gay and lesbian people. When I replayed the voice of my trusted preacher in my head, terms like "offenders" and "abominations" were commonplace. Worse yet, their afterlives entailed the promised hand of God hurling their unholy souls through the gates of hell.

So what would I find in their home? Certainly, there must be some indication of their deviant lifestyle, perhaps inappropriate pictures on their walls or erotic books on their coffee table? Even though my husband hadn't been the best example of Christian values lately, I wondered how he would feel about it, which led me to wonder, would lesbians be jealous if one brought another female home as a friend? I certainly wouldn't go hang around with the male recruits, practicing defensive tactics at their homes.

Was this proper behavior? Honestly, I didn't have much choice if I was going to pass the academy. I hoped we could really help each other.

The next morning was Saturday and our family was home together. I was looking forward to a nice day, as I stood in the closet and slipped on jeans and a tee. My husband's deepest voice bellowed through the bedroom. "I knew something was up! I knew you were being nice for a reason!"

"What are you talking about?" I asked him, racing into the room to see what was up.

I found Garrett standing by his dresser, still holding the knob of his sock drawer with one hand, holding up a pair of brown socks with the other.

"I knew you were sleeping around when I was gone!" he said accusingly.

"What? Why would you say that?" I was baffled.

"These are not my socks!" he cried, waving the brown pair in the air. "I just can't believe you would do this to me!" His eyes, darker than usual, glared across the room as if he were a cruel stranger. I broke into nervous laughter. In all our years of marriage, I'd never even considered sleeping with anyone else. His accusation created a new feeling a stress down deep inside my abdomen. This was a brand-new argument, one not based in any reality. I was very worried, but fought not to let it to show.

"Really, Garrett, why would I do that? I can't believe you would even think that!"

"So who left their socks here, huh? Who was it, Beth? Huh?"

I pulled the socks from his grip and looked them over. "I have no idea whose socks these are. But if I was screwing around, do you really think I would wash *his* socks and put them in *your* sock drawer? Really?"

He was quiet for a moment, then said, "You can't seem to answer my question. Who do the socks belong to?"

"I don't know. I wash what you bring home in your pack and put everything in your drawers. That's it. There is no conspiracy here, Honey, you're being a little paranoid." And I wondered, at that moment, if paranoia was also a symptom of PTSD.

"I'm shocked at you, Beth!"

Exasperated with him, I said, "I didn't do anything! You are being ridiculous!" With that, I left the room halfway laughing to myself, and sick to my stomach. I wanted to feel love for him, part of his team again, but this type of idiotic outburst didn't help. Now, I had an excuse to leave.

I CALLED CARNIE to see when we could meet. Her wife, Deb, answered the phone.

"Hey, yeah, she said you might call. Come on over anytime!" she said in a friendly tone. She gave me their address, and I hurried out to their house.

When I arrived at their home, I was pleasantly surprised to find it in a newer neighborhood. The house looked just like any other home on the street. I really don't know what I was expecting—a rainbow paint job, or a gay flag flying to alert the world about what went on in their bedroom? I felt my face flush with embarrassment at my own thoughts as I pulled my stupid minivan up to the front curb.

As I approached the front door, suddenly it opened and out flew a young boy, scurrying around me in a flash then bounding toward a neighbor's house to play.

A pretty woman yelled after him, "Scotty! Don't stay for lunch, okay? We have leftovers I want you to eat!"

"Okay, Mom!" he called, and was inside the neighbor's home before I was even close enough to the threshold to step into his home.

"Oh, hi! I'm Deb," she said, seeing me approach and stepping aside to allow me in the door. "Come on in!"

"Hi there," I said as I stepped inside and she shut the door behind me.

"Make yourself at home. I'll go get her." Deb hurried upstairs to let Carnie know I had arrived.

I sat down on their leather couch, which was very similar to the one in my own living room, and looked around, prepared to find the evidence of their unconventional lifestyle. Yet no sexually explicit pictures hung on the walls, no alcohol bottles lay stacked on the counters to signify crazy parties, no sex toys lay out in the open; in fact, there were no signs of "abominations" of any sort. Sitting there, in a simple, warm home, I found my beliefs about gay people were beginning to be questioned. If gays were supposed to be ostentatious, pushing their lifestyle on others, perverting children, then these two women had not received the homosexual handbook.

Deb re-emerged and offered me a drink of iced tea. I followed her into the kitchen, noticing the bright yellow curtains, oak cabinets, and blue-and-white dishtowels, just like mine.

"Thanks," I said as she handed me the glass of tea.

"No, thank *you*," she said, and I looked at her puzzled. *What was she thinking me for?* She went on. "I don't know what we'll do if CJ doesn't pass this academy. My job is on the chopping block. I'm so worried right now, I can't even tell you … We're both really grateful for your help."

I was so surprised by her gratitude I nearly choked on my tea. "Believe me, I need her help as much as she needs mine," I assured her. "Did she tell you I won't pass unless I can learn to be more 'bull-dyke'?" I asked, making quotes in the air.

"Yes, I can't believe they told you that. What a derogatory term to use! CJ's neither bull, nor a dyke, but she will be able to help you toughen up, I am sure of that." Her eyes sparkled as she spoke of her partner. "I'm hoping you can improve her study habits."

"Oh, I'm sure, no worries there."

Just then, CJ Carnie entered the room in sweats and a football t-shirt, and said hello. It struck me as funny that until this very moment, I hadn't even known her first name. I wondered what CJ stood for.

"Hey, Deb, where can we do this?" she asked. "How about we move the sofa, push it back toward the stairs? That'll give us enough space in the living room. And get us a pizza, will you, please? I'm not eating those leftovers today."

"You got it, Honey." Deb was on the phone ordering lunch while we rearranged her living room to make space to practice. I thought to use the element of surprise, and I grabbed Carnie's arm, trying to get her into a control hold before she noticed. She dumped me immediately to the floor.

"Man, you *do* need practice!" she laughed at me. Deb came in to watch.

"Darn it! Okay, let me try again." I got up and came at her arm, this time attempting a different hold. Only a second later, I lay on the floor, looking at the ceiling, thrown down like a sack of potatoes. Carnie stood over me, amused. Deb leaned up against the wall, her hand over her mouth, eyes squinting. Carnie reached her hand toward me. I grabbed it and she hiked me up with one yank.

"I gotta go, I can't watch this," Deb said, walking away.

Now, I've done it, I thought, convinced that somehow I'd offended her. Maybe I had accidentally crossed some unseen line, inched over the edge of lesbian correctness into the void where straight people who don't know the rules mistakenly go. I had been afraid that might happen, so I prepared to apologize.

"Why can't you stay?" I asked, apprehensively.

"I just don't want to hurt your feelings by laughing!" she said, chuckling her way upstairs, then called back to us, "You two look ridiculous!"

And from that moment on, I dropped the worry and expectations, the concerns and preconceived ideas, the judgment of right or wrong, and decided to simply see them as people.

"Think back to your academy training, Recruit Dolinsky," Carnie teased. "What have you learned, Deputy Sheriff?"

"Nothing, apparently! Please, show me what I missed that time," I begged her.

"Do the move step by step and we'll see what you're doing wrong."

We walked through each move to find I was repeatedly forgetting a simple action with my arm.

"Do that action alone," Carnie prompted me. "What does it feel like to you?"

"To be honest, it feels like picking up a laundry basket. I scoop the basket, then push my hip forward to balance it."

"Okay, when you put me into the control hold, you're just 'lifting the laundry.'"

"Okay," I said, skeptically. We practiced a few more times, and when I reached that move, I would mimic lifting the laundry.

"*OW!*" she yelped, her arm twisted pretzel-like behind her back. That's it! You got it!"

"Really?"

"Yeah, really! Let up already!"

"Oh, sorry!" I let go, thrilled.

"No, no, that was good! Now, do it again."

Carnie had me do the move many times over, until I was certain not to forget to "lift the laundry" each time. Achieving this peculiar objective, to inflict pain in order to control another person, was oddly satisfying for me. I thought it such a warped milestone, like I was channeling some primitive, cave-woman chutzpa, some strength that wasn't mine at all, but was out there in the universe for any woman to borrow when needed. And just then, I needed it to help me "bull-dyke" up.

"Can we work on gun retention?" I asked.

"Sure, hang on a minute." Carnie left the room for a moment and returned with a plastic water pistol. "This should do; he won't mind if we use this."

She mugged, holding the gun out in front of her with both hands as they had instructed the day before. I tried to grab it away from her, but she moved, as we were taught, and I was unable to sustain my grip as intended.

"Now you do it."

She handed me the gun and I held it with both hands. Carnie tried to grab it from me and conquered me within seconds. Twirling the gun around on her index finger, she gloated. "I know you can do better than that."

"Okay, let me try again."

"This time, you need to swipe your hand like this." Here, she demonstrated the chopping motion that moved my hand off the gun instantly. "It's like, uh … to put it in your terms, grating carrots. How's that?"

"Grating carrots, huh?" I took the gun from her. I held it with one hand and she tried to grab it. I repeated the grating motion, and it worked perfectly. She let go quickly.

"Ha! Yeah, that's it!" she said, and we laughed at ourselves and the absurdity of mastering police work through "lifting the laundry" and "grating carrots."

By lunchtime, I had worked the steps well enough to earn her confidence. As we sat at the kitchen table, we practiced flashcards of ten-codes. I called them out, and she guessed the answers.

"Ten-seventy-six?" I quizzed.

"En route."

"Ten-forty-two."

"Beginning of shift."

"Nope, remember, forty-one is beginning the shift, forty-two is ending shift."

"Shit! I'll never get these memorized!" she worried.

"Yes, you will! If I have to sit here until tomorrow, we will get them in your head. Okay, now, ten-ten." It felt good to switch roles and play teacher for a while.

"A fight."

"Ten-seventy."

"A fire."

"Code four."

"Situation under control, officer is okay."

"Perfect!"

And so it went, every Saturday. We met at her home for our study day, during which she would beat me up physically and I would beat her up mentally, until each of us reached the point of exhaustion. She was a perfect person for me to practice with—tall and husky like a man, but tough on me, unlike the male recruits who tended to baby their female partners, thinking they might break us if they used any muscle at all.

Carnie pushed me to master everything from military marching turns and stances to shrimping, which was a technique we'd learned for escaping being pinned on the ground. That day, Deb giggled as I lay on my back on her floor, her wife kneeling over me, pretending to choke me. I wiggled each side of my body upward along the carpet until I was forward enough to knock her off with a single swing of my leg. Deb applauded for me and we laughed at Carnie falling to the floor for once.

I felt such gratitude for their friendship. These women became my personal trainer and cheerleader. I took on the role of tutor, helping Carnie study whatever the trainers threw at us, discussing it at length at their kitchen table. Even six-year-old Scotty got involved, sharing his own test-taking strategies one afternoon.

"When I have to take a test, I just think about recess. You can do that, Mom."

"Really? How does that help you take a test, thinking about recess?" Carnie asked, grinning at his concern for her.

"'Cause I don't worry about the test if I'm worried about recess. I just answer all the questions, fast as I can, so I can go outside and play." We all smiled at Scotty.

"Thanks, buddy, I'll keep that in mind," she said, smiling.

More than just helping me learn the job, these women taught me about life—even parenting, a subject with which I felt completely adept. Over our many Saturdays, I watched how Carnie and Deb related to Scotty, how they loved, nurtured, and disciplined him. I studied the dynamics of this unorthodox family. Here were two moms, yet he was very much a typical little boy. His room was decorated in blue, his shoes full of dirt that splashed all over the floor when he popped them off after a day of outdoor play. His toy cars dotted the interior landscape of their home. They were a close family, and these creative parents cared for their boy deeply, as much as I cared for my two. So normal, ordinary. What surprised me most was how comfortable I'd become here; though I didn't feel I particularly deserved it, they accepted me.

For the first time in my life, I was coming up with reasons not to attend church on Sunday. "I'm really tired from Saturday's practice," I'd say to my friends, or "I just want to spend time at home with my family." I knew I was now incapable of tolerating the fear-based negativity that had been my norm just a few short weeks prior. A reality wrecking ball had smashed through principles that had been cemented into the foundation of my faith since childhood, leaving shame in their wake. How could I have ever been so small-minded?

The more I experienced Carnie and Deb's healthy relationship, the more light it shone on the deterioration of my own. I felt a stabbing at my heart when I had to return home after a day of practice. Often, Garrett would be in the garage when I arrived home, wiping down his beloved motorcycle until it shined. The garage of glistening metal was clean and sparkling, like the inside of the house I had kept painted and perfect. What we could control, we made lovely and kept in mint condition. But our marriage was out of our control. It was decomposing, rusting, rotting from the inside out. I was starting to feel that it was a losing battle, my family being led by a broken man who now blamed me for his problems. I resented him. Sometimes, I hated him. Within moments, though, my intense guilt would set in. After all, he was just doing his job! Still, I was beginning to imagine living without him. While my heart ached at home, at the academy I finally felt like I had a friend, an ally, someone in my corner. And for that I thanked God.

FIFTEEN

SCENARIOS WERE NERVE-WRACKING, to say the least, now that we were being watched by our instructor-turned-evaluator, and by our peers. But there really was no better way to see what skills had been retained by each recruit. While completing these unscripted skits, the recruits' most common behaviors, good or bad, would ultimately shine through.

Most scenarios were set up to evaluate a specific skill, such as how quickly a recruit recognizes a threat, or how well he or she verbalizes commands to a suspect. But realism was hard to attain in the red-and-blue-mat room, especially when the "suspects" were the same people who had just taught us the skill we were now required to attempt on them. During one such scenario, the trainers wanted to hear our "verbals," or how we spoke to people in different situations we might face one day as officers. Smythe briefed me in the hallway.

"You're entering a bar fight; handle it as realistically as you can—say what you would really say, okay?"

"Okay."

"Oh, yeah, here." He handed me a red plastic Sig Sauer, formed just like mine, which fit inside my holster should I need it for the scenario. It was a dead giveaway that they expected me to use it. Now, I was ready.

Upon entering the mat room, I found Benetti and Waverly in what looked like a fight. He had his arm wrapped around her neck in a choke hold; her life was on the line. I yelled, "Reno Sheriff's! Break it up!"

I ran toward Benetti, pulling the red gun out of my holster. Benetti stopped fighting and put his hands in the air. I had him at pretend gunpoint and was feeling pretty proud of myself, until he began walking toward me.

"Stop right there!" I yelled, sweating. My mouth was dry. I was oblivious to the other recruits, who had already completed the scenario and were seated on the mats around the edges of the room, watching my every move. Benetti crept toward me slowly.

"What are you gonna do about it, huh?" he growled at me.

I'd come a long way in this academy, but not yet far enough. My mind feverishly scanned through mental files to come up with a command to call out, something to stop the assailant and save the day. The only thing that came into my mind popped out of my mouth in the same way as if I were yelling at naughty children.

"Stop! Stop right there! Don't make me shoot you!"

Instantly, I wished I could suck the words back inside my mouth, chew them up, and swallow them. I cringed when Waverly called, "Code four!" and walked up to me.

"Is that really what you would say to a person committing a crime? 'Don't make me shoot you?' Really?"

I was mortified.

"What the fuck do you want them to do, Dolinsky? Give commands for what you WANT THEM TO DO, like 'Put your hands in the air,' or 'Get down on the ground!'" She was yelling in my face, so close that I could smell her breath and her spit landed on my cheek. I stood still and just took it. "You are such a fuckin' soccer mom, this is ridiculous!"

Waverly threw her hands in the air and turned away from me, grumbling, then turned back and again, to my face, said, "Maybe you don't belong here! Have you considered that? People like you … make it hard for female cops like me to be taken seriously!"

Her words stung, like an inoculation, like my mother's words had after a night of drinking. When I was a child I would burst into tears after such an outburst. At that moment, I felt like sobbing and running out of the building. But I would never let that happen. Nothing this woman could say to me would truly hurt me. I'd been conditioned throughout my childhood, by a much harsher critic, one who had loved me one minute and hated me the next, one who was far more quick-witted and had a sharper tongue than this deputy could ever imagine. My mother could make me cry, but not this pudgy little brunette. I would never let them, any of them, see me cry.

Still, her very vocal opinion of me did nothing but harm to my already dismal reputation with the other recruits. In another scenario, I was teamed with a male trainee who was not much taller than me and about half my age. Jarvis was a twenty-two-year-old who resembled a human GI Joe. He was unhappy having to be my partner and made no bones about it, rolling his eyes when they called our names, refusing to stand anywhere near me during scenario briefing. This kid thought he was pretty special, but I thought he was a rude little jerk. The trainers gave us a minute in the hallway to discuss the tactics we would use.

"You cuff, I'll do verbals," Jarvis suggested. I agreed. We entered the mat room to find Deputy Smythe pretending to be a drunk wandering the streets. My partner went right up to Smythe and handcuffed him immediately, with no discussion or assistance from me. The trainers were unimpressed and made us do it again, but using verbal skills this time. And they wanted me to handle the cuffing. In the hallway, I tried to talk to Jarvis about it.

"Geez, you moved fast in there. I thought I was going to cuff him?" I questioned.

"I wasn't going to wait for *you* to do it," he said snidely. *Jerk.*

Benetti called us in from the hallway for our re-do.

"Hey, you! Where are you going?" I immediately shouted to Smythe, who was swaying to and fro before turning away from me. I walked closer. Jarvis held back this time.

"Sir, I want to talk to you a minute," I said, reaching for his arm, but Smythe pulled away, lost his balance, and fell on the mat floor. I wanted to laugh because he looked so silly rolling around on the ground, but I knew not to. I glanced around for Jarvis for a brief second, but it was obvious by his stance, arms crossed and leaning against the wall, that he had no intention of being part of this scenario. I pulled out my cuffs, knelt, and handcuffed Smythe easily. "Code four!" yelled the trainers, and the scenario was over.

Toward the end of the few weeks of Defensive Tactics training, a number of other trainers arrived to help with scenarios as they became more complicated. One of the most memorable occurred at the end of the day, just before the weekend. My partner, Mannington, and I were one of the last teams to go. We were briefed by Benetti in the hallway.

"Okay, the setting is a public park after curfew. A number of robberies have occurred in the neighborhood, and these three kids fit the description. You have to find reason enough to search them."

"Isn't that reason enough to search them … the fact that they fit the description?" I asked. He just glared at me and said, "I don't know, Dolinsky, is it? Will that reason hold up in court?" It was a moot point; they had other plans for us.

Mannington and I entered the room and approached the three, who appeared to be playing dice in the far corner of the mat room. Our fellow recruits who had already finished the scenario were seated against the left side wall. Out of the way, they watched with baited breath to see how we would "fuck it up."

Mannington and I both started speaking at the same time, so I shut up. She would be primary; I would be her back-up. To my right, my partner talked with the three subjects. Then, to my left, I saw a flash, and before I knew it the thing was running up behind me. It was huge—a trainer covered from head to toe in red padding, for his own protection. We were expected to realistically defend ourselves and attack if provoked.

He was running directly at me and I screamed, just like a little girl. "*AAAAHHHH!*"

No! I cursed myself immediately. *Dammit, why did I have to scream?*

Milliseconds later, my partner pulled her stick and was dodging the red man as he came at her. I pulled my stick, too. This guy was enormous.

"You suck, fuckin' cops!" he hollered. "I'll kill you, assholes."

I could not believe how quickly he dodged left, then right, missing most of our stick swipes. When he focused on Mannington, I would hit him in the legs and back; when he turned toward me, she would hit him. This went on for a few seconds, which felt like minutes. Dodging and weaving, I was determined not to let him get too close to me. He was a big man and could easily overpower me and take my pretend gun. We had learned a quick lesson on gun retention already, but I prayed not to have to try to remember the moves right now, with the red man, numerous trainers, and all my peers watching.

I was breathing hard now, adrenaline pumping through every cell in my body, my mind agonizing to think of something, anything to say that wasn't soccer mom language. Nothing came to mind. I felt like a boxer in the ring, moving left and then right to avoid contact with my assailant. We bobbed and weaved for a few minutes; suddenly, Mannington tripped and fell backward on the mat. The red man was right there, climbing over the top of her. Mannington was struggling, attempting to get her legs pulled up under him to kick him off, but it was no use. I pulled my plastic Sig and ran up behind him, ready to "shoot" downward into his red head, when I realized that my partner was directly under him. I would probably kill her, too!

Unable to free herself, she yelled "Kill him!" I moved my Sig to the side of his head and yelled, "Bang! Bang!"

"Code four! Code four!" called Benetti, ending the scenario. Then he turned to me. "Well, Dolinsky, aren't you the bad-ass Betty Crocker? What do you think? How do you feel?"

My heart was still racing and I could barely breathe, much less have a discussion. I nodded to him, indicating I was fine. The red man had climbed off Mannington; I reached down, grabbed her hand, and pulled her up off the floor. We were absolutely exhausted. It had been my first all-out fight and it was over in less than six minutes. Red man removed his large red helmet and I recognized him as one of the trainers from another police agency. He was laughing, as were all the recruits, refreshed from their own red suit experiences. I wished I'd seen some of theirs.

"Now, each of you've been involved in a fight. It took a lot out of you, right?" Benetti said. "And this was a controlled environment where you knew you wouldn't be harmed. Imagine how it feels to be in a fight for your life against a real 'Joe Shit the Douche Bag' out there, on the street, not knowing if he's armed, if he has associates nearby to help him … Good lessons today, nice work, everyone."

As I stood there still reeling from the red man scenario, I knew I would never forget the sheer exhilaration and the intense exhaustion that I experienced that day, in my first "real" fight.

THE LAST DAY OF SCENARIOS I dreaded more than any other day in the academy. It was the day each of us would be sprayed with pepper spray, otherwise known as Oleoresin Capsicum, or O.C. Spray. One of the best tools on an officer's belt, pepper spray was so potent that one small press of the nozzle could clear a very large room. But for us, it would be sprayed directly into our faces.

We had known this day was coming. According to the policy, in order to be certified to use pepper spray, we had to first experience it ourselves. I had fretted about it since day one, and felt a little shaky as they explained the situation that would occur the next morning.

"Deputy Waverly will shoot you in the face, and you will then perform tasks inherent to the job … before you can wash it off," Benetti explained, and I could tell this time he was smiling, not squinting. "O.C. is something one must experience to understand. I'm tellin' ya straight up, be prepared for it in the morning. Get some good rest tonight, you'll need it." Benetti and the other trainers just laughed. *These people are masochistic!*

"Oh, yeah," Smythe added, "baby shampoo works well at removing the sting."

The first thing I did that day after arriving home was hurry to the cabinet where I kept an old bottle of baby shampoo, which I then slid into my bag for the next morning.

The event was staged outside, and it was warm for a winter day. By the time my turn came up, most of the group had already gone before me. Many of the recruits were still crying like babies, even fifteen minutes after they had been sprayed. Big football player types, even little Jarvis, who thought I was a complete waste of time, sat crying like he missed his mama. I almost felt sorry for him.

"Put your right hand over your right eye," Waverly directed as she stood shaking the cylinder of O.C. spray that represented an actual can of whoop ass to me. My knees felt weak as the cool spray landed across my hand, then over my left eye. Immediately, the substance on my skin began to burn and my eyes to water. Trainers yelled instructions at me, but I was unsure where they wanted me to go.

"Punch Joe Shit the Douche Bag, he's to your right!" Benetti's voice was loud in my ear. I turned to the right and began to punch at what looked like a large black blob, which in fact was a vinyl punching bag held by one of the deputy trainers.

After about six punches, I heard Benetti again in my ear. "Call out on the radio, here." He handed me a block of wood to simulate a radio. "Dispatch, Dolinsky, ten-ten behind the academy building!" I hollered at the wood.

"Good, now give commands to the suspect. You need to cuff him."

It was not difficult to put the burning sensation in the back of my mind while I was moving, but it was increasingly challenging to see through the snot and tears running down my face. A figure walked by, but I could just barely make him out.

"Get down on the ground!" I belted out at the "suspect" and he immediately lay on his belly on the ground. My face really hurt now, like it had been smacked, hard. The amount of water drenching my face from my own eyes was astounding. Snot drained from each nostril like lava. As I knelt to place the handcuffs on him, it was as if I was experiencing the worst allergic reaction possible, with sizzling hot pepper blistering my skin. But I did it, and it was over. And it had gone better than I had expected.

I got to my feet and walked into the building, quickly learning that a lack of breeze made the spray feel even hotter, more unbearable, on my cheeks. I fumbled for my bottle of baby shampoo in my backpack, my face sizzling as I went into the bathroom to wash. There was a slight tinge of orange on my skin, along with a few lingering after effects, but for the most part I was fine, and took my place with my peers, who were all still suffering needlessly, back in the classroom.

Taking a seat, I looked around the room, wondering why these twenty-somethings remained so miserable. Jarvis's eyes looked as if he'd been beaten, as did many of these recruits who had been sitting for a half hour or more, writhing with the sweltering heat still on their faces, too manly, too tough, or, most likely, too unprepared to wash it off.

"What did you do?" asked Jarvis, sniffing and coughing. "How did you …?"

"I washed it off," I said, matter-of-factly, to which my fellow recruits looked at me curiously.

"How did you …?" Jarvis repeated, pathetically. I was tempted not to offer my panacea, but that just wasn't my style.

"Here, you're welcome to it." I tossed the bottle of baby shampoo to him. He and the rest of the room collectively made a beeline out the door, tripping over each other as they ran down the hall to the bathroom for some relief.

There are times when it pays to be a soccer mom.

Sixteen

"**WHAT THE FUCK** is taking you so long to get out of this car! You are sitting in a coffin as long as you are in here. Move it, Recruit!" His voice startled me and I dove out of the car, almost landing on my face. If there had been a recent class discussion in which Smythe had gone over why we were supposed to exit our vehicles quickly, I had missed it. Shakily, I got out of the car, stood up straight, and, looking ahead at the vehicle in front of me, mulled over my next step of how to approach it properly. I began walking up to the driver's side window.

"Jesus, Recruit, you gonna walk up like that? You're practically in the travel lane! Pull your head out of your ass, Dolinsky, and take control of this situation," Gruff griped. It was yet another scenario—traffic stops.

I stood frozen on the black top, afraid that my next step would be wrong, again. From where I stood at the center of the tarmac, the asphalt had no markings. The ground was black on black all around me. What was this guy talking about, "the travel lane"?

"Sir? There are no markings for the travel lane, how can I be sure I'm not ..."

"What the hell is the matter with you, Recruit?" Gruff hollered. "Don't you think I know what I'm talking about?" He rolled his eyes. "You're killing me here, just get moving."

I continued my approach, walking as close to the vehicle as possible, until I reached the driver's side window, which was rolled down. Deputy Smythe was inside wearing a black ball cap backward. He began to open the door to get out.

"Sir, shut the door and stay in your car," I said, but he continued to make his way out of the car. I yelled, "Stay in your car!" He sat back down and closed the door.

"Whatever," said Smythe, in the role of Joe Shit the Douche Bag.

"May I have your license, registration, and insurance, please?" I continued.

He handed me two pieces of paper with numbers written on them, as well as his actual driver's license. "Stay in your car, Sir, I'll be right back," I said and quickly walked around my patrol car to the passenger side to run the license and registration.

"Dispatch, Nora one, two, three," I pretended to speak into a radio mic as if "N-123" were my call sign.

"Go ahead, Nora one, two, three," responded Gruff, who was standing behind me.

"Ten-twenty-seven, twenty-nine, white male adult …" and just as I was pretending to call in the information from his driver's license, checking to see that the license was current or whether he had any active warrants, Smythe jumped out of the car and ran back toward me. He was only about five feet from me when I noticed him and yelled "Get back in yo…" But before I could get the words out, Gruff stopped the scenario.

"Code four! Code four! He just shot you, Dolinsky. You are dead."

"Really?" I didn't know what else to say.

"Yes, really! That's a big fuckin' fail for you. You get an 'F' for the day! More of this from you and you'll be baggin' groceries at Safeway. Get back to the class and send out Recruit Phoenix next."

"Yes, Sir."

I returned to the classroom and told Phoenix he was up. He scurried out of the room. As I took a seat in the class with the other recruits, I asked if anyone else had "died" today.

"I didn't exactly die, but he did throw a soda can at me from the car window," said Olin.

"I died. He got all the way to me from the front seat before I noticed him. Gruff called me a knob," Mannington shared. It made me feel a bit better, but I still wondered how I could have missed Smythe getting out of the car.

"He said if I keep this up I'll be …" and in unison five other recruits said with me, "baggin' groceries at Safeway!" We all laughed, but Mannington was frustrated, and it showed on her face.

"I hate the way they train us here. My dad said that I just have to buck up and deal with it. But they don't have to be so mean all the time, making us feel like losers instead of focusing on what we do right," she blurted. I knew it had to be tough for her, having a father on the force.

"Well, let's look at the bright side," I added. "All we can do from here is improve; we've got nowhere to go but up."

"Do you think they're tougher on us because we're females?" Mannington asked.

"I wouldn't know," I said.

"I think they are," said Carnie, "and I think it's bullshit, but what are our options?"

"We just can't let them win." I said.

"That's right. I'll never quit, no matter what," Mannington said, and we all agreed that the only way to beat them at their own game was to succeed.

A FEW DAYS AND A FEW SUCCESSFUL scenarios later, it was the last day of traffic-stop training. I was beat. The stress and rigor of the academy were getting to me, and to my fellow recruits. But there were only three more weeks of training, and the academy would be over.

"Say you call in a license plate, and it shows the car is stolen. Do you pull them over alone?" asked Benetti as he stood on the tarmac with all of us lined up before him. "Watch and see how to handle a felony car stop. You'll want to pay close attention to this demo."

Behind him, drivers were maneuvering two patrol cars, and Gruff was behind the wheel of a black-and-white SUV. The pink car roamed the track, as the SUV and two other black-and-whites pulled in behind it. Suddenly, Gruff "lit 'em up" and pulled the pink one over. The squad cars stopped on either side, and drivers burst out of the doors, red guns drawn.

"Driver, turn off your vehicle!" Gruff yelled at the driver of the pink car. "Toss your keys out the window! Keep your hands up!"

Due to the cars idling and the wind, which was picking up, I could barely hear what the primary officer, Gruff, was directing the suspect to do—something about turning around and lying on the ground. I tried to listen as he ordered commands, yelling at the top of his lungs, but didn't make out much. I caught "code four" when it was over. Then they returned to their vehicles and drove back to the starting positions. Gruff walked up and pointed to me as he said, "I want her to go first." There was no arguing; I was the primary officer, meaning I would lead the first scenario.

I told myself that this time riding with Gruff would be different as I climbed into the SUV and adjusted my seat. This was his own personal patrol car, which was full of knobs and levers I'd never seen in the training vehicles. Since my embarrassing performance in the scenario in which I had "died," I had not had the opportunity to work with Gruff and show him my improvement. I'd advanced considerably since that day, and had some newfound confidence in my mental bag of tricks. The sheer fact that I was still a recruit and hadn't been tossed out of the academy told me that I was on the right track. Unaccountably, it still mattered to me what he thought, and I believed this was my chance to prove to him that I belonged.

Gruff got into the passenger's side. Jarvis and Phoenix were driving my back-up cars. We broke the formation and drove around until I began tailing the pink car and used my made-up call sign to identify myself.

"Dispatch, Nora three, four, five."

"Go ahead, Nora three, four, five," said Gruff. Now to call in my location, the license plate number and state, and a car description.

"On the tarmac, plate number Ida, Charles, Sam, eight, six, six, Nevada, on a pink Ford Crown Victoria," I said slowly to avoid a screw-up. Moments later, Gruff spoke for dispatch.

"That vehicle is coming up stolen out of California, repeat, the vehicle is stolen. I will close the channel for you. Green channel is closed for the deputies on the tarmac."

My adrenaline started pumping and I hit the lights. The pink car pulled over and, remembering how my last vehicle exit had been too slow, I bolted out of the car quickly, stood behind my door, pulled my gun and aimed at the driver through my open window. It was then I realized that, in my haste to impress, I'd forgotten to wait for the other two back-up cars. There I stood alone, gun drawn, Gruff disgusted in the seat next to me. With only the sound of idling cars and the breeze to soothe my stupidity, I felt sick, humiliated. *Oh my God, I forgot to wait for back-up.*

With the knowledge clear in my mind that I had utterly blown this scenario, there was nothing I could do to fix it. I started yelling to the driver to turn off his vehicle. He complied, and just then my back-up arrived, Jarvis on my left and Phoenix on my right. They pulled their guns and, eyes glued to the pink car, asked me what I needed them to do. Gruff was unusually quiet, evidence of his exasperation at my pitiful performance, and I wondered if there was any way to salvage this. My most important scenario, the one I had hoped would be my saving grace, was instead fast becoming my most dreaded nightmare.

"Driver, toss your keys out the window," I yelled. "Sir, I don't think they can hear me."

"Why don't you use the PA system," Gruff said dryly.

"What PA system, Sir?" I had not driven any training cars equipped with PA systems, nor did I know how to operate one. This SUV was an active member of the patrol fleet, not a throwaway vehicle with holes in the dash like those I was used to.

"What do you mean? This car has one right here." And he tossed the mic onto the driver's seat. I picked it up with my left hand, keeping my eyes on the back of the suspect vehicle.

The twisted cord was not long enough for the mic to comfortably fit in my left hand, so I moved my gun to the left and mic to the right. I pulled the mic close and spoke into it, pushing the button on the side, but nothing happened. Gruff sighed heavily and said, "You have to turn it on."

"But I can't take my eyes off the back ..."

"Turn the fucking thing on!"

I tried to peek at the console to see if there was a button or something to indicate where the PA turned on. Gruff saw me and lost it.

"What the hell are you doing, Dolinsky? Watch the fucking car ahead of you! You can ask for help, ya know! Ask me to turn it on! You just gotta ask! Jesus fucking Christ, you are some kind of knob!"

"Would you please turn it on?" I heard a click.

"Driver, toss your keys out the window," I said over the public address system, the curly mic wire stretched tight. I gave directions for about ten minutes, telling the suspect to get out of the car while visually searching for any sign of a weapon or other trouble. Every muscle in my left arm hurt from flexing tightly to hold up the gun throughout the scenario. I directed the suspect to walk backward toward the sound of my voice, and Jarvis and Phoenix got him handcuffed. I'd never been so happy to hear "code four" in my life, but mentally braced for Gruff's honest evaluation. He waited until all of the participants and trainers stood around him in a circle.

"Dolinsky, your performance began as a circus—wait for your goddamn back-up to arrive before you exit the vehicle! What the fuck were you thinking? It's like you just work off impulse, but that doesn't work in law enforcement!"

Everyone around us looked down at the ground; I fixated on a pebble lying near my boot. Even my partners were afraid to make eye contact with Gruff.

"I was embarrassed for you during this scenario. How can you not know how to use your equipment? That is absolutely unacceptable. You *never, ever* take your eyes from the area of responsibility at a felony car stop! You *never* switch your gun to your weak hand! How can you not know how to use the PA system? You've been in the academy now for nearly three and a half months!" He went on for what felt like an eternity but was probably only five minutes, berating my performance.

"Yes, Sir," I said at the end.

I sauntered back to the classroom, defeated, flattened, my newfound confidence crushed down to a fine, pathetic pulp. All the things I knew better than to say to him swam through my head like a school of guppies. *Does he not realize we have no PA systems in the training cars? If he hadn't yelled at me earlier about getting out of the car quicker, I wouldn't have been so quick to jump out. If he hadn't worried about the stupid PA system and just let me try it once first, I wouldn't have switched my gun hand! How come these people do nothing but yell at us? And what is with all the profanity?* My hands were fists when I reached the door to the restroom. Benetti pulled me aside before I went in.

"I hear Gruff was really hard on you," he said.

"Yeah, you could say that. I guess I deserved it." I exhaled a big breath. "Are you here to tell me I'm out?"

"No, but his evaluation is so critical, we need to retest you. You aren't the only one, so don't feel too badly, but you do need to do a better job in order to continue as a recruit."

"Yes, Sir."

I walked into the bathroom and the tears started to flow. After all the work I'd done, all the extra practices with Carnie, all the time away from my kids, to come this far …

I locked myself in a stall and wadded up what seemed like half a roll of toilet paper, then quietly dabbed my eyes, blew my nose, and talked myself out of quitting.

There was no way I could go home and tell Garrett I'd failed. I just couldn't. I couldn't tell my friends I'd failed, either. But despite my conviction, inside I felt so hurt, so fearful that I would be pushed out and have to do exactly that, admit defeat. *Oh, God, don't make me go back out there and try again. I can't take another verbal beating in front of everyone.*

I blew my nose and wiped my eyes, then thought about my mother. A voracious reader, she used to devour true crime and police stories with a vengeance, after which she'd say something like, "I would've made a good detective," or "I should've been a cop." I'd always tried to please her and had rarely been successful, with the exception of giving birth to my children. Grandkids, she claimed, gave her life a purpose. But for as long as I could remember, she had grieved over never having reached her potential in life, and had been ashamed because she'd never really tried.

It would only be a few more days until the two-year anniversary of her death, and I reminded myself that, in that short time, I had placed myself in a position to fight for a career she would have envied. I wondered if the need to please my mother, which was so embedded in my psyche even after her death, had been my reason for this career choice. Could that have been all this was?

I should leave, I thought, as it occurred to me that the stiff sergeant had been right. *I'm being tested like I've never been tested before. And I can quit, right here, right now, just get the hell out of here. And my future would be … I* sighed heavily with the thought. *Well, it would be … miserable. Like Mom's.*

I couldn't quit. My thoughts raced through other questions, searching for answers that might lead me out of this bathroom. I had yet to come up with one.

Perhaps this was some sick game. Maybe they had hired a bunch of women just to meet a quota of some sort. Maybe I was already slated to be fired, no matter how well I did.

Could my life's potential really be here, at this academy, out there on the tarmac, beyond that bathroom door?

What about my kids? I considered what it would be like to be old, on my proverbial death bed. How would my own kids feel about me, my life, the example I had set for them? Would I have earned their pity or their respect? The thought of them believing me a quitter was too much to bear. In their eyes, I wanted to be a doer, an achiever, someone who loved life and strove to better herself. A fighter.

That was it. That's what I wanted—to become the type of person they might grow up to emulate.

It was finally clear to me that I was more afraid of never reaching my own personal pinnacle than I was hurt by any of the harsh words Gruff had for me. It would be an uphill battle, but I would push to see my potential, give myself the chance to struggle, to reach out with everything I had, to stretch and hopefully to grasp my life's purpose at its peak.

Yet there I sat, sniveling on the toilet. I waited in the restroom until I was absolutely certain no sniffles remained, then stepped through the doors and joined the recruits in the classroom, where five women waited to head back to the blacktop.

Motivated with a renewed sense of purpose, I again took my turn. It was time to have my skills retested and do my very best.

It was growing dark outside by now. Benetti sat next to me, and, this time, Gruff played the bad guy in the pink car.

Again as primary, I waited until my back-up was near, and then I pulled over the pink car. Wind whistled through my gun as I yelled to Gruff to get out of the vehicle, without the PA system, which, apparently, nobody else had been badgered to use and was conveniently missing from this training car. I hollered with all my might through the wind and cold that hit as soon as the sun went down.

Tumbleweeds rolled by during the third run when I, as a secondary officer, cuffed the suspect and escorted him to the back of my patrol car. We practiced five more times, with the six of us women switching off primary and secondary positions. By the end of the evening, all six of us had passed.

Though mentally fatigued to the point of impairment, I managed to drive myself slowly home. With each traffic light and stop sign came the expectation to jump out of the car and draw my weapon. Mannington, Olin, and I, along with the three other female recruits, left the academy exhausted but content to have achieved what mattered most: We still had a spot in the academy, an opportunity to try, though I was unsure how much more abuse I could take.

SEVENTEEN

GARRETT HAD CALLED IN SICK from work and the kids got their wish—they walked themselves to school for the first time, lunches in hand. I had to concede. What else could I do? Today was of monumental importance, and one I particularly looked forward to. I was headed to the range for my first day of shooting. Finally I was able to bring my real gun.

It was the final piece of my police puzzle. The last thing we needed to learn was how to shoot our handguns, and I couldn't wait. After my little taste of it at the indoor range, I'd been looking forward to firing my own gun; I just hadn't had time to do it.

"You simply push forward the slide, pop the lever, and the slide will come right off," the range master demonstrated for the class, using his Glock for an example.

He watched me struggling to remove the slide from the top of my German-made Sig Sauer. It took quite a bit of muscle to manipulate, but I eventually was successful. The range master moved to the next desk, where Mannington was attempting to do the same.

The room was alive with sound, the clicking and clacking of gun parts with an occasional clunk of a metal piece dropped on a wooden table top. Once the slide was removed, pieces popped out of my gun. I had to re-act quickly so that none of them fell to the floor and rolled away. With all my gun segments corralled on the desk, I took a minute to look around at the others recruits. Neale and Carnie seemed the only females comfortable with handling their weaponry, which I deduced from the fact that they were sitting at their desks and talking, already done with reassembly.

"Now, put your guns back together," the range master said. His moustache completely covered his top teeth as he smiled widely, as if he had just played a great joke. But we all knew the next step, and were already attempting to rebuild our firearms. More noises, grunts, and groans arose from the group, then sighs of relief once each recruit had achieved gun reassembly. Metal scraped and snapped as we pulled the slides back and let them go to create a loud smack when we snapped the slides atop our semi-automatic handguns, testing our proficiency. Then we did the same exercise three more times.

"Cycle hard! Don't baby your guns, people, let the slide go quickly when you cycle," instructed another range master who had joined us that day from a different agency. I looked around the room and glimpsed several of the male recruits acting like mobsters with their guns held sideways, tipping their heads to match. Others were holding their guns with both hands, aiming at the unoccupied corners of the room. EVOC had been fun, but so far this range stuff had done the most to bring out our toughness. At this moment, I was feeling rather bad-ass.

"Pick up your firearm with your gun hand," instructed the slightly frazzled range master after witnessing some of our novice stances and aiming techniques. "Now, wrap your non-gun hand around the grip, fingers touching the knuckles of your primary hand. Let me walk around and talk to you individually to be sure you have it." I sat at my desk fiddling with my grip.

Two other staff members came in to assist with this all-important lesson. It was essential to be sure we were absolutely safe. One of the staffers was a really handsome guy who stopped at my desk and, watching me handle my gun, rolled his eyes. He reached for my gun, which I handed to him, incorrectly.

"Grip first, geez! What you gonna do, shoot me?"

"Oh, gosh, I'm sorry, I was just trying ..." My face felt hot.

"No excuses, Dolinsky. Stand up, let's do this," he said.

I hopped up and the instructor walked behind me. With his arms around me, he physically placed my hands around the grip of my Sig, in the correct fashion. Still standing behind me, he kicked my boots apart with his foot to the correct distance, knocked the back of my knees to bend them, and turned my shoulders toward the front of the room.

"See how that feels? Your grip is tight in the web of your hand, your right hand pushes away while the left pulls in. Do you feel that, Dolinsky?"

"Yeah, I do, Sir." I replied, still embarrassed. By now he was practically hugging me, speaking with his face very close to my ear.

"Don't lean back, and keep your torso aimed forward. Give 'em the front of your vest, not the side; let your vest protect you. And now you're ready to shoot. How's that feel?"

"Uh-huh … Weird, but good," I said, nodding and blushing. "Good, Sir."

"At least you were smart enough to get night sights," he said before moving to the next person, leaving me afraid to move so that I remained standing there, in position. It felt powerful, not as daunting as I'd predicted. Pretty comfortable, really. But I wondered how long I needed to hold this position for the feeling of it to cement itself into my memory.

Around the room, everyone was getting into this position. I closed my eyes and focused on how it felt, how far apart my knees were from each other, how straight was my back, how closely in my elbows were tucked. I analyzed each finger, each joint as it was positioned, standing there frozen, holding everything in the correct form.

"I would like to get at least one magazine through your guns by the end of today," the range master said. "Go to lunch, and when you come back we'll be outside, so dress appropriately, and bring your empty magazines."

"Do you want to go to lunch?" I asked Mannington.

"No, thanks, I brought mine," she said.

"Actually, so did I," I remembered aloud. "Where do you usually eat?"

"My car, how 'bout you?"

"The locker room. You're welcome to join me!" I figured after saving her from the red man a few weeks back, and sharing felony car stop issues, she might finally consider me friend-worthy.

"No, that's okay," she replied, so I made my way to the locker room once again to have a quiet lunch. Mannington ate in her car with two other recruits. Carnie headed home for lunch, since she lived pretty close. She did that often, and I knew that even if I lived close, I wouldn't want to go to my home for lunch, especially today with a sick husband at home. It struck me as ironic, how I envied her life.

◈

WEARING A BASEBALL CAP and jacket to keep warm, I headed to the range to shoot my gun for the first time. I fervently hoped it worked. I had purchased it without testing it, but instinctively knew it wouldn't let me down. Strangely, it felt like a friend. I was so proud of it.

The range master split us up into two groups, then drove a truck about one hundred yards to the center of the asphalt on the range. It seemed like overkill to me, and I wondered why he hadn't just walked until he opened the back end and said, "Load up one magazine, and be careful to get the right ammo! Only *one* magazine with bullets, people!"

There on the bed of the truck were boxes overflowing with bullets of every shape and size, tiny golden tubes capable of putting a hole through almost anything, a cardboard target, even a human being, sending a soul tumbling into the afterlife. I looked for the nine-millimeter rounds and took a handful, filling a pants pocket so I could get out of the way of the other recruits champing at the bit to load their weaponry. Watching how others did it, I learned to load my magazine, slipping in one bullet at a time.

"Get eyes and ears, people!" hollered the range master. I grabbed glasses and headphone-style mufflers, just like those I had borrowed at the indoor range, which he also had piled in the back of his truck. Once we were adequately equipped, we lined up at the fifteen-yard mark, each facing a large cardboard target featuring a shadow figure. I expected something really state of the art, like at the indoor range—wires and pulleys moving things closer or farther away. But this was nothing glamorous, just a few sticks holding targets at the edge of asphalt. The weather was unseasonably cold; my nose and eyes were both red and runny, and I was thankful that I had grabbed the jacket.

"Do not load your firearm!" the range master hollered from behind us using a bullhorn. "Recruits, use your sights, line up the front one between the two on the back of the gun." We all took a few minutes to aim correctly.

"Using the correct stance and, using your sights, dry-fire your weapon!" Thirteen quiet clicks could be heard down the line. "Keep dry-firing people, get comfortable with how it feels!" I heard clicking sounds around me. Olin stopped and lowered her gun toward the ground.

"You should be in firing stance! No one moves until I give the command to move! Is that understood?" bellowed the range master. His face turned red, and I expected a button on the jacket stretched over his round belly to pop off.

"Okay, okay, sorry!" Olin said, quickly positioning herself at the ready.

The range master continued, "All right, recruits, de-cock and holster your weapon." I pushed the de-cock lever and placed my Sig into my holster, then slid the holster's locking band into place with a click. *Phew.*

Moving one at a time toward the dirt hill to our right, as instructed, we each faced the berm to load our firearm with a full magazine, snapped the slide to load a bullet into the chamber, then de-cocked and holstered the gun. Afterward, I thrust my hands into my jacket pockets to keep warm.

I was incredibly eager to test my gun. I hungered to know if my Sig was indeed the charmed purchase I had presumed it to be, a remarkable, enchanted tool that may one day save my life or the life of another. It was finally testing time.

Lined up in front of my targets, I held still, my heart beating powerfully in my chest. The world visibly shook a little with every beat. While I waited, facing my target, cold air filled my lungs and my fingers felt like ice. No longer in the jacket pockets, my hands dangled at my sides. I imagined I looked like someone out of an old cowboy movie shoot-out. That's how it felt.

"At the word 'GUN' you will pull your weapon and fire three shots into the target, then wait at high ready. Do you understand?" buzzed the bullhorn. We nodded. "Put on your eyes and ears … People, remember, this is not a race, slow and steady! Ready … GUN!"

I grabbed at my holster, pushed the retention strap forward, and gripped the handle of my Sig. Muffled popping could be heard near me as I pulled my gun out and held it straight in front of me. Wrapping my hands around the grip, I placed my right index finger on the trigger and squeezed, slowly. *BOOM!* The nose of my gun bounced upward as I fired.

Shooting sounds carried on around me like a war zone. I focused my sights again on target and squeezed twice more, *BOOM! BOOM!* Squinting, straining to see if my shots had hit the mark, I focused and recognized sunlight shining through three perfect little holes—not in the center, but through the man-shaped print on the cardboard just the same. It worked! My Sig Sauer semi-automatic worked, well, in fact. I had "laid lead down range" and it felt glorious! I wanted to squeal and jump up and down with excitement, but instead I stood quietly, staring at my target.

For the next few weeks of range training, I had very little trouble, partly, according to the range master, because I had no experience and thus no bad habits to break. He was not a Sig fan, though he acknowledged it to be a good-quality gun. From what I gathered, gun owners are extremely brand loyal, and he was Glock man. Still, he was one trainer who practiced consistent patience with me and the other recruits.

There was nothing I disliked about range training; it was the only thing, so far in police work, that came somewhat naturally to me. The smell of gun powder, the feeling of cold metal muscle in my hands, the explosive force … this was sexy in a way I could never explain to my friends. They would never understand. My dad might have gotten it, I thought, and surely Garrett knew all too well what I was feeling, the inimitable power of walking around with a death device on my hip. My firearm was the great equalizer. I would never be as big and strong as the males, but I might very well be as good a shot. Range was a different type of training, and I understood why they saved it for last.

"Okay, you got six shells?" the range master asked as I stood in front of a line of small metal targets.

"Yup." It was the end of our first week of range training; I stood holding a shotgun with some apprehension.

"Okay, pay attention. Bolt goes forward, finger checks the chamber, close it, snap it, load it. It's as simple as that. Now, you hold it and I'll walk you through."

I handled the gun as the range master directed me through the safety inspection and stacking procedure. Before long, I was locked and loaded.

"Now, rack it," he instructed.

I did, just like in the movies, pushing the slide forward with a loud clack and back with force. I held the gun to my right shoulder, Annie Oakley style.

"Squeeze the trigger slowly," he directed, so I pulled my index finger toward me very slowly. A thunderous *BOOM!* erupted. Birdshot exploded from the gun, and recoil knocked the ear covers into a cockeyed position on my head. I had "killed" the first of my intended targets, a metal circle about the size of a salad plate that sat on a frame and, when hit, flipped down and backward out of sight. One was down, but three others awaited my aim. I readjusted the ear muffs and continued racking and shooting until all four metal targets lay down out of sight.

Once I was done with the shotgun lesson, the range master told me to put the targets back up as he called Neale over. I jogged up to the steel targets and lifted them into place one at a time, eerily appreciating being in what only seconds before had been my line of fire. I studied the circles to see if there was any way to distinguish the freshest hit from the thousands of dents covering the face of the metal. Watching our trainer out of the corner of my eye, as he explained to Neale how to load the same shotgun and shoot into the exact location where I now stood, I quickly moved out of the way.

By the last day of range training, we were more than ready to complete qualifications, which consisted of shooting a stationary target from different distances and, to make it interesting, from different heights. Each of us stood alongside twelve other loaded guns; we had to trust each other not to make a mistake, not to open fire in the wrong direction. However, any one of us could have killed the others in a moment, in a flash, and just knowing that enhanced my feeling of belonging in this group.

"Load your weapons! De-cock and holster!" The range master's voice was loud enough to be heard without the bullhorn, but he held on to the thing like toddler with a security blanket. We were locked and loaded, each standing behind a fifty-gallon drum, beyond which sat our targets.

"Gun!" he roared over the bullhorn. I pulled my weapon while running up to the large barrel that was intended for our use as concealment. Still kneeling behind the drum, I peeked out from the right side as if my shadow-figure target would be shooting back at me. The black human form was much less clear from the twenty-five-yard line, but I shot three times, then over the top of the drum three times, and three more from the left side of the barrel until "code four!" came from the range master.

Next, the thirteen of us moved up to the fifteen-yard line, and "Gun!" was called. This time, we each shot three rounds from a standing position, holstered our firearm, and repeated this same exercise three more times. We were moved to the ten-yard line, and then to the five-yard line, completing similar exercises. Finally, we were finished. The range master walked the target line, inspecting each puncture through the cardboard, marking them with white chalk and counting. Some recruits were excellent marksmen, with their bullet holes in a tight circle in the target's center; others were scattered all over the cardboard. Mine were somewhere in between.

We all nervously stood around the ammo truck waiting for the results. The men discussed workout strategies, and Neale and Carnie talked together about their relief that the academy was almost over. Olin bit her fingernails. Mannington talked to her boyfriend on the phone. I prayed in my head, *Please, God, may I pass* over and over, as if repetition meant something to Him.

My heart pounded when suddenly the bullhorn roared. "Nice work, recruits!" he called. "You all passed!"

A collective sigh could be heard. Relief at last. We headed to lunch, but not before we heard the range master holler at us as we walked away, "Don't get too comfortable, people! You have one last lesson, a final scenario. It will give you a good understanding of how to shoot at close range, so upon returning from lunch, meet outside on the asphalt. Got it?"

WE ALL ARRIVED RIGHT on time, no doubt anxious to get our special lesson done and over with as quickly as possible. Once this lesson was complete, I would only have one final test standing between me and my shiny chrome badge.

At the base of a hill lay a small carpet roll bearing a smiley face that had been drawn on with a permanent marker—yet another representation of Joe Shit the Douche Bag. I went first and was called over to the carpet, literally. The range master spoke quietly, only to me.

"You'll jump on the carpet and grab the top of the roll with your left hand. Okay?"

"Okay, Sir."

"Then put the muzzle of your gun up to Joe Shit the Douche Bag and shoot him twice through the face."

"Okay, Sir."

"Dolinsky!" The range master yelled at me, this time for all to hear. "This guy is fighting with your partner! You have a clear shot if you can get close enough! It's you or him! You gonna let Joe Shit the Douche Bag kill your partner?!"

I jumped onto my knees, straddling the rolled-carpet "Joe," and stuffed the muzzle of my gun right up to his drawn-on mouth. I pulled the trigger. Nothing happened. That was expected by the trainer, but there was more for me to learn.

"See, Dolinsky, your gun did nothing!" The range master's voice got louder. "What are you going do? He's killing your partner, it's you or him!

What are you going to do, Dolinsky?" *Oh my GOD!* I thought frantically. *What do I do?*

Then it came to me. I remembered in class that Smythe had said something about getting too close to a target. I pulled the muzzle back a few inches and, with my right hand, shot twice into Joe Shit the Douche Bag's face.

The bullets rocketing through the carpet hit the ground below with such force, it blew chunks of dirt, dust, and rocks over the top of "Joe" and into my face, which was now covered with debris. I blinked and spit tiny rocks out of my mouth, and then I heard the range master speaking close to my ear, so only I could hear.

"That's human blood, bones, and brains all over your face and in your mouth, Dolinsky. Blood, bones, and brains ... Can you handle that? Huh? Can ya?"

I shook my head hard to loosen the fragments from my eyelashes, and, a bit wobbly, I holstered my weapon and stood up.

"Good job, Dolinsky. Go clean your weapon. I'll see you at the graduation."

"Thanks, Sir," I replied, beaming and proud to be done with everything but the final written exam, but also still captivated by what had just happened. While I was cleaning my gun, my mind revolved around the mental image of human brains splattered all over me, in my mouth, on my uniform. Intellectually, I knew it was only dirt, but it had flown at me so realistically, and covered me so completely that the range master's words had branded the experience as real in my mind. My body had gone through the motions of physically killing Joe Shit the Douche Bag, and though I knew it was just a training scenario, the emotional impact stayed with me. I was still processing the lesson in the car on the way home. If I felt this strongly after killing a carpet, what did the men and women in uniform really feel after killing a true, live human being?

Tears began to run down my cheeks, sticking in the dirt I hadn't yet washed off. *Those poor officers,* I thought. *How do they live with themselves after taking a life?* I wondered about those who had accidentally killed innocent people, or fellow officers, or, God forbid, children? Oh God, no one should be put in such a position, just doing their jobs and suddenly, in an instant, scarred for life. Is that what had happened to Garrett? Had he been forced to take a life?

Tears rolled off my chin and landed on my uniform, despite my futile attempt to hold them back.

What if I were put in that position? What if I had to kill another person? Could I do it? Yes, I thought I could. No, I *knew* I could. But how would it change me? How would my family look at me? How would it shake my faith? How would I see myself from then on?

Against my wishes, the floodgates opened, and I drove home from my last training day at the academy a blubbering idiot. I wiped my eyes on my sleeve, feeling a hurt deep in my chest, sadness, grief, even aching for all the officers who had taken lives, and for those who had been killed in the line of duty. I sobbed for their families and victims of crime, and victims' families, and anyone who had ever been a victim of anything. And then, I just cried because I couldn't stop.

The last time I had cried like this was when my mom had been dying. One day, prior to my argument with her doctor and her eventual release to hospice, after having visited her in the hospital, I sat down in my dining room, photos of her spread before me on the table. Garrett walked into the kitchen to grab a beer. He stopped and took one look at me, bawling uncontrollably. I looked up at him just as he popped the top to his beverage, and I watched him walk out of the room. He had offered no comfort, no kind words, no hug. He left me there, alone. Mom wasn't even dead yet, and I already felt that I was annoying him by being too emotional.

So no, it wasn't the war that had changed him, I realized. Even then, before the war had altered him, his lack of empathy had begun to change my feelings toward him. And, I thought, it was much the same way that I would be changed if I had to kill for my career.

I parked in front of the house and took a few minutes to pull myself together. I looked in the rearview mirror and saw the contrast of my deeply reddened eyes against my green irises. After hastily wiping away my tears, I made my way into the house and straight to my closet to change clothes. Then I went into the kitchen to calmly begin preparing dinner.

Eighteen

THE STIFF SERGEANT HAD BEEN TELLING US how difficult the final exam would be for weeks and now it was finally time to take the test. My nerves were shot, as were the nerves of all the recruits. It had been a long and trying fourteen weeks, and I was thrilled it was coming to a close.

On the day of the final, the day before our last day in the academy, I entered the locker room in the morning to get ready for the test and overheard a female recruit bad-mouthing another trainee.

"She has no idea what she's getting into, I doubt she'll make it in the jail," I heard Neale say to Carnie, their backs to me. Neale prided herself on being the resident expert when it came to the detention facility; she had already been working there and claimed to know the literal and figurative "ins and outs" of jail.

"I don't like to shit-talk," Carnie said to her, unaware of my having entered the room. "Besides, I think you're being a little hard on her. None of us have passed the test yet, and that's my main concern right now."

Neale was unmoved. "Passing this academy isn't the same as working the jail. I think she's an idiot when it comes to law enforcement. There's no way she'll make it in Detention."

I heard Neale's locker slam and, with that, they both turned around, stopping dead in their tracks when they saw me. Now it was painfully clear; the target of Neale's criticism was me.

We stood there staring at each other. Then, feeling brave, I started the conversation "Is there a problem?" Four other women who were dressing nearby had stopped and were now gawking at us shamelessly.

"Yeah, there is," Neale said arrogantly. "You don't know where you're fuckin' going! But I do! I do, because I've worked there for *five fucking years* already." Neale stepped over a bench and moved closer to me, now only a few feet away, still another bench between us. She lifted her foot and dramatically rested her boot on it before continuing her rant.

"You don't have a fuckin' clue," she said pointing her index finger at me and leaning into me with every "fuck." "Inmates'll see right through you, Dolinsky. You'll get fuckin' hurt or you'll get someone else fuckin' hurt. I don't think you fuckin' belong in this business, and I don't think you can make it through FTO!"

I wasn't even sure what "FTO" meant, but I knew it had something to do with training. I also knew that if I backed down now, she would forever have the upper hand.

"Whether or not I get through FTO is my concern, not yours!" I lifted my foot to the bench to mimic her stance and leaned forward, resting my arm on my knee. Then I continued, "You know, you'd be taken more seriously if you cleaned up your language." These were the moments I wished I'd been born more like my mother, who always was ready with a quick wit and biting tongue.

"You never even figured it out, that calling you 'Soccer Mom' was meant as a cut! It's not *cute*! It's because nobody likes you here! Every day you come in here all happy and smiling like you're going to a party. The jail is no fuckin' party! You want to be all nice and shit, go be a librarian! Deputies need to be fuckin' tough!"

Her beady eyes squinted with anger so tight that the color was no longer detectable, and her short spiky hair enhanced her tough appearance. I considered just letting her speak her mind and then holding my tongue and walking away, but after my last few weeks, I kind of felt like an argument, so I shot back.

"I have every right to be here, just like you or any other recruit!" I tried to speak calmly, so as not to let her know she had me upset in the slightest. "I thought we were supposed to support each other? Members of the same law enforcement family, each other's 'go-to guys' for the rest of our careers?

Huh? Guess I was just unlucky enough to get stuck in an academy that would rather talk down about each other than help each other." I stared at her, uncomfortably, still mimicking her stance, but with my arms crossed.

She moved closer, her finger inches from my face. "You are so fucking naïve, Soccer Mom. You don't have a fuckin' clue what it's like in jail, but I do! I know what those pricks over there'll do to you, and I'm not just talkin' about the inmates, I mean the deputies, too! They will *tear you up*! You better be fuckin' prepared for it!"

I wanted to grab her finger and snap it off, but I just kept my arms crossed in an attempt to look relaxed, my boot still on the bench.

"Again, it's *my* problem, not yours," I stated, as calmly as possible, though my voice cracked a little. Neale glared at me with those tiny eyes, turned, and stormed out the door. Seconds later, the other women resumed dressing and Carnie looked my way and smiled, seeming pleased with how I'd handled myself. Then she shrugged and left the room.

What was this, high school? There was no way I was going to let some beady-eyed, post-pubescent pain in the ass control my destiny, no matter how idiotic she wanted to behave. Not after I'd come this far. If she was right, I'd simply have to work that much harder in the future.

Careful not to look at Neale when I entered the classroom, I found my usual seat waiting for me and readied myself to take the final exam. After all the build-up, I was surprised to find that it was just a test, like any other I'd taken in school, and it hadn't seemed particularly difficult to me since I had studied hard and was prepared.

After lunch, we returned to the classroom to learn where we ranked in the class. I was ranked in the top half of the class, and Carnie ranked just below me. It was done, we had passed, and in two days we would graduate.

NEARLY TWENTY YEARS had flown by since I had graduated high school. At that time, I'd fully expect to go on to become a college graduate as well, but then I'd married Garrett and that hadn't happened. Having a job and my own money felt good, really good, and now that I'd completed the police academy, a significant achievement, I was confident I could achieve even more. I began to revisit the idea of finishing college, hopefully earning a bachelor's degree before the boys reached college age, so that I could set a good example for them.

Never would I have expected to have earned a police training certificate. It had never even been on my radar as a kid. I considered that irony as I stood on stage in formation on the morning of graduation.

The stiff sergeant spoke nervously about the events that had taken place over the past fourteen weeks, much like the speech he had given us on the first day. My eyes scanned the crowd. My dad joined Garrett, Marge, and the boys near the front, so I could easily see them from the stage. Though I had prepared my uniform the night before, spit-shined boots and all, I had forgotten to make sure the boys' clothing was pressed—another irony. But from where I sat, they looked perfect. While the stiff sergeant explained to the crowd of about one hundred and fifty people the meaning behind all the training we had completed, and described how we would revert back to our training when in crisis situations ("...which is why training correctly the first time is so vitally, so critically, so irrevocably important ..."), I was daydreaming.

Italian sounds good, but we always do Italian, I mused about the options for our celebratory meal. *Maybe Mexican would be better today. We could go to a casino buffet and have both, or whatever we want ...*

I heard something about us being "the best and brightest," and went back to my daydreaming. *What a bunch of hooey!* I chuckled to myself. *They told me I was never going to pass, and now they say this? "Best and brightest," my butt. Hypocrites! If the audience only knew the things they yelled at us, the way they acted with us, they'd be surprised.* Then my rumbling stomach got the best of me. *Seafood sounds good, too. I'd better make sure the buffet includes shrimp, at least.*

Our valedictorian, a female from a sister agency, gave a speech in which she explained how much it meant to her to become a police officer. It was her dream job, she said, and she thanked her family for their support. Though I was on the same stage she was, at what seemed like the same phase in life, I felt a little envious of her. I wished all the work I'd done to get here had satisfied some deeply hidden dream within me, but it didn't feel like it had.

Finally, it was time for each of us to be called up to the podium and receive a badge from the chief commanding officer of our respective agencies. Four different agencies had recruits in our academy, and each chief was in attendance.

"Christie Jean Carnie," was called. *So THAT'S what CJ stands for!* I thought and grinned. As Carnie got up to approach the podium, I could see Deb, Scotty, and a few other people rise and cheer. I felt proud of her, too; after all, I was a bit invested in her success.

"Elizabeth Dolinsky," called the announcer, and I hurried to the podium, where the sheriff shook my hand and offered me my badge.

"Congratulations," he said as I received my badge. "Welcome aboard."

"Thank you so much!" I gushed, full of excitement and pride at that moment, forgetting the negative thoughts that had filled my head just seconds before. I glanced at the coveted badge in my hand, a beautiful, shiny silver star with gold accents and a metal ribbon along the top that read "Deputy Sheriff." Once I'd shaken hands with each of the chiefs, I walked back to my seat. My family cheered, and Deb and Scotty cheered, too, which made me smile. Even though I had completed everything asked of me and had passed, the whole experience still seemed surreal to me.

After the presentation had concluded, the recruits milled around looking for family members. A reporter from a local television station approached with a photographer in tow. I was reminded about what counted for news in a town the size of ours.

"Hey," he said, "would you mind giving us an interview?"

"Okay, I guess," I shrugged, and then looked at my family, who had just arrived at my side. They were all smiling awkwardly, as if they didn't quite know what this interview might be about. So was I, actually. It seemed weird to me.

I spoke to the reporter, a young man probably right out of journalism school, about my experience in the academy. I lied.

"So what made you become a deputy?" he asked. *The gambling, the officer in Colton's class, the jail tour...* "It was just time to get back to work after being a stay-at-home mom for so many years," I said, smiling at him but not looking directly at the camera. The light shined brightly into my eyes.

"And was the academy hard?" he asked.

"Parts were difficult, but other parts were just plain fun. Nothing worthwhile comes easy." Now I was having fun and realized I sounded like a politician.

"What's the next step for you?"

"I'm looking forward to getting to work. The academy was great. I mean. really, what other job allows you get to shoot guns and drive fast?"

And with that, the reporter told the cameraman to "cut."

"I've been thinking of trying to get into the academy in a year or two," the young reporter confided as they packed up their gear.

"You should do it! You might really enjoy it!" I encouraged him, now feeling a little guilty for my not-so-honest answers.

Dad gave me a big hug, which was hard to do considering the thick, bulky ballistic vest I wore under my uniform.

After I changed out of my uniform, we all headed to lunch at my favorite buffet, which indeed featured seafood. I was enjoying all the attention but was anxious to get home, to put my gun in the safe and just be *me* again, for however short-lived a time. FTO was only a weekend away.

NINETEEN

WALKING INTO THE BUILDING for my first day of work in my new green-and-tan uniform, I felt I had earned at least a portion of the respect that came from wearing a badge on my chest. The solid steel symbol of strength, safety, and protection was proudly displayed over my heart. While it impressed people on the street, such as the woman who had made my latte that morning and tried to give me a discount (which I declined), respect from the other deputies was completely different, and not easily acquired. Rather, it was to be hard-earned.

Each new recruit was partnered with a different field training officer, or FTO, for each phase of training. My FTO for this first phase, Intake, was a serious former Marine. A well-built man with a crew cut, Paxton exuded confidence and was completely "squared away," right down to his shirt stays and sock garters. If anyone could get me squared away, he could. I began each day smiling and friendly, just as I had at the academy. I couldn't help it; it came naturally with the excitement that accompanied me to work. This first day began with a discussion of the basics.

"Okay, FNG, my initial concern will be to see if you can exhibit 'officer presence,'" began Paxton with authority. "Being that you're a small female, I'll be looking to see if you have the confidence to control inmates, especially the males and the convicts who have done time in prison. It's a rough crowd in here, lots of players and manipulators."

"Okay, Sir. Excuse me, but what's an 'FNG'?"

"Fuckin' New Guy," he answered simply. "And don't worry if you make a decision that's wrong; just be confident. I won't let you do anything to get yourself in trouble. And don't call me 'Sir' ... FNG."

"Okay, Sir." Then, catching myself, I stumbled apologetically, "Oh! Sorry."

"It's okay," he chuckled. "Now, I want you to work on your game face. Do you know what I'm talking about?"

"I think so."

"I mean, I don't want you smiling at these people in jail," he went on. "These are inmates. They are adults that act like children; treat them like children."

"I smile at children, Sir," I said, smiling at him. My trainer rolled his eyes and said, "Treat them like bad children. This is about safety and security, so be serious, *not* friendly, to these people. I want to see a game face from you today."

"Yes, Sir," I replied, seriously.

"Quit calling me 'Sir.'"

"Sorry," I blushed.

The former Marine walked me down some stairs and into a hallway where gun lockers hung on the walls.

"With a ratio of seventy inmates per one deputy, we cannot afford to have firearms or batons on us. It would be too easy for inmates to overpower us and use our weapons against us," he explained as he placed his equipment in a locker. I followed his lead, chose a locker, and placed my baton, magazines, and firearm inside. Then, with a snap, the locker was secured and its key hung from my belt.

It was an entirely different feeling, standing in front of the blue sliding door to the secured facility, than it had been during my first visit to this facility, when I had toured the jail with Smythe. Back then, I had been full of questions—Would I get this job? Would I get through the academy? Since then, so many unknowns had been answered. This time, walking through the door represented something different and exciting, like another piece to my puzzle revealing itself. I felt giddy with anticipation because once FTO training was completed in just a couple of months, I would be a full-fledged deputy sheriff. Rather than this being a door to a mysterious future, it was now the door to the home stretch.

My trainer pushed a button near the door. We stood waiting in silence.

"Get used to waiting. That's how it works around here," Paxton answered my unspoken questions. "Don't continuously push the button for them to open the door; you won't make any friends in Central. We don't know what they're dealing with in another part of the jail, so practice patience. Otherwise, you'll just piss 'em off."

"Okay," I said, pointing up. "They see us through the cameras?" Three cameras were visibly aimed down at us from the ceiling.

"Exactly."

The door opened with a very loud *Crack!* We walked through the doorway and down a hallway full of doors.

"Wait right here a minute," said Paxton as he entered a room, leaving me alone in the hallway. When he returned a minute later, he handed me a radio.

"You know how to call in?" he asked.

"Uh … well … sort of."

"Okay, listen, then copy me," he said, and he pushed the button on the mic attached to his shirt. "Central Control, Deputy Paxton."

"Go ahead, Deputy Paxton," said the voice on the radio.

"Ten-forty-one, Intake, ten-eight, good morning," said Paxton as he looked at me. Then he let go of the button and said, "Got it?"

I'd never handled a real radio in the academy; we'd only pretended with blocks of wood. So Paxton helped me stick the receiver in the holder on my belt and wrap the curly cord around my back to attach the mic to my shirt like his. Other deputies were wandering up and down the hallway, maneuvering around me in a whirlwind, while the radio was a flurry, with the new shift deputies calling in just like Paxton had done. Finally, I keyed the mic.

"Central Control, Deputy Dolinsky." No response.

"Somebody walked on your traffic," Paxton said. "Try again."

"Central Control, Deputy Dolinsky." Still no response. I looked at my hand on the radio. *Oops,* I thought when I realized that I hadn't pushed the button hard enough on the mic.

"Okay, Probie, let's try it again. Key the mic," Paxton said.

I keyed the mic.

"Central Control, Deputy Dolinsky."

"Go ahead, Deputy Dolinsky." Then I realized, I didn't remember what I was supposed to say after that. I threw a fearful look at Paxton, who was waiting for me to say something.

"Deputy Dolinsky, do you have traffic for Central?" asked the male voice from Central on the radio.

Paxton reminded me, "Ten-forty-one, Intake, ten-eight."

I keyed the mic, then repeated, "Ten-forty-one, Intake, ten-eight"

"Ten-four, Deputy Dolinsky," confirmed Central.

From that simple exchange I felt a surge of excitement running through me as we walked from the hallway to the Intake area.

Paxton wasn't so excited. He shook his head from side to side and mumbled, "You've got a lot to learn, Dolinsky," as we stuffed our pants pockets with black rubber gloves and headed over to the Sally Port. I pushed the button to open another windowed sliding door that would let us into the Sally Port. With a loud mechanical *Crack!* the door began to open.

"I'll do a few searches, you just watch for now," Paxton instructed. Soon it would be my turn, and having learned the systematic quadrant searching techniques during the Defensive Tactics portion of the academy, I felt prepared to give it a try. Another FTO stood there with one of my academy mates, Jarvis, who ignored me as I said hello. The radio sounded.

"One unit in, two J-three's, one J-three-X," a male voice said through the microphone clipped to my shirt. Remembering the codes I'd studied endlessly, I knew we had three arrestees, two males and one female, arriving in the parking lot.

"I'll search one of the guys and you watch," Paxton told me. "Then you search the girl."

"Yes, Sir," I replied, excited to get to work.

A large officer from a neighboring city brought in a male and sat him in one of our plastic chairs, placing the man's cuffed hands behind the back of the chair. Paxton began the search.

"Stand and face the wall, separate your feet," he directed the inmate, and then asked him, "Do you have anything on you that will poke or stick me?"

The man stood up and moved his feet apart, then said, "No." The man looked to be about sixty, but, according to his driver's license, was only forty-five. He smelled pungently of body odor and cigarette smoke, and had an apparent inability to stop his whole-body twitching.

I watched while Paxton checked the man's waistband, removed the man's belt, and tossed it into a gray bin, which sat on the chair.

"Black belt," he said. Jarvis held a clipboard, scribing the inventory while Paxton searched the man.

"When's the last time you used?" Paxton asked as he pulled cigarettes and a lighter out of the cuffed man's pocket.

"I don't know, probably last night."

"Meth?"

"Yeah."

"How much?" Paxton asked as he tossed a black wallet extracted from the man's back jeans pocket into the bin.

"A lot," said the man matter-of-factly as Jarvis picked it up and began going through it, pulling out every photo and card one by one, and tossing it all into the bin.

"Dolinsky," Paxton waved me over toward him so the man couldn't hear our conversation. "See how jerky his movements are? See the scabs all over his arms? Clear signs of meth use."

"Wow, I wouldn't have known that."

"You'll also see it in their teeth, black spots on the teeth; the meth eats right through the enamel and they lose teeth easily. We call it 'meth mouth.' You can't miss it. Go see if he has any drugs in his mouth."

"How?"

"Ask him to open his mouth and look under his tongue," he instructed and went back to work, picking up the gray bin of belongings and placing it behind the chair. He then motioned to the inmate to sit down. Paxton lifted each of the inmate's feet and removed the man's boots one at a time, and instantly a strong whiff of stink hit my nose. I put my shirt sleeve up to my face to prevent my inhaling it, and I noticed that Paxton and the other deputies in the room seemed oblivious to the scent.

The arresting officer who was standing near the sliding door preparing to leave asked me, "What? Is it your first day?"

"Yup, it's her first day," Paxton answered for me.

"That explains it," the officer replied and he chuckled. "That ain't nothin' compared to seep feet." Paxton nodded solemnly. They were obviously friends, and went on to discuss a baseball game they would be attending over the weekend.

A few minutes later, another male prisoner was brought in by a different officer, and Jarvis went to work on him. I could hear his FTO talking about Jarvis to the pretty female booking agent who was responsible for taking the mug shots. She was motioning with her hands to indicate that he should be over there helping his trainee.

"He's squared away, I don't need to watch him," the man said dismissively. "When are you gonna bring cookies in for the deputies again?"

"So you like my cookies, do ya?" she replied seductively.

Their conversation became mute when I saw the female inmate enter, escorted by a female parole and probation officer. I began to give her instructions, as Paxton had done.

"Stand up, face the mat," I ordered. Paxton broke off his conversation and watched my every move.

"Take off her belt, Dolinsky," he directed. "Don't forget the hair tie, and she has a watch on, too." All I could think was how strange it felt to take off someone else's clothing, a stranger's. I could only imagine what it must be like for these people, to be handcuffed, forcibly undressed, and touched everywhere. I had to keep reminding myself that they had committed crimes in order to get here and, in so doing, had earned this treatment.

After I had gone through her pockets, Paxton reminded me to take off the shoes.

"Bring your feet up," he told the inmate, and she did. Paxton and I grabbed her ankles with our gloved hands. I slid off one pump, he took off the other, and we checked between and under her toes.

"Do you know why we take the shoes, Dolinsky?" Paxton quizzed me. "It's because it would hurt a lot less getting kicked with this," he held up her naked foot to demonstrate, "than it would with this," and he held the shoe by the heel and moved it toward my face for effect.

"It makes perfect sense," I said.

At that moment, a call came over the radio. "Ten-Ten in Cell Three!" It was the voice of Jarvis's training officer, the one who had left the Sally Port moments before. Paxton immediately dropped the foot, threw the shoe in the gray bin, and yelled, "Come on!"

Racing through the slider, we ran at full speed across the lobby into the area to where Cell Three was located. I could see a large, heavy, blue door standing open and followed Paxton in to help. A man lay on his stomach on the floor, thanks to the deputies holding him down by kneeling on top of him, each with a knee on one of the inmate's shoulders. Paxton grabbed both ankles and crossed them, then kneeled on the top one.

Jarvis's training officer was yelling at the inmate, "What the *fuck* were you doing?! Battery is a felony in custody, Martinez! Now you earned yourself another charge! You've been here enough to know we would've brought you another sandwich. Why would you fight over a fucking sandwich?"

Martinez could barely speak with these large men on his shoulders and calves. He muttered something unintelligible when the strong deputies stood him up as if he were made of paper. The deputies then walked him into nearby Cell Four, which was empty, and slammed the door, locking it with a large key.

Once they had moved Martinez out of the room, I could see the victim—a small, skinny, older man with a beard and no teeth who was gumming a peanut butter sandwich. His nose was visibly bleeding, but he didn't seem to care. He just sat on the floor in the corner of the room gazing at the sandwich as he slowly ate it. I stood looking around the cell, which was quite large and had been painted an ungodly brown color.

During my tour of the jail, I'd learned about the "Drunk Tank." In here, there were no chairs or furniture of any kind, just brown, cinder-block walls and small cement steps that were about eight inches high and ran the perimeter of the room, just wide enough to hold a sleeping human.

Paxton called me out of the cell, catching me off guard since I hadn't realized I was now alone in the cell with the inmate. I turned and moved out of the cell quickly so that Paxton could shut the heavy steel door.

"You need to understand, Dolinsky … You should've been in there first, not me. To pass training, you need to be *on it*," he said. "I won't pass you until I know you're not afraid to engage in a fight with the inmates."

"I'm not afraid," I piped up. Paxton rolled his eyes.

"Then show me. This is all new to you and I understand that, but I want no excuses." I stood listening, subdued. "I know it's your first day and all, but we only have a few weeks to get you through this phase and into the next one. Next time we have an incident, you need to step up and be involved before me. Got it?"

"Yes, Sir," I answered, forgetting that I'd just broken another of his rules. *How in the world am I supposed to be faster and stronger than these muscle-bound, body-builder deputies?* I wondered. The men all towered over me, the deputies and the inmates. How could I possibly beat them in any fight?

I completed a security check, an every-fifteen-minute requirement to check inside each cell. Paxton stopped at the nurse's station, located directly in front of the Sally Port door, and informed them of the bloody nose in Cell Three. I met him back in the Sally Port.

"Fuck you!" was the first thing I heard coming from the average-sized man in handcuffs being slammed against the wall by Jarvis, who was roughly pushing his elbow into the man's back. I instantly understood the need for the blue mats lining the walls. "You ain't got *nothin'* on me! This is just piddly-ass county shit. I've done time in Folsom! I know tough, an' you ain't tough!"

Paxton directed me to assist in searching this inmate while Jarvis held one side to the mat. Another very muscular deputy, Hoffman, arrived and took control of the inmate's other side, also using his forearm, this time to plant the arrestee's face into the mat.

"Oh, I see!" yelled the inmate. "This make you pricks feel big? Fuck you, I'll fuck you up when I'm outta these cuffs."

While the deputies silently held the intoxicated arrestee to the mat, he continued to yell profanity and threats. I squeezed in between the deputies to search his waistband and took off his belt, tossing it into the gray bin on the seat.

"Girl's gotta do your work for ya, huh? Fuckin' tough guys?" taunted the inmate as I emptied his pockets and felt along each leg. Paxton stopped me after I searched the inmate's groin area.

"Don't be afraid to get in there—you gotta know there are no weapons getting into the facility. Get up *in* there," he urged.

So, holding the man's leg, I re-searched the crotch by sliding my gloved hand up his jeans into the area right next to his penis, then quickly back down. I felt nothing out of the ordinary. The inmate hadn't even seemed to notice.

"Better," said Paxton.

I did the same search to the other leg. Now the man was complaining that he needed to use the restroom, and, by keeping him from doing so, we were violating his rights. This time, I moved up into the groin area with more force.

"*Damn* bitch! You don't gotta knock my nuts off!" the inmate yelled as I completed the groin search.

"Perfect," said Paxton, smiling proudly.

I followed Jarvis and Hoffman as they dragged the still-handcuffed inmate up to the photo area, leaning him back against the gray mat. The prisoner hung his head down so the booking clerk couldn't snap a mug shot.

"Put your head up and look at the camera!" ordered Hoffman.

"Fuck off!" yelled the inmate, refusing to look up.

"Well, that's not very nice. You kiss your mother with that mouth?" joked Hoffman.

"Fuck you!" yelled the man. At this, Hoffman and Jarvis turned him backward and dragged him through the Intake lobby to a cell across the room, all the while with the man yelling, "You mother fucker! I'm gonna kick your ass as soon as these fuckin' cuffs come off!"

The deputies dragged the inmate into Cell Five, and then I entered after them, hurrying to do my part.

"Kneel down!" ordered Hoffman.

"Fuck you," came the inmate's response, fighting the order by stepping forward.

Paxton hurried past me and grabbed the inmate's legs, pulling them out from under him. The inmate nose-dived toward the cement floor below, but the strong deputies held him up by his arms, placed him firmly on the floor, face down, and then knelt on his shoulders as I'd seen done earlier that day. Paxton again crossed the inmate's feet and knelt on his calves, then motioned to me to come in and take over for him. I did, grabbing both ankles and kneeling on the calves before Paxton let go and stood up, moving just outside the door. Hoffman gave instructions to the inmate, who at this point was very still and quiet, no longer fighting us.

"We're gonna to take the cuffs off and place your hands on the back of your head," said Hoffman in a low voice, which echoed through the tiny cell. "You understand?"

"Yes, Sir," replied the inmate. I used all my weight to hold the man's legs in place. Though he wasn't resisting me, I wasn't sure he wouldn't suddenly start up. Hoffman took out his key and removed one cuff, guiding the man's free hand to the top of his head and holding it there as Jarvis removed the second cuff. They interlaced the inmate's fingers and held his hands against the back of his head, then instructed him to stay in that position until the door closed. He didn't respond.

I was nearest the door still holding the feet in place. Jarvis shot past me out of the cell and Hoffman squeezed by me. Before I could panic about being in there by myself, I felt the back of my belt jerk hard, lifting me to my feet. Hoffman was pulling me out of the cell backward with one hand, which I now knew was, tactically, the soundest and quickest way to remove the last person from the cell, who usually was the person holding the feet. Paxton slammed the door and locked it with the key, and I felt myself exhale. We began to walk away when all of a sudden the inmate appeared in the window of the cell door, screaming at the top of his lungs, "I'll hurt you *motherfuckers*, I'm not done with you yet!"

It startled me, but the seasoned deputies just laughed.

"Typical cell warrior," said Paxton as he wiped his forehead with his sleeve and walked out of the holding cell area into the lobby, the three of us following.

IT WAS LUNCH TIME. Paxton had seniority on the shift and chose to go early at eleven o'clock, which meant so did I. He showed me the way to Staff Dining, where the inmates cooked for the staff.

"Meet here at noon," he said to me, and then he took off through the security doors.

It was then that I remembered. Somebody had mentioned in the academy that, as a recruit, you had to be invited to sit at the "deputy table." I scanned the room for any signs of a "deputy table" in order to avoid it, thus avoiding any calamity resulting from an improper seating choice. The problem was, no deputy was in Staff Dining at the time, and I had no clue which one was the "deputy table." So I sat at a long table in the back of the room and proceeded to eat the ham sandwich I'd brought from home.

One table was full of people wearing lab coats, eating quietly. The noise coming from the kitchen was what you would expect—the sounds of drink machines, coffee makers, and grills. Only female inmates worked here, and they were noisy, too, cackling at each other. Most had never held jobs, thus had no idea how to behave at one.

I watched as a sergeant entered and purchased a cup of coffee. He stood talking with plain-clothes officers, whom I recognized only by the badges and guns worn on their belts. Nurses entered through a different door, followed by a deputy who was clearly flirting with one of the nurses. He then walked over to the microwave located directly behind my seat, put a frozen dinner in the machine, slammed the door, and turned it on.

"What the fuck, FNG?" he turned and asked me angrily.

"Excuse me?" I said, not quite sure whether he was talking to me.

"Sitting at the deputy table already? Didn't they warn you in the academy?"

"Oh! Sorry!" I said as I got up to move.

"Relax! I'm just fuckin' with you," he said as he slid into a chair two away from mine. His name tag read "Van Zant." Minutes later, a tall deputy entered the room and slid into the chair next to Van Zant. I couldn't read his name tag, but he had a booming voice and even louder laugh.

"What the fuck?!" he boomed, pointing at me.

"I know," said Van Zant. "Probies are pretty cocky this academy. I remember when I started, we would've never sat at the deputy table without an invite, I'm just sayin'."

I stood up, gathered my lunch and moved to the next table over. The two men watched me sit down, then opened their lunch boxes and began eating.

"No sense of humor, either," boomed the tall deputy. Then he called condescendingly to me, "You don't have to move, we're just bustin' balls."

"I'm fine," I insisted. "Don't want to break any rules."

"Jesus … whatever, FNG," he mumbled, though even his mumble was loud. I sat alone at my table as three more male deputies and Connor, the female whom I'd met in House Five during my tour with Deputy Smythe, arrived and sat with Van Zant and the Boomer. I remained in my seat at the empty table and could only hear bits and pieces of their conversation over the noise of the diner.

"She's such a whore. I can't stand working with her, never could," said Connor. "I would *never* date a deputy, never!" she continued, only to be interrupted by Boomer.

"So your fling in the car in the parking lot with Rosenthal, that wasn't a date?"

All the deputies laughed loudly at this. Obviously irritated, Connor retorted, "Fuck you!" Then she stood up and walked into the locker room, leaving her lunch on the table. No sooner had the door closed behind Connor when Boomer took the salt shaker and poured salt into her soda can. The five men sitting around the deputy table giggled like they were in elementary school as they toyed with ideas of what to do to her sandwich.

"It's no good if she can tell we messed with it," said Van Zant.

"Get the mustard!" Boomer ordered one of the other deputies at the table. The other deputy flipped him his middle finger and remained in his seat. Van

Zant jumped up and retrieved the mustard just as the door opened and Connor re-entered the room. The five male deputies who were huddled over her lunch immediately pulled back and looked away, which tipped her off.

"What'd you do?" she asked accusingly.

"Why, whatever do you mean?" Van Zant responded jokingly as the other deputies snickered. Connor picked up her soda, her eye on the men. She scanned for any movement that would confirm their defilement of her drink, but they were nonchalant, pretending to have no interest in whether she took a drink or not. She lifted the soda to her mouth, scouring her counterparts for any clue. The male deputies perked up considerably, every one of them watching her with baited breath. She walked to the trash and threw it out.

"What? What are you doing? Were you done with that soda?" asked Boomer. Connor just glared at them as she threw away her sandwich and walked toward the door.

"You guys all suck!" she whispered loudly as she walked by the table, picked up her lunch box, and headed toward the exit.

"It was Franko! He dick-rimmed it!" yelled Van Zant, only to be slugged in the bicep by one of the other male deputies at the table, and they both laughed loudly. Connor never turned around. She continued to walk away, but lifted her left hand, displaying her middle finger, to the exuberant laughter of the five male deputies, the other diners seemingly unaware of the drama at the deputy table. I watched in astonishment, eyes wide, mouth hanging open.

"What are *you* looking at, Newbie?" woke me out of my stare. The five deputies were glaring at me. I turned away, continued eating, and waited for my trainer to arrive.

At noon on the dot, Paxton entered through the door and sat down to discuss what to expect that afternoon.

"Dolinsky, you seem a little gun-shy. That's to be expected on your first day. This afternoon, we'll continue to work the Sally Port, try to get you more hands-on experience," he said. "This is quite a culture shock for you. Do you have any questions so far?"

"Yeah, I do, about a million," I said, thinking, *Yeah, what does "dick-rimmed" mean?* We walked downstairs into the secured part of the jail to continue training.

"Did you go code?" Paxton asked.

"Code …?" I asked.

"Did you call out 'code seven' over the radio when you went to lunch?"

"Uh … No, I don't think so."

"You gotta remember to call out everywhere we go in the facility. Hugely important, or Central won't know where to direct help if something were to happen. If shit hits the fan, you push the orange button on the radio. See here." He pointed to the orange button on the top of his radio.

"Push this and the green herd comes a runnin'—no matter where you are—but Central needs to know where to tell us to go. Got it?"

"Yes, Sir."

"Oh," Paxton continued, stopping one more time, "be careful not to key your mic when you're in the bathroom. It seems to happen with every new group of recruits. Don't be a tool. Don't make me look bad, Dolinsky, okay?" he said with a wink.

"Okay, I'll try."

Deputy Connor was waiting in the Sally Port to take custody of female inmates returning from court.

"Hey, want me to teach her to strip search?" Connor asked Paxton.

"Great! That would be great, one more thing off my list."

"Okay, Dolinsky, come with me." Connor led me and the female inmates to a cell. One prisoner went in and we followed, making sure Connor's foot kept the door from shutting behind us. "First, we give the instructions to the inmate, and they do as ordered. Watch me and take notes," Connor said.

"Face away from us," she began instructing the inmates. It was clear that Connor had done many unclothed searches because it seemed like second nature for her.

"Remove your shirt; hand it back to me." The inmate complied.

"We go over the shirt, check every seam. You never know where these inmates'll hide shit." Connor felt the seams with her gloved hands and threw the shirt on a wooden bench in the cell. Next, she asked for the pants, checking each seam and hem thoroughly.

"Okay, turn and face us," Connor ordered. The woman seemed embarrassed, holding her arms around her protruding belly as she stood there in nothing but her underwear.

"Open your mouth, run your fingers between your cheeks and gums." The inmate had been through this before, but moved slowly, clearly not anxious to do it again.

"Flip your hair forward, show me behind each ear," Connor said. The inmate did as ordered.

"Face away from us and take off your bra, then underwear." After this instruction, Connor turned to speak to me.

"Women hide things in 'nature's purse' all the time. Found a driver's license in an inmate's hooch once, but most of the time we find little baggies of drugs."

"Did you say you found a driver's license in a woman's vagina?" I asked, shocked and revolted, to confirm that I had heard correctly.

"Yup. Can't imagine it was too comfortable, but that's where it was stored. We're looking for anything shiny, like a corner of a baggy, paper, or foil … anything that doesn't belong there."

Now Connor gave the final instructions to the inmate. "Turn around and face me. Lift your breasts." Connor pulled her flashlight from the holder on her belt as the inmate moved slowly, and then Connor began to inspect. "Lift your belly … Okay, turn and face away. Bend at the waist … spread your butt cheeks and cough." The inmate didn't expend much effort in spreading her butt cheeks.

"What the hell?" Connor barked at the woman. "Did you not hear me? Spread 'em, goddammit!" The woman did as she was told. The light shone brightly on the inmate's privates as she coughed twice. This certainly had not been covered at the academy, and, I was convinced, couldn't possibly be in the job description. Had I gone to nursing school, I might expect this level of examination, but not here.

I glanced only briefly at the inmate's exposed and pried-open "hooch" until my eyes darted away, flitting around the room as I did everything in my power to avoid a second look.

"See there, Dolinsky?" Connor stood pointing the light at the woman's anus, which was only four feet away from us, as if she were a USDA meat inspector examining a side of beef. "It isn't hard to notice when they have something in there. Just remember, you're looking for anything out of the ordinary." *This whole experience is out of the ordinary!*

Yet Connor was so comfortable in this role, so unfazed, that I wondered if she had always been this way, or whether she had felt as disturbed and self-conscious about this job requirement during her first time as I did now.

"You all right there, Probie?" Paxton teased as I stuck my head out the door of the cell trying to catch my breath. We had six women to search; Connor did four. I wrote notes in my notebook on each step and, after watching Connor, searched two by myself. Thank goodness the inmates were used to this procedure and led me through the process, pointing to the next piece of clothing they were to remove before I could read it in my notes. They were actually helping me and I was grateful, and while the whole experience didn't seem to bother most of the inmates, I'd never known awkward like this before.

Then it was back to the Sally Port for the last three hours of our shift. Paxton watched as I searched new arrestees coming into the facility. He taught me hidden places to look for drugs in shoes, purses, and jeans. He pointed out the ways belt buckles could be used as weapons, and I was too overwhelmed to listen. Once our relief arrived, we passed down any information we had regarding the inmates, including the tale of the "cell warrior" from that morning who still remained in the holding cell, "marinating," not yet ready to be booked.

"Dolinsky," Paxton spoke candidly as we walked upstairs to leave, "you did okay today. I threw a lot at you. Tomorrow and the rest of the week, I expect you to remember the things I told you today, and you should be able to build on what you learned. Any questions for me so far?"

"Not really, Sir." My mind was racing and, emotionally, I was spent.

"What's the goal, Dolinsky?" he asked.

"To make it home to our families at the end of shift, Sir," I responded dutifully.

"That's right. You did that today, Dolinsky. See you tomorrow, and please ... quit calling me 'Sir.'" And then he entered the men's locker room.

I took my overwhelmed and exhausted self home. And on the way, I considered how much this jail was a different world from the one the academy had trained me for. There would be no felony car stops here, no pulling guns on people to protect the public. No, this world, this jail was a gritty, smelly, crazy place where there were no innocents, only criminals, and those of us paid to keep them in order. And after one day it was crystal clear that much of what is considered "normal" for people in custody would never, *ever* be normal anywhere else.

TWENTY

"**I**'M SURE YOU'RE A VERY NICE LADY with a very nice family, but this is a life-or-death situation here. If you can't control inmates, you're a danger to your partner and the safety and security of this facility!"

"Yes, of course I understand, Sir, but …"

"But nothing. You are an officer-safety nightmare. This is unacceptable. I don't want excuses, Dolinsky, I want action," ranted Deputy Franko. "You need to re-evaluate if you want this job. Talk to your family about it. You're going to have to do better than you've been doing to pass our program. Nothing against you personally, but I won't water down our program just so a soccer mom like you can pass. Honestly, not everyone is cut out for this line of work. You think about it, hard, before you get somebody killed."

Closer to his mother's age than his, I offered no asset to the force in Franko's mind. He'd made it abundantly clear that I was not welcome.

It was my third day as a recruit at the sheriff's department, and my assigned training officer, Paxton, had called in sick. In turn, I had been placed with Franko, a perfect example of the stereotypical, knuckle-dragging, hard-headed deputy who displayed limited patience with anyone who wasn't just like him. I knew it would be a tough day when I arrived in Intake and heard my substitute trainer complain to another deputy about being "stuck with a knob for the day." I just smiled at him, like I had with everyone else, and hoped for the best.

This latest tirade from him had been the result of an incident that had occurred shortly after we had arrived downstairs. A female inmate whom I had searched in the Sally Port was taken to the showers to clean up before being moved to a housing unit. I had missed searching a pocket on her shorts, where a tiny crack pipe was later found while she was changing clothes at the showers.

That's when Franko let me have it in front of everyone, and I was mortified. He was right, after all. I needed to be more careful. But did he have to call me out in front of all the other deputies? After the tongue-lashing, he sat down and put his feet up near the deputy station, where I was working on a property inventory. I felt my eyes getting teary as I continued writing down each thing inside the inmate's purse, focusing on the property sheet to distract my mind. *White metal ring with clear stone. Yellow metal ring with four clear stones, missing one. Two white metal hoop earrings …* I wrote until Franko stopped me.

"Dolinsky, give me that."

I looked up to see his big hand waving at me from over the counter.

"The form you're writing on, hand it to me!" he ordered.

I stopped writing and handed him the form over the countertop between us. Still with his feet up, he looked it over and tossed it back on the counter.

"Wow, I'm impressed. I thought you would have fucked that up, too. Why do we write the color metal?"

"Because if I write 'gold,' but it is in fact just costume jewelry, the inmate could claim she arrived with a gold ring and when she left we gave her something else."

"Correct," Franko said. "We are not jewelers, just bucketeers."

Two other deputies walked over to Franko, found seats next to him, and lifted their feet to the counter. The three were obviously friends; all three were drinking protein shakes and discussing their plans to work out during their lunch break. A door to my right opened and a fourth muscle-bound deputy entered. Franko greeted him.

"Hey, Penis. What up?"

"Just livin' the dream," he replied flatly as he continued to walk around the counter and then head back toward the property room where the inmate clothing was stored.

Intake was such a noisy place. Doors creaked open, then slammed shut; metal file drawers banged; three female booking clerks talked cattily of a coworker who was on vacation despite the sound of their phones seemingly ringing off the hook. One-sided conversations could be heard as inmates shouted into the telephone, "Bail me out, man, you gotta bail me out!" I finished the inventory and watched as the day unfolded around me.

Nurses walked to and fro across the lobby, and a pretty one stopped to flirt with one of the Detention Emergency Response Team, or DERT, deputies, who flirted back.

After she walked away, Franko chastised him. "You're crazy to be hittin' that," he said to his partner. "Take it from me, I know what I'm talkin' 'bout."

"I never said I was hittin' that. You *assumed* I was hittin' that. Don't get me wrong, I wouldn't *mind* hittin' that," the man said with a chuckle.

"I hear ya, brotha, but if you ask me, I'm just sayin', that one's trouble." Franko finished and the three men shook the newspaper open and began to read, feet still up.

Suddenly, one of the inmates yelled into the phone, "You gotta come bail me! Oh, yeah? Well, you fuckin' owe me, bitch! Oh, yeah? Well, fuck you, then!" He slammed the receiver down.

Being the nearest deputy to him, I recognized the need to take action, but what exactly to do? Franko and his buddy ran from around the desk, and each grabbed one of the inmate's arms with such force it lifted him off the floor. The phone receiver dangled swinging back and forth as the massive deputies carried him to a holding cell, his feet hanging and running in mid-air as if to keep up.

I followed, knowing that Franko would berate me again if I didn't become immediately involved. They entered a cell with the inmate and tossed him to the floor on his stomach.

The inmate screamed, "What did I do?! I didn't do nothin', you guys! Ouch! Hey, you don't have to be so rough!" I grabbed the legs and crossed them as I had learned from Paxton, still nervous about my skills and hoping I was performing the move acceptably for this FTO. The sergeant showed up a few minutes later with keys to lock the cell, and we exited exactly as we had before—Franko grabbed my belt and pulled me out backward. I returned to write the time, name, and "att" for "attitude" on the whiteboard by the cell door to document why the inmate had been placed in the cell.

Feeling pretty confident about my performance, I eagerly looked for my training officer to say something good. He didn't.

"You should have grabbed an arm and escorted the inmate instead of waiting for me," he growled. "Next time, be on an arm, and be first in. Think you can do that?"

"Franko!" A booking clerk yelled our way from a desk behind him, and he turned to look.

"We have some releases, if you want your trainee to do them." Franko groaned as he motioned for me to go to the desk where the booking clerk stood. I picked up the release forms and took them to the carpeted lobby area where the inmates were seated quietly, none wishing to be escorted in the manner they had just witnessed.

"Delmar! Langundo! DiPietro! Line up!" I called in what felt like my loudest voice to the inmates in the lobby.

"Come on, FNG, use your big-girl voice!" chirped one of Franko's DERT buddies who remained on his rump, feet up, while I worked. His buddies laughed as I called the names out again, so loudly that my voice cracked, which amused them more. The inmates lined up and I marched them single file to the release corridor, having learned the steps for releases the day before with Paxton. Another deputy was already at the release desk, moving other released inmates through the process.

"I hate releases, these fuckers stink," he muttered, and he was right. Multiple people dressing themselves in unwashed clothing that had sat in airtight bags for weeks or even months invoked a pungent, musty smell of body odor so strong I could almost taste it.

After all the inmates had received their items, I directed them to line up quietly and they followed my instructions, standing in the hall facing the wall, waiting for another sliding door to open, which it did with a *Crack!*

Franko waited with the released inmates for me to retrieve my weapons from the gun locker. I took out the collapsible baton, placing it into the holder on my belt. Next, the extra magazines were snapped into place, and, finally, I retrieved my gun and slid it into the holster on my right hip, snapping the retention band into place. Resting my hand on my gun, I called the released inmates through the sliding door, directing them up the stairs and out of the building. All went smoothly, or so I thought.

"What the hell are you thinking?" Franko bellowed at me as soon as the last inmate walked across the driveway toward the bus stop.

"Sir?" I questioned, not sure what he was referring to this time.

"You always, *always* grab your gun first out of the locker. Last in, first out. Say it, Dolinsky. 'My gun is always last in, first out.'" I stood blinking at him.

"Say it!" he prodded.

"My gun is always last in, first out," I repeated.

"Other than that, you did okay. It's time for lunch. Let's meet in Staff Dining at thirteen-hundred," instructed Franko, "and don't be late, FNG." He smiled, and I thought for a minute that he was softening to me, until I realized his buddies had walked up behind me. He had been grinning at them. They disappeared into the staircase that led up to the deputy gym.

Lunch was quiet, with not many people in Staff Dining—there was only me and one other recruit, who had never spoken to me during the academy, so I avoided him. We ate at separate tables in the large room, listening to the banging and clanging of pots and pans and an occasional cackle from the women in the back.

Franko was not there at thirteen-hundred to meet me. As I stood waiting for him, a few deputies, who had left for lunch about when I'd taken mine had returned almost an hour later with fast food in hand, and asked me who I was waiting for.

"Franko," I said, and they laughed.

"You can expect him at thirteen-thirty or later," Connor said. "DERT guys take extra-long lunches and never get in trouble for it. It's just how it is."

At thirteen-forty, Franko and his buddies arrived. "Here's the knob, I mean, my trainee," he said, motioning toward me. "See you guys later." His buddies entered the locker room and we headed back downstairs to Intake.

As we arrived at the deputy station, where the DERT deputies liked to put up their feet, Franko noticed a deputy doing fingerprints and he asked her to take me over to the print machine and teach me. She heaved a big sigh, but agreed.

While Franko and his buddies sat eating their lunches, Deputy Terrence took the time to walk me through the printing process. She was a small woman in her late thirties with overly frosted hair pulled tight into a tiny ponytail, a pronounced nose, and dark, tired eyes.

She called an inmate up to the print machine.

"We roll each finger like so …" The inmate stood next to Terrence as she held his hand and rotated his fingers, one at a time, on a small green glass.

The print popped up on a monitor above, and she pointed at them. "These are digital prints. When I finish, I'll show you how to send them to the state and the FBI national databases."

Now, the inmate started scratching himself. "What the hell? Stop wiggling! Jeez, you're killing me here!" Terrence said, annoyed. The inmate just laughed.

What Terrence lacked in stature, she made up for in presence, exhibiting all the confidence of the male deputies—in fact, maybe more. She encouraged me to try rolling the fingers of the last inmate in line, so that I would get a feel for the machine, and then I learned to tap the button with my foot when I was ready to print. It was pretty easy for me. While I rolled, Terrence talked about her life.

"I've been on the force for fifteen years, and last year I received an award from the Sheriff for exemplary performance. Chased down this guy who stole a purse from a lady on the street. I wouldn't recommend it when you're new, but once you have some experience, you'll see things happen in town, and you'll want to step in."

"I can't imagine chasing anyone down, ever," I said, incredulous.

"That'll change. Do you carry off-duty?"

"My gun?"

"Yeah, do you keep it with you off-duty?"

"Like, in my purse?"

"Nevermind. If anything happens, just be the best witness you can be."

We completed prints and returned to the lounging deputies.

"Dolinsky, get a Barney Rubble suit. We have a female going special watch," called Franko, who was standing up and readying himself to leave.

I had no idea what he was talking about. Terrence saw it in my face. "Come on, I'll show you." And she pulled on my sleeve, directing me to follow her back into the property room, where an older gentleman was seated at a desk.

"Need a canvas suit, Mel," she said, and Mel got up from his desk, disappeared into the shelves of clothing, and returned with a heavy, quilted, dark-green blanket wrapped in Velcro.

"This is what we use for inmates who want to kill themselves. It's indestructible," Terrence said, taking it from him and handing it to me.

We took the suit to Cell Twelve, the "rubber room," where Terrence placed it in a corner. The walls and floor were covered with a tan material, softer than the painted cinder-block in the other cells. No bench, sink, or toilet here. In fact, there was nothing in this cell but a grate on the floor. I only knew it was the toilet because someone flushed it by pressing a button on the outside wall while I stood there.

Two female deputies entered the cell, escorting an inmate by the arms, one on each side. Terrence and I moved out of the way to let them in. The inmate was handcuffed and crying. I recognized one of the deputies—Carnie! The other was her training officer, Deputy Connor, who gave directions to all of us.

"She said she wanted to kill herself," said Connor. "So we need to take all of her clothing one piece at a time. Remember, ladies, slow is fast in this business. There's no hurry, just one thing at a time."

The recruits got to work as Connor then addressed the inmate. "Gloria, do you want to do this the easy way, where you cooperate and take off your clothing yourself?" The inmate gave only more tears as a response, which irritated the trainer and she rolled her eyes. "Okay, we'll do it the hard way," she said.

"I'll start with the pants," said Terrence, who began to pull at the waist of the inmate's gray jail pants.

"Wait, let's prone her out first," yelled Connor. "Dolinsky, Terrence, you get her legs." We each grabbed a leg at the same time, and Carnie and Connor still had control of the inmate's arms and lowered her to the floor. The inmate was now lying face down, and Terrence began tugging the elastic waistband of the pants. I assisted by removing her orange clog-like shoes and orange socks. Then Carnie motioned to me to toss the clothing out of the cell, which I did.

"Hey, Dolinsky, pull the pants from the bottom," said Connor, and I moved near the inmate's feet and began pulling the pants from the hems while Terrence worked the waistband. Our teamwork was effective and they came right off, so quickly they flew out of the cell and hit Franko in the leg.

It was then I realized we had an audience: Franko, my training officer who was evaluating my every move, and two additional sergeants, who had stopped by to assist, all stood outside looking in. I sheepishly smiled at Franko, who stood, arms crossed, shaking his head back and forth.

We removed the stained underpants by sliding them along the sides of the inmate's legs and were quick to cover the inmate's bottom with the canvas suit for privacy. A strong smell of body odor and feces filled the room, and Terrence gagged while I put my shirt sleeve to my nose in an attempt to avoid inhaling what was, by far, the foulest smell I'd encountered in the jail to date.

The only thing remaining was the shirt. Carnie and her FTO worked to remove it, which was not easy since there were no buttons or zippers. The inmate was despondent now, moaning as if we were killing her. I felt badly for her. *How does a person get into this situation, being stripped down by people she doesn't know, just to keep her safe from herself?*

We had to roll her to one side to remove her t-shirt and bra. Because she was not fighting us, Carnie took off the handcuffs and maneuvered the inmate's hands to her head, holding them there with her own gloved hand.

Then Carnie gave her one last order. "Keep your hands on your head until the cell door is closed," she instructed sternly. "Do you understand?"

"Yes," said the woman tearfully.

We walked out quickly and closed the door. I looked in the window to see if she indeed had waited to get up until we had locked the door. Her pathetic, bruised legs stuck out the bottom of the canvas suit, which was covering her body as she lay on the floor, motionless.

"It's good to see a friendly face!" I said to Carnie once the door was secure.

"Hey! What's up?" Out of the corner of my eye, I could see Franko discussing my actions with the sergeant.

"What's housing like?" I asked Carnie.

"Okay. My FTO is pretty cool. I heard you were having a hard time of it."

"Who said that?" I asked, but before she could answer, her trainer called for her, and Carnie scurried off down the hall to return to House Six. Now it was time for Franko to let me know all of the mistakes I'd made, and, of course, there were plenty.

"First of all, you stepped over the inmate's legs! What if she had kicked you? I'll have to ding you for that today. Also, you don't have to move so fast—slow is fast in here. Remember that! It's not a race, we got *all* day."

"But yesterday I moved too slowly in a similar incident, and Paxton said …" I began defending myself, which was a big mistake. Franko got quiet and was visibly angry, his face going red and nostrils flared.

"What the fuck is it with you new recruits? This is the saddest group of recruits I've ever seen from any academy, ever! All you do is spew excuses for your lame-ass behavior and poor performance! It won't be on my shoulders if you become a deputy and one of my brothers goes down because you can't do the job. I will *never* let that happen! Do you understand what I'm saying to you, Dolinsky?"

Just then, one of the female sergeants called him over so that she could speak to him privately. As the two stood there whispering, I watched, trying to read her lips. All I could make out was, "It's only her third day." I stood alone near the door to the release corridor, wishing desperately at that moment that there was some way I could release myself and run out of this building, never to return.

My heart hurt inside my ballistic vest. I felt frustrated and afraid that I might lose the job I had worked so hard and come so far to get. Three deputies nearby just watched the sergeant and Franko. None looked at me, for which I was thankful.

Terrence motioned to the sergeant that she was going to take me up to Staff Dining. Grateful to be excused from the uncomfortable scene, I followed her. As we walked up the stairs, Terrence told me the details of how she had gotten her exemplary performance medal, and about the sexy guy she was dating from a neighboring police agency. It was amazing how much this woman could say in only a few minutes.

Unable to contain my curiosity any more, I interrupted her. "Terrence, was I *that* bad today?"

"No, not at all. Franko has a lot of personal problems right now. His wife kicked him out of the house recently. He was caught having sex with one of the other deputies here in the supply office on graveyard. He was forced to work day shift, and now he's moving in with another deputy, a guy who was forced out by *his* wife once she discovered her husband had impregnated one of the booking clerks."

"Wow," was all I could muster as we sat down at a table in Staff Dining and I tried to follow that bizarre chain of events. It made me feel better to know it wasn't only my performance that had him so upset.

"Look, Dolinsky, here's how it is. You do what the FTO wants, whatever is important to them. Figure out what each trainer wants, do it until they pass you. Then, once you're done with FTO, you can be the type of deputy you *want* to be."

I liked her perspective, the idea of "just get through it and then be yourself." I could do that.

About thirty minutes went by while Terrence and I sat talking in Staff Dining. Finally, Franko arrived to find me.

"Okay, Dolinsky," he said. "We're going back to the Sally Port to finish the day strong."

"Yes, Sir," I hopped up with renewed enthusiasm. I followed him downstairs with Terrence in tow.

We entered the Sally Port to find an uncooperative male subject being held up to the blue mat by two large deputies. The inmate was fighting and was clearly exceedingly strong based on the fact that it was taking all of their might to restrain him. I jumped right in to help and began searching the inmate's pockets while the deputies decided to lay him down in the prone position for the rest of the search. Terrence entered through the sliding door and pulled her taser out, aiming it in the center of the inmate's back.

"Taser up!" she yelled. "Sir, if you continue to resist, you will be shot with fifty-thousand volts of electricity! Do you understand?!"

The two large, muscular deputies were no match for this man. He rolled over with his feet in the air in what looked to me like a karate move, hands still cuffed behind him. He was primed to kick us.

"*Tase him!*" yelled one of the deputies. At this point, time felt as if it was slowing down. There was a clear shot at the inmate's chest, yet Terrence was waiting, and waiting.

"Do it! Tase him!" yelled Franko in what felt like slow motion. He pulled his own taser from its holster on his thigh and aimed at the prisoner. With one move of his massive arm, Franko knocked Terrence out of his way and squeezed the trigger, creating a loud snapping sound that continued for about five seconds. The inmate went stiff instantly, and the deputies on each side were able to roll him over and gain control. Now, five large male deputies were involved in holding the inmate to the ground as I helped search him. Just one five-second deployment of the electrical weapon had been all it took.

The inmate, who had been so uncooperative just moments before, was nothing but compliant afterward, repeatedly begging us not to do it again. Once he was corralled into a holding cell and the door was closed, all eyes went to Terrence.

"What the fuck was that?" said Franko. "You should have tased him!"

"If you can't do it, then give the thing to someone who will," scolded another deputy.

Another smacked her in the back of her vest and said, "Nice work, Rookie," and then walked away with his buddy. Deputy Terrence kept quiet; she was smart enough to listen to them and not make any excuses.

"I gotta talk to Sarge," she said and quickly walked down the hall toward the sergeant's office. I felt terrible for her, but it was good for me to see that these deputies weren't only mean to me—they were mean to everyone.

"One unit in, two J-three," blasted through my radio, and I prepared the Sally Port to receive more arrestees, getting forms and bins ready. When the new arrestee came in, he looked strangely familiar to me.

"Anything sharp in your pockets I need to be aware of?" I asked.

"No," he said, staring ahead at the blue mat just inches from his face. He knew what to do, even though he was twitching wildly. I didn't recognize his voice and couldn't put my finger on how I knew this guy, but I couldn't shake the feeling that I did. I removed his belt and his other belongings from his pockets, tossing them into the bin. I reached into his back pants pocket and removed his wallet, pulled out the license, and instantly realized how I knew him. And my heart broke. I had grown up with this guy! Our families attended the same church. I had babysat him as a child. It had been years since I'd seen him and had no idea what had happened to him.

Tossing the license in his property bin, my thoughts were of his mother and father, good friends of my parents'.

They were such a nice family with good morals, not the kind of people to have a child who gets hooked on meth, I marveled. What happened to him? What had led him to get so high on methamphetamine that he didn't even know it was an old friend reaching into his pockets, taking off his belt and his shoes?

Inside I felt despair, but I fought against letting it bother me as I asked him to open his mouth so that I could look for any drugs hidden near his teeth or under his tongue. I watched as he jerked uncontrollably. Then, once his photo was taken, he was escorted by male deputies to a holding cell to sleep it off. I grabbed the keys off the hook near the deputy station and followed as they passed, gloved mitts wrapped around each bicep. They stopped just outside the cell and removed the cuffs. He walked into the cell and I locked the door behind him, sick to my stomach.

This was the end of my shift, thank goodness. Our relief shift arrived and "pass down," or special information and instruction about what had happened on our shift, was given. Then we headed for the door. Franko didn't have anything to say to me post-shift; he told me he preferred to tell Paxton directly about his evaluation of my performance. *Fine with me,* I thought ruefully. In the locker room, I changed clothes quickly, ripping off my gun belt and tossing it into the locker.

On the drive home, I felt much like I had coming home from the academy, once again disappointed that my performance didn't measure up to the expectations of my trainer. But more deeply felt was the sense of disillusionment that arose from my first-hand look at drug use. The crack pipe I had missed, the distraught suicidal woman, and, mostly, the kid I used to babysit, who was all grown up and completely addicted. He had been a sweet young boy, like any of the others at church, and I wracked my brain to remember anything that would have been a red flag—a memory from the many times I babysat at his home, any bad behavior he might have exhibited, any poor parenting skills displayed by his parents, anything that might remind me of the differences between his family and my own. There was nothing.

I hoped and prayed my own children would never reach the point where they, too, found so little value in their own lives that they would choose to self-medicate like that. Up to this day, I had felt completely confident that they would never make those kinds of choices. If they had faith, if they had parents who loved them and cared for them, if we spoke openly and educated them about these things in our home, my children would *certainly* stay on the straight and narrow, wouldn't they? And this day, I had learned, it just wasn't that simple.

Twenty-One

"HEY, **D**OLINSKY, go look in Cell Twelve," ordered Boomer on an overcast spring day in April. It was my second week of training in Intake, and I was feeling a bit more comfortable in handling inmates, and myself, around the other deputies.

"Why should I?" I asked Boomer as he stood by the door to the release corridor.

"Yeah, Dolinsky, go look in Cell Twelve," Deputy Van Zant hollered at me as he sat at Station Two. Boomer hurried to sit by Van Zant, and I wondered why the sudden interest in me. They were laughing quietly together as I walked over to Cell Twelve, "the rubber room," to peek at the inmate inside.

I looked through the window and saw Mr. Petrov, who was thin, white, and buck-naked, eating something. I watched him lick his fingers, crouched down on the floor like a gremlin or a living, breathing gargoyle fresh from a dormer at Notre Dame. He continued to lick his fingers as I looked back at the deputies, who directed me to this window, as if they would offer some sort of guidance as to what I was supposed to be noticing. Van Zant and Boomer laughed hysterically.

I turned to look back at the naked man in the cell. Mr. Petrov was continually lifting what looked like cookie dough off the grate in the floor. He would press it to his lips, lick his fingers, and repeat the process. It was then that the horrifying realization hit me. He was not eating cookie dough. No, the substance he was consuming did not fit any food group. Petrov was eating his own poop. With the same joy my children found in licking cookie dough from the mixer beaters, this old man was licking his own shit off his fingers in front of me. Now I got the joke, but it wasn't funny. My stomach was curdled, and I thought I might vomit right there on the floor. It was one of the saddest things I'd ever seen.

I turned and looked at Van Zant and Boomer, who were waiting for my response. They seemed so interested in what I would do after witnessing the poop eater, so I had to be tough—no sickness, no sadness. I forced a chuckle and said, "That is the most *disgusting* thing I have ever seen in my entire life," to which the deputies bumped their knuckles together in a sort of triumph and were off to find another unassuming victim they could entice into visiting Cell Twelve.

My family was just as dysfunctional as any other, maybe more so in some ways, but Petrov's type of mental illness was a new and shocking reality that seriously jolted my sensibilities. And this sad man was only the beginning.

Margaret was a short, heavyset, bleached-blonde woman brought into the jail, and I judged, by the state of her clothing and the many layers she was wearing, that she had been living on the streets. Her leathery skin made her appear much older than her fifty-three years, and by now I had already realized that it's hard to tell the true age of a homeless person. She'd been charged with trespassing; it had been a windy, rainy day, so she had lingered in a casino long after security had told her to leave.

"I don't belong here!" Margaret yelled. "You should let me go!"

"Okay, Ma'am, I need to search you. Face the mat and ..."

"You let me go!" she demanded in a deep voice. "Stop it! Just stop it!"

"Do you have anything sharp on you that could poke or hurt me?" I asked.

"No, but I am *so mad* at Cecil! I don't want to cuddle with Cecil, will you tell him?"

"Sure!" I played along. "Who is Cecil?"

"I just don't want to cuddle with him, okay?" she screamed at me as if I had just taken her last bite of food for a month. I was searching her waistband and peeling back her many jackets, checking in each pocket before peeling them back off her shoulders. They couldn't be removed yet due to the handcuffs around each wrist.

Margaret was looking down, watching me as I searched her pockets, when a male deputy ordered, "Face the blue mat on the wall!" She moved her head and stared at the mat just inches from her nose. As I checked for items possibly stashed in her bra, she took her eyes off the wall again.

"Watch the fuckin' wall!" yelled the male deputy, surprising both me and Margaret, after which she began mumbling to herself.

"I don't belong here, you should just let me go. Yes, I know, that's right, we need to go home, if you could just take me home I wouldn't be in the casino, that's right, home, that's right…"

Once I completed the search of her many layers, I sat Margaret in a chair and removed one of her simple canvas shoes, which made her start wiggling in her seat.

"Do you know Brennan?" she asked.

"I don't think so. Margaret, could you quit moving for me so I can get you searched please?"

"Look at my shoes. Please look at my shoes!" she pleaded with me. Then, again, she asked, "Do you know Brennan?"

I had no idea how to respond, so I said nothing, just finished searching her feet and tossed the dirty white shoes in her bin, noting nothing remarkable about them.

"Do you see?" she continued. "Do you see what she's done to my shoes? She never wants me to have anything nice."

"*Who* doesn't want you to have anything nice?" I delved, curious.

"Brennan!" she yelled, inciting the other deputies to look our way as she raised her voice. I held up four fingers indicating we were code four, and continued the conversation.

"Why," I prodded quietly, "would Brennan care about your shoes?"

Margaret then got quiet and looked around to be sure nobody was overhearing her. She grew quite solemn and whispered, "She never wants me to have anything nice. She always wants me to look poor."

"How do you know it's Brennan?" I asked Margaret. Her tired blue eyes lit up at my interest and she turned toward me with excitement as if I had just offered her a prime rib dinner.

"I know it's Brennan because she always leaves a hair behind." *Of course,* I thought. "Then I save it in a piece of paper and fold it up." As she spoke, she made hand motions as if carefully folding incredibly important, delicate material. I continued searching her belongings—a tote containing a piece of newspaper, an ad from a magazine, a flyer for an event long past, each painstakingly folded to match the exact specifications as the next and placed lovingly inside. She probably had fifty or sixty pieces of paper in her collection, all serving as evidence of Brennan's existence.

I unfolded one sheet and found no hair, so decided not to unfold the rest. I wondered whether Margaret was saving her own hairs, too, or if Brennan was a second personality, or if she understood what was going on around her at all. As I removed her handcuffs, I noticed that her fingers were badly misshapen due to arthritis. It disturbed me, especially when two deputies impatiently grabbed her arms to escort her to the booking clerk, seemingly with no effort to respect this poor woman's dignity. Still, I knew we had a job to do and needed to get her through the booking process. She tried to answer the booking clerk's questions, but it was too much for her and she snapped.

"I want a sandwich!" she hollered across the lobby.

Deputy Hoffman retrieved a sandwich and baited Margaret with it.

"You'll get the sandwich once you answer all the questions," he said. We still needed to fingerprint her and, thanks to her deformed fingers, Paxton explained, it would be a chore. Since I had built some level of trust with her, I volunteered to do the prints.

Standing at the digital fingerprint machine, I logged in and began inputting information before Margaret was brought over to me, grunting and groaning, held up by a female deputy on her left and a male on her right. Neither deputy took the time to speak to her like a person; they simply ordered her to "stand up," "sit down," or "shut up."

I approached Margaret and gingerly asked, "Hey, Margaret, how are you doing?"

"Not very well!" she snapped. I continued to talk to her as I returned to the machine and typed in her information.

"Margaret, I've placed your shoes into the bulk property room, so you can be assured that while you're here, Brennan won't get them, okay? I need to fingerprint you now; will you help me with it?"

She smiled at me, lowered her resistance, and was just as cooperative as she could be from that moment on. I rolled each finger on the lighted computer glass and she watched the print image appear on the monitor.

"Brennan ruined my nice warm coat for winter, and my cigarettes and my glasses."

"Well, she won't get your shoes! I can promise you that," I said.

Once the printing process was completed, I handed her the sandwich and said goodbye. I stood speechless as I watched her be dragged away by the deputies to the mental health unit. She had refused to walk, but her stocking feet slid easily on the tile floor, and a gloved hand wrapped around each of her upper arms helped the deputies pull her forcibly down the hall backward. I watched as her wrinkled face smiled victoriously, which I chalked up to her not having to fight for a meal or warm place to sleep that night.

"Good job there, Rookie," Boomer said as he walked by, slapping me on the back.

"Thanks!" I said cheerfully, not sure whether I'd impressed him with my handling of Margaret, or in my response to the poop-eater from that morning. Then he handed me five cards, each labeled with a photo of one of the five rough-looking women who were standing in a line next to him.

"Time to learn about a shower party," he said, beckoning to Connor, who was trainee-free that day, to come over to teach me.

"Oh!" she startled, and moved to my side. "Okay, where do I start ...?" Then, after a moment's thought, Connor waved to me to lead the group back to the showers located halfway down the hall. I directed four of the five women into the shower stalls and locked the doors behind them. They were to wash their faces, hair, everything ... this was policy. The showers turned on with a ruckus of noise.

"This is not rocket science, Dolinsky," Connor yelled over the water. "I'll show you once. Pay attention. I'll get the clothing. You stay here, so you don't leave the inmate in the hall alone." I watched from the hallway through an open window into the property room as Connor picked up five sets of clothing. She maneuvered in and out of the rows of clothes, picking certain sizes, and as she pulled pieces from mid-stack, she destroyed the neatly arranged apparel. The shelves held garments in just about every color of the rainbow, including black-and-white striped, naturally.

As I stood in the hallway with the fifth inmate, who was seated in a chair, she pointed to me, smiling. I couldn't hear what she was saying, between the showers blasting and my effort to pay attention to Connor. The inmate pointed to her own back, and then pointed to me. It was then that I understood her message; something was on my back. I reached around with my right hand and pulled a clean maxi-pad off my back. Now I knew why Boomer had slapped me. And I'd worn the fashion statement ever since. Connor hadn't bothered to tell me, but the inmate had.

Once Connor was deep inside the property room and I was out of her sight, I asked the inmate, "Did my partner see the maxi on my back?"

She nodded as I threw the pad into a nearby garbage can.

"Well, thanks for telling me." I felt discouraged by the silence of the senior deputy, yet thankful for the honesty of the inmate. Connor re-emerged.

"While the women shower, do a quick visual once-over on each inmate to be sure they're not hiding something on their bodies, like piercings or any other contraband," Connor instructed as she pulled open the shower curtain, exposing a wet woman.

"Hey, shut that!" said the inmate as she grabbed the curtain to close it.

"Leave it alone!" hollered Connor. "You got something to hide? Do ya?"

"No, it's cold!" replied the soaking wet inmate, tugging the curtain away.

"You're in jail, this is not some friggin' hotel!" snapped Connor, grabbing the curtain and swinging it open. "Did I ask your opinion? No, I did not! Inmates do not have a say. *We* make the rules and *you* follow them, do you understand?" The inmate remained quiet, but inadvertently touched Connor's hand as she tried to grab the curtain.

"Don't ever touch me! When inmates touch me, I feel like my skin is crawling, like it's on fire," Connor said, which made me cringe. It seemed like such a hurtful thing to say to another human being. The inmate pulled back, eyes wide, wearing a shocked expression. If she'd been arrested, she certainly had made a mistake, I knew that. But really? Did we need to be that demeaning to people?

The inmate nodded as she shivered and tried to cover herself with her hands.

"Turn around and lift each foot," Connor demanded, then swished the curtain closed adding, "If you don't like it, stay out of jail!"

I opened the second shower, moved the curtain, and asked the woman there to turn around. The inmate lifted each foot, having heard Connor's direction, and I thanked her as I picked up her jeans, t-shirt, push-up bra, and boy-shorts underwear. I walked to the cart and shoved it all in a mesh bag with the inmate's name and number on it. Once all five inmates had been showered, the cart was pushed into the property room, where staff would eventually hang the stuffed bags into the rows and rows, like a giant closet.

"Pick up a gray bin and line up along the white wall," ordered Connor. "While in the facility, you will always walk with your right side as close to the right wall as possible. If anyone, deputy or civilian, walks toward you in the hallway, you will turn and face the wall. Do you understand?" The line of women nodded as they traipsed down the hall and through three more sliding doors as we paraded toward Housing Unit Four, with its "HU-4" in big white letters above the door.

"Dolinsky," she said as I followed her, "House Four, Five in route."

I realized she wanted me to say it on the radio, so I keyed my mic. "House Four, Five in route," I repeated.

We were there in a moment. Connor dropped the movement cards on the deputy desk. The five-by-seven-inch cards each featured an inmate's mug shot and basic information, and were required to accompany each inmate everywhere they went inside the facility.

Conner looked at me. "Well? Where are we?" she asked me, clearly irritated.

I snapped to and keyed my mic. "Central, Deputy Dolinsky and Deputy Connor, ten-six, House Four," I blared over the radio. Connor was satisfied. She then greeted the two young female deputies working House Four, neither of whom I had met, but both of whom looked me up and down, as if I were a spy infiltrating their secret society. I grinned my greeting, but the female deputies clearly had no intention of acknowledging me.

Then they began to ask Connor about my performance right there in front of me, as if I were not present and hearing their every word. "How is she? Lame?" asked the tall, thin, blonde deputy, so smugly I was astonished.

"I heard this one sucks, probably'll get extended." added the younger, heavier one who had really bad acne.

Neither woman was very attractive, but each one's demeanor and rudeness made her seem even less so. I didn't know what to say or do, so I remained calm and moved quietly away from their discussion to protect what was left of my feelings while the nasty women finished talking. Eventually, we wandered back to Intake.

"Hey, don't let those deputies get you down, their comments were un-called for," Connor said as we walked. "It's not you. Those two are just bitch-es to everyone. They pride themselves on their ability to be rude."

Her words helped me to feel a bit better. I sat down in a chair at the computer desk for an instant, and that was all they needed.

Boomer grabbed my left wrist and slapped a cuff on it so quickly I didn't even realize that Van Zant had done the same to my right. They attached the cuffs to the bar just under the seat on which I sat. In the blink of an eye, I had been cuffed to the chair, unable to move either arm. I blushed a burning red. The two men laughed and joked through my embarrassment, and I won-dered what Paxton would say if he knew I had let my guard down enough for these two creeps to get the best of me. Not to mention we had a lobby full of twenty-two inmates and I didn't want them to realize I'd been had.

Don't show any emotion, just smile and look normal, I instructed myself. *They can't leave me here forever.* Then I realized I hadn't seen my trainer in a while. *Where the hell is Paxton, anyway?* I waited for the culprits to take the cuffs off, smiling all the while, as if their shenanigans had no effect on me.

"So what should we do now?" asked Boomer, feigning nonchalance as he leaned against the counter in front of me.

"Guess we could go do a perimeter check?" said Van Zant from behind me, pretending to consider leaving me stuck to the chair.

"Hey, Penis! Remember the time I borrowed the nurse's lubricant jelly and rubbed it all over the phone receiver at the deputy desk? Then you called when Terrence was sitting there?" Van Zant reminisced.

"That was fucking hilarious! She put the phone to her ear for like … a second … then screamed like it was a snake!" Boomer added, laughing. "It was all over her hair …"

"Goddammed right, brotha! It was perfect!" stated Van Zant. "She was so pissed! If she'd had a taser then, I'd a been ridin' the lightning that night!"

"Then she went to Dickens, of all sergeants … He never did shit to me, did he to you?"

"Nope, told me to keep up the good work!" said Van Zant, still chuckling.

"That was one of our best!"

"Yeah, that was frickin' great …"

I looked straight ahead and ignored them, an embarrassed smile on my face, as if nothing was out of the ordinary.

"Oh, all right, guess we'll remove 'em now." Van Zant leaned down and took off one of my restraints. I was sure to hide my relief.

His forearms were beefy, well-defined, and rubbed against mine as he removed the cuffs. I giggled a little, rather enjoying the attention, and when he took off the second cuff, it occurred to me that I couldn't remember the last time I had been this close to my own husband.

AT THE END OF THE DAY, Paxton and I completed a perimeter check, walking around the outside of the housing units, between jail buildings and the perimeter fences. It was interesting to leave the noise of the jail for the quiet outside, and I could see the outskirts of the city from where we were walking along the fence line, where all was peaceful and still, only the sound of our boots crunching the ground, getting covered with dust. I examined the fence for anything that looked suspicious. Having never been out there before, everything looked suspicious to me, and I was tired.

"What's your story, Dolinsky? What did you do before this job?" asked Paxton out of the blue as we walked along the outside fence, visually scouring for holes or objects that didn't belong.

"Oh, uh, my story … I was a housewife. You know, a stay-at-home mom."

"Ah, that explains the culture shock. You went from, well, dishrags to dirtbags."

I laughed hard at his comment. It was so true.

"Yeah, I guess I did! That was pretty witty, by the way."

"You liked that?" Paxton smiled, his blue eyes twinkling.

"Yeah, that sums it up pretty well," I replied, still chuckling.

"So, it's been a couple of weeks … how do *you* feel you're doing?" he asked, seriously.

"Okay, I think. Some things I understand, but others I would benefit from some more practice."

"I'm glad you see that, Dolinsky. I don't want you to feel bad, but I'm going to extend you for another week in Intake. It's not a bad thing, but this job is tough. I think it would be better for you to have one more week before moving into Housing." Then he added, "I hope you're okay with that."

"Sure, I understand, it makes sense," I responded, not really disappointed as I had expected to be by such news.

"Okay, then," he said, "I'll see you back here for one more week."

I suspected he felt badly about holding me back, since my academy mates would be moving on to the next level of training while I had yet to pass the first. To be honest, I felt relieved to have a bit more time to master what I'd learned in Intake before beginning another entirely new phase of training, with a whole new bunch of rules and a new FTO. No, I was fine staying one more week in Intake with Paxton.

TWENTY-TWO

IIIIIIIIIIIIIIII

BULBS PEEKED THROUGH THE SOIL, and flowers had begun to bloom in my neighborhood. The air was light and fresh, and it looked to be a perfect spring day. A few weeks earlier, an invitation had come in the mail for a friend's baby shower. Peggy, whom I had known since my boys were newborns, was having her first baby. We had met right after my family had joined our church, and I knew she and her husband had been trying to conceive for years. Thrilled to attend the shower, I had immediately called Mandy to RSVP and see if she needed any help with the arrangements. Not only would this be a chance to step back into my normal life, which seemed like a nice change of pace, and to visit with all the friends I had missed since beginning my training, but I looked forward to seeing Peggy with a baby belly. I knew she would be adorable. We all knew how much this meant to her. Fortunately, I had the day off.

That morning, while standing in my closet trying to choose what to wear to the baby shower, I had a revelation. I scoured the identical hangers, all white plastic, each holding a freshly pressed blouse, skirt, or pants, cleanly pleated. To each item, an unwritten disclaimer was attached. I pulled out a pair of tan khakis and remembered, "These pants don't hide the post-baby belly." I carefully returned them to their previous location. I picked out a pink shirt and thought, again, "Makes me look flat-chested," and put it back. Grabbing a sundress, I immediately looked for a shirt to wear over it, a response to my fear of its label, "displays flabby upper arms." But then it hit me: I was in the best shape of my life! For nine whole months, I'd been running and forced to stay in shape. There *was* no more post-baby belly. I even had muscle definition in my arms. I grabbed the white sundress and slipped it on, slid on some neutral sandals, and grabbed my tan purse, feeling awakened, lighter.

I stopped for just a second to peek in the mirror, and realized that the dress hung on me like a flag wrapping a flagpole—no curves. So I quickly rifled through my dresser drawers to locate a push-up bra I'd once worn to a Christmas party years ago. Finding it, I changed and checked the mirror once again. The girls looked perky, everything in its right place. Satisfied, I headed to the van in the driveway, but before starting it, I ran back in and grabbed a white shirt to wear as a cover-up, just in case. Old habits die hard.

The first stop was at my local book store to pick up two books, *What to Expect the First Year* and a baby book for Peggy to write down all the many wonderful memories we mothers would forget if we didn't keep them written down in baby books. I was a master baby-book keeper. Each of my two books covered seven years of firsts—their first steps, first baby teeth (both growing in and, later, falling out), first haircuts, first holidays, shot records, travels, pets, anything you want to remember about your sweet little one can be documented. My mother had been a master baby-book keeper and I had cherished the one she had slaved over for me for seven-plus years. Though she'd tease me about what a pain in the neck it was to keep up both a book for me and one for Gwen, I knew she did it as a testament to how much she cared for us. These were the days I missed her most.

With the books, I grabbed a pretty blue-and-pink-striped bag to use as wrapping, some pastel tissue paper, and a card, all of which I paid for, and headed to the car to fix the gift. This was the first time in many months my schedule had actually fit into my friends' lives, and I couldn't wait to spend some time with the people who knew me best. After signing the card, I headed to Mandy's home for the party.

Mandy was the perfect hostess, as usual. She had decorated her home with pink and blue balloons, greeted every guest at the door, and provided more food than we could ever eat. I knew everyone there, which was typical when children attended the same school and families attended the same church. I was thrilled to see everyone and felt welcomed at once. Peggy looked stunning in a turquoise maternity dress, which accentuated her red hair. Mandy wore a draped burgundy top with designer jeans and heels. Sylvia was in rare form with her funny remarks, which told me that she had either gotten a screw-top bottle out of Mandy's wine cellar, or she had put on a few pounds. Humor was her defense mechanism, and she had on a new khaki summer suit, which was evidence to the latter.

All was perfect until my friends began drilling me about my new career.

"Oh, come on, Beth, tell us about it," Mandy suggested.

"Yes, let's hear it, what kinds of things do you do? What have you seen in jail?" Sylvia chimed in, unaware of the graphic nature of what I might share.

"To be honest, you wouldn't believe the things I see on a daily basis," I said, anxious about bringing it up here. "They really aren't appropriate to discuss at a party, especially a baby shower."

"Oh, come on, we can handle it!" Sylvia prodded. "Tell us what happened in your world yesterday, for example." Five women, three of them my very best friends, were literally on the edge of the sofa waiting for my response. I had to say something.

"Yesterday? You really do *not* want to hear about yesterday, believe me," I begged, flashing back to Mr. Petrov.

"You act like we aren't good enough to hear your stories," Peggy said nervously. "We're all friends here, aren't we? You can share. If you can't share with us, who can you share with?" *Oh Lord*, I thought, feeling cornered.

"Okay, here goes …" I began, checking their faces. "When I got to work yesterday, a couple of deputies told me to look in Cell Twelve." The women leaned closer. I continued cautiously. "So I crept over to Cell Twelve to see what the noise was about. There was a little old man, naked, sitting like a gargoyle, eating something off of his fingers."

"What was he eating?" asked Sylvia.

"I thought it was cookie dough at first, but we don't serve cookie dough in jail."

"So what was it, then?" asked Sylvia as the women stared at me with wide-eyed innocence, which I hadn't realized I'd lost until that very moment.

"It was … his poop." I said it quickly, like ripping off a band-aid, to make it easier for them to hear.

"Are you serious?" asked Mandy as if I made the whole thing up. "No way! People don't do that! Tell us the truth! I think you made that up!"

"No, that's what happened!" I insisted.

"Yeah, come on, tell us the truth," Sylvia said condescendingly. "You don't have to make stuff up for our benefit."

"Why would I make that up? We see some pretty terrible things. The poop-eater was the beginning of my day. Then I twisted up a guy and tossed him into a cell, did a shower party, a perimeter check ..." I offered these items plainly, as matters of fact.

"Well, I've heard enough," said Sylvia, exhausted with the discussion. She got up to continue her grazing off the appetizer table. Peggy and two others followed, so only Mandy and I remained.

"I told you it wasn't party-appropriate," I scolded her.

"Well, I guess not," Mandy agreed. We sat for a few minutes in silence before she spoke again. "How do you handle it, being around violent people every day? Having guns in your home? You never even get to church anymore." Before I could answer, she stood and said, "You are like ... a completely different person." And she walked away.

How could I expect my friends to get it? Most had never held jobs in their adult lives; they all stayed home to cook and clean and raise their kids. They didn't want to know about people like Mr. Petrov. Why would I think these ladies could grasp how putrid and vile human beings could be? What good did it do them to imagine that someone's brother, sister, nephew, niece, or, worse, a son or daughter could have the potential to become *that* awful, that ugly? When I descended those stairs from Staff Dining each day, I contended with the law breakers, the disease-infested, the embalmed by alcohol. Why would they want to crawl into the underbelly of society with me? I couldn't blame them. My world was the one that had changed, not theirs. Still, I had thought we were better friends than that. I left the party quietly and went home, wondering if there was anywhere I fit anymore.

Once home, Garrett and the boys were entranced by a movie on television. My heart felt so heavy, I needed to talk to someone who would understand, but who could I call? Locked in my bedroom with a feeling of desperation, I called my father. He had spent forty years of his life working in the gaming industry, so, I thought he had no point of reference. At that moment, I had no idea why I felt the urge to dial his number.

"Hello?" he called into the phone.

"Hey, Dad, it's me."

"Hey, Beth! Hold on a minute, let me turn down the TV, so I can hear … just a minute." The phone clanked around for a minute while he reached the television and turned down the sound to focus on the phone call. It was the same thing every time I called.

"Okay, I turned the TV down. Now, what's going on with you?"

I began with, "I just need to vent." I told him about my jail world, the people I'd seen, my coworkers' attitudes, all that I had experienced in recent days.

"I don't understand what she said about you, you were a dame?"

"No, Dad, she said 'lame,' like a loser, not as good as her … you know?"

"Say that again? Was it 'mame'? With an 'm'? That doesn't sound right."

"No, Dad, with an 'L' … L-A-M-E. Like a horse with a broken leg."

"Oh, lame! Oh, that makes sense. What a rude thing for her to say, she doesn't even know you! People are funny, though, Honey. I remember once I had a manager. Every time I had what I thought was a good idea, I would tell him. I thought I could trust him 'cause he was a really nice guy to talk to, you know, really pleasant. I would go to him and tell him my idea in his office. Next meeting, he was presenting it to the boss as his own idea. Never gave me an ounce of credit for a thing, would act like it was all his." My dad stopped and cleared his throat for what seemed like a minute, then added, "At least these people you're dealing with aren't playing you for a fool. You know right where you stand with them."

"Yeah, that's true," I considered. "Guess that's the silver lining in that cloud."

"What?"

"That's the silver lining in that cloud!" I yelled for him to hear.

"Oh," Dad chuckled," yeah, guess so." He cleared his throat again and continued. "As for those poopy people, we had 'em too in the casino business. People would get off those big busses so drunk they peed or pooed themselves before they even reached their destination. Or sometimes, those homeless or street people, they would come in and try to hang around, beg from the patrons. We called the cops to come pick 'em up, many, many times."

"I may be dealing with some of the same people you did just a few years ago!" I yelled so loudly he caught what I said without my having to repeat it.

"That's right! Funny to think we could have dealt with the same folks in sort of the same way. Different, yet, the same."

"But you didn't have to touch them, shower them, and feed them," I added.

"What's that?"

"I SAID, YOU DIDN"T HAVE TO TOUCH THEM AND GIVE THEM SHOWERS!"

"True, I don't think I would have liked that part," Dad agreed.

"Nope, you wouldn't."

"Huh?"

I changed the subject, as it just wasn't worth repeating.

"Hey, Dad, I went to a baby shower today for my friend, Peggy, gave her a baby book. It made me think of Mom keeping my baby book all those years."

"I thought of your mother today, too," his voice cracked. He still got choked up so easily talking about Mom. He had nursed her through the cancer, but on the last night, the night she died, Gwen and I had kept vigil by her bedside, making sure she could breathe and filling her with morphine. Dad had remained in the living room that night. It was harder for him at the end because there was nothing left to do. He was a handy man, a fixer, and she couldn't be fixed. Early in the morning hours, she had started looking at something—at least that was what it had seemed like, and we knew then to call Dad into the room. Then, once we were all three there in the bedroom with Mom, she relaxed and took her last breath.

Dad went on. "I was talking to her when I took out the garbage today. I was saying, 'I should have listened to you and put more rose bushes on that side of the house.'" Now his voice was cracking and he was sniffing.

"Hey, Dad, what do you think she would think of the changes I've made in my life? What do you think she would say about me becoming a deputy?" I asked, knowing exactly what I wanted to hear. I got it.

"Your mother would be so very proud of you, Honey," he said.

I sniffed, paused, a couple of tears slipping out and dripping down my cheeks.

"Thanks, Dad."

"You're welcome, Honey. Call anytime."

TWENTY-THREE

"DEPUTY DOLINSKY, Sergeant Peters," blared my radio, which was out of reach. I'd stopped to use the restroom on my way back to Intake, where Paxton and I were assigned to work for the next six hours. Now, as I sat with my pants around my ankles, the sarge wanted a response. I scooted with baby steps across the bathroom, almost tripping on my wadded up uniform pants, butt in the air, reaching for the mic. I accidentally hit it with my knuckle, pushing it farther away.

Sergeant Peters called again. "Deputy Dolinsky, Sergeant Peters!"

"Dammit!" Stopping to pull up my pants was the only good option. I wriggled them up, took a step, and grabbed the mic.

"Go for Dolinsky," I responded and dropped the mic again to tuck in my many layers and zip up my pants.

"Twenty-five the Sally Port, please."

"Yes, Sir," I replied, washing my hands and drying them with superhero speed.

I needed to hurry back into the Sally Port, so I quickly picked my belt up off the floor, bent forward, chucked it up to my back, and wrapped its awkward weight around my waist. I grabbed the keepers off the sink and, flying out the door, ran right into a male deputy strolling up to use the facility.

"Better hurry, Sarge is looking for you," he said.

"Ten-four," I said, running down the hall, snapping my keepers into place. I found Sergeant Peters waiting for an uncooperative female to arrive.

"Where were you, anyway?" he asked when he saw me.

"The bathroom," I replied.

Peters was short, carried enough extra pounds on his frame that his belly rolled over his gun belt, and had a high-pitched laugh that I'd swear could shatter glass. It would come out of nowhere, loud and clear. I overheard a deputy say it was the sarge's way of warning his staff he was coming so they could quit doing things they weren't supposed to do, so he wouldn't have to write them up for bad behavior. Regardless, it made me chuckle every time.

"Oh, well, ha ha ha!" There it was, loud enough to be heard a hundred yards away in the parking lot. "I need you in the Sally Port, you know, we have an uncooperative female coming in." Resisting the urge to make a smart remark, I replied, "Yes, Sir."

Deputies Paxton, Terrence, and I waited. Olin entered to help. Her perfume was as toxic as the sarge's laugh, and made my eyes water in the few seconds since she'd entered the room. Finally, two officers dressed in blue uniforms from a sister agency escorted a small Hispanic woman into the Sally Port who was yelling in Spanish, but not fighting nor uncooperative.

"This is our uncooperative?" Peters asked them.

"Yup," said one officer. "She was kicking earlier, but seems to have calmed down once we got her out of the car."

Deputy Terrence began to search the right side while I simultaneously began on the left. We pulled pockets inside out, shook her bra from the bottom so that anything that was not attached would fall out, and placed her into a chair, her handcuffed wrists up and over the back. After removing her shoes, she kicked at Terrence, who straightened the inmate's leg, tipping the woman back in the chair.

"What the fuck? You think it's fun to kick at an officer? That's a felony in here! You'd better shape up unless you want another charge!" yelled Terrence, who was fighting to hold the inmate's leg as she continued to kick. I grabbed her other leg and held it straight out and up as high as I could. The inmate's chair tipped backward, but she continued to kick at us, so we dumped her onto the floor.

"She's going down!" I heard as Terrence yell as she leaned the woman's leg toward me and we rolled the foul woman out of the chair and onto the floor with a thud. Olin immediately threw her body over the inmate's legs to keep them from kicking one of us. Terrence knelt on one of her shoulders, and I on the other.

The woman was now screaming in thickly accented English, "You fucking cops, you are hurting me! You fuckin' bitch cunts!"

"Check her shoes and socks well," Terrence instructed. "Maybe there's something she doesn't want us to find!" I left the woman's shoulder to help Olin cross the woman's legs and put on some ankle restraints, which were like extra-large handcuffs. I stood on the restraint chain and we removed the shoes and socks, tossing them to Paxton to inspect.

"Nothing remarkable here," he reported and signaled, by pointing to the gray mat on the wall, that it was time to take her mug shot. Terrence and I each grabbed an arm and picked her up, but once steady on her feet, the inmate spit at me, leaving a good-sized phlegm glob squarely on my right cheek. I wiped it off with my gloved hand and transferred it to the inmate's pants.

"Spit hood, please! Need a spit hood here!" I called to Olin, who found one and placed the mesh hood over the inmate's head. She again spit at me, and even through the spit hood, I felt the liquid, like a mist, landing all over my face. I told myself to remain calm, but the feeling of wanting to beat the crap out of this woman was overwhelming. *Keep it together! Be cool!*

Holding her arm as tightly as I could, my nails certain to leave marks, and with Terrence's help, I dragged the woman, who was in custody for child abuse, to a holding cell.

"Fucking bitch, you dyke cunts, AAAAAHHHHHH!" she continued to yell.

"That's all we ever get! I'm waiting for a really creative taunt, but 'fucking bitch cunts' is all we ever get," joked Olin. I laughed, but I was sure she saw the fury on my face. This peach needed to be housed alone, so we dragged her and dropped her in the rubber room on her stomach. Sergeant Peters came in to assist.

"Taser up!" the sarge yelled. "Ma'am, if you resist, you will be tased with fifty-thousand volts of electricity. Do you understand?"

"AAAAAAHHHH! AAAHHHH!" the woman screamed, as if we were killing her, and I didn't understand why. Once again, Terrence and I were on her shoulders, and Olin had the woman's legs crossed, as we always do. The metal band wrapped around her ankle was digging into the bone on the other ankle, but so be it. Olin's weight was slight, but enough to gain compliance with the help of an ankle cuff, and the inmate screamed at the top of her lungs.

Once we removed all the restraints and were out of the cell, I pulled Olin out by the back of her belt. Sarge gave me some instructions.

"You need to head over to the hospital lab to be tested. Later today, we'll get her blood as well. There is a policy. I'll get you the forms and you head out right away."

"Okay, Sarge."

I began to follow him to his office when Paxton grabbed my arm. "You did well during that incident," he said. "But you wanted to kill her, didn't you?"

"Oh yeah! So much! I was surprised by how badly I wanted to hurt her."

"Well, you did well, Probie. I'll give you a lot of points for the fact you kept your cool under pressure. I think you're ready to move on and begin special housing training tomorrow with Rowland. You've passed Phase One."

I wanted to jump up and down and give him a hug, but that was just not done.

"Thanks!" I said instead, and Sergeant Peters returned with the forms so that I could get my blood work done at the hospital. I left Intake and waited at the sliding door, feeling nervous about the spit incident and yet excited about moving forward to new training. Just as the slider opened, Sergeant Peters' high-pitched laugh floated down the hall, making me smile.

A QUICK PRICK OF A VEIN at the laboratory, a hamburger gobbled while driving, and I was back at work, still on break time before having to return to Intake. I sat on a bench in the locker room and contemplated, remembering the feeling of some scummy person's spit on my cheek. *I hope that bitch didn't give me a disease,* I thought, morbidly. My head reeled with the reality of my surroundings. I needed to calm my nerves. I needed chocolate.

Dressed in my uniform, I meandered downstairs, but not before picking up a candy bar out of the vending machine. This whole spitting thing had freaked me out. Of all the things I'd considered about this job, I hadn't thought of that risk before. But it was indeed a risk I needed to consider every day while working here.

"One unit in, three, J-three," blared my radio. I ran into Paxton as we headed to the Sally Port. A drunk was being escorted in by a deputy and a trooper.

"Oh my God! What is this?" I cried out as they brought in a man who smelled so strongly of urine I had to hold my breath. He was extremely intoxicated, obviously homeless, and dressed in five layers of pee-drenched clothing.

"I got the PBT," Olin said as she picked up a Preliminary Breath Test, a hand-held machine for checking blood alcohol levels, and brought it over to where Terrence, Paxton, and I stood. The drunk's name was Merle, and he was a "frequent flyer" at our facility. This time, he was here for Civil Protective Custody, a "Seep," which was appropriate as he certainly couldn't care for himself. Merle only needed to sleep it off, sober up, and we would release him. But by the looks of him, it wouldn't be any time soon.

"Okay, Merle, blow into the tube," Olin held the tube to his mouth. He was oblivious and nearly slid out of the chair. The gray-clad trooper and the deputy held him in the chair by his shoulders, and Olin tried again.

"Blow in the tube!" Olin yelled this time. "Close your lips on the tube and blow!"

The drunk gave a blow that was feeble at best. The digital numerals on the machine were racing as we bet on how high he would be.

"Three-point-zero," said Olin.

"Nope, he drinks like this daily. I say four-point-two," guessed the Trooper.

"You better hope not," said Paxton. "We don't take anyone over four-point-zero, so that means you take him to the hospital from here."

"Oh! I take that back, I say three-point-eight-nine," replied the Trooper, smiling.

Meanwhile, the subject of this discussion sat looking down, his hair lousy with grease and dirt, mumbling to himself.

"Close, but no cigar. Three-point-eight and a partial blow at that," confirmed Olin to everyone, "and his levels may be going up." He was under a four, so he would be staying with us, which meant we needed to search him. This would, no doubt, be unpleasant.

Over the past few weeks, it had become clear to me that a subculture existed in the city that believed it was entirely too much trouble to take off their clothing before urinating or defecating. Merle was a member of this club, and searching him unleashed the foulest smells I had encountered to that point, which by now was a real accomplishment. We engaged a few deputies just to hold him up to the mat so that we could get everything out of the pockets of each of the five layers of pants and shirts. Jacket after threadbare jacket came off … a sweater here, a shirt there. Not only did he reek of urine, but it was like peeling an onion, with each layer releasing more vomit-inducing odors than the last. The pants were the worst. My eyes watered as we removed first his ski pants, then the stained sweats, then another pair of sweats, and, lastly, jeans so encrusted with bodily fluids that they were stiff. There was no underwear. We got him down to one layer and the male deputies took him directly to the showers.

"Going commando, eh, Merle?" Paxton joked as Merle's poopy jeans fell to the ground halfway to the shower, exposing his red, rash-covered rump for all to see. I had never come across anyone quite that revolting, but this was just the beginning. The officers on the street had done a homeless sweep and two more waited in the car, though they claimed that Merle was the most foul.

Next was a man who smelled of body odor, but not urine or feces. The trouble with this arrestee was, unbeknownst to us, that he had bugs. I searched him with the help of a tired male deputy who just arrived, in early for the night shift. He and I checked the inmate's pockets, took his belt, and, when I was searching his waistband, I put my hand in the back of his pants and felt my glove catch on his crusty skin.

"Nurse! Medical, please!" I hollered, and within moments a nurse arrived, pulled up the man's shirt, and checked his scabby back.

"Scabies," she said. "Oh, and he also has lice in his hair."

"WHAT!?" *People live like this in Reno? My town?* How could all this be going on around me? And what would I do, the terrifying thought now occurring to me, if I unknowingly brought the vile little pests home?

"Just be sure, deputies, when you're done with him, you wash every exposed part of your skin," said the nurse plainly, this just a normal part of her everyday routine.

"Guess he's yours now!" said Paxton. "You two finish him up so no other deputies are exposed; we don't need to contaminate anyone else."

Contaminate? Exposed? "What?" I asked, looking around while holding the seep's right arm as the tired deputy held his left. Together, we escorted him to a cell. No sooner had we shut and locked the door when we high-tailed it to the closest sink.

"What did she say? *Every* exposed part?" I asked my partner, who was moving so quickly I was certain he was awake now.

"I picked a shitty day to come in early!" he laughed as we scrubbed our arms, hands, and faces with soap. "What can we do for our hair?"

"Uh …" I looked around the sink, "how 'bout this?" I grabbed a bottle of sanitizer and squeezed some onto my open palm.

"Great!" We loaded our hands and rubbed the gel through our hair as best we could. I felt disgusting, itchy, and smelly, having been spit on and now with my hair glued down with anti-bacterial goop. How I wished I could go home to take a shower; I'd had enough exposure to diseases for one day.

About twenty minutes before it was time to go home on this very long, last day of my Phase One training, I was handling a release. A very tiny, old woman named Jane, who was a known drunk, was in the dressing room putting on her own clothes in order to leave, and it was taking forever.

"Jane, are you done yet?" I called to her. She didn't respond, so I opened the door and looked inside. Jane was standing, bent over, pulling on a long, high-heeled boot, but she had so little strength in her upper body that the task was daunting to her. I watched the frail woman, who was oddly dressed in a mini-skirt and halter top, leaning over to pull at the boot that, like her clothes, had clearly been designed for a twenty-something. Jane's thin, white hair hung limply, with whole patches missing all around her scalp. She was deep in concentration, grunting as she heaved, but no closer to her goal than she had been minutes before. I couldn't let this woman back into the world without something more appropriate to wear.

"Mel, do we have any clothing I can give this lady to wear?" I asked.

"What sizes do you need?" Mel replied.

"Small or extra small. How about shoes, Mel, do we have any?"

"Sure, we save all the stuff that don't get picked up by family when somebody goes to prison. I have tons of stuff, whatcha need?" Mel shouted over the country music blaring from the radio on his desk.

"Smallest shoes you have, and a large shirt to use as a cover-up."

He returned in a moment with the items in hand. "How's this?" he asked, displaying them for me. I unfolded a large men's button-down shirt and a pair of Converse shoes, size five.

"Perfect!" I said, and handed the items to Jane.

"What's this for?"

"I just thought you might like something to cover up with, and some shoes without the big heels. They could help you get around a little easier."

"I don't want this shit! Get it away from me!" screamed Jane in her scratchy smoker's voice and she threw the items back at me, as if they were radioactive. "I know what I like, and that ain't it! If I want help dressing, I'll ask for it, sweet cheeks."

Rebuked, I stood there with my mouth open. "I was just trying to help!"

"I don't need anyone's help!" Jane yelled, shooing me away. "Get this fuckin' shit outta here."

Paxton, who was nearby watching and listening, began to laugh hysterically.

"Nice try, Rook, can't fault you for trying." He laughed louder. "That was priceless." And with that, I walked Jane out of the building, watched her struggle her way to the bus stop in those much-too-high-heeled boots, and at last my very long workday was over.

TWENTY-FOUR

T**HREE FEMALE DEPUTIES** were discussing the events of their weekend, and one showed off her new tattoo, as I entered the locker room. I walked by and smiled at the ladies, who promptly shut up and turned away from me.

Near my locker there was plenty of open space; all my locker neighbors worked different shifts, so I had sort of semi-private area for changing into my uniform.

As I turned the combination lock, one of the women hollered from across the room, "Hey, Rookie, who's your training officer?"

"Rowland," I said.

"Whooo-eee, lucky you!" she replied as the other women chuckled, hidden from sight by the rows of lockers.

"Trade you places, Rook!" said another voice, and the women cackled.

"He's a hottie!" said the first voice. "I'd do him."

"But he's fucked half the sheriff's department," said another voice.

"*I* haven't fucked him yet!" said the first voice.

"He must be the only one you missed." There was a burst of laughter, and then the sound of slamming locker doors. Their laughter dissipated as the parade of women headed toward the exit and the door banged closed behind them. Silence.

I was learning to shelve all the rules I had followed prior to embarking on this career. This job had a whole new set of rules, and here I was learning a new one: Nothing is off limits for discussion in the women's locker room, even one's sex life. In fact, it not only was considered appropriate, it seemed preferred.

Rowland had been the deputy in charge of investigating my background when I had first gotten this job. At the time I didn't think of him as being particularly attractive, but next to Garrett, not many men were. All I knew of my new special housing FTO was that he was one of Franko's friends, who sat with his feet up in Intake and exhibited no interest in teaching new recruits, or in working, for that matter.

Today, I met him in Staff Dining, where he completely ignored me. Two other recruits in the room sat across from their trainers and were involved in deep discussions; mine was on the phone to his wife. With biceps the size of my thighs, Rowland was an impressive guy, tall and blonde with dimples that showed when he smiled. And from what I could tell from the phone call, his lack of punctuality was due to his wife's inability to handle their children, which took precedence over his teaching me. I waited patiently for him to hang up so that we could head downstairs.

The deputy mailboxes hung on the wall in Staff Dining. I took this time to check the bank of slots to see if I had been given a box, and sure enough there was my name, stuck with tape on the box between Cunningham and Evanson. Even better, I had mail, a letter from the health department indicating, thankfully, that I would not need to stop in for more blood testing; the lab work following the spitting incident had come back clean. *Phew!*

Finally, at twenty-five minutes past eight, Rowland nodded at me and said, "Come on." I followed him through the secured doors and down the stairs into Detention.

The SHU, or Special Housing Unit, otherwise known as House Eight, was a hardened unit built to house the most high-risk inmates. Each door had a meal slot that opened outward—we didn't even need to open the doors to feed these people.

Due to the nature of the criminals housed in the SHU, it was the DERT deputies who were primarily assigned to work here. But for training purposes, all recruits were required to do a stint in this Special Housing Unit. DERT was a specially trained group, sort of a SWAT team for the inside of the jail. When an inmate flooded his cell or threatened to fight, the DERT folks were the ones to go in with shields, bean-bag or rubber-pellet guns, and whatever other non-lethal weaponry was necessary, and they handled the situation. From what I'd gathered in my three weeks working in the jail, or, as we called it, "The Bucket," many of the DERT members had reputations for being pretty lazy, as was the case with Rowland. Since I knew I would be expected to complete all the security checks today, I would get a crash course in dealing with rapists, murderers, gang leaders, and cop killers, and I would need to be alert at all times.

Once we arrived in House Eight, Rowland promptly went into the office and greeted our partner with the standard male greeting around here: "Hey, Penis." Then he sat down and opened his lunch box to have a morning snack, his blonde head facing the computer and away from me.

This greeting had been directed at our partner for the day, Deputy Valdez, a medium-sized man who seemed small compared to the many workout-obsessed Neanderthals roaming the halls of the jail, with thick brown hair and a moustache like a 1970s television cop, the type who would smile and reveal a set of teeth so perfect they'd sparkle, almost with a *Ding!* like in one of those toothpaste commercials. Valdez was every bit a police parody, right down to his perfectly shined boots.

While Rowland stuffed his face, Valdez took me through the housing unit, down a small white hallway that led to four blue, steel doors marked with the letters "A," "B," "C," and "D," each opening into separate wings. Valdez grabbed the door to "A" wing and yelled into the air, "A, Adam!" The door popped open and I marveled at this cool trick.

I walked into the room and looked around to familiarize myself with the layout. It was pretty much the same as the other housing units, with blue-painted stairs with railings to match. Each wing held fourteen cells, seven on the top tier and seven on the bottom.

"So this is A wing; they're all the same except for D wing," Valdez explained.

"What's the difference?" I asked.

"Females in D. The rest are males. Since we're here, might as well do a security check," he said.

So I headed upstairs to check inside each cell. Valdez walked the bottom tier quickly, but the cells were so dark and dismal, I had to get close to look inside. Peeking in the first light blue door, I was startled as I saw a male inmate peering back at me. I gasped. The inmate cracked up, and a chorus of laughter came from many of the surrounding cells. It was then that I realized that all the inmates were watching me through their windows.

I finished walking the top tier and met Valdez before moving out of A wing.

"If someone plans to attempt suicide, the most common mode would be hanging by sheet," he explained. "We walk the unit looking for a hanger. You need to check every cell, and always think of where you are, and what you would say on the radio if someone was hanging. What would you say?"

"Deputies to House Eight," I replied.

"Medical emergency, possible code fifty, House Eight, Cell A-three," Valdez corrected. "Don't forget the wing and the cell number, gotta have all three for the green herd to find you in here. *Comprende?*" He pointed to Cell One and continued. "So imagine you're walking by this cell and you see the inmate on the floor. It looks like he's having a seizure. What do you say?"

"Medical Emergency, House Eight, 'A' Wing, Cell One," I said.

"Perfect, but you might add 'possible seizure' to it so Medical knows what equipment to bring. Also, never, *ever*, open a door by yourself. It's an officer safety issue and against policy; plus, there are inmates in here that would take any opportunity to kick our asses. We must always have two deputies when a red is out of their cell." I processed the sobering thought while Valdez went on.

"Inmates will try to trick you and may stage a fake seizure to get you into the cell, to stab you with a shank or something. You can't be too careful in the SHU." A shiver of uncertainty and cold fear flowed through me, and I asked myself, for the hundredth time, *What am I DOING here?*

My reverie was broken when I heard the Ogre assigned to me calling my name. "Dolinsky!" I scooted to the office, leaving Valdez to complete the walk around.

When I reached Rowland, he tossed me a set of keys and said, "Here! Go figure out where they work." I took the keys and left Rowland in the office.

I knew from Intake which keys opened closets because I had been given the task of retrieving toilet paper there about a week ago. The same key, I was told, opened all the closets throughout the jail. I investigated the different closets, pipe chases, and doors leading to the next housing unit or the cement yard. I tried keys for about ten minutes, wondering whether this was just a way to get rid of me or if this was somehow going to play a part in my training. When I returned, Valdez told me to follow him into the hallway. He grabbed the door knob of what I thought was a closet and again yelled into the air, "Tower!"

"Yes?" a female voice spoke over the intercom.

"Pop your door, please," said Valdez, and magically the door popped open. Inside was an extremely steep staircase; Valdez nodded for me to go ahead. I went up the stairs to find a landing where a woman was seated behind a desk, much like the deputy station in Intake, with many monitors in front of her. I smiled and she seemed friendly enough, though she stared at the monitors as if she couldn't look away.

"This is Betty. She opens all the doors, including the wings and front slider to this unit. She also schedules inmate tier time, when they're allowed out of their cells to pick up supplies, shower, make phone calls, whatever," said Valdez.

"So you opened the door to A wing?" I asked her.

"Yes, Ma'am! And you shoulda seen your face, I was cracking up, you looked so amazed. That was pretty funny."

"I thought it was some sort of voice-activated thing ..." At this, they both chuckled.

It comforted me to know there was an all-seeing "eye in the sky" watching, listening, and opening doors by touching a screen.

I CAN HARDLY PUT INTO WORDS the feeling of walking up to a door and knowing the person on the other side might possibly kill you if the opportunity presented itself. Then, there was the bizarre experience of peeking into the room and locating the person doing any number of things people do—getting dressed, exercising, or using the toilet, which was placed just inside the door, directly in front of the window. I was told to complete security checks as quickly as possible, so I hurried through A Wing and, upon leaving, closed the large steel door. Next to the door to B Wing, I grabbed the door handle and yelled "B, boy!" Right on cue, the heavy steel door popped open and I entered.

I walked by each cell on the bottom floor and peeked in to locate each inmate. One, a small Hispanic male with the name "Gonzales" tattooed across his shoulders, was standing with his back to me making his bed. He didn't see me, though I suspect he sensed my presence. In another cell was a white man with a swastika tattooed on the left side of his neck. His arms were so heavily tattooed that they looked like sleeves.

"What time is it?' he asked, seated on his bunk and waiting for me to pass.

"Uh, about ten," I told him.

"In the morning?"

"Yup, a.m." He came to the window and watched me walk away, which gave me the creeps. In the next cell was a large black male who was asleep on his bunk, his back to me. And the next held another Hispanic who was waiting by the door for me to arrive.

"Hey!" he called. "What eez your name?" He had a heavy Mexican accent. On his face, near his right eye, was a teardrop tattoo, and the name "Maria" was printed in script on the right side of his neck.

"Deputy Dolinsky," I said as I pointed to my name tag on my uniform.

"Hey, Deputy Dolinsky, you eez new?" he asked, his voice muffled through the door.

"Maybe," I said. "Why do you ask?" I stopped and stood in front of his window. He was so close, I could see his breath fogging up the glass.

"I can tell you eez new, yaaaah," he said in a melodic voice.

"How can you tell?"

"Isss easy to tell, I joos know," he said.

"That's cause everybody's new here. There's a whole bunch of new hires coming through here," a voice yelled from above, as an inmate on the top tier piped up, adding to the conversation through his door.

"Yeah, you win, I'm new!" I said loudly for both to hear as I broke our stare and continued walking to the stairs to check the two males inhabiting top tier cells. The fellow who had yelled down was a Native American man, very large and quietly smiling through his window. It struck me as strange that he, or anyone really, would seem so happy and content in this environment.

The check in the "C, Charles" wing went about the same way the first two had. It was as much about them watching me as me watching them. It felt peculiar to walk by the cell that I had been told housed a man who had killed an officer with a high-powered rifle during a stand-off. He was asleep, to my relief, but the male in the cell next to him was urinating as I looked in. The inmate held his penis and looked directly at me as I sped by.

It was obvious that women didn't often work this unit, for when I closed the door to C Wing, I heard a number of cat calls and whistles coming from the residents.

"D, David!" I hollered and the tower popped the last door open. Instantly, I could hear the women chatting through their doors. Not interested in me, they only asked about the whereabouts of Deputy Rowland.

"He so fine," announced one toothless woman.

"Oh, yeah, I'd do him in a heartbeat, and I'm gay!" said another, and laughter erupted. As soon as I knew all was well, I exited D wing, relieved to get back to the office.

"Sounds like you have a fan club in D Wing," I said to Rowland, which made him smile. I mentioned that one male inmate had been peeing toward the window as I had walked by.

"They do that on purpose," he said. "Next time that happens, you stop and, in a loud voice, say, 'Hey, looks like a penis, only smaller!' I guarantee he won't ever do it again."

That made me burst out laughing.

"I know, it's a good one, and it works," said Rowland, who maybe wasn't such an ogre after all.

For the rest of the day, I was responsible for walking each wing twice an hour. Any time an inmate needed toilet paper, a toothbrush, toothpaste, or any hygiene items, I would pass it into the cell through the food slot in the door.

"Go open food slots," said Rowland, tossing me the keys again. The inmates were pacing around in their cells before lunch arrived, and as soon as I opened their food slots, they were kneeling at their doors, yelling back and forth to each other through the hole in the door.

"Deputy Dolinsky, pleeeez, could I get another sang-weech?" yelled Gonzales.

Rowland watched as I delivered the food, and he shook his head back and forth at the question.

"Nope, sorry," I answered. But it seemed every inmate asked for something—another orange, or more juice. They were certainly game players, and Rowland told me not to push the food cart too close to a door, or they would steal things off of it, the food slot being just large enough for an arm to fit through.

Rowland and I went to lunch at thirteen-hundred hours. I was to meet him at fourteen-hundred in Staff Dining, which was convenient for me since I wanted to buy a meal and stay. As I stood in line at the register, I called, "Central Control, Deputy Dolinsky, code seven" over the radio.

Today's special was "Breakfast Burrito made with eggs, sausage, bacon and cheese, wrapped in flour tortilla served with salsa and sour cream," which sounded divine. The female inmates who were working the grill outside on the patio looked clean to me, and were supervised by a civilian woman. Her job, it seemed, was to run back and forth between the inside kitchen and outside patio all day long. The food smelled wonderful, so I ordered, paid, took a number, and then took a seat, staying clear of the deputy table where Van Zant and Boomer had already parked themselves. It seemed to me they were always together; at least, I'd never seen them apart.

"Mother fuckers! How can they write me up for saying 'fuck'? It's fuckin' un-American," said Van Zant.

"Goddamn right, brotha." Boomer concurred.

"It's hypocrisy at its best! Welcome to county!" said Van Zant.

My burrito arrived, courtesy of a female inmate, who picked my number off the table and hurried back to the register. After my morning, I was hungry and ate as much as I could, then got up to toss the paper plate in the trash. When I returned to the table, Deputy Van Zant was standing there, swinging keys on his index finger.

"These yours?" he asked, straight-faced. I felt my belt where keys should be and they were missing. My heart sank.

"Yes," I said, chagrined.

"Nice work, leaving them where an inmate can get them, Probie." With that, he tossed them at me and I caught them. Boomer walked up at that moment.

"What? Did she fuckin' leave her fuckin' keys on the table?" They turned to leave and I could hear the words "FNG" and "What a tool" as they walked away.

Rowland was only five minutes late—on time for a DERT guy. We were only ten minutes behind when we arrived in the SHU for the second half of the day.

"You won't believe this!" Valdez announced as we entered the unit.

"Won't believe what?" asked Rowland.

"The doors in B wing are acting up. When you were at lunch they all popped at once!" Valdez told us.

"Betty didn't …"

"Nope, she said it wasn't her, and I believe her. She's squared away in the tower."

"True. Shit. If the inmates know the doors can open, we'll have a major fight on our hands," Rowland said. "Wow, this is not good."

"Maintenance is on their way to fix it, see you in an hour," said Valdez, turning to leave for lunch.

The possibility of all the doors opening, freeing all the inmates at the same time, possibly when I was completing a security check, terrified me. I couldn't shake the fear. It hung, suspended in my mind, as I prepared to complete the next security check. I was even more nervous as I walked from cell to cell. I looked in at Gonzales, who smiled, crinkling his teardrop tattoo. The inmates said nothing on this round, which made me wonder whether they knew what was up. Sergeant Paulson, a black female who was a little heavy and very friendly, came to visit us at about fourteen-thirty to see how it was going with the B Wing doors. So far, we told her, we had no incidents to report.

With Valdez at lunch, it was just me and Rowland working House Eight, so I was happy to talk a bit with the sergeant.

"How's it going for you so far?" she asked.

"Okay. I've never seen so many tattoos. Crosses, naked women, swastikas, teardrops …"

"You mean the teardrops near their eyes? That means they killed someone on the outs," said the sarge.

"Really? Why would they want to advertise that?"

"Sarge, I think it used to mean that, but now it's how many times they've been to prison," Rowland chimed in.

"Oh no, it's something to do with death," the sergeant insisted. "Maybe it's to signify the death of a loved one. Now I'm confused. Well, I think it's a murder thing. Anyway, see ya!" She turned to leave, in order to make her daily rounds through all the housing units.

Valdez returned from his lunch and it was time to do another security check, while we waited for maintenance to address the door problem. I was halfway up the stairs in B Wing when the large steel door to the wing closed behind me. I gasped! *Oh shit!*

Stunned at the prospect that my trainer or partner would actually consider it funny to lock me in the wing where security might be compromised, I completed the check and, heart in my throat, walked down to see if the door was actually open. I tried hard to open it, but it was locked. I had no way out.

I repeatedly told myself not to panic. My mind raced back to memories of things we'd covered in the academy that would help me in this situation. There was nothing, not a flipping thing. I briefly considered using the radio to call the tower and ask them to pop this door, but then everyone in the facility would know I was locked in, which would make me and my trainer look like idiots and maybe get him in trouble. I needed to play it cool and wait until they opened the door. They knew I was in there.

I waited by the door … and waited some more. It wasn't long before the inmates had noticed I was locked in there and were peeking out their doors at me.

"Why you no use yo radio?" Gonzales asked me.

"They're testing me," I said, feigning confidence. "If I use my radio, they'll think I'm worried."

"You look worried!" laughed the white inmate with the racist tattoo.

"Worried about what?" I asked, trying to seem nonchalant, as if the thought hadn't occurred to me. "You guys? Nah."

As a matter of fact, I was very worried. But, I reasoned, I'd be even more worried if the inmates had known about the door issue. I remained by the exit, waiting.

"Hey, you'll be all right, you can sleep in here tonight!" offered Gonzales.

"No, she wants to sleep in here with me tonight," added the white inmate.

Deep laughter came out of the doors upstairs, and another deeper voice got in his offer. "Hey, Deputy, you need a place, I'll move over and share a bunk."

"Gee, guys, you're all so kind!" I joked back. "Thanks, but no thanks." The men laughed even harder. I knew they could hear the fear in my voice, because I could.

I bet Rowland's testing me to see if I remember which key gets me out of this room and into the next wing, I thought. Then I reconsidered. *The main doors will be closed in all the wings, so that won't help me much. Maybe the doors aren't even really broken, and they made it up for my benefit, some sick training tactic. Or is Rowland up in the tower watching me through the giant window and laughing? To him, I probably look like a bug squirming under a magnifying glass, feeling a little warmer with each passing moment, until I have a complete meltdown and he can finally fail me, once and for all. I'd be one less "knob" to worry about. No, no way, I'm not going to let that ogre get his way.*

My eyes darted between the cell doors, and my ears were pricked, listening for the familiar "pop" of a door, any door. I leaned heavily against the exit. I tried not to look at the men's faces peering out at me, and instead focused on the big blue numbers on their cell doors.

Moments later, the steel door behind me clicked and I tumbled into the hallway.

"You all right in here?" Rowland asked, laughing.

"Sure, just making friends," I replied stoically, and the inmates laughed. Relief pumped through me, but I was determined not to let my trainer know that his joke had had any effect on me whatsoever. About twenty minutes later, maintenance strolled in to see if they could fix the problem, which they did, fortunately just before I needed to complete another security check.

THAT EVENING AT HOME, the thing I'd been most worried about since taking this job happened. Colton handed me a flyer about a trip that his class would be taking to the museum in two weeks. I knew there was no way I could go as a chaperone, and, again, I felt my heart in my throat. I'd never experienced a day when I was unable to be there for one of my children. It was like one of the creeps in B wing had stabbed a knife through my chest.

"Mom, you'll like this museum, because they have dinosaurs and everything."

"Hey, Colton, remember when we talked about my working? And I told you that I wouldn't be able to go to some of your events? Well, I can't go this time, sweetheart." I held my breath until he spoke, nervous that I would break his little heart.

"Oh. Okay," Colton said. He shrugged and walked away, and that was it. Surprisingly, it didn't seem all that big a deal to him—nowhere near what I had anticipated. If it had hurt his feelings, he didn't show it. And, in a way, that hurt mine.

Once the boys were in bed, Garrett and I were alone. I realized that we hadn't been physically intimate in any way in months. While we got ready for bed, I wondered if I should try to show him some affection, reach out for him. After all, how could we ever get our marriage back on track if we never reconnected? I reasoned that sex could be healing, therapeutic, restorative.

But in the end, my simple fear of rejection won out. I chickened out, and just went to sleep.

TWENTY-FIVE

▛▊▊▊▊▊▊▊▊▊▊▊▊▊▜

ONE OF THE MEMBERS of our own law enforcement family had passed away, and I was told that it was appropriate for everyone on the force to pay tribute. The former sheriff had died the previous weekend, and today was his funeral, which, unbeknownst to me, would most certainly be attended by all of our community's most high-profile members. The current sheriff wanted a good turnout at the service, and allowed anyone from Detention to attend, as long as we wore our long-sleeved uniforms with ties and hats. The sheriff even went so far as to bus us to the church, for what became our first assignment of the day.

Immediately upon arriving at work, Deputy Rowland handed me a black elastic band to place over my badge. It looked like a hair tie to me and I had no clue what to do with it.

"What's this for?" I asked.

"When we go to a funeral for one of our own, we shroud our badges as a sign of respect," Rowland explained. "The band goes top right to bottom left, at an angle." I took off my badge and wrapped the tie around it. With seven points on our star-shaped badges, there was no really perfect way to place it. No matter where I put it, the badge would have four points on one side of the band and only three on the other, which looked uneven. I glanced at Rowland's badge on his uniform, and thought I'd copied his placement of the band, then pinned mine back on my uniform, to the chagrin of my trainer.

"Oh my God, give me your badge right now, Probie," he ordered.

"Why?" I asked, taking it off again and handing it back to Rowland.

"You have the band between the wrong points of the star, ya dork," he said, grinning like he was helping his little sister. He fiddled with my badge for a moment and handed it back to me, pointing to his own badge on his chest. "See, here … it has to be worn between these exact points. Now you are properly shrouded. Put your badge back on, can't have you embarrassing me in front of the sheriff."

With each passing day, I realized more and more that every little thing in the police world, even a tiny piece of black elastic, had a proper and an improper use.

The deputies, including Rowland and I, met in front of the building with hats in hand; my hat fit my hand much better than my head. Resembling a milkman's hat, it sat on the top of my head and sort of just balanced there. The wide, black, patent-leather bill showed every fingerprint, and the green fabric top that matched my uniform pants stuck up higher in the front than the back, in order to clearly display the large, official-looking badge pinned to the front. I wondered why we didn't shroud that one.

Rowland and I waited together amid the crowd of about thirty deputies, some of them my former academy mates, in front of the building where the bus would be picking us all up to take us to the funeral. The bus opened its doors and we trampled aboard, not unlike the boarding process for my children's classroom field trips. Rowland sat with a friend up front, but I kept walking and found an empty seat in the middle by a window. Placing my hat in my lap, I watched people come up the stairs, quickly scanning the heads of those seated before them, seeking people they recognized. A male deputy sat beside me, but I never saw his face; he kept his back to me so that he could flirt with the female deputy across the aisle.

We filled the old overworked bus that was often used to haul inmates to court and back. It rattled loudly as it started out of the parking lot, thanks to the built-in cage lining the walls and the metal door that locked us all in, as it usually did the inmates. Once again, I had no ability to leave on my own steam. I noted that, at one time, that would in and of itself be an unusual thing, but it was now just a regular feature of my workday. To be seated where inmates regularly sat, bouncing down the street, peering out the windows as they did each day, gave me the creeps. I tried to imagine for a moment the experience of being an inmate headed to court, listening to the loud rattling of that metal cage surrounding me, on the way to learn my fate.

The bus stopped in the parking lot of a beautiful Catholic church, and I was reminded that I'd not attended my church for months. We'd arrived early, and I thought it might be a good idea to use the restroom before the service started, since it was such an ordeal to get undressed to go to the bathroom and then get dressed again in my weighty uniform. So I located the ladies' lavatory in the back of the church and did my business, exited the stall, and looked for a place to put my hat while I washed my hands. There were three sinks standing in a row, but not an inch of counter space. I placed my hat in a dry sink for just a moment and washed my hands in the nearest one. That's when I realized that I had missed the sound of the automatic faucet turning itself on and filling my hat with water.

"Oh my God!" I exclaimed and quickly grabbed my cap, careful to turn it upside down over the sink to pour out the water that had soaked into the material on half of it, leaving what resembled a fault line down the middle of the top of my mandatory, official headgear.

"Shit!" I cried, surprised at how easily the curse word had slid out of my mouth. Then, catching myself, I said, "Oh, oops! Thank God I'm alone in here." I chuckled and proceeded to shake the water out of my hat into the sink. It was then when a frail, elderly lady came out of the last stall.

"Oh!" I stumbled, surprised and worried I might have offended her. "I am *so* sorry, Ma'am!" I held up my hat, as if for proof that the offensive word had been justified. "I was an idiot and put my hat in the sink!" The old woman, unassuming and quiet, only walked up to the sink, washed her hands, and left the room, oblivious to my worries. She seemed to be in a fog, and for a second it occurred to me to check whether someone was in attendance to care for her, so I peeked my head out the door after she had left the restroom, to make sure she met up with a caring friend. Indeed, she did.

With my head out the door, I scanned the faces in the crowd to see whom I recognized—the mayor, several prominent legislators, the sheriff and his captains and lieutenants, media personalities and photographers. *Dammit!* I cursed again, under my breath, as I looked at my two-toned hood. *I have got to fix this!*

So I drowned the hat in the sink, thinking the water damage might not be so obvious if my topper at least appeared as one solid color. Then I used paper towels to blot it dry as much as I could, praying I didn't miss a pocket of water that would burst during the ceremony and pour down my face. Feeling stupid, my frustration got the best of me. *Goddammit!* I thought, and clapped my hand over my mouth as if I'd said it aloud. What was wrong with me? Now I was taking the Lord's name in vain, in his own house? I realized that I had been using more and more foul language lately. I also knew it was an unfortunate by-product of my new environment. Still, I reasoned, that was no excuse, and I resolved from that moment on to clean up my mouth. I stuffed some paper towels in my back pocket, just in case, balanced the wet cap on my head, and left the room, hoping nobody would notice that my milkman's hat was now several shades darker than everyone else's.

The funeral began as the color guard proceeded to roll up the flag that had been draped atop the coffin at the front of the room. Stoically, they walked over and handed it to the same elderly woman I'd seen in the restroom. *Shit,* I thought, my new resolution flying right out the window. *Of course, she's the widow of the deceased!* I berated myself for not having once considered that the poor woman could be grieving. Perhaps I could have been of assistance, or at least expressed my condolences. Instead, I'd been too preoccupied with that stupid flippin' hat, and now I felt even more miserable.

We took our places, side by side, lining the back of the room from one side of the church to the other. As the funeral progressed, I wondered about the "law enforcement family" that I kept hearing so much about. So far, my experience hadn't been much like being part of a family, though the deputies had frequently used the term in the academy and even in the jail. If this industry resembled a family at all, it was in that it produced terribly dysfunctional relatives. But standing there, at attention, in our spiffy uniforms, we all looked the same, like a wall of tan and green. I thought that perhaps this was what that word "family" meant: a strong sense of force in the background, supporting the many people who were grieving our lost brother.

As the mayor spoke of the many ways our community had benefitted from the work of our former sheriff, sergeants and lieutenants who had previously worked for the man sniffed, looked down, and wiped their eyes.

I learned how the deceased had rallied his troops during hard times, demanding no more from them than he was willing to give of himself. I heard how he had built many partnerships with children's organizations and was himself a Big Brother to a number of troubled youths. The positive difference his leadership had made in our agency was evident from the many speakers who shared, through tears, their appreciation for this sheriff. It was then that I began to comprehend that perhaps I, too, was a necessary piece of this massive puzzle.

As I stood under my wet hat in the back of the room, at attention, legs straight, eyes staring forward, arms down at my sides. I marveled at how many of us there were encircling the room. And I realized that, had I not been there, it would have been noticed. There would have been a hole in the wall of tan and green. New or not, at that moment, I was equal to all the other deputies. We each held a place and today it was clear that we were more like a team than a family, and I was definitely part of the team. Geez, thinking about it, we had locker rooms, uniforms, gear … that sounded like a team to me.

But back in the jail it was a different story. I had yet to discover the place where I'd fit. The position I would play on this team was still a mystery. Hopefully, it would be clear once I had passed my training. That's when the game would begin.

Being here at the end of one sheriff's "game," I could see how the life of that family continued on, as did the life of the agency he represented. Maybe it wasn't as much about what happened on the field as it was about who was there with you. I looked around me and thought about how these were the folks I was learning to rely on to train me properly, to show me the ropes, to pull me out of a cell by the back of my belt, and sometimes to beat me up a little or to fix my badge when it's not on correctly. Like teammates, they were the players who would be there during good and bad, through the daily grind of the job, or when we got spit on or kicked by an inmate, or, worse, when we lost a partner, a brother, or sister, and had to say goodbye, like today. The Ogre, Franko, Paxton, Carnie … these were the people I would remember when they retired from the game, and they would remember me. Now I was getting it; this family stuff was beginning to make sense, and with my law enforcement family, as with any other family, you don't get to pick your siblings. Simply put, we were stuck with each other.

◈

MY AFTERNOON BACK IN THE SHU with the Ogre and Valdez began routinely. While completing a security check, an inmate, a white guy with a medium build, was out for his tier time in A Wing as I walked the area to do my first check of the day. I smiled, as I typically did whenever I encountered people, and he watched me like a hawk from his seat near the telephone on the wall. The phone began to ring, echoing throughout the unit. A woman's voice answered and could be heard over the speaker. I looked to see why her voice was so loud, and noticed no handheld receiver was connected to the phone. It was only a box attached to the wall with a keypad and a speaker grill. I also noticed how the inmate continued to stare at me as he said, "Hello, Ma." I completed the check quickly and left the wing.

With the exception of that guy, all the same characters were in the SHU that day as had been there the week before; there were a few more women in D Wing. I completed one more security check during the new guy's tier time, and he stopped me coming down the stairs before I left the wing.

"Deputy, I know you," he said in a leering, taunting voice.

"No, I don't think so," I said, my voice friendly. I smiled and left the wing, slamming the door behind me.

Back at the office, I asked Rowland about the inmate in A-3, and he looked up his file in the computer.

"He's a freak," he began, reading from the screen. "In for stalking, attempted murder, home invasion, and false imprisonment out of California." Rowland looked at me. "Why do you ask?"

I explained what had just happened, and how this weirdo had stared at me with unusually strong interest.

"Yeah, I've been meaning to talk to you about that," Rowland began, rubbing his chin. "But since I know you won't be working the SHU permanently, well, it didn't seem to matter. But … well … you need to have more of a poker face."

"Poker face," I repeated. "Yeah, I know what you mean. Quit smiling, be more serious, right?"

Yeah, quit smiling at the inmates. Sometimes they think you like them. Who knows, Dolinsky, you may have your very own stalker by the end of the day." Then he smiled at me.

I knew he was teasing, but the man's stare had been so disturbing, I was sincerely worried. Rowland seemed to see that in my expression.

"Honestly, Dolinsky, don't let any inmate get to you. Let him know by your actions that you aren't afraid of him. Remember, no smiling, and you might want to use the f-word once in a while."

"I'd rather not," I replied quickly. Always wanting to set a good example for my children, and knowing, biblically speaking, that cursing was frowned upon, I had always been determined not to engage in it. I'd also never had a need to.

"You don't have to, but it is effective. And it's how 'jeeters' talk. You want them to understand you, you gotta speak 'Jeeter.'"

"Jeeter?" I asked.

"Yeah, you know, an asshole, scumbag, scrote, fuckstick, dirtbag ... a jeeter."

I started to laugh, "A scrote? A *what*-stick?"

"Jesus, you didn't get out much before this job, did you?" Rowland looked up at me with exasperation. "Just think of parts of the male anatomy, you can figure it out." He turned his back to me and began typing on the computer.

During my next security check, I grabbed the handle on the big blue door to A Wing and called "A-Adam!" The door opened with a *Pop!* As I moved the heavy door, I could see the inmates were all locked down; nobody was out of their cell. Rowland watched from behind me as I walked the unit, peering into each cell as I passed. As I approached Cell A-3, I was startled to see that the inmate inside had his face pressed right up against the window and he was watching me.

"I know you. I know who you are," he said. I stopped and looked back at him, to convey that I wasn't scared of him, though inside I felt quite the opposite.

"No I don't think you do," I replied, straight-faced, staring back at him and trying not to blink, hiding my shaking hands behind my back. He had black hair and dark eyes, long eyebrow hairs that curled up to his forehead, and a messy moustache.

"Do you know me?" he asked. His eyes looked crazy, like he had an inferno blazing inside his head.

"No, I don't know you, and you don't know me," I said flatly, and then continued the walk around, checking the other cells, where the inhabitants seemed unaware of my presence.

"I know who you are!" he called out as I walked into the hallway and shut the door to A-Wing, leaving the inmate and all his crazy inside.

"Yup, a fuckin' freak," said Rowland as we walked back to the office.

That evening, Rowland had planned to do some cell searches … that is, he planned on me doing the cell searches with our partner, Valdez. I was to look for any contraband, anything not authorized for an inmate to possess—leftover food from meals, dice or chess pieces made out of toilet paper and toothpaste, stuff like that. Then, after we searched each cell, the inmate would be moved to a different cell for the sake of security.

"It's your lucky day," smiled Valdez. "A-3 just happens to be on the list." I immediately felt my hands get clammy and my mouth went dry.

The three of us entered A Wing and walked over to Cell A-1, which was empty. Rowland watched while Valdez taught me how to do a systematic search of the cell, which was much like when we performed inventory searches, one area at a time, overlapping for accuracy.

"You got gloves?" Rowland asked. I didn't, so he handed me an extra-large pair from his pants pocket. The gloves floated around my tiny hands.

"Always start at the same point. You want to do it the exact same way, every cell, every time," Valdez explained. "That way you don't miss anything." I began at the door and checked all around the door frame. Valdez produced a small mirror, the kind dentists use, to look in those hard-to-reach places, such as the tops of door frames and behind sinks and toilets.

I moved clockwise through the cell, wiping my gloved hand along surfaces, using the mirror everywhere I couldn't see. Valdez pointed out the tiny hidden areas where he had found contraband in the past; there was nothing there this time. I searched the sink and toilet, then moved to the metal bunks covered with thin vinyl mattresses. Actually, they weren't really mattresses, more like mats that were only about three inches thick. I checked all the seams for holes or anything out of the ordinary. When the search was complete, we visited A-3.

The inmate was standing at the door when I approached. Even though the guys were with me, I felt anxious about addressing the "jeeter."

"Have a seat on the bunk," I ordered through the door. He did it, then I grabbed the door handle and said "Cell Three!" so the tower would pop it. Nothing happened.

"Just use your key," said Valdez. "Tower is probably hitting the head." I must have looked confused because he clarified, "Using the restroom."

My hand shook a little when I opened the cell door using the key.

"Come on out and have a seat in the chair," I directed the inmate, who followed my instructions, walked across the room, and sat in the lonely chair. Rowland watched him while I searched his cell, with help from Valdez. We didn't find any contraband, though we hadn't expected to, since he had only moved in the previous day.

My concern now was to break this inmate's interest. I walked out of the cell and over to Rowland. The inmate watched me with the same deranged gaze.

"Go get your stuff, you're moving to Cell One," I told the inmate sternly, making sure I showed no trace of a smile. Rowland nodded approval, so I knew I was doing this right. The inmate stood up and walked into his cell, emerging moments later with a mattress under his arm.

"Where are you going with that?" I asked, sounding annoyed.

"To Cell A-1, where you told me to go," he snapped back.

"I told you to get your stuff, not the mattress. It stays here in Cell Three," I replied firmly, wondering when, and if, I would have an opportunity to insert the f-word that my trainer wanted to hear from me so badly.

"Well, I don't like that one and I want …" he started.

"What? …" I interrupted. "Put down that …" I gathered my fortitude, "that … f-f-fucking mattress and do as I said!" I bellowed, knowing I sounded completely out of character. My knees were weak, and I held my hands together in front of me so he couldn't see them shaking.

"I just want to move mattresses," he replied, visibly irritated.

"It's not about what *you* want, or what *you* like!" I said, more authoritatively. "It's what *I* tell you that matters! Get your shit and move to Cell One!" My body naturally reacted in the way a ticked-off mother would, with my right hand on my hip, my left arm pointing to Cell One. He hadn't yet moved so I ended the order with, "Do it FUCKING NOW!"

The inmate scowled, turned his head, and looked at me in much the same way one of my kids looked at me right after being disciplined, just before he reluctantly did the thing he was told to do in the first place. Valdez stepped closer to the inmate, who moved away from him and back into A-3, dropped the mattress, and re-emerged from the cell with only his gray bin of linens. He hurried into A-1 and slammed the door behind him.

Phew! I breathed an incredible sigh of relief, and Rowland smiled and nodded at me to let me know I'd done all right. I also knew my days of smiling, even accidentally, at passersby were over, especially when it came to inmates. And as much as I wanted to believe I didn't need profanity in my life, I learned that there indeed was a valid use for, and almost magical power in, the f-word.

Twenty-Six

‖‖‖‖‖‖‖‖‖‖‖‖‖

IT WAS A PERFECT SUMMER DAY in the desert—not too warm, but still sunny. I grabbed a frozen bagel and cup of coffee, and headed out the door to work. I spent the entire car trip mulling over my recent choices with regret and guilt. It was Colton's field-trip day, the first one I'd ever missed, and I was missing it in so many ways. I hoped to God that my little boy wouldn't feel my absence as much as I was feeling it. I was anxious to get through the blue slider door into the secured facility, because I knew that I wouldn't remember much about the outside world once I had the jail surrounding me.

On this day I had been assigned to Housing Unit Seven, the Mental Health Unit, with two other deputies, Hoffman and Terrence, and still under the not-so-watchful eye of Deputy Rowland. This day, we were in charge of sixty-five inmates who had been deemed mentally ill by our nursing staff during the booking process, many of them off their meds, unpredictable, and violent.

During the afternoon, Rowland left me alone for a few minutes so he could visit with a friend in a nearby housing unit. I wondered if he was testing to see how much he could get away with before a recruit would complain about him to the administration. It wouldn't be me. I just wanted to pass, not fight the establishment.

Hoffman, an FTO as well, was my babysitter and really sore from weight-lifting the day before. His walk was so stiff that Terrence teased him.

"Dude, you look like my son does when he has a loaded diaper!" she hollered at him as he unbendingly headed up the stairs and around the top tier. Shrugging back at her, he continued, opening cell doors, asking specific inmates inside whether they wanted tier time. They could take it or leave it, but this was the only time that it would be offered today. Only certain prisoners could come out together; others needed tier time alone, and Hoffman knew the difference.

Tier time was a busy time in any housing unit, but especially in House Seven. This morning, while high-security male inmates mulled around one side of the housing unit, minimum-security women sat at tables and colored in children's coloring books on the other side. The two groups were unaware of each other due to the thick wall built down the middle of the unit. Centered at the end of the wall was the deputy station, so we could sit at the desk and see both sides simultaneously. This was where I sat with Terrence.

"I'm letting Mr. Coleburg out for his tier time, but if he comes out naked again, he's losing it," said Deputy Terrence as if it were normal thing to say, and she pushed the button to open his door on the touch screen. Coleburg was in his seventies and had been incarcerated for throwing rocks through the windows of the county courthouse. It happened the same way each time he was released; within a few hours, officers would get called to head down to the courthouse to pick him up, and a window or two more would have been shattered.

"Hey, this is a good one today, Mr. Coleburg," Hoffman told him and the old man smiled a mouthful of crooked, brown teeth, then walked away. The deputy brought the note to the desk and showed me. It looked like some sort of code. "He writes one every day and gives them to us," said Hoffman. I watched him open a drawer full of papers, stuff the note into it, and slam it shut.

"Deputy, can I have a deodorant, toothpaste, and toothbrush?" asked an older female inmate who was standing before the desk. She looked up at me, a gummy grin on her face. I could see from where I sat that her shirt was on backwards, her hair was stringy, and her feet were just over the red line.

"Sure, but don't forget, you can't cross the red line," I said, and as I handed the items to her, she jumped back a few steps to be in compliance. "That's okay, just be more careful next time," I told her, and she reached to take the items, then turned to go.

"Hi," said the nineteen-year-old woman who had just stepped up. Her eyes were opened wide, not out of amazement, but due to the pain of mental illness.

"Hi," I responded, "what do you need this morning?"

"The pills I'm taking here are making me high," she said. Her brown eyes were as big as saucers and stared not at me, but almost right through me.

"Oh yeah? Do you take meds on the outs?"

"Yeeaahh ... I do ... not these meds ...other meds."

"If you don't feel well, you don't have to take the meds. You can refuse them, you know," I informed her, feeling her discomfort as she struggled to look me in the eye, but instead focused somewhere behind me.

"No, I feel worse without them ... Can I have some deodorant, please?"

I handed her a clear packet of gel, enough for one application, and she left the desk. She was quickly replaced by another female with matted hair and unbelievably bad breath.

"I need soap, a comb, and toilet paper..."

And so it went, inmate after needy inmate, throughout the day.

As in each housing unit, a security check was to be completed every thirty minutes, and it was my turn to perform one. I walked out from behind the deputy station and up the pink staircase, holding the railing, arriving at the first cell. Peeking in the windows in House Seven could be difficult at times, as it was in the SHU, depending on the lighting. As long as I saw normalcy inside the cell, I was free to move on to the next. When I walked past Margaret's cell, she smiled. I wasn't sure whether she recognized me or not. I stopped.

"How are you doing, Margaret?"

"Okay. Can you get me a sandwich?" she asked as she aggressively picked her nose.

"Lunch will be here soon," I said and kept walking.

A few cells later, I noticed a woman sleeping by the toilet in her cell. She had a mattress on the bunk, but she had instead chosen to wrap a blue blanket over her head and attempt to squeeze herself behind the toilet. She was alive, which in my mind was good enough, so I continued my stroll.

After having checked each occupied cell on the female side of the housing unit, I keyed open and moved through a heavy duty door in the center wall. Entering the male side was a bit unnerving for me. Four unshaven, dirty-looking men dressed in red shuffled around the floor of the housing unit, and a shot of red jetted out of a shower in my peripheral vision. It was a hurried inmate heading to his cell, oblivious to my presence, which freaked me out a little. I continued toward the nearest cell: two beds, two inmates, good … next cell, one bed, one inmate, good. And so it continued on the top tier.

Downstairs, where the men were wandering around, I entered cautiously. Through the third window I witnessed a tall, thin black man bumping up and down on his bunk. Initially my thought was that he might be having a seizure, but after a second glance, I realized he was humping his mattress. I called over to Deputy Hoffman, "Hey! This guy …"

Seeing my location, Hoffman interrupted me, "Yeah, I know. He does that all day long. What can we do? If we give him a different mattress, he just puts a hole in it." It took me a second to grasp that this odd and disturbing scene was considered normal, in House Seven.

"O-kay," I replied with trepidation, shook my head, and continued my walk.

Before I reached the deputy station, I was stopped by an inmate calling to me through his window. "Deputy, what time is it?"

I stopped by the window to find a heavyset white man peering out with a confused look on his face.

"Eight-thirty," I replied, then added, "in the morning." He had a juvenile quality about him as he looked outside the window, trying to see around me into the day room.

"Why are you here?" I asked.

"I lost my temper and broke the door at the hospital," he replied, laying his forehead on the six-inch-wide window between us.

"Oh, you did, huh? What's your name?" I asked.

"Sil Jacobs," he said, and I thought I recognized the name. "Sil, are you related to Deb Jacobs?"

After a long pause, he responded, sadly, "Yes, she's my sister." His sister had been one of my high school friends. I thought she'd be crushed to know her brother had been incarcerated.

It was evident, by the way he spoke and the time it took for him to respond, that he was slow to comprehend my questions. I remembered Deb telling me about her brother and had seen photos of him before, but I had never met him.

"Sil, does she know where you are? Would you like me to tell her you're in here?" I asked.

After a long pause, Sil said, "Yes, would you … um … tell Deb I'm here?" He looked at me pitifully, his face still pressed against the glass. I thought I caught a smile on his squished face.

"Sure, I'll e-mail her," I said and walked away. *I work in a human zoo.*

WITH NOTHING REMARKABLE having happened in House Seven for the rest of that day, I sent my old friend a note to let her know that her brother was in custody. Rowland took off to visit another friend, while I continued working with my two partners. It was almost quitting time.

"Hey, do you mind if I have some of your nuts?" Deputy Terrence asked Hoffman. Very health conscious, Hoffman nibbled raw almonds continuously as he sat in front of the computer at the deputy station. He chuckled at her words.

"Sure," he said with a grin, not about to miss the opportunity for an obvious sexual joke. "Get down on it!" The three of us giggled.

"Thanks," she said, grabbing a few from the bag.

"Hey, you want some meat with those nuts?"

I looked up to see him offering her the tuna he had been devouring directly out of the can, and I had to laugh. In fact, the three of us laughed so hard, Terrence almost spit out the almonds, which sent us over the edge. Now we were in stitches. On the computer, Deputy Hoffman pulled up the song "Get down on it" by KC and the Sunshine Band and blasted it as Terrence and I sang along, swinging our hips, keys clanging loudly on the heavy belts. It felt good to share a bit of levity in this gloomy place.

The tune blared from the crappy computer speakers as we squeezed a bit of fun into what had been a routine day. It was then that we heard a loud, awkward moan coming from an inmate in the day room. I eyed my partners for a clue as to what to do. Hoffman turned down the music while Terrence and I gloved up in preparation to address the source of the noise. A second loud moan erupted into all-out yelling.

"You walked away from me! I'm not stupid! You were mean to me and made fun of me!" The voice came from Sil Jacobs, who was yelling at an older man who had been seated with him at a table. Hoffman pulled some gloves on quickly as the three of us raced around the deputy station and into the day room to calm the situation. Hoffman ran up in front of Sil.

"Jacobs, don't do this! It's okay, Sil!" he yelled as he grabbed Sil's arm and began escorting him to his cell.

"Lock down!" yelled Terrence. Three male inmates who were seated at a nearby table jumped up, scurried to their cells, and shut the doors. The older man who had been the object of Sil's outburst was still seated at the table.

"I'm not stupid! I am not!" Sil insisted, looking at Hoffman as he walked toward his cell door.

"Move it!" I hollered to him as I walked closer to the old man, who slowly got up. I helped him back to his cell and closed the door. Everyone had locked down but Sil.

Sil was large, and difficult to control alone, even for a strong man like Hoffman. Terrence grabbed Sil's other arm and I joined my partners, though Sil seemed compliant. Just before he entered his cell, Sil abruptly turned toward Terrence and screamed "I'm not going back in! Fuck you!"

Now the fight was on. Sil stiffened his body, pulling his arms toward his chest, and Terrence and Hoffman took him down to the cement floor with a thud. Sil's screams pierced the silence as he lay on his side on the floor.

"Get his feet!" Hoffman yelled to me. I could barely hear him over Sil's high-pitched screaming. My partner knelt on the cement, his arms wrapped under Sil, trying to gain control of his left arm, which he had pulled underneath him. Sil's jerking and kicking made it difficult to grab his legs, and as I attempted to grab an ankle, he kicked my finger, forcing it backwards, which sent a zing of pain up my arm.

"OW! Shit!" I yelled. Now I was mad.

With one partner's arm pinned under Sil, and one working on gaining control of the other arm, I realized that grabbing Sil by the feet was not going to work, This required a different tactic.

The ballistic vest was not the most comfortable part of the uniform, but it was tough, kept me safe from harm, and was all I had. I threw my upper body onto Sil's legs to gain control of them and, almost immediately, once he felt my weight on him, he stopped kicking. I was able to maneuver to a position of straddling his legs, my knees on the floor with my back to my partners, both of whom were still fighting to get Sil's hands and arms out from underneath him.

"Let me have your arm! Stop resisting!" both partners yelled. "Stop resisting! Stop resisting!"

But Sil remained stiff and fought with his upper body. I wrestled with his legs so that they were finally crossed at the ankle and placed my left knee, and all my weight, on the calf muscle of his top leg.

"Ow, my leg! Get off my leg!" screamed Sil. I'd hurt him, which had been my intent. With his attention diverted away from my partners, Hoffman and Terrence were able to safely gain control of Sil's arms.

Though it felt longer, it had only been about one minute of fighting before the three of us had Sil incapacitated and rolled onto his stomach, right there on the cement floor. Just then, Terrence yelled, "Don't bite me!"

I heard a thunk, something like a melon hitting the floor at the grocery store. I looked at the floor to see what had fallen, and I could see a large pool of blood forming under Sil's head. Terrence had elbowed him in the nose. My mind racing, I called out on the radio, "Escort deputies to House Seven." I heard my blaring voice come through on my partners' radios.

Time seemed to slow for a few moments, the three of us breathing heavily, looking at each other to be sure everything was going in our favor. I could hear my partners huffing as we waited, using our collective body weights to hold a moaning Sil on the floor. For a moment I could hear my own heartbeat.

Deputies arrived quickly, the great thundering green herd to the rescue.

"Central, Valdez, ten-six, House Seven," came out over the radio. Valdez was here somewhere, but we couldn't see him yet.

"Over here!" Hoffman called and Valdez ran to our side. Sil groaned as Valdez pulled his arms behind his back to click on handcuffs. Rowland arrived with ankle chains and clicked them into place while I kept Sil's legs still. Sergeant Paulson arrived and called the three of us, the first responders on the scene, to meet with her. Valdez and two other deputies relieved us so we could stand up and follow the sarge.

"So, what exactly happened here?" she asked.

"Well, Sarge, it started like this ..." Hoffman told her the steps of the incident while I watched as three muscular deputies lifted Sil into a wheelchair with ease, each muscle in their chiseled arms seeming to work independently of the others. They wheeled Sil out of the housing unit and down the hall to the Infirmary, where medical staff could care for his bleeding, possibly broken, nose. A crime scene investigator arrived to take photographs as the sergeant ushered in the inmate workers who had arrived to clean up the bloody mess.

Word travels fast in jail, and the phone began ringing as deputies called to congratulate Terrence on her heroics, avoiding a bite by elbowing the inmate in the nose. Deputies and staff assigned to nearby housing units arrived to check it out. As I stood there listening to the sergeant praise her, I realized that the middle finger on my right hand was throbbing. Shift was over and it was time to go home, so Sergeant Paulson sat at House Seven's computer and printed up papers for me to take to the doctor, if need be, over the weekend.

"It was bad-ass," I heard Hoffman say as he was busy discussing the incident with the mob of deputies remaining. I walked around the housing unit for one final security check. Margaret waved to me through the window of her cell door as I passed and I waved back. All else was "normal" for House Seven. I said goodnight to my partners, who were still knee-deep in storytelling, then walked out the blue slider, down the hallway and out to my van, which had never looked so inviting.

When I arrived home, I found Colton watching television. "Where's my young man?" I called to him. He jumped off the couch and was at my side in a millisecond. As I hugged him, I asked, "How'd your field trip go?"

"Mom, it was so cool! We had the best hot dogs for lunch, you would have liked them because they had cheese on them, the gooey kind like on nachos."

"Yeah, cool, but how was the museum?"

"It was so cool, Mom! We saw a mummified cat and real dinosaur bones. They were bigger than the roof of our house!"

"Wow!" I said. "So you were okay without me there today?"

"Oh, yeah, it was really super fun!" And with that he ran back to his perch in front of the television.

"Great, Sweetie, I'm glad to hear it," I said to his receding back. I meant it when I said it, but deep down, I felt a little piece of my heart break.

TWENTY-SEVEN

WHEN I'D FIRST STARTING WORKING at the jail, I thought often about how creepy it would be to have to work in House Five, alone while inmates walked around freely, the closest back-up two doors and a cement yard away. But of course, eventually, I was assigned there with Deputy Waverly, my former Defensive Tactics instructor, as my trainer.

I tried to nap that day in an attempt to be ready for my new shift. Waverly worked graveyard, which meant that now I did, too. But I hadn't been able to sleep. I figured I'd better get used to it, since that was the shift where most new hires ended up once training was completed. After the fight in House Seven the previous week, I had iced my finger over the weekend and it felt fine by Saturday evening, my new Monday morning.

We arrived in House Five after dinner had been served and the inmates were watching TV.

"In any General Housing Unit, movement cards are the first thing we address," Waverly explained. "Count them first and be sure the number of cards matches the number written on the log before the deputy leaves to go home." She pointed to the log, which was just lined paper on a clipboard. I picked up the binder and began to flip through the six-inch-by-eight-inch clear sleeves filled with the inmate movement cards. Black-and-white mug shots drifted by with each flip as I counted.

"Sixty-eight," I announced to Waverly, who pointed again to the log. It read sixty-eight as well.

"Now walk around and match faces to photos. This is called a formal ID. We do two a day." Waverly ordered this as she set up her e-mail in the computer. She was known for being fair, and though we hadn't hit it off in the academy, I was happy to have a female trainer for a change. "You need to tell them to lock down first, and, Dolinsky, did you call in?" I hadn't.

"Central Control, Deputy Dolinsky," I said into the radio. It screeched with ear-piercing feedback and Waverly turned her radio down.

"Go ahead, Deputy Dolinsky," said a female voice over the radio.

"Ten-forty-one, ten-eight, Housing Unit Five."

"Ten-four, Deputy Dolinsky."

Now, to get them on their bunks.

"Lock down," I said in a voice that sounded loud to me. Still, no one seemed to have heard me. "Lock down!" I yelled. The women who were seated by the television moseyed to their bunks, and a few came out of the bathroom with towels on their heads and sat on their bunks. Nobody was in a hurry, that was for sure. Waverly was not happy.

"Is that how fast you move when a deputy yells 'lock down'? Ladies, consider this a warning! You think you're going to slow-play Deputy Dolinsky because she's new? You had better think again! I expect you to move your asses, or you'll be on your bunks the whole night. Do you understand?"

"Yes, Ma'am," a chorus of female voices filled the room. I walked over to the bunks about twenty-five feet from the deputy station. With only about five feet of space between them, I walked through, calling the names of the inmates. As I did, each one would smile, nod, or raise her hand. This was my debut here, and I hoped I seemed fearless enough, despite how creepy it felt to me being so closely surrounded by criminals, all watching my every move. I carried the white binder full of cards and flipped them to see their mug shots as I walked between the bunks.

"Severson," I called, and a rough, toothless woman in her fifties nodded at me from a bottom bunk.

"Christian," I said, to which a young white woman with acne and long blonde hair lifted her hand in acknowledgement. I took two more steps.

"Deitch?" A young twenty-something woman with the image of a gun tattooed on her neck gently smiled my direction.

"Acebedo?" Her bunkmate, a Hispanic woman in her thirties, waved down at me from the top bunk.

As I walked between seventy bunks, I tried to get a feel for the unit and who currently resided there. Some of the women didn't acknowledge me at all, even when I called their names, and I wondered if they might be the ones to give me trouble.

Upon returning to the deputy station, I confirmed with Waverly that everyone was accounted for, and she explained more about how House Five worked.

"This was built to house the boot camp, when we had one. It's since been eliminated. That's why it's so different from the other units. Also, the inmates have freedom to go to the bathroom at will, unless on lock down. When they pass this station, they must say 'passing' or they'll get locked down for the rest of the night. Understand?"

Then she turned her attention to the inmates. "Okay, ladies, you may have tier time," she said loudly, and the unit was immediately abuzz with activity. "Passing" was heard repeatedly in different voices as the women walked by the deputy station into the restroom behind us.

"Why don't you familiarize yourself with the unit while I call my husband for a few minutes?" Waverly suggested. I figured she probably wanted to check on her baby, remembering that she had come back from maternity leave during my academy. I stepped down the three stairs and left the safety of the deputy station, again to find myself eye to eye with inmates. I wandered among the busy women, who were setting up chairs to watch TV, resuming card games, and braiding each other's hair. They were careful not to walk up behind me, which was smart, and one of the rules.

When approaching House Five from the outside, it felt like entering a tent, due to its shape, but inside, House Five felt solid. But an absence of windows made it seem dank and dark. Fluorescent lamps lit the room with an unnatural bluish glow, and just above the lights, metal pipes, which made up the sprinkler system, swayed with every turn of the ceiling fans. To me, this felt more like working in a storage space than a housing unit.

The whole place had the feeling of a high school woodworking project. Seventy bunk beds were lined up around the room, and the center was filled with mismatched tables and chairs, in various levels of disrepair. Heavy posts riveted to the cement floor held phones. I walked back to check out the inmate bathroom and was surprised to find that showers were center stage; the toilets lined the perimeter, and sinks and tall mirrors were in between them, to create the aura of privacy. Gray paint peeled off the cement pad floor in the showers, too, and I wondered why anyone would bother painting cement gray anyway.

It didn't take long for me to appreciate a fundamental benefit of House Five, which was that we could look around the room and know almost immediately where everyone was—no walking from cell to cell and peering into windows, as in the other units. Security checks were a snap. But all that sitting in the dark with only a desk lamp to light the room made me sleepy, especially once the inmates were locked down for the night and were fast asleep. After that, all I heard for the rest of the night were typical nighttime noises—snoring, sleep-talking, and an occasional fart. I felt more comfortable once the criminals were unconscious, and I sporadically caught myself dozing off. Such a calm, quiet, peaceful experience was a new one for me in this jail, and one of the paybacks of graveyard shift; my trainer saw me struggling to stay awake and started talking.

"Without cells, sound carries, and they learn a lot about us when we're on the phone or talking with coworkers," Waverly explained. "If you ask the inmates, they can tell you which deputies have been arrested or who's in a romantic relationship with whom, so watch what you say in here."

"Deputies have been arrested?" I asked, drawn out of my sleepiness. Waverly laughed, and all I could see was her shockingly white, almost glow-in-the-dark teeth.

"Most of their observations are baseless, but once in a while they'll get one dead on," she said. "They have nicknames for certain staff, too, but they're usually just stating the obvious. You know, like, 'Big Bertha' for Karen—do you know her?"

"No."

"Well, the minute you see her, you'll understand why they named her that … Do you know Lonna?"

"Uh, I don't think so." It seemed weird when she called the female deputies by their first names.

"She's called 'Burnt Barbie' because she bleaches her hair and looks like she sleeps in a fuckin' tanning bed."

"Do you have a nickname?" I asked.

"Not yet, but I rarely work this unit; tonight was simply for training purposes. Anyway, I want you to understand, many of these women are not inherently bad, they just made poor choices. And they do it over and over again, often because of drug use. The majority are here for crimes directly related to drugs."

"Like, they steal something to trade for drugs?" I asked.

"That, or they were selling drugs, or they prostitute for drugs. Most, you'll find, blame their drug habit on someone else, usually their boyfriend or husband."

Waverly was particularly knowledgeable on this topic that was as foreign to me as Lederhosen. She explained that this was a working unit, and by the time an inmate arrived in House Five, he or she would have been in the jail long enough to detox and were now ready to work.

While Deputy Waverly spoke, I recalled how, the previous week, during my lunch break in Staff Dining, I had heard a lot of giggling and noise coming from the back where the food was being made. One of the deputies hadn't liked it, so he had fired all the women working, lined them all up, and marched them downstairs to House Six, where they spent their time locked in cells and lost the privileges and freedoms of House Five. Once word got around, the inmates had been on their best behavior, and I hoped it would continue throughout my training.

DURING THE EARLY MORNING HOURS, an inmate woke and approached the deputy station. "Deputy Dolinsky?" she began, standing on the red line and startling me from my pre-sleep state. It was Sherman, a woman whom I could tell had once been pretty, but had lost her looks to drugs.

"Yeah?"

"I'm restless. Could I please make a phone call?"

"At this time of night?" I whispered, trying not to wake the other inmates.

"I haven't heard from my husband at all. It's been over three weeks since I've been in jail. He's never dumped me like this before, and I was hoping I could call ...?"

I could relate to that feeling well. Though Garrett and I were still living under the same roof, these days we'd been acting more like roommates. "You think he's gonna be up at this ungodly hour?" I asked Sherman while Waverly listened in.

"He works, and I can never get him during the day. I really do love him, and I'm worried that something might have happened to him to keep him away. Please, Deputy? Please, may I make this call?" Her eyes were pleading and contrite. I glanced at Waverly.

"It's your unit," Waverly said, earnestly "You make the decision."

I shrugged. "Okay, just make it quick," I said to Sherman quietly. "And use the closest phone, over there." With that Sherman ran to the phone to which I was pointing.

"*I* would never have let an inmate use the phone so late at night, but it's *your* unit, so run it as you see fit," Waverly said after Sherman had left.

"Why not?" I asked, wondering if I'd just made a mistake.

"They can do it on tier time. Besides, they lie all the time."

It was my empathy that had gotten the best of me this time. I like to give people the benefit of the doubt. I watched Sherman as she sat at the bank of inmate phones, pausing a moment as if to get her bearings before picking up the receiver and dialing. She contacted her husband who, I assessed from her voice, was not happy to hear from her. He didn't let her speak much, and it wound up being a very one-sided conversation.

"But Baby, where are you? But Babe, I … but … I was … but …"

I felt badly for Sherman. She wanted to pour her heart out to him and I could tell she had received no warmth from him. For a few moments I could sympathize with her heartbreak, convinced that I was witnessing proof that inmates and deputies really were more similar than we were different.

Then she said it. "Baby, I don't care if we have to live in your car, I just want to be with you." And it was at this point that my empathy came to a screeching halt. As if living in a car could, in any way, ever, be the right choice. Now, the woman's heartbreak seemed childish to me, her willingness to be homeless for a man completely unacceptable, ridiculous, even idiotic.

Waverly could see the disgust on my face and smiled.

"Considering her history of drug use, she's probably cowering to him so she can keep her high once she gets out," my trainer said.

"So you think it's not about him as much as it is about the drugs he gives her?" I asked.

"Yes, I do." Waverly lowered her voice even further. "Look her up and see when she's getting released. I bet it's soon and she's hedging her bets. And he knows it, so he's not necessarily happy to hear from her." I looked Sherman up in the computer and, sure enough, she would be out within days.

In her desire to escape reality, she had brought me back to it; our lifestyles were, in fact, quite different, irreconcilable.

A sleeping inmate whose bunk was located near the phone heard Sherman talking and approached the deputy station. "Deputy, can you look up my out date?"

"Right now, in the middle of the night? Why would I do computer checks at this time of night?" I whispered.

"But Deputy, I thought since you let her use the phone ..."

Deputy Waverly had her head cocked as if reading, but I knew she was watching me over the top of her book, waiting to see what decision I made.

"No, no computer checks right now, lock down."

"But Deputy, I need to know what time I get out so I can ..."

"You need to get your butt back in your bunk," I glared at her.

"But Deputy, I ..."

"One!" I whispered with force. The inmate looked unsure about what to do. I continued counting.

"Two!" I said louder, now holding up two fingers. The inmate turned and scurried away from the deputy station, hopped on her bunk, and threw the covers over herself. I caught the smirk on Waverly's face.

"Did you just *count* to an inmate?" Waverly asked as she stood up and made her way toward the deputy bathroom, popping off her keepers as she did so. "I can't believe you just counted to an inmate. Now I've seen everything," she muttered, shaking her head and chuckling as she entered and quietly shut the restroom door.

At three-fifteen a.m., Deputy Neale and her FTO arrived to relieve us for lunch. I gave her the pass down, and then Waverly and I stepped outside, into the cool night air. I looked up at the stars, which were beautiful through the concertina wire, coiled in circles around the top of the chain-link fences. The wire sparkled in the moonlight, and it was actually pretty.

Once in Staff Dining, I sat at a table alone, and Waverly sat at the deputy table alone. She called to me to come over.

"Hey, Trainee, come over here," she said. "They won't give you shit if you sit at the deputy table. We don't do that on graveyard. Besides, you look pathetic over there by yourself."

I grabbed my lunch and moved to sit in the seat across from Waverly. Within moments, we were joined by three male deputies, one of whom shot out a loud fart as he sat down just a few seats away from me. I couldn't believe he had just acted so casually in front of someone he didn't even know—much less at the dinner table.

"Good one," praised his buddy in a calm voice, as if this occurred during every meal.

"Nice!" said the other.

Relieved that these men weren't sitting directly next to me, and a bit stunned by their behavior, I reminded myself that this was graveyard, a whole new team and a whole new set of rules.

A few minutes went by in silence. I'd finished my sandwich and was working on a yogurt when a sergeant came over to sit with us. He was carrying a basket from Staff Dining that held a breakfast burrito, one of my favorites. Sergeant Dickens, which I read off his name plate, sat next to me and was very friendly.

"How are you doing?" he asked.

"Okay, Sir, just my first night on graveyard, so I'm kinda tired," I confided.

"You'll get used to it," he went on. "We all do. So, you in Five tonight?"

"Yes, Sir."

"Waverly, you teachin' her to keep an eye in the bathrooms?" the sergeant asked my trainer.

"Of course, Sir," Waverly answered. "We haven't had much of that lately, anyway."

"Still," the sergeant went on, "We don't want them going 'gay for the stay.'"

"Gay for the stay?" I repeated, not sure I had heard correctly.

"Yup, really common in the female units, and we've found some ladies fooling around in the showers of House Five in the past. Gotta keep a good eye on the bathrooms," he said.

"Hey, FNG, don't look so shocked," one of the male deputies joked. "We aren't talking about deputies in the bucket going gay, just the inmates."

Sergeant Dickens elbowed me in the arm and joked, "It doesn't make ya bad, everyone's gotta have a hobby! Besides, doubles your chances on Friday nights!" Everyone at the table laughed out loud. It was obvious this was one of the favorite sergeants, and I could see why. He was tall and thin, with a thick head of curly hair, a huge smile, and a great sense of humor.

"Hey, Sarge, whatcha eatin?" asked the farter.

"Why, I am enjoying a lovely breakfast burrito," said Sarge, sarcastically.

"That'll pack a turd," the farter said, and his buddies laughed.

"Not in front of the young 'uns!" said Sarge, again poking me with his elbow as he smiled. It sure felt good to laugh at work for a few moments, and to feel accepted.

Sarge finished his burrito quickly; the rest of us finished our meals, too. We sat discussing our families. The farter was selling cookie dough for his daughter's school, and his buddies were planning their purchases. One of the guys asked Waverly if she wanted to have a fifth child with him, to which she jokingly replied, "Sure, but you need to talk about it with my husband first."

"You're no fun," he mock pouted and sat grinning mysteriously, and I wondered if fatigue or lack of sleep played a part in my thinking that these people were so hilarious.

The hour had passed; it was time to get back to our stations. Sarge stood up and addressed us.

"Well, you guys have a good night. I'll be walking around, so use the radio if you need me. I'll come out to Five and visit you ladies later."

"Okay, Sarge," said Waverly, smiling and pretending to salute him.

"And you ladies," Sarge spoke to the men, "you ladies know what I always say."

"I may be ugly, but I tuck it in my sock!" replied a raucous chorus of male deputies.

"That's right!" Sarge replied. "Carry on." And with that, he disappeared through the doors to the stairwell, back to his office located deep down, inside the bucket.

As we returned to Housing Unit Five, an inmate was having a bad dream, which could be heard loudly and clearly in the huge, echoing, tent-like building. It was about four-thirty, and out of nowhere a woman, Deitch, had begun yelling as if she were being beaten as she slept.

"NO! No, leave me alooo …" she yelled. I quickly moved to her bedside to be sure nothing was happening. Deitch was asleep, and her head was turned at just the right angle to highlight the gun tattoo on her neck. It resembled a Glock, I thought. It definitely wasn't a Sig Sauer. I touched her shoulder and shook her gently, hoping to wake her. She startled awake and had tears in her eyes.

"It's okay, you were dreaming." I whispered. "Just dreaming, it's okay."

"Oh, sorry," she looked at me with an expression of fear, as if she thought she was in trouble as I knelt by her bed.

"You okay?" I asked.

"Yeah. Well, no, not really. Am I in trouble?" she asked.

"Of course not, you were dreaming," I whispered. "How can you get in trouble for something you have no control over?"

"You'd be surprised," said her top bunkie, who was hanging her head over the edge of her bed to see what was up.

"Really?" I asked.

"Yeah, it happens, with some of the other deputies," the bunkie added.

"Well, get back to sleep, ladies," I said, standing and heading back to the deputy station, where Waverly gave me an earful.

"You should always glove up before touching an inmate! *Never* kneel beside the bed! What kind of officer safety tactic was that? Not very smart. That could have been an ambush where they planned to hit you over the head when you got to that bed. You just never know. I'll have to ding you for those on your progress report." *Dammit!* I scolded myself. *I always forget they aren't just people!* It always felt so natural for me to show kindness to people in this way, and I didn't like thinking the worst of people. But, in here, I needed to make it a habit.

AT FIVE O' CLOCK, the breakfast cart arrived carrying oatmeal mounds that had been plopped onto dingy gray trays.

"Ladies! Breakfast cart is here!" I called to the sleeping women as I flipped on the overhead lights. "Wake up and get moving, you'll be eating in a few minutes."

Four workers got up and slowly made their way toward the cart. There was coffee in a large plastic container with a dispenser so that each inmate could help herself. Another container filled with poorly stirred powdered milk was placed next to the coffee. The workers maneuvered the cart with learned precision to the location best suited for the inmates to walk up and be served. With a thumbs up, the workers signaled to me that they were ready.

"Ladies, it's breakfast time. If you want breakfast, line up at the foot of your bunk," I bellowed, piercing the quiet of the morning. After a few minutes, all the inmates had positioned themselves in line. I waved my arm like twirling a lasso to begin.

As women approached the workers, they were each handed a tray and then turned toward the coffee, which smelled wonderful. I took a deep breath in the hope of perhaps reaping the benefits of caffeine via scent. I watched as each filled her small plastic camp-style cup with coffee and, occasionally, milk, then took a seat at one of the tables in the center of the room. The room was filled with the sounds of slurping and scraping; no one was to leave her seat until I said it was time to do so. The women were quiet, respectful even.

"All right, ladies, bring back your trays," I called when breakfast was over. In an orderly fashion, they walked to the cart, returned and stacked their trays, and went back to bed, and within a few short hours, my shift ended.

On the drive home, I thought about my night. Waverly had given me some tips, and aside from her irritation over my moment of weakness, kneeling by Deitch's bed, she was satisfied overall with my performance. That coupled with the deputies being friendlier to me made me less worried about working graveyard. After another uneventful night in House Five, I felt confident that I could pass General Housing. The next day, I would be moved once again, back with Paxton to a male housing unit and back on day shift.

I had trouble sleeping through that night, so I was so exhausted I couldn't think straight. But Paxton needed to see me take control of a housing unit. I had to prove that I had what it took to get out there, among a bunch of male inmates, and holler to get their attention. And on that day, I got out from behind the deputy station and screamed the f-word across the room to inmate Rodriguez, who had continually been leaving his cell not fully dressed. The word did its job. In most workplaces, such an outburst might have gotten me a write-up. Here, it meant that I had passed my training, period, all thanks to Mr. Rodriguez.

It's hard to explain the feeling of passing FTO and becoming a full-fledged deputy sheriff. It was a victory; I'd done what I'd set out to do, and now I had a new career. The bad news was that I was assigned permanently to graveyard, as I'd expected, with Tuesday and Wednesday now being my "weekend." But the good news was that I received a pay raise with my new title, a raise substantial enough that I could now support myself, and the boys, if need be.

I felt empowered, physically and mentally strong, and capable, all of which were new sensations and a little scary for me. Suddenly, I found myself drawn to checking out the flyers of homes for sale in the area during my morning runs. I thought about trading in my mini-van and flirted with the idea of going back to school. I was changing, in a way not necessarily conducive to maintaining my current life or marriage. Within me, I struggled with the dissolving "soccer mom" persona. I yearned to embrace the woman, the seedling cop, who was just breaking through the soil, ready to feel the sunlight and take in a big drink of water.

TWENTY-EIGHT

ϜϜϜϜϜϜϜϜϜ

MOST DEPUTIES HATED WORKING House Five. But after a few months on graveyard, I'd added a new title, college student—with a predicted two and half years to complete my bachelor's degree in social work—to my resume, and I found I got a lot of studying done in House Five. I volunteered often for the spot when other deputies voiced their less-than-ecstatic opinions about it, as Sergeant Dickens announced their assignments to Five during the night's briefing. This was one of those nights; the female who had been assigned didn't want it, so I raised my hand and asked to claim House Five as my own.

It was a hot and stuffy night. The inmates had been taking showers throughout the day, and the moisture remained in the air all night. Inmates were doing what inmates do on tier time—braiding each other's hair, playing cards, talking on the phones, showering, and watching television. I was seated at the boxy deputy station when I heard the dreaded words come over my radio: "Deputies to House Two, possible code zebra. Deputies to House Two, possible code zebra."

There had been an escape!

At first I thought it might have been a test, not an actual escape. It was simply too improbable. How could someone break out of House Two, a building made of reinforced cinder-block where each inmate resided in a secured cell with tiny windows reinforced with a steel bar through the center? Escape would be impossible! Besides, management had been known to test a new group of recruits just out of the academy to see how they handled a crisis. I shrugged and figured it was most likely a planned scenario.

But as I listened, I heard the K-9s called out. Then the command staff alerted their presence in House Two. The big wigs were here. This was no scenario.

My phone rang.

"House Five, Dolinsky."

"Dolinsky, we've had an escape," said Sergeant Dickens with an urgency I'd never heard before in his voice. "There's a male inmate loose inside the perimeter, and we think he may be coming to your unit. We believe his girlfriend may be there, and we don't know if he's armed. Secure Five now! Do a formal count and call me with your numbers."

"Yes, Sir!" I called and then I hung up the phone. I turned to the inmates and yelled, "Lock down!"

The inmates scurried to their bunks. My mind sputtered, trying to make sense of what he'd just said. House Two was a secured facility with block walls and steel doors. How was it possible for anyone to escape? Was I supposed to tell the inmates? What if his girlfriend really was in here and had a plan of her own? What if there were more inmates in on the plan? I scanned the room. I didn't even have cells to put them in.

One female inmate started for the bathroom without permission. In my loudest, deepest jail yell, the one I'd honed for months, I bellowed, "Get back on your bunk! We are in *lock down*! Don't make me roll you up!" She looked at me with terror and flew back to her bunk. I had gotten everyone's attention.

There was no way to securely lock the doors to House Five, at least not that I was aware of. Apparently, there was a switch at the deputy station to master-lock the doors, but nobody had told me how it worked and I had never thought to ask. Initially, it hadn't been built to house inmates; there had never been a need to lock the simple double doors that served as the entrance, very different from the blue sliders used at all the other units. I scrambled to come up with some way to secure House Five.

Pretending to secure the doors, hoping that the inmates would not know the difference, I opened them and slammed them shut as hard as I could, which rattled the walls and made for a nice dramatic effect. All eyes were on me.

I walked back to the deputy station and called Area Control, who I knew had the ability to watch House Five on a monitor. I knew it, because there was one camera posted high above the deputy station and I knew they could see me.

"Hey, Rachel," I called up as I looked right into the camera. "Would you mind keeping an eye on Five's monitor while I do a formal?"

"Sure, no prob."

If an inmate attacked me as I walked around, it would be seen.

Most security checks could be done from the desk, but a "formal" needed one-on-one contact, meaning that I was required to walk around between the bunks. If I ever needed "officer presence," it was now. I grabbed the book of movement cards off the desk, cringing at the memory of the fear I had shown when I'd been locked inside B wing of the SHU, at how the inmates had taunted me. I did not want that type of situation here. I breathed deeply and walked quickly but calmly around the outside of the collection of beds. These women had to see that I had no fear. I put on an air of serious concentration and high alert, or at least my best version of them. Still, I was scared and thought it wiser to stay out of the spaces between bunks. The fact that the women had not done anything yet was a good sign, but any weakness they perceived in me would heighten the chances of them going through with their plans, and I was busy forming a plan of my own.

My radio was crazy with traffic. The inmates could hear the helicopter hovering above and the adrenaline-filled voices of deputies speaking in codes through my radio from all around our housing unit.

"K-9 three, did the dog hit on the fence?"

"Negative, we're still tracking west of House Nine."

"Where is the Man-Tracker? Do we have our Man-Tracker on scene?"

"Ten-Four, Man-Tracker is ten-twenty-three, he's tracking up the wall and over the tunnel. Our suspect might have gone over the roof."

The inmates began stirring and growing excited, which made it clear to me it was time to say something and defuse the situation. I decided to make a general announcement that would show them I was absolutely in control, despite the fact that my heart was in my throat. I was unarmed. I looked down at my pepper spray, which was all I had to defend myself. Cold terror raced through me at the idea that an inmate who was slick enough to escape a heavily secured building could be coming to my not-so-secured building, and he might be better armed than me.

This was my moment to show them I was no weak link, no pushover. To me, this meant meeting them at their level. Standing on the floor, in front of the deputy station, I cleared my throat first, as to not have my voice crack, and loudly spoke.

"Ladies, I know you're wondering what's going on. We've had an escape from Housing Unit Two." A few cheers erupted in the corners of the room. I ignored them and pressed on. "Hold your comments, ladies. When we find him—we *always do*," I emphasized, looking meaningfully at them, "he not only will have earned himself a felony, which brings a lot of prison time, but the dogs will tear him up. They're after his ass right now, in our perimeter, which is just outside that door." I pointed to the doors that I'd pretended to lock; you could hear a pin drop.

For a little insurance, I softly added, "If you listen really carefully, you'll probably hear the bite." Aside from the helicopter noise above, there was not a sound in the room. "Anyone in here want to join him?" I looked around expectantly. There was no response, not an inch of movement.

With the women quiet and motionless, I walked through the unit authoritatively, around the bunk beds where they lay, ensuring their presence and exuding mine. My eyes dashed between bunks, on the lookout for any action. I never turned my back to the nearest inmates. I watched and listened, my nerves on end to notice any tiny clue from anyone that would tip me off as to who might have been expecting this. They looked up at me apprehensively, their expressions like those of children, uncertain. Some smiled at me; I internally congratulated myself that I didn't crack so much as a smirk.

Everyone was accounted for. I returned to the deputy station and reported to the sergeant, who told me to "remain locked down and stay alert!" He said that they had confirmed that the escapee's girlfriend was not in our custody, but in the case of anything out of the ordinary happening, "and I mean *anything*," he added, "you call out for immediate assistance on the radio."

"Yes, Sir."

I could relax a little. I exhaled. I allowed bathroom breaks for those who asked.

Investigating what I could from the computer at the deputy station, I learned very little about what was going on just outside the doors. The radio was my best source of information, and listening to the event unfold was fascinating. We had our K-9 teams hot on his trail, actively following the scent of the escapee, while deputies armed with shotguns were on the roof, tactically searching the perimeter.

Suddenly, there was a sharp cracking sound that rattled through the building, startling the inmates and sending my heart pounding through my chest. Something had hit the outside of the housing unit. To maintain my outward calm and to prevent alarming the inmates further, I rationally tried to figure out what the noise could have been. I told myself that it was only deputies banging on the wall outside, knowing full well I would be sitting inside on high alert.

Now I was faced with a predicament: If I called out on the radio that someone had just banged on the wall, I will be tagged as a "tool," a title I had fought hard not to earn with this graveyard team. If the sound had indeed been deputies, they would also get in trouble, which was another unwanted outcome. Still, I had to take some action to confirm that the noise was friend rather than foe.

I called Central Control by phone, and asked them to focus the outdoor cameras in the general area, to see whether any staff members were visible.

"Hey, Dolinsky," a voice replied. "Yeah, it appears Deputies Van Zant and Guinness were in your general vicinity just a few minutes ago. They must have banged on the wall, nothing out there now."

"Thanks, I really appreciate you checking it out," I said, and I heard Central hang up on me. I turned my attention to the inmates.

"It's all right, ladies, just deputies playing a joke on us in here," I announced.

Guiness had always been "Boomer" to me, though I would never tell him that. While I thought they were jerks most of the time, it felt good to know they were just outside ready to help if necessary.

It didn't seem long, but hours passed before our dog teams and deputies confirmed that the escapee had left the premises. He had slipped through a gate and into a waiting car driven by his girlfriend. The facility was taken off lock down and resumed normal operations sometime in the early morning hours.

About four o'clock the next morning, breakfast arrived. The inmates in House Five ate and went immediately back to sleep. It was still dark outside, and with all the commotion of the night, we were all beat. I'd opened the double doors for ventilation, the same doors I'd pretended to lock earlier that evening. They opened to the cement exercise yard, which was deemed secure by deputies after the escape was over. It was perfectly still outside, only sparkling stars above and the sounds of the city could be heard softly in the distance. As I sat at the deputy station, a tiny bird flew into the room and landed on the metal sprinkler tubing about twenty-five feet above the inmates as they lay sleeping. I could feel the slightest breeze blowing in, clearing out the stuffy post-lock-down air. The tiny brown bird twitched its head around, looking all over the room. I could just make out a yellow patch on its chest as it looked down and chirped at me.

The bird came and went through the double doors as it pleased, simply and easily. I could have sworn that little bird had done it to taunt the inmates who had no such freedom even to go to the bathroom without permission. For about an hour, the bird flew around the unit and back out the door, tweeting and mocking all of us.

As I watched the bird come and go with the breeze, it occurred to me that, technically, I was just as incarcerated as the inmates, unable to leave or use the restroom without calling for a relief deputy to take over my watch of the sleeping women.

Never had I been so energized after a full day's work. Upon arriving home, I turned on the morning news so my family could see what I had dealt with throughout the night. As Garrett and the boys prepared for their day, I lay down on the sofa, in front of the TV, and fell asleep waiting for the story to air.

TWENTY-NINE

⊓⊓⊓⊓⊓⊓⊓⊓⊓⊓

I BOUNDED DOWN THE STAIRS, secured my weapons in a locker, and waited by the big blue slider door. Central was taking their time opening the slider, and all I could think about, while I stood there waiting, was that I couldn't wait to get to my duty station.

"Come on …" I mumbled to myself as my knees twitched with anticipation. For me, freedom lived behind the slider—no stress from my crumbling marriage, no kids with their multitude of needs, no housework, no cell phones, even. Here there was nothing but me and my job. Being secured inside the white walls of jail, I felt liberated. For me, custody equaled freedom, and the irony of it began confronting me head-on.

The job wasn't the only thing influencing my feelings of liberation. Twice a week, after my shift ended in the morning, I scurried off to the local university for my classes. I was thrilled to be done with police training and on to new and different levels of learning. Today was one of those days.

Finally the slider opened. I took a deep cleansing breath and headed to the deputy station to stuff my pants pockets with gloves before entering the Sally Port. Deputy Van Zant was working Station Two and would be the brains of Intake for the night, answering phones and telling us what tasks needed to be completed. I was concerned for two reasons: He had been a real jerk to me in the past, and his sidekick, Boomer, was working House One. I speculated about how much more of a jerk Van Zant might be tonight without his best buddy by his side.

"There's an X in the Sally Port!" he yelled at me. *Geez,* I thought as I turned on my heels. *I just walked in!*

"Okay, I'm on it," I said and hurried to get the female prisoner searched. About halfway through the search, a small, elderly man was brought in by an officer I remembered as having graduated from the academy with me. The officer was handsome, muscle-bound, and of definite interest to Mannington, who had run to join us the second she had recognized him. While I worked, she flirted up a storm.

"You look great! So, how have you been?" Mannington asked him, batting her eyelashes and playing coy with the officer, while I finished searching the arrestee and began searching the man who had just been brought in for civil protective custody. He was a tiny, wrinkled, Asian fellow, in his eighties and not very coherent as he mumbled unintelligible phrases.

While Mannington and the officer continued their flirtation, I tested this man's level of intoxication. "Sir, put your lips around the tube and blow," I said as I held the breathalyzer to his lips. He blew hard and, to my surprise, the machine registered all zeros. He was stone sober.

"Oh, you are so funny, Charles!" Mannington giggled to the officer while grabbing one of the inmate's arms. She stood the old man up. "We'll take him in," she said to the object of her affections, and began walking the inmate into the facility.

"Oh, hey, wait!" I stopped her. "We can't take him, Mannington, he's not drunk." I showed her the machine in my hand, which clearly showed all zeros.

"Oh, that's okay, we'll take him for Charles," she said, winking at the officer from our academy and proceeding to walk the little man into the CPC facility, located directly next to the Sally Port. She removed his cuffs, pushed the old man into a cell, slammed the door, and wrote his name on the whiteboard on the wall. Then she wrote ".100" next to his name. I was astonished.

Sergeant Dickens was playing music on his computer across from where the nurses sat. Realizing the old man who had just been placed into a cell might have health issues, I walked to the nurse's station.

"Um," I meekly asserted myself to the nurse, "the little man in Cell Fifteen is not intoxicated." The nurse in her fifties looked questioningly at me. "I tested him, he was all zeros."

I explained what had happened, without mentioning any names, and then went back to work. The nurse immediately got up and approached the sergeant's desk.

A moment later, a loud "Mannington!" came from the sergeant, who was now standing and hollering across the room. His voice bellowed through Intake. She ran over to him, and they left the area to speak in private. Mannington never returned to Intake that night.

A few minutes later, Van Zant, seated at Station Two, received a phone call. He hung up and immediately yelled at me, "Dolinsky, get the man out of Cell Fifteen and put him in a chair so we can keep an eye on him in the lobby! Patrol deputies are on their way to take him to his hotel of choice."

"Okay," I said obediently, and began walking toward Cell Fifteen.

"Dolinsky!"

"Yeah?" I looked back, just in time to catch a huge set of keys thrown at me. "Check the other cells, too. Let's get the jeeters out of holding, and take someone with you."

Deputy Olin was nearby, so I asked her to come. Inmates only remained in holding cells until they sobered up enough to be officially booked; then they were let out to congregate in the Intake lobby until a booking clerk called them over to begin the process.

We approached Cell Two, and I peeked in to find an inmate lying on the wooden bench inside the cell.

"How ya feeling?" I asked, but got no response. I kicked the door, making a loud *bang!* There still was no response, though I could see his chest moving, which told me he was at least breathing. Then we checked Cell Three, where a short Hispanic male with a gang tattoo on his forehead was at the door waiting for us. He seemed ready to come out, so I opened the door.

"Sit in the tan chairs and watch TV," I instructed him. "Do not speak to the ladies in the lobby or it gets you thrown back in here. Do not cross the red lines on the ground or you will be back in holding. Do you understand?"

"Yes," he agreed and wandered to the tan chairs to have a seat. Then, at the last minute, he decided to lean against a wall.

"Sir, you need to have a seat," I reiterated, to which he waved his hand at me dismissively, as if he could do whatever he wanted.

"I'll stand," he said.

"I need you to have a seat," I repeated firmly. "That's a rule of the lobby."

Again he waved me off.

"Have a *fucking* seat! NOW!" I yelled across the lobby, and the little tough guy threw his butt into a tan chair as quickly as possible. *The f-word works every time.*

At last, patrol deputies arrived and the little Asian man's story ended with his release. I felt measurably better after he'd left the jail. If something had happened to him here, when he had no reason to be in custody, I would have found it hard to live with myself.

"Dolinsky! Can you fingerprint this person?" Van Zant called, and then came to hand me the print paperwork. I completed the prints on the inmate, and then Van Zant was there to give me another order.

"Dolinsky! Could you escort an inmate from House Seven to Four?"

Am I the only person working Intake? Why doesn't he pick on someone else? I thought resentfully.

"Dolinsky! Go to code!" Finally, it was break time.

"Central, Dolinsky, code seven," I called on the radio, and then wandered across the street to the convenience store to buy a dinner of coffee, a hot dog, and cheese puffs, which I carried back to Staff Dining to eat. Staff Dining was empty—a product of my lack of seniority was that I got the last break slot available. Carnie, the only person on the shift that night with less seniority than me, arrived after me.

"Hey!" I called enthusiastically to my old friend. "Have a seat! What's up with you?"

She sat down and took out her food. "Nothing," she replied, coldly.

"Nothing? Really?" I probed, unable to leave well enough alone. "How's Scotty? How's Deb doing? It's been so long since I …"

"She left me," she blurted out.

I was so stunned I almost fell off my chair. An icy cold spider of unaccountable fear crawled down my spine. "What? How … why?"

"She up and moved out. We weren't happy for a long time. I just thought it would get better, but she moved to Oregon and took Scotty with her." Carnie looked crushed as she sat staring at the table while she spoke.

"Oh, Carnie, I am so sorry! I … I can't believe it! You should have called!"

"Why? There's nothing you can do."

"Can you fight for Scotty?"

"He's her biological son, not mine," she said. "I have no rights."

"None?" I asked in disbelief.

"None," she confirmed, shaking her head.

I grappled to comprehend the meaning of all this, and for something to say. How could a couple that seemed so perfect end up like this? She had to be wrong. "There must be *something* you can ..."

"I've been in touch with a lawyer," she interrupted. "I'm screwed, unless Deb wants to allow visitation. It's all up to her, the ball is in her court. And right now, she's refusing to play."

"Oh my God! I can't believe it!" I said, sounding more outraged than her. "That is so wrong! I just can't believe it!" My heart hurt for my friend as I struggled to come up with a word, a phrase, anything that would help, but there was nothing.

"It sucks! No ... it *fucking* sucks!" she said.

"Yes, it does *fucking* suck."

All this time, I had been envious of their relationship, and in a sick way, I still was. It should have been me suffering the anguish of a break-up, not her. One day, she was a wonderful mother, and the next, she was alone, her son taken to Oregon, out of her life, just like that. I felt such pain for Carnie and worried that, one day, I might be in her shoes. I couldn't survive losing my children like that. I thought about how often the D-word had been creeping into my thoughts. *I can't split up the family, I just can't,* I thought as I still reeled from Carnie's news.

Back in Intake, Boomer had come out to visit Van Zant, which seemed to warm him up; at least for a few minutes he wasn't telling me where to go and what to do.

But before I could get too comfortable, I heard, "Dolinsky! Check the seeps! See if any are ready to leave."

"Don't you ever say please?" I snapped.

"Whoa! Did you hear that?!" he said in surprise to Boomer and then turned to me. "You don't want to start shit with me, *junior* deputy! I will chew you up and spit you out." As he and Boomer stared me down, I wanted to crawl under a chair. To avoid letting them see the red creeping into my face, I quickly made my way to the CPC unit and started the process of releasing those who were ready.

Three frequent flyers and two young college students who wore perma-nent marker moustaches were the only people in civil protective custody that were sober enough to leave. The scents of barf, morning pee, and pu-trid socks filled the room as the seeps walked by, their hair matted as if it had never been combed and their clothing filthy and disheveled. The frat boys had come in many hours before, completely trashed, with alcohol lev-els above point-three, and had slept it off. But the moustaches on their faces would prove harder to remove.

As I walked the penned men out of Intake, Boomer couldn't resist. "Hey guys? What happened to you?"

"Sorority party," said the first kid.

"I hope this stuff comes off," said the second. Both boys walked with heads hanging low as they aimed toward the door.

"Thanks for coming by, and for choosing our jail," Sergeant Dickens joked.

"Hey, everybody's gotta have a hobby," Boomer chided.

"Some people collect stamps!" added the sarge with a chuckle. It was easy to see that these two students felt horrible; we could only hope they had learned their lesson. The other seeps would probably be back tonight. Boomer headed back to House One, leaving Van Zant, Dickens, and five female deputies, me included, in Intake.

I was gearing up for my class to begin, looking over the syllabus and flipping through the book. The shift was almost over—only thirty minutes left.

"Dolinsky, come with me," Van Zant ordered. He was handling a large male shower party and needed to get them moved to housing so as not to leave work for the next shift. He needed to have someone nearby in case any inmates got "froggie." There were no other male deputies in Intake, so I waited in the wings while he quickly organized ten men in and out of the showers, all dressed and ready to walk down the halls to the door marked "HU-1."

"Pick up your shit and follow single file!" he ordered. "I'll go over the rules as we go." The inmates lined up, gray bins in their hands. I followed behind the large group as they moved like a snake through the hallways.

"Heeeey," Van Zant addressed a young white man who was acting tough as he walked the hall. "What is *your* problem, guy?"

"I got swagger," the kid, who was all of eighteen, replied toughly. "It's just what I do. It's how I walk."

"Not in my house! Unless you got one leg shorter than the other, you got no reason to be swaggering through the halls. Got it?" Van Zant told him forcefully.

"I just can't help it, I ..." His words were interrupted by a crash. Deputy Van Zant had the kid up against the wall in the blink of an eye, one hand holding the kid's collar, lifting him up so that the kid's toes barely touched the ground. His gray bin filled with necessities—cup, toothpaste, toothbrush, comb, and bed linens—fell and the items were strewn all over the floor.

"Face the wall!" I yelled to back him up, and the other nine gawking inmates quickly turned to the wall, their noses barely touching the painted cement block.

Van Zant was speaking softly but so quickly that I only caught a few words and the last sentence. "You wanna act tough? In my house, you follow my rules. Got it? You act like a punk-ass bitch, I'll treat you like one." With that, he released the kid's collar. The inmate's feet hit the floor running.

"Yes, Sir," said the kid, reclaiming his issued items from the floor and lining up quickly to face the wall with the other nine inmates. His swagger noticeably disappeared as the inmate parade continued to move down the hallway toward its temporary home, escorted by Van Zant, who, if I wasn't mistaken, seemed to have a bit more swagger to his own step. I was thoroughly impressed at his ability to squash attitude and take control, and wished I had some of that boldness flowing through my own veins.

A few weeks later, I was called up to the Office of Internal Affairs. Too new to be nervous, I arrived early without a representative, which I learned later had not been a good idea on my part. The sergeant in charge brought me into an office and explained the investigative process, swore me in, then conducted an interview with me about the elderly Asian man who had not been drunk, and Mannington's involvement in his arrival in the CPC unit. I answered all the questions truthfully, though I felt like a snitch. Any guilt I had evaporated, though, when they showed me the video of Intake that night, in which I could be seen administering the breath test and showing the results to Mannington. It was easy to tell what was taking place when I could be seen shaking my head in protest as Mannington walked the old man into the facility. I don't know what she had said during her interview, but a few days later, Mannington was fired.

Thirty

IT WAS AUTUMN, my favorite time of year, and this one had begun on a high note. While sticking to our strict budget, I had managed to just about completely replenish the boys' savings accounts, which had been emptied on Garrett's gambling spree, and had saved a good amount of money for myself, too. I felt strong and a whole lot less dependent. And while Garrett seemed to have curbed his gambling, his drinking remained an issue, as did his lack of interest in receiving help. I decided that it was up to me to get him some help, so I made plans to attend an Al-Anon meeting on a Friday, right after work. I hoped that someone there could share an idea or piece of advice about what I could do to help my husband. I fervently hoped that maybe they held the key to sobriety. One thing about our marriage that I knew for sure was that I had to give it every attempt, every ounce of effort within me, to keep our family together. I felt a great sense of relief to have made the decision to do something proactive, with or without Garrett.

Gwen agreed to attend with me. I'd been wanting to get the most out of my first visit, and thought two sets of ears might be better than one. I felt so alone, so anxious. I wanted her to know what was happening in my life, but most of all, I wanted her support. As I drove to Gwen's house and then to the meeting, I was quietly, nervously praying to myself that I would come out of the meeting enlightened. If only he would stop drinking, he would be happier and I would feel close to him again. I reminded myself that this wasn't a miracle cure, but deep down, I hoped it was.

Walking into the building, we heard laughing and joking. *These people have figured something out if they can enjoy themselves like that!* I thought, cheered by the sounds. We entered and were greeted by a heavy, dark-haired woman who introduced herself as Jennie and welcomed us to the group. Jennie immediately took us to a table to sign in and get name tags.

"I don't really think we belong here," Gwen whispered to me as we landed in chairs, part of a large circle. I guessed maybe fifteen people were there, and by the looks of this very diverse group, no nationality was immune to alcoholism. Tissue boxes dotted the room. *Oh boy, this should be fun,* I thought sarcastically.

"Hi everyone," Jennie began. "I see a lot of new faces and that makes me happy. We like to tell our visitors, please come at least six times. You may get something from one visit, but things reveal themselves to you as you return. We are thrilled you came this morning … welcome." Her arms were outstretched like she was inviting a hug from each person in the room. She went on to explain the rules. Each person was invited to share their story, anonymously and confidentially, or we could just say, "I pass." The rest of us would listen, with no judgment, only support. And they began.

Just as a black gentleman began his story of his wife's drinking episode, a woman came running in the door. She was breathing heavily and hurried to the name tag table, raced over to the group, and positioned the tag on her blouse as she took a seat.

"Hey, Cheryl," said many voices in the group.

"Sorry, everyone! Child care issues," she said and then I realized … *Cheryl!* The hairdresser and wife of Garrett's friend, the woman who made me feel tiny, inadequate, and uncomfortable in my own home! That Cheryl was here, with me, at an Al-Anon meeting! I wanted to leave, run for the door before she spotted me. There was no way I would give her any ammunition to throw back in my face later. There would be no sharing for me today.

Many people told their tales, and I could relate to a few, but nobody had the same story as I did. I started to think that maybe Gwen was right; maybe we didn't belong.

After a while, we adjourned for a break and Cheryl came over to say hello. "Elizabeth?" she approached cautiously. "I thought that was you."

"Hi, Cheryl," I said reluctantly, realizing there was no escaping this conversation, and introduced Gwen.

"Uh, I've been meaning to call you, Beth," she began. "I feel that I owe you an apology."

I stood blinking, silent and confused.

"I wasn't very kind at your house that night you had us over for dinner. I wanted to impress you and Garrett, since Jeff always talked so highly of his buddy. I was nervous and I'm afraid … well, I acted like a snob. I am truly sorry."

I didn't know what to say, so I stood looking at her, wondering if this was a joke.

"I don't know how you've been, but my world has fallen apart since Jeff came home from Iraq. He drinks constantly when he's home, which is less and less since the baby arrived. I even caught him gambling and spending a bunch of our savings."

"Really?!" I said, actually relieved by this terrible news. "They must go to the casino together, because Garrett gambled *all* of our savings!"

"Really?"

"Yes! Really!"

We looked at each other, stunned, and then we both started to laugh. To finally know someone who understood exactly what my life was like gave me an overwhelming rush of relief and comfort. I thought about how difficult the year and a half had been, and wished I had swallowed my pride and called Cheryl months ago.

Gwen, seeing we had things to discuss, got up and began mingling. She was good that way. I remained deep in conversation with Cheryl, who told me her story, which was so much like mine it was scary. She said the group had helped her to accept that it wasn't her fault, that she couldn't change Jeff's behavior.

"You mean these folks haven't … well, *fixed* their loved ones?" I asked.

"Oh, God no." she said quickly.

"How can they be so happy?" I wondered.

"I'm still trying to figure that part out. But I do know it's about learning to let go of what you can't control." She pointed to our leader. "Jennie left her husband recently."

"I really don't want to do that," I snapped, a little too quickly.

"Me neither, but it may be an option if it means keeping my child safe."

ON THE WAY HOME, Gwen gave me her impression of the events of the evening.

"I don't know why you didn't tell me things were so bad since Garrett got home.

Maybe I could have helped?" she said, trying to be supportive.

"I guess I didn't think you would understand," I said honestly. "Your husband would never act the way mine has. I wasn't sure how to tell you."

"You should've just said *something* to me."

"Gwen, it's easier said than done! I didn't mean to leave you out, but it was hard, you know? I kept thinking he would snap out of it, but he hasn't. I feel like a jerk." At this point, my eyes teared up and my voice cracked. "He was fighting for our country, for our *freedoms* … he didn't ask for this! I … I'm afraid of what's happening to my family, but I just can't keep going on this way!" Tears hit my blouse. "We don't even *talk* anymore. We just argue!"

"Well, I think I know what you need," said Gwen, and I sat up to listen. "A boob job." *Typical Gwen!*

"Oh, sure! That's just what I need, a rack like yours!" I said as I grabbed a tissue out of my console and blew my nose.

"You don't have to be rude about it!"

"Sorry, but I doubt bigger boobs are the answer."

"Seriously, Sis, after I got my boobs, the Professor couldn't get enough of me! He loves them! Besides, you're always doing for everyone else. It's time you do something for yourself."

"Thanks for the suggestion," I said, dismissing the idea. "I don't think it would work for me."

"Think about it," she said, smiling as she shut my van door and walked up the beautiful walkway to her massive home. I had to hand it to her, she and the Professor had a good thing; maybe she was on to something. I'd think about it.

Three days later, I was starting a new work week and I needed to take a nap during the day to be ready and at my duty station by eleven that night. I was folding towels in our bedroom to get them off the bed before I hit the sack when Garrett came in and flopped on the bed, turning on the TV.

"Why did you turn on the TV?" I asked.

"Why not?" he asked distractedly as he switched channels.

"I was about to go to bed."

"I forgot, everything is about you," he chided.

"Not now, I gotta go to work. Do we always have to start an argument right before I sleep?" I asked.

"Just because you work graveyard doesn't mean it has to change all of our lives. Sorry if I ruined your day!" he snapped as he clicked off the TV, got up, and left our bedroom.

"You didn't. Nice try, though," I said under my breath, picking up the empty laundry basket to put it away.

My husband was right in many ways. I had changed remarkably over the last eighteen months, in some ways I couldn't believe myself. There was no going back. I would never again be a stay-at-home mom, and our traditional ideals concerning what married life should be had been shattered. The word "divorce" had always, in my mind, been as distasteful to me as the f-word, yet, sadly, both were becoming familiar and useful terms for me. And there was one other thing concerning me of late: the opportunities at work, by which I mean the attention of other men.

Walking out of the jail with a large group of deputies, I'd overheard a male deputy whom I didn't know say to his buddy, "Hey, did you catch Dolinsky in those jeans? Nice!" *Wow!* I beamed to myself. *Someone just noticed my behind!* I smiled all the way to the car.

That same morning as I stood in the bathroom in my underwear brushing my teeth, Garrett passed me on his way out of the room. Holding his arms above his head, and edged out of the room by hugging the wall, as far away from me as he could get and without uttering a word, determined to avoid even an accidental brushing of skin. This had, unfortunately, become our norm. It had been a long time since my husband, or anyone, had noticed me, any part of me, and I was flattered to have my ass be worthy of comment. It was the first bit of attention I'd received in as long as I could remember.

When I got home, I wanted Garrett to know that I had been noticed, for him to realize there was a person in the world who might be interested at least in my rear end.

"Honey, I gotta tell you … this was funny … one of the deputies made a comment about my butt today."

"What? How do you know that?" he said, perking up.

"I heard him as I was leaving work, something about my jeans."

"That's really low, to talk about somebody else's wife like that."

"I know, I just thought it was kinda funny."

Later, after dinner, when the boys were in bed, Garrett brought it up again. "I'm still a little surprised some dude would make a comment about your ass today. He probably just wants to get in your pants."

"Maybe, but I'm not interested in that; it just made me feel good to get noticed."

"Yeah, I bet! Probably the guy you were with when I was gone!"

"Oh, not this again," I said, exasperated. "For God's sake, what's it going to take for you to understand? I wasn't with *any* guy when …"

"You know what?" he interrupted me, his anger escalating. "Fuck you then! Just … fuck you!" he sputtered, pointing a finger at me. Then he darted out of the room, out the door to his garage, and onto his Harley. He started it up and rode away.

I wondered where he went on those evenings, but after six Al-Anon meetings, I'd learned not to worry about things that were out of my control.

I stood staring at the spot where Garrett had been standing moments before. I remembered Gwen's advice. How often my mother had said to me over the years, "You are such a pretty girl … it's just too bad you're so flat-chested." My sister's comment still rattled around in my mind. Maybe a boob job would get my husband's attention. I looked down at myself, inspecting my body. *And while I'm at it, I might as well have a tummy tuck, too,* I thought. I looked up, astonished at myself for actually considering cosmetic surgery.

When I returned to work that Thursday night, I ran the idea of surgery through my mind, over and over. I knew that a number of female deputies working the jail had fake boobs. The ballistic vest made me feel so masculine. I thought it would be nice to feel sexy once I removed my uniform. A few curves, fake or not, might just make a difference to me and my marriage.

On my way home, I called Gwen and told her the good news.

"They are fabulous, I *love* having boobs," she said, sounding so proud. "Go to Doctor Echols, he's the best in town. You won't even believe how much you love them once you have them."

It seemed such a ridiculous waste of money, a superfluous charade to think that nobody would notice when I returned from taking vacation time and had to ask for a new vest to fit my new body. But maybe it would spark up my marriage enough to make me want to stay. I needed to do everything in my power to save this situation, and if tits were what it would take, so be it.

The fact that I had even entertained the idea of a boob job to begin with bothered me. Was I being honest with myself? Was this about my marriage, or was I craving the attentions of other men? Or did I secretly believe that nobody, including Garrett, would want me and my flat chest, in a world of young, vibrant, implant-loaded women? Whatever the case, to Doctor Echols I went for an initial consultation.

Known around town as "The Boob Doc," Dr. Echols put me right at ease during my initial consultation with him. After we had discussed the surgery and any risks and costs associated with it, he asked what bra size I wanted to have after surgery. Starting from my meager A-cup, I figured I'd be happy with a B.

"Do you want to look like a Victoria's Secret model?" he asked.

"Who doesn't?" I joked. "But a B will be just fine."

"I think you should go bigger," he said. "How about a full C? I'm not trying to convince you, but let me tell you, virtually all my patients wish they'd gone bigger after surgery. I want you to be happy with them, so you might want to go bigger now."

"I don't want to look like a freak," I said. "I don't want them to enter a room a minute before I do."

"These are going to look great, Beth! You have strong shoulders and your body will be proportionate in a full C, and I think you'll be happier with a C. But it's ultimately up to you."

"Okay," I shrugged, now decided on the surgery. "You're the expert. Let's do the full C."

After my consultation with Dr. Echols, I met Mandy and Sylvia for lunch at what had long been our favorite little Italian spot. I had called them and arranged this lunch. I missed my friends and wanted to fill them in on what was happening my life, and to hear all about theirs. We'd greeted each other with hugs, and once we'd gone around the table and gotten the updates on kids and church over with, we got down to the real girl talk, the serious business.

"I'm getting a boob job," I blurted out right after Sylvia had taken a big swig of water. I half expected her to spit it on me.

"What! Oh Honey, why? You're not the type to get fake boobs!" Sylvia said after a quick swallow. Mandy was unusually silent.

"I know," I said, shrugging putting my hands out, palms up, as if it was just as much of a surprise to me. "I feel a bit weird about it, but here's my reasoning: I work in a man's uniform forty-plus hours a week. When I take off the suit, I want to look like a woman."

"Not a good enough reason to mutilate your body," Sylvia argued. Mandy still hadn't spoken.

"Also, I haven't told you two this, and, in fact, I've never even said it out loud. But, over the past few months, I've often thought of leaving Garrett," I went on, watching their faces as I continued. "Granted, it's not what I want for my family. And I feel like I need to do everything in my power to try to keep us together. My sister says it might be the key to boosting his interest in me. You know … light a fire? Spark things up?"

My friends sat silently, clearly not sure what to say.

Finally, Mandy spoke up. "Well, since we're confessing … I had a boob job before we met."

I was dumbfounded. "Really?"

Sylvia, speechless for once, sat there with her mouth hanging open.

"Doctors often trade services so it didn't cost us anything, I've been thrilled with them ever since I got them. I'd do it again in a heartbeat. But I don't think yours will save your marriage."

"Well, mother of God! You think you know people! Then they throw this out there just like it's nothing," Sylvia joked, then turned to me. "Beth, I can't say I agree with it, but if it's what you want, as long as you're happy, I will be happy for you."

"I'll drink to that!" Mandy held up her empty wine glass, and looked around. "Where is that waiter, anyway?"

I smiled, pleased. It felt so good to reconnect with my friends. Since the baby shower, we hadn't really spoken, and I'd thought our friendship might have eroded, but maybe I was mistaken. After all, they were here now, supporting me, and I was grateful.

THE NEXT NIGHT AT WORK, I put in my vacation request to the sergeant, and a few days later, I was working House Five when the phone rang.

"House Five, Deputy Dolinsky?"

"Hey, it's Van Zant. I got your vacation request in my mailbox. You're gonna have something done, aren't you?"

"What?"

"Don't do it," he urged. "You're gonna ruin the package."

"What do you mean?"

"Every chick that starts working here gets fake tits. You are too new in your career to take two weeks off, unless, of course, you're having something done, which I know you are. I'm just sayin', don't do it. You're gonna ruin the package."

"Uh, well …" I stammered, not sure what to make of the comment, "not that it's any of your business …"

"Ha! I knew it!"

"Well, it's not *your* package to worry about!"

"Okay, you're right, I'm just sayin' … you don't need to do it."

"Uh, thanks, I think."

I hung up, and sat in shock. *Wow! Now two men have noticed me.*

The next evening on my break, I sat with a female deputy I had never met before. She and I sat quietly eating our dinners, she reading the newspaper while I attempted the crossword puzzle from the same paper, which lay strewn all over the table in Staff Dining. After about half an hour, in walked three impressive male deputies in tight black tees, pumped from their workout in the gym. They looked at us, obviously to see whether we were looking at them. It was a parade of muscles—defined, sweaty, well-worked physiques. I intentionally looked away, but I peeked, just as the last man was entering the locker room and caught his eye. He smiled and winked. *There's three.*

THIRTY-ONE

IIIIIIIIIIIIIIIII

IT WAS MY LAST NIGHT IN INTAKE before my two weeks off for surgery. After recuperating, I'd be back on dayshift. I arrived, put my sports water bottle on the counter, and turned to grab some gloves when Sergeant Dickens hurried over to me. He grabbed my water bottle, lifted his leg as a dog would at a hydrant, and squeezed the open bottle, shooting a stream of water at my fresh new uniform pants. Sarge had "peed" on me. A few weeks prior, I might have been stunned by that, but now I was ready for it.

"Oh, so sorry, must've been something I ate," he joked.

"Why, thank you!" I said, barely glancing at him, and continued to fill my pockets with the gloves provided for my shift. I handed one to the sarge.

"Here, put this on the bottle," I said. "For your and my protection."

"You never can be too careful, right, Doctor?" he said, taking the glove and sliding it over my water bottle, then putting it back on the shelf.

"Right, Doctor. I'm headed to the Sally Port stat, Sir."

"Right! Carry on!" And with that he departed through the door, making a beeline for the sergeants' office. I was left to get to work, with about a third less water in my sports bottle, one soaking wet pant leg, and a great feeling of acceptance.

A young, beautiful woman of just twenty-three years of age was brought in on the charge of Driving under the Influence Causing Death. Her story nauseated me in a way I will never forget. She had been driving her new luxury car, which had been purchased by her father, when she hit a fifty-two-year-old man as he made his way across a downtown crosswalk. The man, who was married with three children, died on scene.

"How long do I have to be here, anyway?" the woman asked. Adorned with fake nails, fake eyelashes, and hair extensions that gave her gorgeous blonde locks that streamed down her back, she clearly had been afforded every luxury in life. I was alone in the Sally Port at the moment, and the only female working in Intake that night, so I was in charge of dealing with her.

"It depends on whether you get out on your own recognizance or you get bailed out," I told her.

"Last time I was here, it only took a few hours," she said as I began my search, checking her waistband and taking off her gaudy, rhinestone-encrusted belt.

"Last time?" I stopped my check for a second to ask. "So, you've been here before?"

"Yeah, this is my third DUI," she said proudly. "I beat the other two. My dad's an attorney."

As I stared at the blue mat, stone-faced, anger welled up inside me. Her crime was of no more importance than a game; it was something to "beat."

"Well, again, there's no way to know how long you'll be here," I reiterated, holding my tongue. "This time, your charges are more serious."

She rolled her eyes at my words.

"Stay here, I'll be right back," I said and hurried into the report-writing room next to the Sally Port, where her arresting officer sat typing. I stuck my head in the door.

"Hey, does she know what happened?" I asked him.

"Oh, yeah, she's under the impression that daddy can buy her out of this. She killed someone else's dad tonight and has no remorse whatsoever," he said.

"Wow," I said, digesting this information. "That's just ... horrible."

"She was only a point one-o-nine blood alcohol level on scene—real peach."

I returned to the inmate and began to take off her jewelry.

"You'd better take good care of my jewelry! It's expensive!" she demanded.

"Oh, so we'd better, huh?" I said to her, dismissing the internal voice that told me not to let her get to me. "What are *you* going to do about it?"

"Like I said, my dad's an *attorney*," she said pointedly. "I will sue the shit out of this place if you don't take good care of my things."

I'd had about enough of her little twenty-something entitled attitude.

"Look, you're not in any position to make demands. We treat everyone's property the same." I said as I abruptly sat her in the chair and slung her cuffed hands around the back of the chair.

"Look, Bitch, you've been warned," she said petulantly.

"Watch your mouth," I said, "and you *will* call me 'Deputy.'"

"I'll call you anything I want, and don't be thinking of taking any of my jewelry!"

"Hate to break it to you, Princess, but no deputy is going to risk a job to take a piece of your jewelry." After removing her earrings and necklace, I knelt behind the chair, twisting her rings around her fingers as if to unscrew them.

"Ouch! That fucking hurts! Some of those rings don't come off!"

"They'll come off," I said.

"Oh, no they won't!" she snapped and pulled away from me.

I took a moment, stood, retrieved some lotion from a nearby shelf, and returned.

"Oh, yes they will!" I said softly. "Nobody goes into a holding cell with rings on."

"Holding! You're not putting me in a cell! Why can't I sit out and watch TV like the others?" she whined.

"Because of the nature of your crime, you have to be placed into a holding cell. It's our policy," I explained, trying to be patient though hating her more with each passing minute.

"Well, I don't think I should have to go into a holding cell like some *lowlife*."

"Oh, well, you'll get over it," I said. I had peeled off her rings, and was standing her up by the cuffs. I walked her toward the gray mat on the wall to get her mug shot. She smiled as if it mattered. Though she was physically lovely, I now thought she was one of the ugliest people I'd ever met.

After I escorted her to the cell, she stood in the doorway, where I uncuffed her wrists. Sergeant Dickens stood by. Then she stepped into the cold, cement room and immediately turned and asked, "Can I have a ..." to which I slammed the door in her face.

"God*dammit*! My dad will have your badge! You fucking bitch!" could be heard from the cell as we walked away. *Please God,* I prayed, *don't let my children turn out like that.*

WE HAD NEW BRASS. Sergeant Loewe had been moved to our shift and, as the junior sergeant, and he had something to prove. He assigned me to work Station Two. I'd worked the desk a few times with no problem, so on this shift, as I had done for many months, at two a.m., I again headed out to House Five to break Deputy Neale for lunch. Waverly covered Station Two while I did that week's homework—reading about the life of Cicero for an hour until Neale returned from lunch. That's when I hurriedly went to lunch myself, excitedly bounding up the stairs to Staff Dining to order my newest favorite, chicken tenders dipped in barbecue sauce. That's when the radio blared, "Deputy Dolinsky, Sergeant Loewe." He sounded angry.

"Go for Dolinsky," I said into my mic.

"Your twenty for twenty-five." He wanted to meet with me.

"Staff Dining, Sir."

"Ten-four."

Moments later, Loewe burst through the door. His eyes fixed on me and didn't blink until he stood across the table from me, his bald head shining from the fluorescent lights.

"What were you doing earlier in House Five?" he demanded.

"I relieved Neale for lunch."

"You had no authority to relieve House Five. You abandoned your post!"

"Sir, I ... uh, I've been the relief for Five every night for the past few months."

"I will be writing you up for this, Dolinsky. It's unacceptable behavior, absolutely unacceptable."

"But, Sir, the other sergeants have never even warned me that there could be a ..."

"I'm NOT the other sergeants!" he yelled. And with that, he turned and stormed back downstairs to his office. Disturbed and worried, I looked around the room. A few nurses eating nearby quickly looked away.

Back at Station Two, I mentioned the write-up to the other Intake deputies.

"That guy's a fuckin' dick," said Van Zant. "He wrote me up once for saying 'fuck,' the fuckin' tool."

"Yeah, he's on a big time mother-fuckin' power trip," added Boomer. "You know why, right?"

"Why?" I asked. Boomer wiggled his pinky finger at me.

"What does that mean?" I asked.

"Means he's hung like a field mouse," said Van Zant as he sat reclining in the chair, arms behind his head, his legs spread enough to rest one boot on his other knee. His crotch faced me, and my eyes rested on the substantial bulge in his pants as he spoke. *I wonder if that's all him or if he stuffs something in there to make him look bigger,* I ruminated, forgetting myself for a second until the realization hit me that I'd just been looking at a coworker's dick. What was *wrong* with me? Had I lost my mind completely? I desperately hoped no one had noticed.

"He's gotta get his frustrations out somehow," added Boomer, and the two men left for the Sally Port. My cheeks were still pink.

Waverly was listening nearby and looked up the reason for my write-up in the General Orders in the computer. "I wouldn't sign the write-up," she offered. "It says here, Station Two is not a post, it's an assignment. There's a difference. Don't sign anything that suggests you abandoned *anything*. I'm just sayin'."

"Deputy Dolinsky, Sergeant Loewe," his voice blared over the radio.

"Go ahead," I said, my stomach in knots. I was still freaked out by my recent lurid thoughts.

"Twenty-five, my office."

"And there he is," Waverly said. "Good luck."

"Ugh," I said, bracing myself. "Thanks a lot for your help." As I stood to go meet with the sergeant, she slid into the seat at Station Two to cover it.

I moved through the halls nervously, not exactly sure what I should do.

"Come on in," I heard Loewe yell, so I opened the door.

"Sir," I walked toward his desk, noticing photos of kids smiling from frames on a bookshelf nearby. He didn't look at me as he spoke.

"Read this," he said, handing me a form. "It's unfortunate I need to do this, but hopefully you learned something."

"Sir, may I just say ... I don't understand how something I've done for months, with the blessing of the other sergeants, would suddenly warrant a write-up?" Loewe shrugged and simply handed me a pen.

I read the words on the paper, which made no mention of "abandoning a post"—only that I had "relieved House Five without approval." *Whatever.*

I felt wounded as I signed the paper, then turned to leave. I was angry and afraid, and I couldn't get away from him fast enough.

The rest of the night, the fact that I had received a write-up hung over me like a bad smell; I couldn't shake it and it dragged me down.

It was time to leave for home and I was trudging through the hallway, headed toward the blue slider to retrieve my weapon from the gun locker. Deputy Franko was coming into the facility to start his shift. He had been my toughest former trainer and I still got nervous just seeing him there, walking toward me in the hallway.

"Wassup, Penis," he said in his low, growly voice. I looked around. Nobody else was in the vicinity. The hallway was empty with the exception of me.

"Me?" I asked.

"No, the *other* Penis," Franko joked and disappeared through the slider into Intake.

I stood there overjoyed when the realization hit me: I was "Penis"! A tickle went through me. "Penis," the name he called any one of the guys! If Franko, of all people, considered me worthy of the title, then I'd finally arrived! The biggest asshole deputy at the jail had just made my day.

When I arrived home that morning, the boys were fighting, Garrett was locked in the bathroom, and Magnum was barking. I walked into chaos and had brought no patience home with me.

"Jake took my socks, Mom! He can't wear my socks! I don't use *his* socks!" Colton whined the second I entered the kitchen. I opened the fridge, poured a glass of milk, and took a swig, pretending I hadn't heard him.

"I'm out of socks, Mom, he has five pairs! It won't kill him if I ..." Jake whined in return.

I just couldn't take one more complaint. Not one more issue, not at that moment.

"Lock down!" I yelled at the top of my lungs. The boys froze, with no idea what this meant.

"Lock down! *NOW*, Goddammit!"

Mom had clearly lost her mind. But by now it was clear what they should do. Startled, the two ran at full speed to their room and slammed the door.

I curled into a ball on the sofa and enjoyed my milk in peace.

Thirty-Two

INALLY, IT WAS SURGERY DAY, and boy, was I nervous. I had a lot riding on this procedure, but I knew what I was doing. Garrett seemed supportive. Though he didn't go to the pre-op meetings, he drove me to the surgery center that morning and waited with me for a little while. He was heading to work, so Gwen would meet me there and take me home. Dad was watching the boys for a couple of days, so everything was set. Once I was dressed in a gown and hooked up to the IV and a number of other gadgets, Dr. Echols came in to see me.

"You can give her a kiss now," he said to Garrett, who was hanging around until he had to leave. "She'll see you in a couple of hours." Garrett bent down and gave me an awkward peck on the forehead, and then they wheeled me away down the hall.

The next thing I remember is that everything was very fuzzy, and when I tried to sit up, the nurse wouldn't let me.

"No, dear, you need to lie down, don't want you sitting up quite yet."

"Buuu, I waaannnnaaa siiiii up," I slurred, still heavily under the influence of anesthesia.

My chest felt engorged, much like it had when I was a breastfeeding mother and had missed a few feedings—it was almost unbearable. My abdomen was wrapped in a huge Ace bandage, and my gut felt just like it had after the boys' c-section—sore, but it was pain I knew how to handle.

And then, in what felt like amazingy rapidity, I was in a wheelchair, then in the car, and then home, only a couple of hours post-surgery.

"Here, let me help you," Gwen said, holding my arm as I gingerly stepped out of the car. I was leaning on her as walked into the house, and, I realized, leaning on her in more ways than this lately.

"Can I get you a drink? Another pillow? Anything?" she asked once I was tucked into bed.

"No, thanks, I'm okay."

"I'm still pissed off at Garrett for not taking this week off to be with you," she said.

"I'm not. He would just drink too much or drive away on his motor- cycle. Believe me, it's for the best. Thanks for everything," I told her, and meant it. And before long, I was asleep.

Gwen stayed with me that night, and the next day Garrett came home unexpectedly.

"Hey, Babe," he said in a caring tone, one I hadn't heard in his voice for a couple of years. "The boss thought I should be home with you, so he gave me a few days off."

"Thanks, Babe, that's nice of him." I was curled up in bed, actually wish- ing that he was still at work and that Gwen was still with me.

That evening, he came into the bedroom and climbed onto the bed with me. As we spooned, I could smell beer on his breath—the last thing I need- ed. I couldn't trust my own husband to stay sober when I needed him the most. The next morning, I called Gwen and asked her if I could stay with her for a few days while I was still recuperating. This time, for a change, I would be the one leaving.

I lied and told Garrett I was going to Gwen's for the day, but planned to stay at least until I felt strong enough to do some things on my own. I needed people around me that I could trust to be sober. When she arrived, I made my way to the car as quickly as I could, and we were gone. My heart hurt along with my breasts and abdomen as we drove away. I told myself it was the pain medications making me emotional. What was most important was that I healed in a safe environment, which meant away from Garrett. I called him that evening and told him I'd be staying at Gwen's for a few days, which pissed him off. I didn't care.

Honestly, I was glad to be away from my job for a while, too. The crazy stress, constant state of alertness, and playful flirting had clouded my thoughts. Without all that, I could really focus on my home life. As I worked to get physically stronger each day, I second-guessed myself. Why had I gone through with this surgery? What had I been thinking?

Gwen drove me to the doctor for my follow-up exam a few days after the surgery, and my "unveiling" a few days later. We both went back to the examination room and waited until Dr. Echols came in.

"Hi there! How's it going?" Echols said as he entered the room.

"Not bad, little sore still," I said.

"Let's take these bandages off, shall we?" he said as, with the help of his nurse, he unwrapped my middle and held a mirror up for me so that I could see what I looked like. To me, my chest looked stuffed, like a turkey. Echols stood back away with his arms folded, an artist checking out his own masterpiece.

"Yeah, these are nice," he said, holding his hands cupped in the air, as if underneath holding up my breasts. "These are going to look really natural when they settle. Very nice!"

Now I knew what the inmates felt like when we examined them: weird.

After I'd been at Gwen's for a week, it was finally time for her to drop me at home. Dad brought the boys home, and things were getting back to normal.

I'd been home for a few days, and now it was the evening before I started back to work. I expected Garrett to arrive home at any minute. We'd had no contact for a week. He'd made no phone calls to see how I was doing, had showed no interest at all for the entire time we had been separated. His lack of interest in my surgery, and in my life, could no longer be ignored. At this point, I wasn't even sure how I felt, nor how I was supposed to feel, but I knew it would come to a head soon.

I stood in the bathroom, wearing only my panties and a robe over my shoulders, examining myself in the mirror. My body looked like a face with two taught-nippled eyes, a belly button nose, and a big pink scar for a smile. Definitely not sexy. It was as if my body was laughing at me, a ridiculous, uncomfortable smiley face. *Oh God, what have I done?*

Garrett entered the bedroom. I could hear his bag thump onto the floor and the door shut. "Hey! I'm home! How's my little Emerald doing?"

"I wish you cared, but I know better," I responded flatly.

He ignored my words and stared at me as I walked out of the bathroom, closing my robe around me.

"I don't know what they look like underneath, but they look pretty perfect from here." He was trying to be light, but I wasn't biting.

"Yeah, I don't feel perfect."

"It's going to take time," he said, as if he knew. "I think you'll like them more when you get used to them."

I just stood there looking at him as he gawked at me. I felt a whole new hurt. This hurt was deep and frightening, and it was one that I didn't care to get over. It was nobody's fault, I was just done pretending, done doing what was right for the family but not me. Just … done. I picked up my pillow, grabbed a quilt, and moved to the sofa bed, permanently. Clearly, my marriage was coming to a close.

STILL SORE AND WRAPPED around the middle, I arrived at work, my first day back on day shift, in the largest clothing I could find. I was nervous that I might walk into Staff Dining and hear someone say, "I see you got some souvenirs on vacation," or "Nice rack." Or, like Van Zant, "You ruined the package." I'd been uncomfortable as an A, and I was still uncomfortable as a C, and I had no idea how my ballistic vest would fit. I would need it today, since the sarge had me scheduled to go to the hospital with a pregnant inmate who would be having her baby.

In the locker room, I opened my locker to find my lifesaving vest rolled into an odd shape and remembered two weeks before; Connor had shown me how to bend it so that it would fit post-surgery. I unfolded it and looked at the front, which looked completely flat, then looked down at my bulbous body. *Oh my.*

My abdomen was wrapped in an Ace-style bandage, which fit tightly under my uniform pants; my breasts were wrapped as well. I placed the vest over my head and attached the sides with the elastic straps. Surprisingly, it wasn't as bad as I had expected. The heaviness bothered me more than anything else, thankfully, and it still fit under my shirt.

As junior on the shift, I had been the one ordered to take the inmate, who was in labor, to the hospital, and then sit with her while she gave birth. In Staff Dining, I met with the sergeant, and she gave me keys to a van and directions to the hospital and parking. Then, as I hurried toward the door to go downstairs to collect the inmate, the sergeant said to my back, "And be careful. She's is a very high-risk inmate. She's looking at some serious time—killed her own kid."

"What?" I bellowed as I stopped dead in my tracks across the room.

"Hurry up, she's in labor, get a move on!" the sergeant ordered, and I, as carefully as I could so as not to harm myself, ran through the door and down the stairs to House Six.

The inmate was in the day room waiting, and the deputy who had been waiting with her had everything ready. I placed the belly chains under her belly tightly, due to her risk level and the fact that she could always have a plan with someone on the outs to try to escape. The inmate, Lionelle, a pretty young black woman, sure did not look like a murderer—more like a pregnant cheerleader. She smiled at me with bright eyes and perfect teeth. Who would ever have known?

I could see an inmate in Cell One watching me through the door wearing light blue, the color for protective custody, which is what we called complete segregation from the general population.

"What's her story?" I asked the day-shift deputy, nodding toward Cell One.

"Name is Melanie Barrett. Picked up for a child porn charge. They say she lured her own ten-year-old daughter to be pimped out by her boyfriend." I gasped and the deputy nodded in agreement, then went on. "Lucky for the kid, they were hooked before she hit the streets."

"That's horrendous!" I exclaimed, completely disgusted by her crime. I was glad she'd been placed into Housing Unit Six, a location I rarely worked. She didn't look like what I would have expected, either, with dark hair in a short bob, thick glasses, and big, gray eyes—much more like some studious, nerdy kid at school than a criminal.

I ushered Lionelle out of the unit and to the van. We arrived at the hospital quickly and I signed her in under an alias to be sure no family members could locate us. I would be the only line of defense if she did indeed have an escape planned, and I knew it; so did she. Judging by her tattoos, she had gang affiliations, and her gang friends would probably have more fire power than I would, though I would most certainly have better aim. At least, that was what I told myself to ease my mind.

Nurses hurried us into the room where she would remain throughout her labor, and we began the arduous task of waiting for something to happen. If she was in labor, it was just starting, because she wasn't in much pain. A talkative little gal, she filled me in on all the details of this pregnancy—the baby's name, the sex, about her husband who had recently been imprisoned for the murder of their youngest child.

"You might have read about it in the paper," she said, almost proudly. I *had* read about the case in the paper—shaken baby, one of the worst child abuse cases in Reno's recent history. Through her entire commentary, Lionelle grinned from ear to ear, as if all this were normal.

A few hours went by, and finally I was summoned out of the room by a very young, handsome doctor.

"I'm not sure you know this, but the baby is not expected to live," he said.

A sick flood of relief went through me as the doctor spoke. I shook my head to indicate that no, I hadn't heard. "The baby has a genetic disorder severe enough that it's only expected to live a few minutes, up to an hour, once delivery is complete."

"Yes, Sir, what do you need from me?" I asked.

"How do you feel about her being able to hold the baby after delivery? Is there a policy against that, or could she be allowed to hold the child until it passed away?"

"Sure, I don't know of any issues with that …" I guessed, trying to determine whether that violated any rules. I could think of none.

"After all, it may considerably upset her to watch her baby die," he said, with sincere concern on his face. I asked him if he knew her charges, and he said he didn't.

"Doctor, this inmate is in custody for murder, and the victim was her own child." Now I could see his face wearing the same pained look I felt in my gut. The stunned doctor was silent.

I answered his original question. "We have no policy against it, and I wouldn't object if she wanted to hold the baby."

He thanked me and went about his work. This kind, caring attitude toward a murderer disturbed me to the core, but I reminded myself that she was innocent until proven guilty, and walked back into the hospital room.

Chained by the ankle to a metal bar on the bed, Lionelle watched television.

"That's my favorite restaurant! I love that place." she said loudly from the bed. "I have those, I love them!" she would exclaim in tandem with the commercials, remaining so strangely good-natured. Whatever they were selling, it didn't matter; she had a comment about every product, and it was usually that she loved it.

My mind hurt trying to make sense of this situation. How was it that this person got free hospital services because she was in jail? Child murderers shouldn't be allowed to have more children, should they? Could any hope come from this situation, anything at all? I wanted to vomit up answers to all these questions at the same time to relieve my sour stomach, but it was not to be. I was forced to sit with her for eight hours of mental turmoil, after which I was, at last, relieved by a night-shift deputy.

"Hey," I said, handing her the radio and preparing to do pass down. "It's been a quiet day …"

"I know everything," she interrupted me abruptly. "My sergeant filled me in. You can go." Then she shooed me out the door with the wave of her hand. *Ah, deputy rudeness at its best.*

I hurried home to my own children, whom I'd missed terribly that day. I brought home pizza, wanting to have something quick and easy for dinner. Garrett ate and went out with his band buddies. He was not yet home when I laid down on the sofa bed to sleep. In the dark, as I lay on my back staring at the ceiling, I wondered why. Why did babies have to suffer? Why did this society cater to criminals? Why would anyone lure her own daughter into prostitution? My head swam with unanswered questions, preventing me from sleeping.

The next morning, back at work, I was irritated to be assigned to House Six. The deputy who was typically assigned there during this shift was Golander, a friendly, cute, slightly heavy woman and solid deputy who challenged the administration occasionally with some of her questionable style choices, such as dying her hair odd colors or piercing her nose. When I arrived, Barrett, the PCer, was out for tier time by herself, which was a requirement; she was allowed no other human contact besides deputies.

"So what's the story on her?" I asked the night-shift deputy.

"Golander's fighting classification on her PC status. She's pissed about it."

"Why? What's it to Golander?" I asked as I counted the movement cards.

"She said a person, not yet convicted, being held in practically solitary confinement is wrong. They use it in prisons for disciplinary reasons, but not in jails. Golander thinks the PCer is losing it, being stuck in Cell One. Personally, I don't give a fuck." Then she shrugged and turned to me. "See ya." She tossed me the keys to the unit and left. I noticed a civilian in the Area Control bubble and waved at him. He ignored me. *It's going to be a long day,* I thought, sighing.

It was time for a formal ID. I called on the intercom to every cell, telling the inmates to be ready to call out their names as I walked by their doors. I tapped the screen to transfer power to the guy in the AC, then began my first of many checks to occur during the day. Keys on my belt shook, which alerted the inmates to my location as I walked up the green painted staircase on the left side of the day room. On each step, the paint was worn down and shiny silver metal peeked through. I held the movement card book in one hand and the railing in the other. As I approached each blue metal door, in my mind I practiced making a call out about some possible event that might be occurring inside, just as I had been trained to do.

As I made the rounds, I noticed the PCer watching me. She was seated at a table below, watching the flat-screen television that was attached to the top tier railing, and which I was now standing behind, having stopped on my way back to the deputy station.

"You all right down there?" I asked.

"Yeah, good as can be expected." She spoke with a slight accent that I didn't recognize.

"Good enough," I said, not interested in speaking with this person any more than was absolutely necessary.

A half hour later, I made the rounds again. The PCer was still watching the TV, and when I walked behind it, she called to me.

"Deputy?"

"What," I said curtly.

"When will you be locking me down?"

"Don't know. Why?"

"I wanted to make a phone call."

"So hurry up and make your call before I lock you down," I looked at my watch, "in ten minutes."

"So I have ten minutes to talk to my kids?"

"Well, no, now you have nine ... " With that, the PCer hopped up, ran to the nearest phone, and feverishly pushed the buttons to make her call. I chuckled to myself. And yet, as disgusted as I was by her charge, I knew I needed to get a feel for this inmate, just like the rest. Her health and well-being were now my responsibility, at least for the next eight hours. *Innocent until proven …*I reminded myself. *She's not had her day in court yet.*

Later, after lunch, the PCer was out during another hour of tier time and, again, during a security check, I walked near her.

"When do you go to court?" I asked, continually moving toward the stairs on the right side of the room.

"Not sure, but you might not want to talk to me," she said.

"Why is that?" I asked. "You got cooties?"

"If I do, I got them here," she replied jokingly. Then, getting up, she gathered her things off the table and started walking back to her cell. "The last deputy who worked in here, Brighton, she loaned me a book, and now she's under investigation."

"No way! Really?" I asked skeptically, reminding myself that inmates often lie. "That's awful." I faked concern, all the while reminding myself that you can catch more flies with honey.

"I feel terrible about it," PCer added, stepping just inside her cell. "Feel like it's my fault, like I got her in trouble."

"Let me know if you need anything," I offered, "besides a book."

"Ha! Very funny. And if you need me for anything, I'll be right here in Cell One," she said with a big smile, under those huge glasses, which kind of made me laugh.

"Indeed you will," I replied and she closed her door.

Later, after dinner, when tier time was occurring for the rest of the inmates, PCer watched through the door, doing her best to be a part of anything going on outside of her cell. She had been living in Cell One for an uninterrupted five months and the inmate workers acted concerned about her mental health.

"Couldn't we just talk to her, Deputy Dolinsky? Just for a minute?" begged two girls who worked to clean the unit. "She's probably losing her mind, with no contact for five whole months."

The same thing had occurred to me. "Just through the door and just for a minute," I replied. "No passing notes, ladies, just a quick conversation."

The two young girls, one in for burglary and one for possession of meth, stepped carefully toward Cell One as if stepping up to a lion exhibit at the zoo, like they were fearful something might jump out at them. The PCer bopped up to the window and was thrilled to have a visit from anyone. The girls chatted through the cell door window, which reminded me to do a little checking.

I called the sergeant to find out about the PCer's claim regarding Deputy Brighton, who had been a deputy for nearly thirty years and had worked House Six for most of it.

"Yup, that's exactly what happened," Sergeant Paulson confirmed. Brighton had borrowed a book from an inmate, read it, then loaned it to the PCer, who read it. Barrett later mentioned it innocently to another deputy, who turned Brighton in. Apparently, the veteran deputy, who was one of the few I'd met that I truly respected, had put in her resignation after the ordeal. The Office of Internal Affairs was investigating her, and she didn't need the hassle for something so minor. I couldn't blame her, but I felt sad to see her go.

The dinner cart arrived. I locked down the unit and got the six inmate workers out to serve dinner. They brought the cart through the slider, prepared the juice, and set the special diets for diabetics, vegetarians, etc. on a table for them to pick up one at a time. While the girls worked in the day room, I popped Cell One with my key. Melanie Barrett was seated at a wooden desk attached to the right side cell wall and reading a book. Not only did I need to hand her a dinner tray, but I was intrigued by her accurate knowledge of Brighton's retirement.

"So, what's your story?" I asked her, standing in the doorway to Cell One, holding in my hand a thick gray dinner tray that was heaped with something resembling chili mac.

"What do you mean?" she asked, putting down the book and getting up, pushing her thick, round glasses on her head.

"I don't think Brighton did anything wrong, but why would you feel guilty?" I prodded.

"She didn't, but I mentioned it to Deputy Connor, and next thing you know, Brighton is gone." Barrett's face showed the strain of worry as she took the tray.

"Not your fault!" I insisted. "You didn't know it was an issue, you couldn't have known they would make a big deal over it. It's not your fault." Then PCer tried to respond to me but I cut her off. "Don't get that guilt in your head—you have enough to worry about without taking on deputy issues as well." She smiled unconvincingly and looked down at her tray.

"Mmmm, chocolate pudding!" she said.

Not your fault," I repeated as I shut her door.

Protective custody inmates were required to get the same treatment as general population inmates, meaning the same amount of time out of their cells. I had to lock the unit down after dinner to let Barrett out for a while, alone, but when I opened her door she declined the offer. I stood in the doorway to Cell One and asked her why she'd pass up the free time.

"They stand at their doors and stare at me. It's hard when people are watching me and I know the people behind the doors would hurt me if they could get out."

"Yes, I know that feeling," I said, remembering how I had felt locked in B wing of the SHU.

"It's uncomfortable, they don't even know me. They don't know my story at all. And every now and then someone yells something horrible out their cell door, and I know it's directed at me. I would rather avoid that." Barrett seemed pretty introspective to me compared to other inmates. *Not surprising,* I reminded myself. *She's had five months alone to think about things.*

She added, "I just want to play Scrabble with someone."

"I'll play Scrabble with you," I said.

"You can't! I used to play with Deputy Carnie, but she was told not to do that anymore." Why was I always finding out about changes in policy from this inmate?

"What? I was recently told by a sarge, we were supposed to mingle with you guys. Nice how you know the rules better than I do!" I said, a bit aggravated.

"Well, if you find an inmate I can play Scrabble with, I would be up for it," she added.

"I'll think about it," I replied, feeling absolutely certain there was not an inmate in the facility that I would trust to be around the PCer.

THE NEXT DAY, I was again assigned to House Six.

"If you need to shower or make a phone call, now's the time," I told her first thing in the morning as I stood in her doorway.

"No thanks," she said. Then, leaving her door ajar, I headed back to the deputy station to work on an essay for school. Barrett must have reconsidered because she took a shower and was drying her hair with a towel on the way back to Cell One when I noticed her again. She was slightly taller than me, chunky, with Asian features, maybe Pacific Islander, I wasn't sure; she was definitely mixed-race, but her skin looked more like white than anything. Her thick, black hair hung to her shoulders but was tousled all over her head. She stopped and asked for a comb. I handed her one.

"If you don't mind my asking, whatcha doing?" she inquired.

"Writing an essay for my Western Traditions class," I replied. "But it doesn't sound right, and I'm just not sure why."

"Read it, I'll give you feedback," she offered.

"That would be a thrill for you, I'm sure. Doubt you want to hear about Roman society compared to American society post-World War II," I said, doubting she'd be knowledgeable enough to offer feedback of any value, anyway.

"Look, I got nothing but time," she replied.

I couldn't argue that, and figured it wouldn't hurt to let her hear it, so I agreed. I cleared my throat and attempted to stand up, but my boot was wedged in the bar at the base of the high black office chair in which I was sitting. I fell to the floor with a loud *thunk,* bouncing my arms off the desk as I went down. To the PCer, one minute I was there, the next I had disappeared behind the deputy station.

"Oh crap! Are you okay?" she asked, trying to hold back the laughter and refraining from helping me up; she would have had to cross the red line, and that could get her locked down. I pulled myself up to the desk with my arms, as if I were getting out of a swimming pool, and I was so embarrassed I felt my face glowing red. Unharmed, but in the throes of laughter, I placed myself back up in the chair. I was laughing so hard I was crying, barely making any noise and almost unable to catch my breath. The PCer was now laughing hysterically, too; her gray eyes were squeezed tightly, her nose crunched up, and her hands, which she held to her mouth to cover her laughter, revealed tattoos on both wrists—a butterfly on one, a gecko on the other.

It took a moment, but eventually I composed myself enough to read the essay, breaking up a few times as I replayed my not-so-graceful fall in my head. Barrett listened and then proceeded to give me and incredibly easy idea for improving my essay, which involved simply rearranging two paragraphs.

"It would make more sense if you put that idea second and that other one first," she said, and I could see immediately that her suggestion made all the difference.

"How did you know what to do? Did you study English or something?" I asked, amazed at how much her little suggestion had improved my paper.

"Nope, I've just read two to three books a day for the past five months— you know, a lot of the classics are on the book cart in here."

"Thanks for the help," I said, genuinely impressed. "So you've taken this time to educate yourself while you're in here?"

"You're welcome, and yes, I have made some big changes since I came here. I'm not the same person who was arrested months ago. And I'm so very grateful for this opportunity," she said, sincerely. "Jail is the best thing that could have happened to me." Then she stepped away from the desk, said, "See you tomorrow," and locked herself down for the day.

Moments later, I heard her laughing in the cell, which made me giggle. With a smile on my face, I yelled over the desk toward her door, just loud enough for her to hear, "You can stop laughing now!"

"I wish I could, but you looked so stupid …" then more laughing, "when you fell down!" she yelled back.

All I could do was snicker along with the PCer. I kept my eye on her cell window as I left the deputy station to walk around for my last security check. She was seated at her desk, with her back to the window, and her light blue smock moved up and down with her shoulders as she chuckled.

A week or so later, Sergeant Paulson informed me that Golander had been accepted to participate in a special assignment and needed a permanent replacement in House Six. I was happy to volunteer. Although at first I'd been reluctant to work here, the more I thought about it, the more I was looking forward to getting a break from the constant influx of arrestees, the searching, and the horrific smells of Intake. It was the holiday season and nearly my two-year anniversary with the sheriff's department. It was time for a break.

Each day in House Six, the slider shut behind me, locking me inside with up to seventy-two "pre-trial detainees" who were in custody for everything from trespassing to domestic violence, sexual assault, and murder, and all were innocent until proven guilty. The PCer was still housed in the unit, and each morning during her tier time, we would laugh at silly things. It was unusual for inmates to be as upbeat as she was, especially someone who was in segregation from others. She never spoke of her crime, and though I was curious, I knew not to ask. It was apparent that, under her cheerful exterior, she carried a heavy weight. To keep things light, she would joke about her "cellie" stealing her commissary.

"Deputy, would you move my cellie, please?" Barrett would ask, her gray eyes bright. "The bitch keeps stealing my stuff!" Once, she laid her extra uniform out on the top bunk to make it appear that someone was there, so she wouldn't feel so alone.

During dinner meal service, the rest of the inmates exited their cells and stood by their doors, cups in hand. A few days into my stint as the new House Six deputy, I decided to let them eat dinner at the tables in the day room, just for fun … with the exception of Barrett, of course, who ate in her cell.

Dinner consisted of beans and franks, salad, bread, and a cookie. Every night when franks were served, a woman would comment, "Look, ladies! Dinner *and* a date!" This night was no exception. Many of these women had little restraint and fewer manners. I walked around in between the tables, which were filled by the sixty-eight female inmates, each dressed in a navy-blue t-shirt and gray elastic pants, each eating her beans with a bright orange spork from a dingy gray tray. The smell of barbecued beans filled the room, and the sound of inmates slurping their juice and scraping the trays were all that could be heard.

I felt the need to build the inmates' trust for a number of reasons. Since I was the provider for everything they needed, from toilet paper and pads to food and water, they would eventually come to see me as their caregiver. If I played my cards right, they'd keep me abreast of the issues brewing in the unit. One thing was for sure: It would have to be done at their level.

"How many of you ladies are in here for prostitution?" I asked. A few hands shot up.

"Okay, ladies, I'm just curious … What do you charge for your services on the streets?"

Some snickering could be heard in the crowd. A large black woman, Jude, who was in custody for drug charges and prostitution, began.

"It depends on what services you mean, Deputy," she said, her dark skin shining.

"Okay," I said, addressing Jude, who seemed to be the expert in the room, "what's the going rate for a blow job on the streets of our fine city?"

Cackling had now erupted; I was a little unsure about how far I could safely go with this line of questioning, but my curiosity got the better of me.

"Oh! Hmm …" she pondered as she dramatically scratched her head. Then she leaned her elbow on the table, cradling her chin in her hand, and asked, "Why you askin', Deputy? You thinkin' a changin' jobs?"

I smiled and stood in the center of the room as the ladies laughed loudly. I needed to show them no fear, as I got to know the players in this housing unit, to uncover which of these inmates were the leaders.

"Well, I don't know, but I hear it pays better," I replied dryly.

"Depends if you workin' fo' crystal or cash?" Jude replied.

A tiny, white, dishwater-blonde woman named Delmar piped up, "By crystal she means a hit, not like jewelry or nothin', just dope."

"How do you know what I mean?" snapped Jude, stereotypically moving her head from side to side.

"I was just sayin', you know, clarifyin' for the deputy," replied Delmar, looking a bit intimidated. She and Jude were complete opposites physically, though both spoke with the same street-style inflection.

Sherman, who had been released and then re-arrested since I had allowed her that late-night phone call in House Five so long ago, added, "I get anywhere from one hundred to five hundred dollars for a blow job, no dope."

"Your skinny ass don't get no five-hunned dollah for no blow job!" Jude responded.

At this the room erupted in laughter, my own included. Sherman got up and glared at Jude as she walked to the dinner cart, placed her tray on top, and headed to her cell to lock down. I attempted to calm the giggles, appease Sherman, and gain control of the conversation.

"Okay, ladies, settle down!" I hollered, then added, "I just wanted to know the going rate for my own curiosity. Not many of my friends would know this information. I could be a big hit at dinner parties from now on!"

"Sho you will!" said Jude, "you'd be a bigga hit if you knowd how to perform."

As if on cue, Delmar picked an enormous banana off the table, a left-over from lunch, and quickly peeled it. Before I could say anything, the tiny blonde had the entire banana in her mouth and down her throat, to the amazement of us all. The room was silent. I stood speechless. Even Jude's mouth hung open. Delmar bit off the banana and smiled a big, fruit-filled smile. The room roared with the loudest laughter I'd heard in jail, or anywhere. Every woman in the room was giggling with amusement. White, black, Asian, Native American, and even the Hispanic women who didn't speak a word of English were laughing loudly. Sex was absolutely a universal language, which I'd never considered prior to that moment. Even Sherman and the PCer watching from their doorways doubled over in giggles. It was an impressive show.

"Wow," I managed to stammer between my own tear-inducing giggles.

"Please don't do that again! Delmar, that banana was half your size! What would have happened if you had choked on that thing?" I pleaded, still in disbelief. "Oh, yeah, I can hear the bosses now, 'Why, Deputy Dolinsky, did you know about this?'" I mimicked. "What the hell could I say? 'Why, yes, Sir, I stood there and watched her get intimate with a banana!'" The women roared. "Please, ladies, out of respect for my career, no more examples!"

After a few more moments of raucous laughter, Sherman got us back on topic. "Approximately one hundred to a hundred and fifty dollars, I would say, would be the going rate for most things," she said, returning to the table. When she sat down, she went on, "I think most of us have done it for money at times, other times for drugs. It depends."

It surprised me, just how much these ladies would admit to over a dinner tray.

"Depends on what?" I pressed.

"On a lot of things," she added vaguely.

"On whether or not you were already high?" I asked.

"Maybe, or sometimes you do it for a place to sleep," added Jude, "or for dinner … or so yo' man don't hit you." At this, two other inmates, including Delmar, nodded in agreement. Their expressions told me more than their words ever could. Many of these women had also been forced to perform sex in exchange for their safety. I didn't know what to say and hoped my face didn't show the shock I was feeling inside.

"Uh … so, um, when you do it for money, do you just go buy drugs?" I prodded.

A few voices answered, "Yup, drugs." Then Jude added, "I bought a cell phone last time."

Delmar added, "That's so she can call her dealer," after which the two women high-fived and cackled in confirmation.

Trying to steer the conversation, I said, "So I could feasibly do eight BJs in one night and rake in eight hundred bucks?"

Jude smarted. "Well, I don't know if *you* could … but *she* could," she said, pointing to Delmar.

"Indeed she could! After that exhibition, I have no doubt!" I replied. Seeing that dinner was over, I reluctantly brought things back to the matters at hand. "Ladies, bring back your trays and head to your cells."

I was standing next to Jude as she got up to return her tray. She was a good six inches taller than me and at least three of me in width, and while she had a strong personality, you could see she had a soft side. She looked down at me and smiled. "You would be surprised, Deputy Dolinsky!" she said, making a sweeping, clockwise, circular motion with her massive arm, adding, "There be a HO wide world out there!" The ladies and I hooted at the pun. Jude walked her tray back to the cart and swaggered over to her cell. Even in the academy, I had never imagined myself and a handful of hookers talking about sex over dinner.

The inmates were entertaining, but there was more to this conversation than just a laugh. These women were so tough, so hardened, with histories I could only imagine and so very different than my own. On the drive home, it dawned on me how these female inmates had done me a favor. Never had I attempted to place a street value on my sex life, but after twenty years of marriage, I estimated my level of expertise would rival a more experienced hooker. Pricing my wifely duties oddly elevated my self-esteem.

THIRTY-THREE

FIRST THING ON A CRISP NOVEMBER MORNING, I had just arrived at work and counted the cards, then the people. All were sleeping, with exception of the PCer, who was out for tier time. As I sat down at the computer to look at e-mail, Barrett stepped up to the deputy station and said, "Good morning."

"How's it going?" I replied, not taking my eyes off the computer screen.

"Could be worse," she said with a smile, which made me smile. After all, our jail was considered "hard time" by the inmates, and her solitary situation made it one of the worst places to be within the facility. How could she be so cheerful?

"Thought of anybody to play Scrabble with me yet?" she asked.

"Nope, haven't really been focused on that, to be honest." I replied, still not looking at her.

"Well, if you do, you know where I'll be," she added, sounding a bit disappointed.

The phone rang and it was the visiting desk.

"You have a visit for Cell Forty-six, Inmate Hallister. She'll be on the first video monitor."

"Can't do it right now, I have my PCer out ..." I tried to explain, but the man hung up.

On the left-side day-room wall hung two video visitor monitors, which were like television screens with telephone receivers attached. I was frustrated because I knew the PCer was, by law, entitled to tier time like any other inmate, but she would need to lock down now for visiting time. This happened with more and more frequency, and I was being pushed into a corner. I called Sergeant Paulson to see what she would have me do.

"Make it work," was her response.

Looking at the schedule for the day, with med-pass, two meals served, and visiting times in the morning and afternoon, I saw no time for Barrett to be out alone. I called her to the deputy station.

"How did Golander get your tier time in when she worked here?" I asked her, knowing the former deputy must have had the same trouble.

"She just let other people out while I was out, if she knew the particular inmates and they were the type that didn't really care about me," she said. "Most won't jeopardize their visits with friends or family to beat me up."

She had a point, so I walked over to the right side of the room and keyed an empty cell open.

"You need to jump in here if you hear the slider opening, got it?" I instructed, knowing the sarge would be making rounds, and to "make it work" I would need to get creative.

"Got it," she said and took the newspaper to the right side of the room to sit near the open cell, where she continued her tier time. I was nervous all morning, but it was clear that this was common for the inmates. Nobody gave the woman in the light-blue shirt a second look.

Med-Pass, a large cart loaded with medicines pushed by a nurse, arrived each day, morning and evening. I would have the PCer get her meds first, then lock down while the other inmates came out for theirs. Handing out medication in a custodial environment was tricky, with so many of the "patients" being drug addicts or even dealers on the outs, and that demographic didn't change once they arrived in jail. After administering the meds, the nurse and I checked inside each inmate's cup and inside her mouth to thwart any "cheeking" of meds. Next, they locked down and went back to sleep. Barrett reemerged from Cell One to resume her tier time. This dance went on every day.

During her tier time, Barrett would glue herself to the television and devour old movies. A wonderful Cary Grant film would take her away from the eventualities of her own life, or a musical with Esther Williams or Debbie Reynolds. Being an old movie buff myself, I would discuss with

Barrett the merits of musicals, our favorite singers versus dancers, and the idealization of women and relationships portrayed in those types of films. Eventually, we got creative, imagining how funny it would be if the inmates suddenly broke into song and dance in the way people did in all our favorite films.

"How about a beach scene where we haul in sand and dump it all over the day room, then each table has a unique dance sequence going on?" I suggested. "And the grand finale, surfboards come down from the ceiling, complete with go-go dancers on top!"

"Love it! Okay, I got one!" squealed Barrett. "Women from rival gangs would dance it out in the center of the day room like *West Side Story*. You know, like this," she said, adding a dance move in which she spread her arms wide and shook her hands, with the most serious look on her face, which cracked me up. "You never know, Deputy Dolinsky … maybe we're living in a musical, but we just keep missing our cues!"

"Could be!" I agreed.

After a few weeks, Barrett was reading the paper and hurriedly approached the deputy station. She stood on the red line, holding the paper in one hand, pointing to it with the other, as if I could read it from where she stood, some five feet away.

"*Gone with the Wind* is on tonight! Do you think we could do a movie night?"

"Maybe, but how does that work for you, since Cell One is so far from either television?" I asked curiously, certain she had a solution already devised.

"Cell Fourteen! You put me in Fourteen first, and I can peek out the window while everyone sits in the day room. I've done it before. Oh please, Deputy?" pled the animated inmate. She dropped the paper, letting it float to the floor. The tips of her straight black hair bounced back and forth as she excitedly bopped on her toes, hands held together as if praying in anticipation of my answer.

"Please, Deputy? I was named after a character in that movie!" She threw it in as if to sway my answer. I thought for a moment about what rule this might possible break.

"All right, let's do movie night," I agreed, and Barrett bounced high on her toes like a little kid. I continued thinking out loud. "It'll be interesting to see how the rest of the girls take to the film. Wonder if it'll hold up? This will be fun! Let's do it!" Then I added sarcastically, "By the way, I was named after a character in *Little Women* … not that your comment swayed my answer in any way."

She giggled all the way back to the television to finish watching an old black-and-white western.

That afternoon, once my lunch break was done, I explained over the intercom the details of our planned event and had the workers come out and set up a "theater." The cheap plastic chairs were lined up in front of both televisions, and I chose inmate Sherman to be "keeper of the remote" so she could mute the commercials. We only had one remote for both televisions, so she sat in the middle of the day room and blasted the thing at one TV, then the other. Only during commercials would showers, phone calls, or any noisy business occur, and once the mute was over, quiet was the rule. I escorted the PCer into her "vacation home" across the room. She had packed her gray bin with blankets, her pillow, and some commissary snacks. She entered fourteen and looked back at me, her eyes huge through her Coke-bottle lenses. With an excited grin, she began to set up her home away from home.

I popped the rest of the doors just as Tara's theme started, and wondered whether I ought to read the script ascending on the screen for this uneducated crowd. An inmate took control and read, freeing me to return to my perch near the slider in the back of the room.

About three hours into the movie, the women were engrossed, snuggled up in their blankets in the plastic chairs. I was thrilled. Sergeant Paulson entered for the daily check and saw the door to Cell One was ajar. Her eyes got big and she asked me in a parental way, "Dolinsky? Where's your PCer?"

"Oh! Light Blue? She's in Cell Fourteen, Ma'am."

As if she didn't believe me, Sarge walked into the day room to see for herself. There was the PCer, her head resting on a pillow up against the door. Her black hair was pressed against the cell window as she dreamily escaped into the trials and tribulations of Scarlett and Rhett, through a plate of steel and glass, safely locked away.

"Wow! Good job!" she said as she left the unit. Another hour after Sergeant Paulson left, Lieutenant Reed entered the unit. Sarge had to have mentioned it to him and he wanted to see for himself how this was working out. Reed was a nice fellow to work with, probably because we rarely saw him.

"Dolinsky, how's it going this afternoon?" he asked.

"Great, Sir," I said. I explained the workings of "movie night." All fifty-six ladies watching the classic film were captivated and behaving beautifully. He seemed impressed that the women had been at this for four hours already, and would sit for five before it was through. I told him it was the PCer's idea, and he agreed it was a good one before leaving the unit.

The film ended at shift change. I told the ladies to get supplies and lock down quickly while Deputy Olin counted the cards. Once the women were safely inside their cells, I popped Fourteen and the PCer came out with her bucket of stuff.

"Thanks, Barrett, for the great idea. You made me look good to the brass today," I said. She smiled, hopped into Cell One, and closed the door.

The next morning when I arrived, I called the department that handled visitations, to check on whether or not they needed the day room for visits. So far they had nothing scheduled. I set up a table near Cell Fourteen and popped the door to the empty cell, leaving it ajar. Then I spoke to an inmate named Vann, who was in for minor offenses and had worked for the school district. She was educated and I knew she had chatted with Barrett through the door during the movie the night before. Maybe she might be up for a game of Scrabble?

"Absolutely!" she exclaimed when I asked and bolted out of her room.

I popped Cell One and Barrett emerged. I explained that if either of them heard the slider open, she would have to hop into Fourteen and close the door as quickly as possible. She looked at me as if I had given her a fabulous gift, put on her glasses, and hurried over to the table to play the game with Vann.

About an hour went by before I got a call from Visiting. Game over. Barrett and Vann both headed toward their cells to lock down, as I let out the inmate who had a visit. PCer stopped at the desk to thank me and told me she would not need to do that again.

"Why is that?" I asked.

"Vann sat there and spoke of nothing but how she doesn't belong here, how she was set up, through the whole game. She hasn't owned her crimes, and I'm not interested in hanging around people like that," Barrett confided.

"Nobody's guilty in here, just ask them," I joked.

"Exactly! That's why I am glad to be in Cell One alone. I know what I did was wrong, and I wish I'd had the strength to recognize the red flags earlier. I'm a different person now and I know, I will *never, ever* be that person again."

Introspection was rare among inmates, and true change even less common.

MOST INMATES RETURNED TO JAIL over and over again, but this was Melanie Barrett's first time in custody, and over the next few months she would confide many things to me, her only confidant. Sitting in Cell One, directly next to the deputy station, she overheard many conversations and had a prime vantage point of the inmates on tier time. She knew which deputy was wearing what costume to the Halloween party, which one just got a new puppy, who was considering having an affair, and who had already succumbed to the temptation. She knew which inmates were sharing commissary or "hooking up" as couples, who were bullying, being bullied, or trying to emerge as a leader in the unit. This was invaluable to me, the only deputy among so many inmates.

"Have you spoken to your kids since your arrest?" I asked.

"Oh, yeah, they live with their grandparents, my former in-laws, back in Ohio. About a week after I was arrested, I called them, just to see if they would take my call. They did and even told me they believed in me and ... well, they knew what kind of mother I've been ..." Here she got choked up. "That meant a lot."

"Is that what your tattoos represent? Your kids?" I guessed, trying to change the subject and avoid tears.

"Oh! Yes." She showed me her wrists. "The gecko is my son, the butterfly is my daughter. How did you know?"

"I've seen a lot of tats and heard a lot of stories. Anyway, it's good they support you. That kind of support is rare in here, you know that, right?"

"Oh, yeah, I am very lucky. And their grandparents have been true to their word, allowing me to talk with my kids by phone. Even my daughter, we've been building our relationship back and she has forgiven me ..." Again, she choked up. "As a family, we are moving on."

Barrett spoke often of being grateful for being arrested. It had ended an escalating situation before any irreparable damage had occurred. In addition, she had learned much about her boyfriend through reading court documents, horrific details regarding the child pornography on his computer and things he was planning to do.

"I hate myself for allowing things to intensify," she told me, clearly grieving and beginning to put things into perspective. She often tearfully told me tales of the abuse she had endured at the hands of this man.

"I woke up once, and he was standing over me with a knife to my throat. He also threatened to kill himself in front of me. One day, he doused my cat in gasoline, held her in one hand and had a cigarette lighter in the other. I gave in. I don't even remember what he wanted me to do." Deep loathing was evident in her eyes and voice when she spoke of him. Then she added, "You ever try to clean gas off a cat?"

"No, can't say I have."

"Well, it ain't easy!" We both smiled, uncomfortably.

She told me how she wrote to her boyfriend at her attorney's request because he would absolve her in almost every return post, claiming he was sorry for implicating her.

"Look at all this!" She showed me his cards, disgust evident on her face, and I read how he claimed she was not to blame for the mess they were in.

"You know, the deputies read your mail, too, right?"

"Oh, I know, most of them think I'm evil based on what they read."

She was right. More than once, I had heard deputies commenting on her letters, how disgusting she was to write to him, never scratching the surface of the person to reveal who she was inside, never knowing why she wrote what she wrote.

There were a few deputies who never would let her out for tier time during their shifts, even though this was a blatant violation of our policy. One went so far as to tell Barrett that she "planned to make her life miserable." Then, after a few days, I would come back to work, and in the early morning hours the PCer would fill me in on what I had missed; then throughout the day, per my sergeant's direction, I would "make it work" for Barrett's tier time.

In the following weeks, we discussed what her future plans would be if she were indeed convicted. How she could capitalize on the many programs they offered in prison? How did she intend to continue her personal growth? We also watched a number of old musicals, like *Paint your Wagon* and *Annie Get your Gun*, which I forced to one side of the day room, near Cell Fourteen. Also, the makeup of the housing unit had morphed throughout these last several weeks; it now had a different feeling, because most of the women who had watched Scarlett and Rhett weeks before had been released or gone to prison. This new group preferred sex-driven reality shows on cable networks.

I began gearing my discussions with Barrett toward her plans for a new life when she got out. Her attorney was recommending probation, and he seemed to feel confident she would get it, yet she was terrified of going to court.

One morning I got the phone call.

"House Six, Dolinsky."

"I need Melanie Barrett for court in five."

"Okay," I said, pointing to the PCer, who was at the window to her cell. "Get yourself together! It's time for court!" I called.

"Oh my God!" she exclaimed, looking like she was about to cry. Soon she would know her fate, be it probation or prison, either of which had to be better than sitting in here all alone.

An Intake deputy came to House Six to escort her to the room where other officers would transport her to court. All day while she was gone, I wondered how it was going.

The other inmates had often confided in me information about their lives, their spouses, their children, even their crimes. Usually I detected no remorse, just feelings of frustration at having been caught. Recently, a woman had explained to me how she had scammed hundreds of thousands in retirement money from a local senior citizen, all of it conveyed with an attitude of entitlement—she saw it as being owed to her. Another in for burglarizing people's homes whined to me when her cellie had "borrowed" a ramen soup from her gray bin, the irony lost on her completely. And another young mother argued that it wasn't she who had put out a cigarette on her infant's skin, and then had no trouble asking me to order her some clean underwear after she'd had an "accident." It was my job to care whether a child abuser had clean underwear. "Innocent until proven guilty" was my daily refrain. I was only their babysitter, not their judge.

When Barrett came back from court, Golander went out of her way to walk "Light Blue" from Intake to the housing unit. Barrett appeared to be smiling, but as she got closer, I could see her gray eyes were red and puffy.

"Six years," Barrett said to me as she entered the housing unit. Golander nodded.

"What happened?" I asked, as apologetically as I could.

"I need to be by myself for a little while," she said, shaking her head and scurrying to Cell One to lock herself down. Golander filled me in. Apparently, the prosecution had been relentless on the grounds that Barrett had "failed to protect her daughter." The female judge had studied the case and was ready and willing to give Barrett probation, but the prosecution had changed her mind.

The next day, the boyfriend went to court and got sentenced to twenty years.

Thirty-Four

IIIIIIIIIIIIIIII

THE MORNING HAD BEEN AVERAGE in every way. It was my first day back to work after the weekend, and as I sat reading the newspaper, the inmates slept, all but the two women in Cell Twenty-Six, who were giggling and chatting and seemed to be bouncing off the walls—strangely energetic for this time of day. The monitor buzzed to indicate that an inmate wanted to come out of her cell. It had come from Cell One. I hadn't talked to my PCer since her day in court.

"What is your emergency?" I asked teasingly, watching her face peeking through her cell window from where I was standing.

"Toilet paper," she replied.

I touched the button on the monitor to pop her door and out came Barrett, her hair knotted and uncombed, her clothing wrinkled. She hurried to the cupboard behind the deputy station where I sat. I kept an eye on her while she knelt down and grabbed a roll, then shut the door and hurried back to the other side of the desk to stand on the red line.

"Good morning," she said, faking a smile.

"How are you doing today?" I asked. "I was a little worried about you over the weekend."

"Well, I had a lot of time in my cell and figured something out that I need to share with you." She smiled but seemed seriously uncomfortable, so I gave her my attention.

"What is it?" I asked.

"Nobody was in the courtroom when I got sentenced, no family or friends, and I felt very thankful for that. But the prosecuting attorney repeated over and over how I had 'failed to protect ...'" Melanie broke down for a moment, then regained her composure. "I have thought of that fact every moment of every day that I've been in here. It haunts me, and I'm trying to forgive myself." Tears rolled out of her eyes.

"You'll have time to work on that in prison," I reminded her.

"No, I know, but that's not it ..." she said, holding up a hand, palm facing me, while she stared at the floor. I wondered what could be so difficult to say. "All weekend long I thought about it, why it had hit me so hard. I know that the person the attorney spoke of, the woman I used to be ... is not who I am now." Melanie took a big breath, exhaled and swallowed.

"Just spit it out," I said.

"Okay ... um ... I had ... sex with ... well, multiple partners ... and made videotapes." She paused, took a deep breath. "Those tapes were presented in court." She wiped her eyes under her glasses.

"Okay, so your past choices helped to convict you ... is that it?"

"No, I'm not done," she emphasized, frustrated that I wasn't getting it. "I knew about a lot of the porn my boyfriend had on his computer, but I ... I didn't do anything ... I did nothing ... And there were drugs involved, we did meth ..."

"You and three quarters of this unit," I joked, interrupting her. But she was serious.

"Deputy, you've made such an impact on me. I am just so ashamed. The reason it hit me so hard was because, well, I didn't want you to know the truth about me." She took another breath and tearfully said, "I just didn't want *you* to know."

In any other situation like this, hearing such a personal confession, I would have come from around the desk and given her a hug, but this was no ordinary circumstance. I was prohibited from doing such a thing. My eyes felt misty and I looked down at the papers on the desk between us, pausing to gather my composure. Touched by her confession, I wondered how I had allowed an inmate to affect me like this! As a deputy, I could never let my guard down. But as a person, I couldn't help it. Barrett and I had spent three to four hours a day together for several months discussing life, helping each other, watching our musical world go by, yet we could never be friends. I could never communicate with her again, once she left this facility as a convicted felon.

After a few moments, I spoke up. "I didn't exactly think you were sweet and innocent when you got here, ya know." She chuckled through her emotions. I waited until she looked me in the eye and went on. "It's not just me, *remember*? Three deputies here have seen promise in you. You practically have a fan club here, Melanie," I teased, wanting to keep her focused on the positive. "Remember, your past can't be changed. It's your future that matters now."

We stood stiffly, her on the red line, me behind the deputy station, waiting silently. Finally, she asked, "Can I write to you here at the jail when I'm in prison?"

"Sure, just don't expect a response," I told her. She nodded, understanding the policy.

"Deputy, you're an amazing woman," she said, and smiled.

"Likewise, Melanie."

Suddenly, our attention turned to another matter—that of Cell Twenty-Six and the girls giggling loudly inside. "Now," I began, wondering what could possibly be so funny at seven-thirty in the morning, "tell me what you know about Cell Twenty-Six."

"There are drugs in there," she said, held up her hands as if to deny a connection, and without another word stepped back into Cell One and closed her door.

"**DRUGS IN HOUSE SIX?**" the sergeant repeated after I had informed her of what I had just discovered.

"Yes, Ma'am, that's what I hear."

"Guess it's time for a shakedown," she warned. "Turn off the water, I'll get it going."

Being the deputy assigned to the unit, I was the one who had to orchestrate a way of retrieving the drugs. I wanted to do it quietly, before the inmates woke up and got wind that we were onto them. I'd seen shakedowns done in the past, and I knew that, usually, the inmates saw it coming. Eight or nine deputies entering any housing unit wearing gloves was a dead giveaway. Another was when an inmate tried to flush the toilet and it wouldn't flush, or the sink didn't work; it told them we'd turned off the water, and they knew it was done on purpose, to keep them from flushing any contraband. The inmate who made the discovery would then usually yell "Shakedown!" to alert the entire unit.

I knew deputies were coming and would take over my unit; I wanted to get the drugs quickly before the green herd arrived. Deputy Olin entered the housing unit early, and I filled her in on my plan. "Hang out at the deputy station while I do a security check and pull the inmates out of Cell Twenty-Six casually."

"Okay," she said.

I walked around the unit and stopped at the door of Cell Twenty-Six to peer through their window.

"Ladies, why are you up so early?" I asked nonchalantly, smiling at the two young women inside.

"Deputy Dolinsky, whaaaat tiiiiime is it?" asked one of the inmates, stumbling as she stood with her face at the window, mere inches away from mine. Meth had not yet taken her looks, though obviously dyed black hair had grown to reveal an unattractive two inches of blonde roots. Her cellie was a Hispanic woman with bleached hair who giggled incessantly while lying on the top bunk and repeatedly kicking her feet up and down.

"It's only seven-thirty in the morning," I whispered. "Everyone else is asleep." They giggled some more as I opened the door with my key and summoned them to come into the day room. "Ladies, come out and hang with me, let's chat," I said.

As if they had received some special privilege, the two women excitedly hurried to my side. I directed them to a table in the day room, where they sat and looked up at me with the largest pupils I had ever seen. Bingo.

"Well, ladies, you need to know, I think you're both high as a kite," I began, "and I'm giving you an opportunity to come clean now and tell me about your drugs, before I search you and find them myself."

Neither seemed nervous about my threat. They both insisted that they had no drugs nor had used any. Deputy Olin and I took the women into separate shower stalls, where we completed unclothed searches.

"I have it!" Olin said suddenly, and I looked down to see a small baggie with clear crystals inside lying on the floor near her boot.

Because Olin had found the drugs, she would be writing the report, and I would do a supplemental. We had the women sit at separate tables and write statements in which each would tell her story; then they were escorted to the SHU.

The green herd arrived shortly thereafter and completed an entire sweep of the housing unit. The sound of inmates coughing could be heard while female deputies completed strip searches in two nearby cells. Then came the loud smack of vinyl mattresses against the wooden bunks as male deputies stripped off sheets. From my location at the deputy station, I could look in one direction and see out the window, on the other side of which stood searched inmates, shivering in the cold cement yard. If I looked in the other direction, I saw bedding, toilet paper rolls, books, and other personal items fly out the open cell doors and accumulate on the floor of the day room. Socks and underwear, half-eaten sandwiches, salt and pepper packets, and a handful of pencils came rolling out of one cell, clicking along the cement floor and nearly tripping a deputy walking through. Out of another cell were chucked three oranges, which rolled around in the day room, while sheets and blankets flew out another. And so it continued as deputies leap-frogged through fifty-six cells. Another deputy tipped over the book cart, sending paperbacks flying to land twenty feet away. Trash lay near two large, upturned garbage cans in the day room.

Once each cell had been sufficiently searched and each inmate put back into one, the unit looked as though a hurricane had gone through, leaving every table and chair upturned amid a mountain of contraband.

Notes that had been passed between inmates had been located and studied. We looked for any tidbit that might lead to information regarding a safety and security issue, such as a planned escape or drugs in the unit. Though we found no threats to security, I was enlightened about a couple of budding relationships between ladies who were trying to "hook up" in the unit, which was now under a twenty-four-hour lock down. I was assigned to stay in House Six the rest of the day. The unit was inordinately quiet, with the inmates not being allowed out of their cells and only the workers who cleaned up being allowed to move around.

Just before lunch, I needed to read the statements from the two inmates that had been involved, in order to paraphrase their claims in my report. Each woman in Cell Twenty-Six blamed the other for bringing meth into the unit; naturally, neither one claimed responsibility.

But one's description of the incident particularly struck me: "My cellie handed me a baggie of rock so I put it in my pussy."

And there it was, as if it were quite normal to store things in her vagina, just another pocket like any other. I laughed out loud. The Prison Purse I'd heard tell of in training was indeed real. I had it in writing. Of course, we'd all suspected that this was how the drugs had gotten into the facility, but I was astounded and amused, all the same.

TERRENCE CAME IN TO RELIEVE ME in House Six so that I could meet with Sergeant Paulson in her office and watch the videotapes of the day room cameras. Olin and I viewed the tapes and noticed a number of people taking things from Cell Twenty-Six during a two-hour period on the night before my shift had begun. In the black-and-white surveillance video, an arm could be seen repeatedly handing something out of the cell. The receiving inmates walked straight to their cells, only to return later to Cell Twenty-Six with "payment"—a soup, candy, or some other commissary purchase.

Two truths came to light through scanning the tapes: First, five more inmates were involved, and second, there was strong likelihood that there were still drugs in my housing unit. People do crazy things when they're high, things they would never do otherwise—desperate, violent things—and people were still getting high in House Six.

After my weekend, I returned to discover that the five women Olin and I had been able to identify had already been moved into the SHU. The remaining inmates in House Six had been locked down for twenty-four hours straight, again. Most had slept the time away, but some were going stir crazy, which you might expect from any two adults who were stuck together for twenty-four hours inside a box approximately fifteen feet by twelve feet in size.

At lunchtime, the lock down ended, so I let them go outside to the yard to eat. It was a nice day and I wanted them to feel some relief. As the women ate their lunches in the cement yard, unbeknownst to me, two dog teams and numerous deputies were lining up in the hall preparing to complete yet another search of my unit.

The ladies came in from the yard and were all standing by their doors, when suddenly the slider door behind me produced a *Crack!* In came the troops, led by Sergeant Paulson. She marched in, followed closely by two dog teams and six other gloved deputies. They ordered the inmates back out to the yard. Then, cell by cell, the dogs entered and searched. One K-9 team searched the top tier, and the other the bottom. The German shep-herds were beautiful animals and fun to watch as, noses upturned, they sniffed at the air. Sergeant Paulson ordered me to follow one team and take notes of anything the K-9 located that was suspicious.

"Don't box us in, he may bite," said the deputy dog handler. I stayed back and watched with suspense; I'd never seen anything like this before.

The dog team I followed, Deputy Metcalf and K-9 Chuck, were well known in the jail. Chuck would immediately jump on the bottom bunk in each cell and bite the pillow on the bed. The handler explained, "It's his thing, just what he does." The dog was funny about leaving his mark—claw holes in the blankets and slobber on the pillowcase—in each cell. Suddenly, from Cell Fifty, Chuck sat and barked. I volunteered to search the cell be-cause, if there were drugs in my unit, I wanted to be the deputy to find them.

The cell was clean, each bed made nicely and everything else neatly stacked in each inmate's gray bin. I tore the linens off the beds, checking the seams on the blankets, sheets, and mattresses for rips or holes sufficient for hiding drugs. Next I began searching the paperwork in the cell. One inmate had a stack about a foot high containing legal papers and letters from her kids. She had temporarily lost custody and was fighting to get them back.

The inmate, Emmett, was a beautiful, young, Native American woman with long hair that flowed down her back. Though pleasant, she was often in the thick of whatever drama was taking place in the unit. If there was trouble, she usually had some part in it, and had visited our facility seven times in her short twenty-six years of life. Still, she was a hard worker and sincerely loved her children, the faces of whom lined the cell walls, thanks to the photos she had stuck up there with toothpaste— cute, but against the rules. The children seemed to watch my every move as I transferred the stack of paper, one piece at a time, from the desk to the beat-up mattress piled high with inspected bedding. If drugs were here, I was determined not to miss them.

As I searched, I began to doubt Emmett's participation in this crime. She had letters, notes, and drawings set aside for each child. She had self-help books that had been sent to her from ministers outside the facility, a book on how to be a better parent, and another book that she was currently reading as part of earning her high school diploma; it now lay open on the wooden desk to reveal her notes written throughout. Hers was the bottom bunk, and she had used the stickers from her bananas to adhere photos of her kids to the base of the upper bunk, so that she could gaze at her babies before she fell asleep at night, and see them first thing when she awoke.

As I searched the edges of the bunks, behind the toilet, and under the sink, I remembered that Emmett spoke to her kids daily by phone. A week prior, she had asked me to call and check on her daughter and son because she had been unable to reach the foster family who was caring for them. I verified that all was well and Emmett thanked me. She never missed any of the classes offered in jail, which covered topics like Substance Abuse and Women's Empowerment. While I was well aware of her bad reputation for being in the mix, I thought that this time she seemed different, more mature, more committed to her family, and less mischievous.

I was also aware that the next day, Emmett was scheduled to have a contact visit with her children, which had been set up by the state's child welfare office. They wanted to see how the kids reacted to her and vice versa. This was a critical step in the process of reuniting the family, and Emmett was so looking forward to holding her two young children. It had been many months since she had seen them face to face. She had been charged with child neglect, due to their homelessness and a lack of resources that could help them, yet the state believed in her, and so did I.

The search ended with K-9 hits on three separate cells, all of which were searched from top to bottom, and no drugs were found. The sergeant was frustrated and called another twenty-four-hour lock down. This would mean that Emmett would miss her visit, the visit that could define her future and her children's futures. I couldn't let that happen.

After the deputies, dogs, and sergeants had left the housing unit, I was sitting at my perch when I got a buzz on the intercom. It was an emotional Emmett, who wanted to know about her pending visit. I walked up to Cell Fifty and opened the door. Her cellie was sitting on the top bunk, which was still a mess, while Emmett was making her bed underneath. She was crying and looked at me with bloodshot eyes.

"Deputy Dolinsky, what does this mean? Will I miss my visit? You *know* I can't miss my visit! For the first time in my life, I'm actually staying clean, doing what's right, working hard, *so* hard …" *sniff*, "to get my kids back, and because some person brought drugs into this unit, *I'm* being punished!"

She stopped and blew her nose on a piece of toilet paper, then went on. "I need to see my kids tomorrow, Deputy! I just *have* to see them!"

"I know, I know," I said. "You gotta trust me here, Emmett, I have a plan. I can't go against the sarge, but I can try to soften her up in the morning."

"Do you think it'll work?" she asked, still sniffing and trying to compose herself.

"No promises," I answered, "but I think if I talk to her tomorrow when all the stress of the shakedown has worn off, well … just trust me on this one. Okay?"

She nodded and I pushed the cell door shut. I felt disappointed for her, but I knew it would be considered insubordination if I went against any sergeant's order. And while some other deputies might not have cared, I'd made the decision to help her.

If any inmate showed me that she wanted to better herself, I would go to bat for her, although it rarely paid off. A few weeks prior, another female in House Six had been on my radar. A fetal alcohol syndrome baby, the inmate was academically slow and was having a tough time of trying to earn her GED. After she'd returned from class in tears a few times, I arranged for an educated inmate to tutor her during tier time to help her learn. Eventually, the tutor began going to class to assist her even further. After discussing the plan with the sergeant and feeling quite proud of my effort, I was dismayed when the sergeant's response was nothing but a heavy sigh and a dismissive, "Just guard them."

I knew that getting her to approve this visit for Emmett would take some creative thought.

The next day, I came to work early. Sergeant Paulson was seated at a table in Staff Dining, as she was every day, waiting for us to arrive to give us our assignments. She saw me and muttered, "House Six, and let's not have any issues today. All right, Dolinsky?"

"Yes, Ma'am!" I responded. "And, may I ask, exactly what time is the unit off lock down?"

"Come on, Dolinsky, you know the drill. Twenty-four hours from yesterday, when the shakedown ended," she said.

"Sarge, they had just come off a twenty-four-hour lock down when I arrived yesterday, just before the K-9 shakedown. And another last week. So I'm hoping to get them a little air this morning, if that would be all right with you?"

I knew no sergeant wanted to break a law, and though I wasn't sure exactly how many hours the inmates could legally be locked down, we had to be getting close. Paulson thought for a minute.

"Yeah, why don't you let them out this morning, that's good enough," she said. Smiling, I agreed and hurried downstairs to the housing unit to tell Emmett her visit was on. The night watch deputy was relieved to see me; it had been a long, boring night due to the lock down. As soon as she left the unit, I went to Cell Fifty to share the news. I popped open the heavy door with my key and looked into an empty cell.

Emmett was gone.

THIRTY-FIVE

I QUICKLY COUNTED THE MOVEMENT CARDS, and then walked the unit and peered into each cell through the window, figuring Emmett had been moved to a different cell and I would find her when I did my walk. No such luck. She was no longer in this unit. I checked the forms from the night before— maybe she'd been released. But her name had not been written down as a release. There was only one more thing to check, so I logged on to the computer and typed in her name to see where she was in the facility. Emmett had been moved to the Infirmary. Inmates in the Infirmary's cells were not allowed visitors.

I had some time before it was necessary to walk the unit again, so I headed to the Infirmary to talk with Emmett. I entered to find Deputy Carnie working the unit that day and reading the newspaper. I walked to the deputy station and asked to borrow her book of movement cards.

"Why?" she muttered.

"I want to talk to Emmett, so I need to know what cell she's in," I said.

"Why?" she grunted, never looking up from the paper.

"To tell her something. Is she really sick, or can she have visits today?"

A nurse walking by at that moment overheard our conversation and asked, "You looking for Emmett?" I nodded. Deputy Carnie looked relieved not to have to look up from her paper. It was coming up on two years since we had begun the academy, and she and I had grown apart. At that moment, I realized how much I missed her.

"She's in Cell Three, but she's scheduled to go back to House Six soon. She had chest pains last night, so they kept her here for evaluation. Stress-related, but nothing serious. The doctor has already released her from here," said the nurse.

I walked over to Cell Three to see Emmett peering out the window with a concerned look on her face. "Hey! Your visit is on, Sarge gave us a break," I said through the glass. Her face lit up and she grinned from ear to ear.

"How'd you do it?" Her voice was muffled by the heavy steel door between us.

"I have my ways," I said slyly. "See you when you get back to the unit." I left the Infirmary and headed back to House Six to let the inmates out for tier time, per Sergeant Paulson's instruction. They were happy to come out of their cells and promptly lined up on the red line in front of the deputy station to start the barrage of requests.

"Deputy, I need to get a rag to clean my room? Oh, I need bleach, too," asked one inmate. I motioned to the inmate to look under the sink to my right. Another inmate approached, her navy-blue tee on backwards, which was evident by the tag under her chin.

"I need toothpaste. Oh, and a pencil."

I handed her the items, and another arrived.

"Can I get pads?" Again I motioned to look under the sink.

Then another asked, "I need a kite and a comb." I handed her the inmate request form and a comb.

Not a second later, I was interrupted again. "Can you check my release date?" I checked the inmate's file in the computer, and we discussed what date she was scheduled to get out of jail and at what time.

Another inmate saw me looking in the computer, so she raced up with three of her friends to have me check whether they had release dates, too. Some ladies asked every day, as if somehow, overnight, their dates of release had magically changed. They were needy people; they would continue with the requests until I told them to go away.

"I need a deodorant," came another request. I handed it to the woman, who took it with one hand, the other busy picking at her black, meth-affected teeth.

"I'm out of toilet paper," said another inmate. I motioned to the cabinet under the sink.

"Permission to go outside?" another asked.

Their neediness consumed my morning, and about an hour later, Emmett arrived at the slider door with her bin full of linens and personal items. I called to Area Control to open the slider and ushered Emmett into the unit, motioning with my hand to her to go up to Cell Fifty again. She obliged and bounded upstairs as I popped the door from the touch screen.

The inmates were locked down at noon for my lunch break. Just before thirteen-hundred hours, as I walked in from lunch, the phone rang.

"We have a visit for a Emmett out of Cell Fifty. Send her to Area Control One," said the person working the visitor desk.

They were here! I felt excited for Emmett and clicked her cell door open, knowing full well that she would be ready and waiting. She flew down the stairs so quickly that she forgot to shut her cell door.

"Hey, woman! Shut your door!" I reminded her, and she raced back up the stairs, taking two stairs at a time. Her long, dark hair was pulled back into a braid and swished like a cat's tail across her back. She moved at hyperspeed to the deputy station. I gave her the movement card she needed to leave the unit, and she headed toward the slider, appearing really nervous. Area Control One was less than fifty yards away. I walked the hallway with her because I wanted to see how this visit went.

"My son will be mad at me," she said as we walked toward the visiting room. "I'm worried it might be tough to get him to warm up to me again."

The door popped and we entered a tiny room with little space to accommodate anything but the small table and two chairs that filled it. I stood against the wall and allowed Emmett to sit at the table, with the empty seat remaining for the social worker. We waited.

Suddenly, the door to my right opened and in came an adorable little four-year-old girl. Her shining brown eyes glistened with innocence, and her face was framed by big bushy curls that bounced as she walked. The social worker carried the baby boy, who was just eighteen months and the spitting image of his mom. I squeezed my back closer to the wall to make room as the social worker sat down, and it was then that the oldest realized who else was in the room.

"Mama!" she screamed and literally climbed over the table to reach her mother's arms.

"My baby! My baby!" Emmett exclaimed as she comfortably scooped up her daughter and kissed her on both cheeks. Emmett squeezed her little girl tightly, and the girl had both her little arms wrapped around her mother's neck. As the inmate snuggled her daughter, she had one eye on her baby. She loosened her grip and her daughter climbed down off her lap to play on the floor. Emmett stood up and reached her open arms across the table, beckoning to hold her baby.

"Hey, Sammy," she said softly as the social worker handed the baby to his mother, and he made a face like he was about to cry.

"Hey, Sammy, I got something for you," Emmett said as she cradled him in her arms before he could make a sound. She reached into her mouth, which made me wonder what in the world she had in her cheek. She popped out a tiny piece of candy, and with her fingers she placed it into his mouth like a mother bird. The baby loved the candy and smiled up at her, and that was all it took. Naturally, taking candy out of the housing unit was unacceptable behavior by jail standards, but I thought it was ingenious, and exhibited how well she knew her son. It was a trick I certainly would have used if I had been in her circumstance.

Emmett was engrossed in her children, and her eyes darted back and forth, inspecting them from head to toe, as mothers do. She took a moment to thank the social worker for bringing them, at which time I knew I could leave, which I did, undetected.

Once back down the hall, I sat on my stool at the deputy station and took a minute to think about what I'd just seen. Weeks before, when I had begun working this unit, I had looked in the computer at Emmett's file to see whether she could satisfy the criteria to be a worker, but she could not; her arresting officers had claimed she had "violent tendencies." I had asked her about it, and she told me she had fought the officers when she'd been arrested.

"They were ripping my family apart, taking my kids from me, all because we didn't have a place to live," Emmett told me. To hear her tell it, police saw her record and took her in. She fought like a mother bear defending her cubs, and while she had committed many crimes in the past, from burglary to possession of marijuana, obstructing, and resisting, and I knew she was no angel. But after seeing her kids, I understood. The truth was, I might have done the same.

When the visit was over and Emmett returned to the unit, she had tears streaming down her face.

"It's okay deputy, they're good tears, happy tears," she said, seeing my concerned face as she entered and kicked off her shoes. She separated her feet, and put her hands on her head with her fingers interlaced, ready for a pat search. I took her movement card and told her I was not going to search her this time.

"Thank you, Miss Dolinsky," she said and slowly walked up to her room.

From then on, she called me "Miss Dolinsky," rather than "Deputy Dolinsky," and I wasn't sure why.

THIRTY-SIX

IT WAS THE FIRST WEEKEND IN **D**ECEMBER and the boys and I were busy putting up a Christmas tree in the living room. Both children were responsible for decorating from a large box of ornaments given to them by my mother before she passed away. The year she died, she gave each of them a truck ornament with his name on it. When you pushed the button on it, the headlights lit. This year, I would have to continue the tradition, and knew I would never find anything quite as cool as those ornaments. I called them over and handed them each a gift.

"Oooooh, what is it?" Colton beamed. Ambitious Jake didn't hesitate to rip his open to find a green train engine ornament. Colton followed suit; his was red. As they positioned their newest pieces on the tree, I felt my eyes watering up once again. This happened every year. The boys lost interest quickly and went to their room to play. I lit candles and played Christmas music, and began to mix up a batch of sugar cookies—another traditional must-have.

But this year was different in many ways. Garrett was at church practicing with the band while I pulled the garland and lights out of beat-up boxes and ever-so-carefully placed them on the five-foot Austrian Pine, standing gloriously on a box in the front window. Though we hadn't formally discussed our situation, I knew this would be our last Christmas together.

Once the tree was sufficiently adorned, I got the boys and we ran out into the street to check out our newfound curb appeal. After dinner was over and we had eaten what seemed like half of the cookie dough, it was time to relax. I fell asleep on the sofa bed and woke up extra early the next morning.

It felt so peaceful with the house quiet. The sound of wind outside could be heard, but though I was cozy and safe, I couldn't get back to sleep. I had to be at work in three and a half hours.

I lay there awake until five a.m., when finally, puffy-eyed, I got up to start the day. I slid off my makeshift bed, wandered into the kitchen, put the dog out, and hit the bathroom to see whether my eyes looked as bad as they felt. They did.

Moving slowly, I made coffee, let Magnum back in, and headed to my bathroom to fix what I could. My uniform felt like lead, my ballistic vest heavier than usual. I slid it up over my head and lost balance, and it crashed down around me, covering the black half-tee I slept in.

Eventually, I found my shirt, pants, brass name tag, badge, and watch in the usual places. I got in the car and pulled out of the driveway, only to realize that I was missing my gun belt, and had to stop the car to run in and retrieve it. I snagged a few cookies and a to-go cup of coffee on my way out.

When I reached work, it was difficult to find a parking place, which was irritating. I arrived in Staff Dining just in time, barely, and hurried over to the sergeant for my assignment. Because I'd volunteered, I was always assigned House Six. Trudging downstairs, I smiled at the familiar nurses as they quickly walked up the stairs, squeezing past me in a hurry to get home. Moving steadily from the staircase through the shiny white hallway, I reached my post at the deputy station and dumped my backpack full of snacks and a book to read for school. *Two more years of school, lugging books around the jail, had better be worth it*, I thought. Deputy Olin was there. She had bid the graveyard shift, had no pass-down information, handed me keys to the unit, and took off. I couldn't blame her; I wished it were me.

All inmates were accounted for and all were sleeping, at least until Med-Pass showed up and the nurse pushed her heavy cart into the unit, making a racket. As the inmates walked out of their cells to get their medications from the nurse, I received a call from House Four. The deputies needed to move a large number of women over to my unit to make room for those coming from Intake. It had been a busy night.

"Sure, no problem," I grumbled on the phone.

In a matter of moments, fifteen women had come down the hallway and lined up along the wall, carrying gray bins piled with bedding. The slider door cracked open, and Carnie entered and handed me their movement cards.

"Hey," she said.

"Hey," I responded. "How are you doing?"

"I'm okay. Visited with Scotty yesterday. Deb was in town, we had lunch. It was good." She was smiling and I was happy to see her, but she quickly headed back to her housing unit. I smiled as I watched her walk away.

The nurse was calling up the last of the inmates for meds, so I began assigning the newest residents to the empty cells.

Inmate Moore was among them, which concerned me. A small, meek, middle-aged black woman, Moore was unpopular as a cellie because she refused to wash her hair, which gave her a distinct smell. This meant I needed to put her in a cell alone. She had spent some time in House Seven, due to being a little ten-ninety-six, or mentally ill, but this day, she cleared medical and psych, and here she stood in the hall with fourteen other inmates being moved back into House Six. I finished assigning cells and went into the hall to speak to Moore about how she felt about living in House Six. She said she was going to "be the bigger person" and not let the girls get to her this time.

"Okay, you're in Twenty-two, and keep me posted if you have any troubles, all right?" I said as I pointed toward her cell. "Oh, and Moore," I stopped her. She turned to look at me with her big, dark eyes, and I saw there was sadness in them. "It's shower time, so go wash your hair, okay?" Moore nodded in agreement and walked to her cell. I popped the door and she went in, closing the cell door behind her.

There were other inmates who had hygiene issues already in the unit, and I had to remind them to shower periodically. It wasn't uncommon when you worked with street people, and with folks who had been brought up in homes where their parents were more interested in drugs than parenting. Still, Moore was a unique case, because she was self-conscious of the fact that she smelled, while most were oblivious.

Once the women had made their beds and I finished my paperwork, I started tier time by tapping the intercom and setting the doors to be opened from the inside. A few cells popped, and out came Delmar, Sherman, Emmett, Deitch, and about twenty others, plus a few of the newbies, all gearing up at the red line to ask me for something.

"Deputy Dolinsky, can I have the remote for the TV?"

"Deputy, I need toilet paper."

"I need a comb and pads."

"I need deodorant."

"I need to call my public defender, do you know the number?"

Moore approached the deputy station. "Deputy, they were talking about my smell," she said, pointing to a group of women seated in front of the television who were deep in discussion about something. I watched the women; they appeared to be discussing what to watch on television, and none so much as glanced at where the inmate stood. I told her that I didn't think that she was truly the topic of their conversation. She disagreed and, mumbling to herself, walked back to her cell and locked herself down.

I took the opportunity to complete a security check and headed back to the deputy station to read e-mail. A few minutes later, I heard some ladies in the day room laughing loudly. I looked up to see Delmar and Sherman slapping hands in a high five. These ladies were not the same women Moore had just pointed out to me, but a different group located on the other side of the day room.

"Hey! Keep it down over there!" I hollered.

Just then, I heard yelling from the same group of women, aggressive yelling that sounded like a fight.

"Lock down!" I yelled as I moved quickly from behind the deputy station toward the commotion. Nobody moved.

"LOCK DOWN!" I hollered even louder, my voice scratchy as I gave it all the air I could muster. My face turned red, and I was surprised not to pee my pants, shouting with that much force, but it worked. The group disbursed quickly and I could see Moore in the middle of it, her sad eyes big as saucers. The women were hurrying to their cells, and I reached Moore, who was now alone in the center of the room.

"It's okay, Moore, you'll be all right," I said in a calm, motherly voice as I placed a handcuff on her left wrist. She quickly got agitated, and as I reached for her right arm, she pulled it away from me.

"No! I always have to move! Why don't you move *them*?!" she screamed at me.

This was the key moment. If I don't get her right arm cuffed now, there would be a fight. It would be just me versus Moore, with nearly thirty inmates watching. For a split second, I wondered whether they would help me or her in an all-out brawl. But I couldn't afford to find out.

"Hey!" I yelled loudly. She looked at me, startled, which was the break I needed. I grabbed her right wrist and pulled it behind her back, and with a click she was cuffed.

"You'll be just fine, Moore," I said in the calm voice. "We'll move you to a housing unit where you can feel comfortable and where the girls don't talk about you." I walked her to a chair by the deputy station.

"Arms up and over the back, there you go," I directed as she sat down.

"They were talking about my dead father!" she yelled at me as I called Station Two for escort deputies. Hearing the hollering, Deputies Valdez and Hoffman, who were in the hallway, rushed in to help. One stood at the touch screen, opening doors so the inmates could enter their cells. The other escorted Moore from the unit as she screamed at the top of her lungs, "It's not fair! You *always* move me! Why don't you move *them*?" I could still hear her bellowing as she headed down the hall, "They were talking about my dead father!"

Moore would be taken to the Infirmary for an evaluation, then cleared to move to House Seven, the mental health unit. I felt sorry for her. She just couldn't understand.

Once all was under control and I had a moment to think about what had just occurred, it dawned on me how close I had come to a possible incident in which I might have been seriously hurt, or worse. It was a sobering thought to realize that I had control of a housing unit because the inmates let me.

Partly because of Moore's outburst, and partly because of the numerous shakedowns and K-9 searches we had experienced over the past few days, there was a melancholy feeling in the unit. We were all tired, emotionally drained. Certainly, being locked down for many hours, usually with some irresponsible, untrustworthy, or unhygienic person, could darken one's mood. I wanted to lighten the atmosphere and have a little fun, so I called to the ladies on the intercom. I had an idea.

"It's been a stressful few days, and I think it's time we have a little fun," I said. "Let's play some music. If any of you ladies have a request for a song I can find on the Internet, let me know."

Cheers came from the cells as I ate my cookie breakfast and opened the doors from my perch near the slider. The line in front of me was immediate and followed the red line all the way around the desk. The women were very enthusiastic to hear their favorite songs, since many had been locked up for months, some closer to a year. The PCer stood at her door and watched the action. Jude made the first request.

"Please, Deputy Dolinsky! I gotta hear some Tracy Chapman," she said.

"Great choice, Jude! How about 'Fast Car'?" I quickly found the song on the computer and turned the speakers way up. I could see the smiles creeping across their hard faces as Tracy Chapman's voice bellowed out of the crappy computer speakers. The music was universally accepted, no matter what race or ethnicity, and I realized I'd hit on something great.

The next request was for Matchbox Twenty. About sixteen women squeezed as close as they could get to the speakers. I walked around to complete a security check and looked down from the top tier as they swayed. It made me happy to watch the women, who were taking in the tunes much as they would the smell of cookies baking, with eyes closed and grins on their faces. Many who were normally self-conscious about their meth-affected teeth today smiled widely. It was all about the music and nothing else. For a moment they could imagine themselves being anywhere.

But I still had work to do.

"Emmett, Xavier, Jolan ... Line up, it's time for court," I spoke through the intercom.

The three women arrived at the deputy station. I handed them their movement cards and they wandered down the hall to the end, where escort deputies would collect them, chain them up, and take them to court.

Sherman requested a country song, which got a similar response, and by the last few beats, serious dancing had commenced. Two young black women in the back of the group were doing a booty shake that got roars from the ladies seated in the day room.

"Deputy Dolinsky, can you do a booty shake? We'll teach you, come on," said one of the young dancers.

"I guess I could try, but *no laughing!*" I said loudly to my audience as I walked out from behind the desk. With that, I turned on a song and the girls started shaking their rear ends with such speed I had to stare.

"There is *no way* my white ass is gonna move like that!" I said and headed back to the deputy station, which earned me hoots from the ladies in the day room. Then the girls requested "Pop, Lock & Drop it," by Huey. It wasn't familiar to me. I went back to the computer, found the song online, and turned it on. The women near the speakers erupted in excitement; many knew the song and were very able dancers.

I watched the two young black women, whose ages together equaled mine. One was in for burglary and the other for possession of a controlled substance. Both were moving their hips from side to side. This made me feel gutsy. I came back out from behind the desk and attempted to copy their actions. Two white and three Latino girls joined us on our makeshift dance floor near the deputy station. They shook it, too, but there was something about the two black girls' movements when it came to this particular dance that nobody could surpass. I mimicked them by moving my hips to the left and right, as quickly as I could, but my movements paled in comparison.

"Come on, Deputy! You can do this!" they yelled, and the girls each locked one leg out and dropped to the floor, only to pop back up immediately. *Oh no, maybe I'm in over my head!* I thought.

At forty-two, I might not have been able to pop back up immediately, but I decided to try. As the booming bass filled the room from the tiny computer speakers, I locked my right leg out straight and dropped to the ground, touched the tile floor, and popped back up, twice. The dancing girls stood for a moment with their mouths hanging open.

"Did you see that?" one asked the other.

"Holy shit! Deputy Dolinsky, I didn't think you would really do it!" said the other.

The audience applauded and the phone rang. I bowed to my fans, then hurried behind the deputy station to grab the phone. It was Lester in Area Control, who was laughing so hard he could barely speak.

"I have worked here a long time and … ha, ha, ha! I have never seen anything like that. You got the *moves*, girl! Ha, ha, ha!" and he hung up. Apparently, he'd been able to see me down the hall and through the slider as I popped, locked, and dropped. I laughed so hard out of embarrassment that tears ran down my cheeks.

We played many songs that morning. Then nurses brought in meds, inmates went to classes and then returned. Though we'd had a dismal beginning, the day was picking up.

In the midst of our fun, the lunch cart arrived, so I locked the unit down and, when I did, Emmett returned from court. She was smiling broadly.

"I'm getting out today! The judge let me out with time served! I'm so excited!" she beamed as she walked in the door. I did the mandatory pat search on her and she headed to her cell as the workers prepared for lunch.

After the juice was made, the four workers got into the usual places, each woman ready to hand her peers a sandwich, a cup of salad, an orange, and a cookie as they passed. I called the top tier out, then the bottom. The women paraded single file, as they did every meal. They were excited and still singing their favorite songs, and many still had smiles on their faces as they came down the stairs. Once the women had received their food and locked themselves down, I walked around the unit, peering into windows to be sure every inmate was alive and well, then I went to lunch.

Staff Dining was quiet. I sat alone at the deputy table. A new recruit came in looking lost as his FTO walked out the slider to leave the building. I could tell the recruit was fresh out of the academy. I remembered the feeling. The recruit was looking for a place to sit, so I waved to him. He walked over and I motioned for him to have a seat.

"Thanks," he said. "I didn't want to sit in the wrong place."

"FTO told you about the deputy table, huh?" I replied. He nodded. So I explained the "rules" to him. How some deputies would be rude to him no matter what he did, so "don't take it personally." I told him about the deputy table, and to never leave his food alone if certain deputies were present. I told him how FTOs would test him extensively to see if he had what it took to work there. I told him everything I wished someone had told me when I had been brand-spanking-new. He seemed grateful, but I didn't care. It was just the right thing to do.

Later that evening, back in the housing unit, I let the girls out for their final tier time before I left for my holiday break. *It's a Wonderful Life* was on television; few of these women knew anything about the movie. I gave them the option to come out and watch the film or stay in their cells—no showers, no phone calls. It was this movie or nothing. Some growled as I popped the doors open.

"Deputy Dolinsky, no phones? Really? None?" Delmar whined.

"Only through the commercials," I replied, since I knew she was hoping to talk with her husband that evening.

"Thanks, Deputy Dolinsky," Delmar replied as she took her seat in front of the television. I was curious to see whether the movie would hold up for these young women as well as *Gone with the Wind* had. Fifty-eight women watched the film from start to finish, including Barrett in Cell Fourteen. During every commercial break, the ladies ran to their cells, refilled their drinks, got more snacks from their commissary stash, or made quick phone calls. Then it was back to the movie.

The deputy phone rang.

"House Six, Deputy Dolinsky."

"I have a release for you. Emmett out of Fifty. She's time served."

"Emmett, roll it up!" I called out. She was down at the base of the stairs with her bin full of linens in what seemed seconds.

As she approached the deputy station and I handed her movement card to her, she handed me a folded piece of paper and said, "Thanks, Miss Dolinsky." Then she hurried out the blue slider and down the hall, anxious to get back to her life. I was happy for her. Would she stay on the straight and narrow? I could only hope.

Once Emmett was out of sight, I opened the paper. It read:

Deputy Dolinsky,

I want to tell you thank you for being a blessing in my life. You have made a difference in here. Thank you for seeing change in me. It's not how we start but how we finish that matters. It has been a pleasure having you in my life based on my circumstances.

Sincerely,

Renee Emmett

It warmed my heart to read the note as the movie ended and the theme song played. The ladies disbursed and walked to their cells. My day was almost over and they needed to lock down for shift change. A few of the inmates clearly had not appreciated the movie, but most loved it, and would speak about it for weeks to come, how they, too, would "earn their wings."

The inmates were locked down, the unit was quiet. In the morning, five of the ladies were scheduled to go to prison, Jude and Sherman included, and they were restless to start the next leg of their incarceration experience. I probably would not see them again.

My relief, Deputy Waverly, came in to take over. The inmates had told me she was usually happy to lock them down for any small offense. She counted movement cards as I gathered my lunchbox and coat.

I began to walk out of the housing unit when suddenly an unknown voice yelled, "Merry Christmas, Deputy Dolinsky!" It was an inmate calling to me from her cell.

Waverly perked up. I could see that she would have liked nothing more than to be given a reason to leave them inside for the night. The inmate knew what a chance she had taken in yelling out her cell door. I waved in the direction of the cells and began to leave again when a chorus of voices flooded the room, with inmates calling through all of their doors.

"Bye, Deputy Dolinsky!"

"Have a good weekend, Deputy!"

"Thanks for everything, Deputy!"

Some said thanks, others wished me a Merry Christmas, and some wished for me a simple good weekend. The girls knew what they were doing, and still they had chosen to risk their evening tier time to wish me a nice holiday weekend I was touched. I turned and smiled at Waverly, who was just waiting for me to leave, but I stopped at the intercom one last time and addressed the inmates.

"Ladies, we had a pretty good day today, very positive. Have as good a Christmas as you can in your rooms." Some chuckles could be heard. I went on. "I challenge you to see if you can keep your hearts filled with this positive spirit through the holiday weekend, no matter what. Thank you for today. And I'll be thinking about you, all of you, on Christmas morning."

The inmates cheered. I stood there for a minute to acknowledge them. Waverly looked perplexed, maybe even disgusted, but I didn't care. I turned to leave, wearing a huge grin, and walked out of the housing unit feeling like a proud mama.

On the drive home, it dawned on me. My job was about more than just controlling and keeping order. It was about people, and caring, and change. *Anyone* could improve if they wanted to, no matter where they happened to be in life. It had taken a transformation for me to earn my position working in the jail. Now, I could motivate others to make change in order to stay out of jail. This was why I had to become a deputy sheriff, and I couldn't imagine doing anything else.

ACKNOWLEDGMENTS

TO MY HUSBAND, SEAN: I owe you big! You kept the laundry done, the house clean, the yard groomed, and the dogs and me fed, when all I could think to do was type like a crazy person in the hope of finishing this book. You do more than just balance our lives—you care, and you continue to show me how much every single day. I am a very lucky woman. I love you. Thank you!

Without my sister-in-law, Jessica, and our "Friday Writing Workshop," I would still be on page ten and clueless about how to proceed. Having your skill and expertise sitting across the table, one day a week, made all the difference. You listened, encouraged, and mentored as I crafted my story. Then, as copyeditor/project manager, you took over and made it lovely, wrapping it with ribbon and adding a beautiful bow. You've given me quite a gift! Thank you, my sis, for everything.

Abundant gratitude is due Lucky Bat Books owners Cindie Geddes and Judith Harlan for sticking with me and not losing faith that I would eventually produce a work worthy of publication. Your sincere trust and patience have meant the world to me. Thank you so very, very much!

To editor Dayle Dermatis: Without your gentle guidance, my manuscript would be as dry and dull as the paper it is printed on. I am forever grateful for your assistance, which freed me to write the best version of the story within. Cheers! Also, thanks go out to artist Nuno Moreira for his talent and vision in designing a cover with exceptional artistic flair.

Much appreciation is due my father, John, and brother, Dave, who heard much more than they ever cared to about this book. Thank you for your genuine patience and love, and for getting me through the tough times. You two are the best!

I also send many thanks to Delaney and Shane for inspiring me to continue striving forward, and to the Keasts for their unwavering support.

To my many friends and family members who sustained me through the grueling writing process: Jeanie Knowles, for being such a great sounding board as we ran mile after mile; Roe Pope, for her positivity and wonderful example; Merri Kay Beard, for her inspiration and insight; Ray, Michelle, Peggy, Tami, Carolyn, Ron, Dana, Mike, Jenny, Laurie, Sharon, Shaun, Holly, and Anita; the Sierra Sunrise Toastmasters; the band Asphalt Socialites; aunts, cousins, neighbors, co-workers, and any of you who cared enough to ask how the book was coming—you know who you are—Thank you!

A shout out to my law enforcement family, from FTOs to FNGs and everyone in between. While none of you are directly represented in this book, I believe every single one of you will be able to relate to some character, in some way, somehow, no matter where you train, where you work, what color uniform you wear, or in which community you serve. Stay safe.

And thanks to the inmates. All the inmates in this book are completely fictitious, but real inmates did help me to depict an accurate account of jail life. They were human dictionaries when I needed real street terminology or information on what drugs really do to a person's life, and they helped by being interested and positive about the project. Ladies, I appreciate your input, more than you will ever know.

Lastly, there is one person who would have been even more enthusiastic about this book than I am. The most avid reader in the family, she'd be my harshest critic, yet my greatest cheerleader. And inside, right now, she would be bursting at the seams with pride at my achievement. Love to my mom, Patricia … I miss you.

ABOUT THE AUTHOR

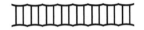

Dishrags to Dirtbags is Brooke Santina's first novel. She is a wife, mother, and deputy sheriff residing in the Reno, Nevada area with her family and three dogs. Learn more about this book at www.dishragstodirtbags.com, or read more from this author at www.brookesantina.com.